The Rose Trilogy

Tenth Anniversary Edition

by

Tish Thawer

Amber Leaf Publishing

First Edition
First Hardback Printing, 2021
ISBN: 978-1-0879-1666-8

Cover Design by Emily Wittig Designs
Blur by The Blurb Doctor
Originally edited by Kara Malinczak
Updated editing by Sharon Kay

Amber Leaf Publishing, Missouri
www.amberleafpublishing.com
www.tishthawer.com

Tish Thawer

A vampire's love…
An innocent's guilt…
A secret no one could've imagined.

"With Tish Thawer's vivid storytelling, I was dropped straight into the new world of *drifting* vampires!"

- Caris Roane, bestselling author of the Guardian's of Ascension series.

Scent of a
White Rose

Book One of The Rose Trilogy

Scent of a White Rose

(Book One)

***

Rose's eye blinks, an idea blooms.
But who could've imagined the impending doom?

CHAPTER ONE

(Rose)

I opened my eyes and felt death. The presence of it, the weight of it, the sadness of it all. I couldn't believe my mom was gone. I thought *the weight of it* described it best—like a pressure sitting on my chest that would never get lighter.

Dad said we'd be okay. *"Time heals everything, Rose,"* he'd told me time and time again. But I didn't believe him. How could I when I could tell he didn't even believe it himself? And honestly, I didn't want time to pass. I just wanted to lay here on my bed, wide awake in my black funeral clothes and stare at the ceiling—remembering when Mom and I had painted my room and hung these stars and moons.

They weren't the stick-on, glow-in-the-dark kind, but instead, beautiful crystals in all colors and sizes, strung from my freshly painted black ceiling, dancing and gleaning just like we'd imagined. Well, just like *she'd* imagined. It was her idea... my mom, the crafty one. With a spark of wonder in her voice she'd said, *"It'll be beautiful, Rose. You'll feel like you're sleeping under the twinkling stars every single night."* At the time, I wasn't convinced. But when we pulled back the curtains and let the moonlight flow in, I was speechless. She'd been right. Amazed, I watched the beautiful little stars and moons twinkle and spin right there in my very own room.

God, I loved my mom.

No, I didn't want time to pass. I wanted it to reverse.

* * * * *

My mom, Loraine Reynolds, was killed in a 'freak accident'. Someone broke into our house in the dead of night, and when they found my mom coming out of her room, they killed her.

Doesn't sound too freaky, right? Your average burglary gone wrong? Well, what made it 'freaky', I guess, was *how* she was killed.

The cops were baffled, as the only evidence of violence was two small puncture wounds on the side of her neck. At first, they thought she'd been stabbed by an ice pick, which was strange enough, but then came the *really* strange part. Her body had been drained of all its blood. See… *freaky,* right?

Besides that, the robbers didn't take anything. The cops said they must have panicked and fled in a hurry. There were no fingerprints or DNA left at the scene and no trail for them to follow. So, after receiving countless apologies, we faced the fact that we were never going to get an explanation as to how, or *why,* my mom had been killed. It was just something we had to live with.

It's been six months since the accident. Dad has gone back to work, and I've gone back to school. My college is about twenty minutes away, but you'd think it was in a third-world country from the way he'd been treating me. I understand that he's freaked, and, I understand that I'm now the only family he has left—a fact he reminds me of on a daily basis. But damn, I'm twenty years old, and not a child.

But… every time I look at him and see the sadness in his eyes, I watch the emotions roll across his face and hold my tongue. Because he's right; I am the only family he has left. So, if he wants to treat me like I'm ten instead of twenty, that's okay. If he wants to have one of his company cars take me and pick me up from school every day, that's okay. And if he insists I live with him until I graduate college, that's okay too.

But I'll be damned if he's going to stop me from seeing Christian.

CHAPTER TWO

(Rose)

"Dad, I just want to go have dinner with some of my friends after school. Why is that such a big deal?" My voice rang with exasperation.

"Why is that such a big deal? Really, Rose? You have the nerve to ask me that?" Clearly, he was just as frustrated as I was. "It's a big deal because this is a dangerous world, and you of all people should understand that. I'm sorry, but I just don't like the idea of you being out after dark."

I tried to smooth my voice into a mature, compassion-filled tone. "Dad, it's been six months. I miss Mom too, and I will *never* forget what happened to her. But we can't continue to live our lives in fear."

"I'm not living in fear, Rose; I'm living in reality. I lost my wife, and I refuse to lose my daughter to the evils of this world, too." Sad and defeated, he scooted his chair away from the table.

I knew this was how the conversation would go, but you can't blame a girl for trying. I really wish he would've said yes, though, because I'm so sick of lying to him and sneaking around. But what am I supposed to do? I have to get on with my life... it's what Mom would have wanted. But, as I watch him pile his breakfast dishes in the sink, place both hands on the counter and hang his head, I know I can't fight him on this. So, as usual... Dad wins.

Resolved to be the innocent 'white rose' he pictures me to be, I gave in. "Okay, Dad. I'll be home before sunset. Do you want me to pick something up for dinner, or do you want to do it?"

"Actually, I have a meeting to attend, so just have the driver stop for takeout on your way home. And no calling for delivery. I will not have strangers coming to this house, even if it is just to deliver food."

I started to protest, frustrated he could totally dismiss my plans and insist I come straight home, when he wasn't even going to be here. But then it dawned on me... this was the perfect opportunity. It looked like I'd be skipping dinner with my friends and opting for a little road trip instead.

"Okay, I'll just grab something for myself, but what time should I expect you?" I asked innocently.

"Probably around nine." He spun around, straightened his shoulders, and plastered a loving smile on his face. "I love you, Rose. Thanks for humoring an old man who cares too much."

Well now I just felt like crap. "You're welcome, Dad. I love you too."

I listened to the front door close and looked into the sink, watching as our breakfast slid down the drain. White, runny eggs swirling their way down into the dark hole toward the disposal. That was me... a white substance, fading and running like watercolors down a drain into the dark. Man, I wished I didn't have to lie to him.

As I climbed into the shower, I realized not only would I have to figure out a way to ditch my driver today, but also how I was going to get a hold of Christian to let him know I was coming down. He'd always said, *"Don't try to reach me before dark. I'm dead to the world."*

I knew he slept for most of the day because of his job, but man did it make trying to plan a spontaneous rendezvous a little tricky. I suppose this time I just wouldn't tell him I was coming, and surprise him instead.

Christian worked at a nightclub on the outskirts of town. I'd been there plenty of times, but had never gone in. Not for the obvious reason I was only twenty, but because we were usually *preoccupied* in the back seat of his car. Most of my visits revolved around us spending time together during his breaks, but I remember the first time I ever saw him.

It was a night I'd never forget.

Dad had arranged for my friends and I to be driven in one of his company limos to a concert in Masen—the big city about two hours away. We didn't have a curfew, but we were expected to stay with the staff that came with the car. I saw it for the compromise it was; he was letting me go, but with supervision. I guess he'd always been protective, even before Mom's death.

After the concert, we were driving back when Jillian—my best friend—loudly announced that she had to use the restroom. The only place around was the nightclub up the road. It was called "The Rising Pit."

Once we reached the club, Jill thanked the driver for stopping, bounced out of the limo, and made a beeline to the club's front door—accompanied, of course, by one of the 'car crew' as we'd taken to calling them.

After Jill disappeared behind the door, it swung open again and a man stepped outside. He was carrying a girl in his arms. I watched from the car as he placed her on her feet, steadying her with a light touch to her arm before letting go. Though I couldn't hear was they were saying, we were close enough I could tell she was crying, and he seemed to be talking to her in a very gentle manner. Reaching up, she rubbed the tears from her cheeks and nodded, and the guy smiled.

Like an angel bathed in moonlight, the clouds broke in the sky. He was so incredibly gorgeous; unlike any guy I'd ever seen before. He had to be about 6' 2", and solid muscle from the looks of him. Not bulky like those beefed-up body builders, but very athletic with wide shoulders, a broad chest, a thin waist, and what I was sure would be strong, muscular legs. With the moonlight shining on him, I could see he had dark blond hair with golden highlights, cut short and sharp. I hadn't realized I was hanging half way out the limo when he suddenly turned and looked right at me. My breath caught, and I thought I would die.

His eyes so were beautiful. Mesmerizing. And even at this distance, his gaze pierced me. A rich brown with golden highlights mixed together like swirled caramel and honey, creating the most intriguing amber color. He was easily the most beautiful thing I'd ever seen.

Jillian came barreling out of the nightclub in that moment, her escort closely in tow. "I only wanted a quick shot," she said, causing the rest of us to burst out laughing. As she walked past the beautiful man, he reached out and tapped her gently on the shoulder. Stopping, she listened to what he had to say, continually glancing back at the car with a huge smile plastered on her face. After a brief moment, he handed her something, then disappeared back inside.

I was so anxious to see what he had said to my friend, and wondered if it had anything to do with her only using the facilities instead of being a paying customer. It was obvious that he worked there from his all-black uniform.

When Jill got in the car, she sat there for a moment, smiling like the Cheshire cat, then handed me a business card. It was shiny and smooth and had the nightclub's logo on the front. I turned it over and found a hand scribbled note. *"Roses are red, but I'll be blue, if I'm denied the pleasure, of meeting you. ~ Christian."*

My jaw dropped. Jillian was still smiling at me as my other friends passed the card back and forth, then proceeded to tell me that guy had asked her my name, then scratched out that poem so fast she could barely see his hand move. He had also included his phone number on the back and asked that I call him in two days after sunset—which of course, I did.

After that, I started seeing Christian every week, visiting during his breaks and getting seriously serious within those first three months. But then, Mom died and everything changed.

My dad, Jeremy, is the Vice President of a marketing firm here in town, but all his best clients come from the big city, which is why he has to take an overnight business trip once a month to schmooze their egos. It's only during these trips that I get to see Christian, as Dad has me stay overnight at Jillian's house whenever he leaves town.

So, with Jill's help once a month, I lose all sense of morality and am forced to sneak out to see my boyfriend while lying to my dad.

Yeah… it pretty much sucks.

CHAPTER THREE

(Rose)

Once focused long enough to actually get dressed, I came up with a plan to ditch my driver after school. It would take some bad behavior on my part, and then some sweet talk immediately after, but with a little effort, I thought I could pull it off.

At school, I was your average college student—never stood out much, kept my nose in the books, and made pretty good grades. But today was a different story. Today, I was completely disruptive, chatting when I shouldn't be, constantly dropping stuff and apologizing loudly, even smacking my gum so hard it was starting to hurt my jaw. But finally, I got what I wanted.

"Rose Reynolds... see me at the end of the day," Mr. Thompson snapped.

YES!!

I felt like a complete deviant for causing this much trouble, especially for one of the few professors I actually liked. But I knew his biggest pet peeve was students disrupting his lectures, and that's exactly what I'd done to perfection.

Immediately after my last class of the day, I made my way back up to the third floor and to Mr. Thompson's classroom. He was waiting for me at his desk, his nose buried in his day planner. "Ms. Reynolds, I was not pleased with your constant interruptions in my class today. Is there an explanation you can give that will keep me from tacking on an additional 500 words to your thesis?"

I sat down and tried to make myself look a little shaky. "I'm so sorry, Mr. Thompson. I think it had something to do with my low-blood sugar. It doesn't happen too often anymore, but after my mom's accident, sometimes I would just forget to eat, and then I would end up all shaky and hyper. I'm really sorry." Sincerity dripped from every word. .

Did I say deviant before? I meant criminal.

I couldn't believe I'd actually played the *'my mom was killed'* card, just so I could go see my boyfriend. I hated it, but it worked.

After being dismissed with a feather-light warning, I made my way to the girl's bathroom around the corner. Taking a few, guilt-ridden deep breaths, I refreshed my makeup and changed out my jeans and t-shirt, swapping them for the dark blue sundress I'd stuffed in my bag earlier this morning. The black flats I had on were going to have to do. I was taller than average at 5'10", and didn't wear heels very often anyway. Looking in the mirror, I thought I looked pretty good. The sundress hugged my ample curves just right, while my light blonde hair hung past my shoulders, falling below my collarbone. I wore it straight most of the time, but today I had braided it for school. Now, when I shook it out, it was nice and wavy, just like I planned. I loved that trick.

Taking one last glance in the mirror, I applied a final dab to my cherry-colored lipstick, smacking my lips. "Time to go see my man!" I laughed out loud. Yep, I was giddy.

As usual, I had to borrow Jill's car for my trip to see Christian. She was such a good friend, and completely felt for me and the strict rules I had to live by. So, whenever I could squeeze out from under my dad's thumb, she was totally supportive. *Huh.* Now that I'm thinking about it, I'm not sure if that makes her a good friend or a bad one.

Pulling into The Rising Pit's parking lot, I parked next to Christian's car, a '67 Mercury Comet Caliente—and yes, it lived up to its name. It was hot! After checking my lipstick one last time, I jumped out of my borrowed ride, and began the search for my man. Opening the club's front door, it took my eyes and ears a minute to adjust. The lighting was dark and seductive, and the only sound present was a slow mechanical grinding.

Looking around, I noticed I was alone on the main floor and quickly pinpointed the source of the noise. The stage in the middle of the room was moving, but I couldn't tell if it was going up or down. And honestly, I didn't care. Instead, I was completely focused on all of the people coming out from underneath it.

I could barely make out the circular staircase that ran around the inside wall beneath the stage, but that's where everyone I recognized as The Rising Pit's staff was coming from: Bobby, the sexy, blond DJ; Tori and Dominique, the adorable redheads and sister bartenders; the gorgeous owner, Evangeline; her muscular, right-hand man and bar manager, Dax; and then of course, Christian, the head of security and my boyfriend.

They were all talking and joking, looking more like a family than coworkers, as the stage rose the rest of the way up and locked into place with a loud bang. Startled by the shock wave it sent up my legs, I sucked in a breath.

Everyone's heads snapped in my direction at the exact same time.

Busted, there was no point in acting shy. They all knew I was Christian's girlfriend, so I cleared my throat, cocked my hip, and gave a little wave directed just at him.

Christian looked surprised, happy, and wary, all at the same time. Once everyone got over their initial shock of seeing me, they dispersed into the club, leaving only Christian and Evangeline staring in my direction. Leaning in, Evangeline whispered something in his ear, then moved off. His eyes held mine as he smiled, so I figured whatever she had to say couldn't be all that bad. I certainly didn't want to get him in trouble for me showing up unannounced, but come on, this *is* a nightclub… party central, and the front door *had* been open.

Evangeline headed toward the back of the club while Christian stood there for a moment longer, not moving a muscle, and looking like a Greek god. He eyed me up and down—admiring my dress, I guess—since his smile just kept growing. I think he liked what he saw.

Finally, he made his way over and wrapped me in his arms. "Wow, this is an amazing surprise!" He pulled me close, nuzzling my neck.

"Yeah, I escaped and thought I'd ditch my friends and come see you instead. This once-a-month shit is for the birds." My voice was playful as I reached around and grabbed his butt.

Christian and I had made out enough that we were comfortable touching each other, but I needed to let him know it was okay if we took things all the way. As a matter of fact, I was aching for it. It's not like I was a twenty-year-old virgin for Christ's sake, as crass as that may sound.

He jumped a little as I squeezed his perfect ass, then looked around to see if anyone was watching… and they were.

Promptly grabbing my hand, he flipped off Bobby and Dax as they continued to laugh, then pulled me out the front door.

"I'm really glad you came, but you should have called. We're not allowed to have guests here until after 8 p.m. when the club opens." He guided us across the parking lot and back to his car.

"I thought the club was open. The front door was unlocked, and the outside lights were on."

Right then, Terrance, one of Christian's security staff, stepped out of the woods just a couple of cars down from where we stood. Christian's eyes narrowed and his body tensed. "Terrance, is there a reason why you're out here alone and left the club's standing wide open?" he snapped.

Terrance looked flushed. "Sorry, boss. I forgot something in my car."

Christian squinted and looked around the small lot. "We'll talk about this later," he said.

Terrance gave him a clipped nod and walked back inside.

"Maybe he was making out with his girlfriend in the woods," I teased, trying to lighten the mood. It must have worked, too, because in the blink of an eye his hands were all over me. With his mouth crushed against mine, our tongues fought for dominance. It was amazing.

"Wow, I guess you really like the dress," I panted between kisses.

"I love your dress, but I'd love it more if it was on the ground," he growled.

His voice was lower than I'd ever heard it before, and there was an urgency in the way he kissed me. Grabbing the hem of my dress, he raised it slowly as he licked my neck. And while this was definitely what I wanted tonight—here, outside against his car, wasn't exactly the fantasy I'd envisioned.

Settling himself between my legs, Christian reached for his belt when the club's front door slammed open wide. I jerked my head up to find Evangeline staring directly at us.

"Christian," she snapped, "I'm sorry to interrupt, but we need to finish opening."

Hands stilling, he slowly raised his head from the side of my neck with the most serious look on his face. And even though it was dark outside, in that moment, it seemed like *he* was darker too. His eyes were smoky and had lost their honey swirl. Even his hair seemed darker, like the highlights had completely disappeared. Suddenly, I wasn't too upset by Evangeline's interruption.

Christian quickly shook his head and kissed me one last time, himself again. "Sorry, babe. I gotta go."

Feeling slightly relieved, I smoothed my dress back into place. "No problem. I guess I should head home anyway, in case my dad comes home early. Sorry if I got you in trouble. Next time, I'll be sure to call."

"That would probably be best." He winked and sauntered across the lot and back through the club's front door.

Evangeline ignored him as he passed, instead watching me fumble for my keys.

I heard the club's front door shut and felt a moment's relief… until I looked up and saw her walking my way.

Evangeline was a beautiful woman. In her early thirties, with silky brown hair, slate grey eyes, and a petite frame reaching to only about 5'5". At one time I wondered if I should be jealous of her, but Christian told me she and Dax were involved and had been together forever. That made me feel better, but right now, that was *not* the feeling I had.

"Hi, Evangeline!" I tried to sound light and upbeat. "Sorry for just showing up tonight. I truly thought the club was open or else I wouldn't have just walked in."

Evangeline smiled. "That's okay. I'm sure Christian was happy to see you, and you're always welcome here, Rose. We just aren't allowed to have any visitors before normal business hours. County rules. But if you'd like to wait here, I can send Christian back out for his first break as soon as we open in about thirty minutes."

I thought about it, but—

"Thank you for the offer, but unfortunately, I have to get back home." Yeah, I just wasn't feeling it. Evangeline seemed nice, but I truly did have to beat Dad home. This wasn't like one of his overnight trips, and I didn't even want to think about what would happen if I wasn't there when he arrived. Besides… Christian just didn't really seem like himself tonight.

CHAPTER FOUR

(Christian)

With the smell of blood in the air, and Rose's body beneath me, I couldn't help but to nuzzle her neck a little more. She moaned as I started to lift her skirt, and that's when I heard, "Christian. I'm sorry to interrupt but we need to finish opening."

Really, Evie... right now? Her voice carried the Sire command my brain needed to hear in order to stop where this was headed. I lifted my head and looked at Rose. She was flushed, and even though she tried to hide it, I caught the look of uncertainty that had flashed across her face. I was sure she was questioning my darkening appearance, so I quickly tried to shake it off. With a final kiss goodbye, I headed for the club before she could notice too much... *hopefully.*

That was one of the many things that sucked about being a vampire... no pun intended. When you started to 'drift' from light to dark, your physical appearance actually showed traces of it. It was in our nature to drift when we feed, or were sexually aroused, or angry. But most of the time, when the deeds were done and the emotions passed, we drifted back to our natural state pretty quickly. These naturally-occurring appearance traits made it easy to tell who was in control and who wasn't. But if we were caught off guard, or drifted in response to some uncontrolled cravings, it could be a real pain in the ass.

I rushed through the front door and almost ran straight into Terrance. He was on his knees, held in place by Dax and Bobby with his arms splayed out wide, unable to move. I assumed Evie had issued the commanded before she made her way outside to get me.

"What the fuck did you think you were doing leaving this club to go feed in the woods?" I demanded.

I'd known exactly what he'd been doing the second I saw him. Both his hair and eyes were pitch black, and besides that... Terrance didn't own a car. His normal coloring was a medium to dark brown, and because he naturally ran darker, we tended to keep an eye on him. But apparently tonight, he'd risen before the rest of us tonight so he could sneak out and have a bite. I cringed at the thought. This was how Rose was able to get into the club tonight—and he could have just as easily grabbed her instead. "Answer me! You left this club wide open, and by doing so, you put us and our maker at risk. What if guests had shown up early? They could have just waltzed right in and saw where we all sleep."

"Like Rose did?" Evie's voice was smooth as ice.

I knew we were going to have this conversation soon, but I'd hoped it could wait until after we'd dealt with Terrance.

"Rose didn't say anything about the stage. She doesn't know a thing about the pit. She's innocent, Evie, and if she *had* questioned it, she would have asked me about it directly, and she didn't."

"I believe you, Christian. I had a little talk with Rose, and did a quick scan for myself. And you're right, she doesn't suspect a thing. But that doesn't change the fact that we could have had a serious problem if anyone *other* than Rose had showed up early tonight." Evie's gaze landed on Terrance, causing him to tense as he sensed the change in her voice. "Dax, Bobby... escort Terrance back down to the pit and chain him up in the cell. I'll decide what to do with him after closing tonight. Oh, and Dax... make him sing."

Terrance visibly slumped when he heard her command. *"Make him sing"* were not words you ever wanted to hear.

Evangeline—our Sire, and Dax—her consort, were the only two vampires in our clan who possess the ability to 'scan' or invade someone's mind. They could choose to gently read your thoughts, like she'd done with Rose. Or, they could *make you sing,* forcibly pulled thoughts from your mind whether you wanted them to or not. It excruciating, and there was no way to hide your intentions or lie about what you'd done... Terrance was screwed.

Dax and Bobby escorted Terrance back down to our actual rising pit—the area where we all slept during the day. It was located underground, far beneath the club, and had only two entrances. One, beneath the circular dance floor, and the other, hidden behind the bookcase in Evie's office. I started to follow Dax and Bobby toward the pit, but Evangeline nodded her head in my direction. I guess we weren't done talking about Rose's appearance tonight after all. Following her into her office, I shut the door behind us.

"I like Rose very much," Evie started, "but I'm concerned she's witnessing too much for her own good."

"You just said you scanned her. So if she had any questions or suspicions about me or The Rising Pit, you would have heard them then."

I wasn't about to let Evie ruin the best thing that had ever happened to me. Rose was the sweetest, most caring, and sexiest person I'd ever met.

The first night I saw her leaning out of that limo and smelled her scent drifting on the breeze, I thought I'd died again. I wrote her some cheesy poem in hopes of capturing her attention, but what I truly remember from that night was her scent. She smelled of innocence and hope: like fresh cotton and sweet tarts, sunshine and rain, all mixed together. I'd found myself immediately drawn to her for reasons I couldn't explain.

"Yes, but while doing my quick scan, I could sense something just below the surface: a wariness, or apprehension of some sort. I'm just concerned that *we* may be the source of that," Evangeline stated.

I crossed my arms. "Or maybe it's because her mother was killed six months ago. And it probably didn't help that she was worried about getting me in trouble. Especially when the owner of the club makes a trip across the parking lot to talk to her about it. Honestly, with everything she's gone through, I'd be surprised if she *didn't* spend the rest of her life wary and apprehensive." Yeah... I was feeling a little defensive.

Evie cocked her head and took in my frustrated tone and stance, a gentle smile slowly spreading across her face. "You're in love with her."

"Damn straight."

I wasn't embarrassed to express my feelings, especially in front of Evie. She and Dax had a wonderful relationship that made the rest of us long to have someone in our lives that we, too, could share eternity with. Unfortunately for me, an eternity with Rose wasn't going to happen, but I didn't care. A normal lifetime with her was something I'd be happy to experience—until my true death, or hers.

"I haven't received any signs of the new Sire emerging, but when they do, you could always petition them to change Rose for you."

Woah. I hadn't even thought about that. Mainly because *I* couldn't change Rose, and at this point neither could Evie. But dang, if she could become a vampire... that would be amazing.

When the Sire of a clan reached a certain age, their ability to share the life blood required for 'the change' disappeared. A new Sire within the line would eventually be triggered to take their place, but sometimes that could take hundreds of years to happen. It had been eighty-five since Evie last created a new vampire, and we hadn't had any signs of who the new Sire could be. Honestly, I think we'd all forgotten about it, as our little family was pretty content.

"I hadn't even thought about that, but I guess when the time does come, I *could* petition the new Sire to change Rose." Hope took root in my chest.

Evie smiled. "Well, it's certainly something to think about. I, for one, would welcome Rose with open arms. I've never seen anyone make you so happy, and she does seem to be as sweet as you say. I think she would make a wonderful light vampire, and it would please me very much for you to be able to spend eternity with the person you love."

I immediately started to fantasize about a life with Rose, but Evie snapped my attention back to the present. "Now, what should we do about Terrance?"

The air left my lungs. "Honestly, I don't know. He's always been a little darker than the rest of us, and even though we've monitored him successfully in the past, I really don't see him changing back this time. When he stepped out of the woods, his hair was pitch black and his eyes were the same, and I could smell and hear the woman he'd left behind. She was bleeding, frightened, and whimpering. I could tell he hadn't made their interaction a pleasant one."

"Is that why you were drifting, because of the effect the woman in the woods was having on you?"

"Yes. With the scent of blood in the air, and Rose in my arms, I couldn't control it. Thank you for stopping me when you did."

I hadn't drifted in front of Rose before, mainly because I'd always made sure to feed before she arrived. Plus, even if I did get really worked up, she usually had her eyes closed and didn't seem notice. But tonight, she'd shown up before I had a chance to feed, and with the bleeding woman in the woods not far from us, I hadn't been able to control myself.

"I think I'll wait to hear what Dax gathers from Terrance and make my decision tonight after closing as planned," Evangeline finished.

As a rule, Evie didn't kill vampires just because they drifted from light to dark; it was in our nature and couldn't be helped. But she did have one strict rule: if any of us started to revel in hurting people and went *permanently* dark, we would face the true death. No exceptions.

For a vampire to permanently drift dark was a rare thing, but it did happen every now and again. It meant they'd given in to their cravings and shut down their emotions. After that, it wasn't long before they started reveling in the kill and became truly evil. If it happened, it was their Sire's duty to deliver the true death, and it looked like Terrance was out of time.

CHAPTER FIVE

(Rose)

Driving home, I couldn't stop thinking about Christian and how great it felt to finally have him let loose a little. His kisses were more intense and the way his hands moved over my body was pure heaven. But there were other things that happened tonight that were occupying my thoughts as well. Like my lying and scheming, my seeing Christian and his co-workers coming out from underneath the stage, Terrance's sudden appearance from the woods, and especially Christian's random darkness and odd mood swing. It's not that these things had exactly stressed me out, but tonight had been so different from any of our other visits, it all just felt a little off.

But, off or not, right now I had bigger problems.

I'd gotten so lost in my thoughts, I'd driven straight to my house instead of Jillian's, and now, I was out of time.

As far as Dad was concerned, I was supposed to have gotten a ride home from Jill after school, so how in the world was I going to explain me driving her car alone instead?

In a panic, I raced around the block, parked the car, and frantically dialed Jill's number.

"Hey, where are you?" The tension was thick in her voice.

"I screwed up! I accidentally drove straight home instead of coming to get you. Is there any way you can come get your car? I'll leave it around the block to the east of my house with the keys under the floor mat. Is that okay?"

Silence stretched between us, and I really started to freak out. Maybe I had pushed her too far this time. She was always looking out for me, especially since the nightmare with my mom, but this may have been asking a little too much.

"Okay, I think there is still one more bus that runs in that direction tonight. But Rose... you owe me big!"

"I know. And thank you, thank you, thank you!" I snapped my phone closed, turn off the car, and put the key under the mat. I wasn't worried if it would be safe here—we lived in a pretty nice neighborhood. As a matter of fact, my mother's death had been the only bad thing to ever happen in the vicinity.

As I rounded the corner, I noticed that Dad's car wasn't in the driveway yet. *Thank God!*

Creeping to the back of the house, I let myself in and headed straight for the kitchen. How was I going to explain the lack of food, when I was supposed to have stopped for takeout? As I rummaged through the refrigerator, I heard Dad's keys unlocking the front door. *Shit, shit, shit.* I quickly shut the fridge, turned on the faucet, and began washing my hands just as Dad came around the corner and stopped in the doorway.

"Hi honey, how was your day?"

I wondered if the driver had given him the heads up regarding the change of plans after school. I was pretty sure he had, so I decided to stick with that for the basis of my story.

"Not great. I wasn't feeling well today, and because of it I ended up having to stay after school. But Jillian gave me a ride home."

He looked at me with a tilt of his head, but after a moment, he shrugged and replied, "Yeah, that's what Dennis told me. So, what's with the get up?"

Oh good. He was just questioning my appearance, not my story.

"Oh, nothing. After I got home and ate, I was feeling better, so I decided to clean out my closet. I've been trying on clothes and messing with my hair. I thought maybe I'd wear this the next time I go over to Jillian's." I smoothed down my blue dress. "The whole family goes out to dinner whenever I stay over," I said as my stomach growled.

"Well, I think it looks great. And actually, you should be headed over to Jill's next week. I just have to confirm some arrangements for my business meeting in Masen first, but then I'll let you know."

"Okay, sounds good." I hung up the dish towel. "I think I'll turn in. I want to make sure to get up early enough to have a decent breakfast. I think that's why I didn't feel good today. I hadn't eaten enough."

God, I hate myself.

"Okay, honey. Get some rest; I'll see you in the morning, and how about I cook this time? Give my girl a break."

And now I was feeling sick for real.

CHAPTER SIX

(Christian)

After the club closed, Dax came out of the rising pit and headed straight for Evangeline's office. They were in there for about fifteen minutes while the rest of us cleaned up the evidence of tonight's good time. The puzzled look on Evie's face left me cautious when she waved us over.

"After receiving Dax's report, I've decided to keep Terrance around for further questioning." Evie's voice was sharp and to the point.

This was a first. Evie usually didn't give second chances, and as far as I was concerned, I thought Terrance had already been pushing it for a while.

"What did Terrance say?" I asked, curiosity getting the better of me.

"His revelations about tonight were exactly what we thought they'd be. He woke up and snuck out early, made his way to the interstate, and sliced that poor girl's tires. When she glided her car to a stop along the woods, he grabbed her. He was not gentle and he planned to leave her for dead all along."

The anger lacing her tone was so thick it almost left a bitter taste in *my* mouth.

"Then why are you letting him live?" I crossed my arms. "His actions tonight not only put us in danger, but it's obvious that he is starting to revel in the kill."

Closing her eyes briefly, Evie took a moment to composed herself. "Christian, please know that I have yours, and everyone else's best interests at heart when I make my decisions. There is something within Terrance's mind that I have to explore," she replied calmly. "But once I get my answers, he *will* meet his true death."

I noticed Dax was quieter than usual during our meeting, and now his head hung even lower with Evie's last words.

It had been Dax who'd petitioned Evie to change Terrance when he found him in the old world, working as a blacksmith. After an accident left Terrance's hands terribly burned, his livelihood was ripped away, and he could no longer support his family. But... if he were to die, his wife could remarry and gain the stability she and their children needed to carry on. Dax explained this Evie, and so the two of them—with their caring hearts—decided to add Terrance to our clan, freeing both him and his family from a terrible fate.

"Terrance will remain chained in the pit until further notice. No one is to talk to him unless I or Dax say so." Evie didn't raise her voice or repeat herself, since the command in her tone was enough to paralyze us all into doing exactly what she wanted—another benefit to being the Sire. Luckily, it was a skill she didn't use very often.

Dismissing us, Evie headed toward the front of the club, taking Bobby and Dominique with her. I assumed they were headed out to gather the girl's body that was still in the woods and dispose of her car, so I walked over to Dax and placed my hand on his shoulder.

We'd been together for so long that I didn't have to say a word in order to express my sympathy, but I thought I'd better apologize for sounding so 'pro-death' when it came to Terrance. "I'm sorry. I really wish he'd drift back to his old self so we could stop all this."

Dax took a deep breath and ran a hand through his hair. "He's not going to. Since about six months ago, Terrance has had trouble drifting back after he feeds. Evie and I noticed it and were keeping an even closer eye on him than usual, but then this happened." He gestured to the front door. "Not only is he terrorizing and killing his prey, but he has now lost all regard for the rest of the clan's safety." Dax shook his head. "There's no way to save him now."

"What do you think happened that would cause him to change so much?"

"We're not sure. But that's what Evie's gonna find out." He pressed his lips together, then clapped me on the shoulder and walked away.

As I headed out to help Evie and the others, I heard Dax whisper something under his breath. I couldn't quite make it out, but it sounded like, *"Man, I wish I knew how he was keeping those thoughts from me."*

Now I understood. If that were true, Dax hadn't been able to pull *specific* thoughts from Terrance, which was highly unusual. I could see why Evie wanted to question him further, and personally, I couldn't wait to find out what Terrance was hiding.

CHAPTER SEVEN

(Rose)

The following week went by fast enough. I didn't get into any more trouble at school, and every morning Dad had made sure I ate a good breakfast so I wouldn't get sick again. *Yes, I know... I made my bed, and now I had to sleep in it.*

I talked to Jill earlier in the week and made sure she had retrieved her car with no problems—which she had—and I was scheduled to stay with her again later tonight, which was the topic of our current conversation.

"If I'm going to help you sneak out to see Christian again, you're going to have to take me with you!" her voice blared through the phone.

Wow. Looks like she was already calling in the favor I owed her. Not that I minded, I just wasn't expecting *that.* "Um... okay, sure. I think that could be fun. And, since you are twenty-one, you can actually go inside while I *visit* with Christian."

Jillian laughed. "Okay, sounds good. I'll see you in a bit."

Dad had already left for his meeting in Masen, and his driver would be here to pick me up shortly to deliver me to Jill's just before six. Stuffing in a few random pieces of clothing in my bag, I thought about the last time I went to see Christian, and hoped things would be back to normal this time.

I never truly had serious boyfriend before, and after receiving Mom's blessing before she died, Christian was the one thing that kept me sane during this sheltered existence I was now forced to live.

Finished packing, I raced downstairs just as Dennis rang the bell.

"Ready to go?"

"Absolutely."

After plotting with Jillian, we explained to her parents we wanted to skip dinner so we could take in a double feature at the movie theatre instead. A total lie.

This was going to be the most time I've been able to spend with Christian in months. Usually, I had to wait for Jill's parents to fall asleep, then with her help, sneak out without waking them, setting off the dog, or tripping the flood lights. Once all that was accomplished, I would only have a couple hours to get there, see Christian, and get back. But tonight, we had checked the movie times, and after taking our drive time into account, we had gotten the okay to be gone for almost four hours.

But honestly, I really didn't know what Christian and I were going to do to fill the time. I mean, sure, don't get me wrong, I had plenty of ideas, but it wasn't like he could take a four-hour break. Suddenly, the thought of being stuck outside in the car waiting while Jillian and Christian were both inside, didn't sound too great.

"Hey, does this look okay?"

I turned around and gasped.

Jillian was on the volleyball team at school and had a great, athletic body: lean and muscular, with minimal curves and a small chest, so I barely recognized the person in front of me now. She had darkened her makeup quite a bit from the last time we were in front of the mirror, and her deep, chestnut hair hung loosely to her shoulders instead of being pulled up at the sides like it was before. But even more shocking than that were her clothes. I didn't even know she owned clothes like this. A red leather miniskirt and a silver sequin halter hugged her frame, while black, knee-high boots made her at least four inches taller than she already was.

"Um, yeah! You look really hot actually." I tried not to sound as stunned as I felt.

"Cool. The last time I was in that club to go pee after that concert, the people in there basically oozed sex. I just want to make sure I fit in."

Well, shit. Maybe I should rethink my outfit too. I'd never really thought about the patrons of The Rising Pit before, since Christian and I were always alone, but I had to admit, her comment sparked a bit of insecurity in me. Maybe I *should* be more worried about the people who surrounded Christian night after night. What if I wasn't the only girl in his life? *Oh, God.* I felt nauseous. "Give me a sec... I'm going to go change."

After trading my plain jeans and tank top in for a black, sleek fitting dress and heels, Jillian and I headed out.

"So, have you and Christian done the deed yet?" Jillian's smile was reflected in the window.

I knew she was teasing, but I huffed out my answer. "Unfortunately, no. Not that we're waiting for any particular reason, we just haven't exactly had the... space." I laughed.

"Well, maybe if Christian can talk Evangeline in to letting you in tonight, you guys can sneak off to one of those private booths they have upstairs and finally seal the deal." Jill tongue was pressed between her teeth, showing her most onery smile.

"Wait. How do you know there are private booths upstairs?"

"When I was in there to use the restroom, someone was talking about them, saying that she wished she could get an invitation or something. I just thought that since Christian has access, it would be the perfect place for you guys to score some alone time tonight."

Suddenly, I felt a rush of energy pulse through my veins. "Well, *if* Evangeline lets me in tonight, I think you're right; a private tour sounds like the perfect plan."

After parking, Jillian went inside to let Christian know we were here, and I couldn't stop thinking about what she had said. I knew the club had a reputation for being a very sultry place, but honestly, I'd never really spent much time thinking about what went on inside. Maybe I should.

I looked up and saw Christian walking toward the car. *Damn, he looks good.* Suddenly, I hoped that what I was thinking about was *exactly* what went on inside.

"Hi gorgeous!" He greeted me with a kiss that effectively weakened my knees. "I've got a surprise for you." He held up a black rubber bracelet. "Evie said that from now on you're welcome in the club whenever you want, as long as you wear this. She had it made for you after checking with the liquor board."

I looked down at the black band which had the club's logo on it, and the words UNDER 21 painted in white.

"This is great, but how did Evangeline know that I wanted to come inside the club tonight?" I asked.

Christian had a huge smile plastered on his face. "I think she decided to have it made after the last time you were here. She actually had a bunch of them made. She's planning to bring in some extra revenue by opening the club to 18+ kids a couple of nights a week." With a fake pout he continued, "I'm just not sure I'm ready to share you with everyone else."

He pulled me close, placed his hands on my hips, and looked me straight in the eye. "I like having you all to myself."

I couldn't tell if it was from his honeyed tone, or from the way his body pressed into mine, but I was suddenly flush and covered in goosebumps. Just then, Jill stuck her head out of the front door and yelled, "Hey you two, get in here!" Christian smiled and took my hand, then led me to the club's front door. I took a deep breath. *I don't like sharing you with anyone else either.*

The club was dark and sexy. A thin layer of smoke drifted in the air as multi-colored lights pulsed from all different directions. The music was sensual and had a very 'bump-and-grind' beat to it, and the guests were just as Jillian described... oozing sex. There were amazingly beautiful women and men dancing and making out everywhere I looked. Suddenly, I didn't like the idea of Christian working here at all.

"Come on, Evie wants to talk to you," he yelled over the music.

Making our way toward Evangeline's office at the back of the club, I got a weird feeling everyone was watching me. It was like they were waiting to see what I was going to do... or what Evie was going to do to me.

We entered Evangeline's office, and she gracefully rose from her chair. "Hello, Rose. I'm so glad that we could accommodate you tonight. I'm sure Christian already told you, but I want to extend my invitation personally. You are welcome at The Rising Pit whenever you'd like, as long as you wear your bracelet."

"Thank you so much, I really appreciate you thinking of me. I'll be turning twenty-one in a few months, but until I move out of my dad's house, I won't be down that often, but this is such a generous thing for you to do in the meantime."

"What? You're moving out? When?" Christian's tone was sharp and serious.

"Well, yeah. As soon as I graduate college., which will be at the end of May. Remember? I told you—I'm graduating early because of all the AP classes I took in high school. I only agreed to live with Dad as long as I was in college."

Christian seemed upset at my news, and I couldn't understand why. I thought he'd be happy for me... for us. Once I was out on my own, we'd be able to see each as much as we wanted. But instead, he stood there frowning, and I was more than a little annoyed by the change of subject.

He reached for my arm. "I don't like the idea of you living alone. Not after what happened to your mom."

And now my evening was ruined.

"Really? You sound just like my dad. What, do you think the guy who killed my mom has been keeping tabs on me this whole time? Just waiting for me to move out so he could strike?" I shook my head. "Be realistic, Christian. Just because I've had to face tragedy in my life, doesn't mean I'm different from any other twenty-one-year-old living out on her own. Besides, I'm tougher than you think." I yanked my arm away and headed for the door. "Thanks again for the kind gesture, Evangeline, but it looks like I won't be needing it after all."

I rushed out of Evangeline's office and spotted Jillian at the bar. Realizing she'd just ordered, I grabbed her arm and apologized. "Sorry, change of plans... forget the drink. We need to go."

CHAPTER EIGHT

(Rose)

Christian reached for hand just as I made it to the front door. "Rose, what's wrong?" His face was lined with genuine concern.

We had never fought before, so this was his first taste of my temper, and right now... it had just started to burn.

"What's wrong is that I'm sick of everyone treating me like a kid!" I screamed over the music. "You don't seem to think I'm too young when your tongue is down my throat or your hand is up my shirt, now do you?"

Taken aback, he gasped and dropped my hand. Standing quiet for a moment, he cocked his head toward the door. "Let's go outside." He walked out, leaving me standing there wondering if we'd survive our first fight.

I glanced at Jillian standing next to me with wide eyes and a concerned look on her face. Leaning in, I raised my voice and shouted, "I'll be right back." She nodded and quickly returned to the bar, reclaiming her seat and drink.

Once outside, I popped my ears, adjusting for the void of the loud music and spotted Christian leaning against his car with his arms crossed over his chest. We locked eyes as he tracked me from across the lot.

The moment I was within range, he said, "I don't understand why you're so mad." Thick emotion laced his voice. "I love you, Rose, and it's only natural I'd be concerned and worried about you."

Listening to him express his feelings so openly made me realize, I'd probably just ruined our entire night. "I'm sorry," I whispered. "But after living with my dad's strict rules for all these months, I guess I'm just overly sensitive to anyone trying to coddle me."

He took my face in his hands. "Rose, I'm not trying to coddle you. I'm just worried about you living on your own. I'm your boyfriend, I love you, and that gives me the right to be concerned."

He loves me. A warm sensation spread throughout my body as the fact settled deep in my bones. I pulled his hands away from my face and stepped into his embrace. "Can we talk about this later?" I reached up and laced my fingers through his hair. "I just really need to be close to you right now."

I didn't wait for his response.

Leaning in, I brushed my lips across his... gentle and hesitant to gauge his response. When I pulled back, his eyes were closed and his breathing was shallow, as a sexy smile spread across his face.

Pulling me close again, he hugged me tightly. "All I ever want is to be close to you," he whispered in my ear.

Wrapping my arms around his broad shoulders, I leaned up and kissed his neck. He reacted by running his fingers through my hair and tilting my head so he could do the same. The feel of his lips and tongue sliding along my skin gave me goose bumps. He pulled away, looking concerned. "Are you cold? Do you want to go back inside?"

I didn't. Not at all. I just wanted to stay out here in the dark with him—where Christian and I were the most comfortable. But, I knew I had to get back to Jillian, and Christian needed to get back to work. So, after a few more kisses, I said, "Yes, we should probably go." I couldn't hide my disappointment.

After double and triple checking that I was okay, Christian led me back inside. He went straight back to work, and I went looking for Jillian.

She wasn't in her seat, and her drink had already been cleared from the bar. So, after waiting my turn, I flagged down Dominique—the older of the two sister bartenders. "Did you happen to see where my friend went?" I yelled.

She lifted her chin, gesturing toward the bathroom.

"Thanks," I shouted back. I didn't know Dominique very well, but during the few run-ins we'd had, she'd always been really nice.

I headed toward the restroom, hoping Jillian was okay. Once inside, I called her name, but there was no response. After checking under the stalls and verifying they were all empty, I headed back out to the dance floor.

A sea of people covered the space, writhing together, either lost to the music or to the throes of passion. Finally, I glimpsed a speck of red out of the corner of my eye. Jillian, in her red leather miniskirt, was currently making her way up the curved staircase that led to the club's second floor. And she wasn't alone.

Pushing through the crowd, I struggled to keep my eyes on her and her mystery companion, but kept losing them as I elbowed my way to the base of the stairs. Finally, breaking through, I glanced up just in time to see them dip behind a thick red curtain. But as I started up the stairs, Evangeline appeared.

Placing a hand on my arm, she motioned for me to follow her. I really didn't want to go, but thought it would be a bad idea to refuse Christian's boss. So, feeling frustrated and with one more glance upstairs, I turned away and let her lead me back to her office again.

"Are you okay, Rose?" she asked as soon as we were inside.

"Yes, I'm fine." I tried to sound as convincing as possible.

"I'm sorry that Christian's concern was upsetting to you. He tends to wear his heart on his sleeve, and as with most men, that can often translate into a fierce protectiveness. It's obvious that he's very much in love with you." She sounded more like his mother instead of his boss.

"I love him, too." I replied softly. This wasn't exactly a discussion I thought I'd have with Evangeline, but it suddenly felt good to have someone older to talk to. "That's why I thought he'd be happy I was moving out. We'll be able to spend so much more time together."

"I'm sure that he'll come around. As a woman who's lived alone for years, *I* know you'll be fine, but it's always hard to convince the men who love us that we don't need them 24/7," she joked. "Why don't you go wait at the bar? I'll let him know he can take his first break."

"Okay, great. Thank you."

As we left the office and headed back toward the bar, it took me a moment to muster my courage. "Evangeline, would it be alright if Christian gave me a tour of the club tonight? Since it's officially my first time inside, I'd really love to see more of the place."

She hesitated briefly. "Sure. I think that'll be fine. I'll send him your way."

I smiled and sat down just as Tori placed a drink in front of me. I waved my bracelet at her. "Thanks, but I'm not allowed."

"It's just soda," she yelled, smiling as she headed toward the man struggling to get her attention from the other end of the bar. Right then, I made a conscious note to myself; once I moved out and could come here more often, I would definitely be getting to know her and Dominique better. They seemed like a couple of really cool chicks.

I sat there waiting for Christian, thinking about Jillian and what the hell she could be doing up there with a complete stranger. Not that I didn't have an idea... she *was* older than me and way more experienced. But she was my best friend, and I had brought her here, so yeah... I was feeling a little overprotective, I guess.

How ironic.

"So, I hear I'm to give you a tour." Christian's smooth voice floated to my ear.

"Yes, you are." I slid off my stool and into his arms. "Let's start upstairs."

Of course I wanted some alone time with him, but this was also where I'd last seen Jill—two birds, one stone and all that.

As we rounded the top of the staircase, I heard noises indicating everyone in this vicinity was having a *really* good time. "What are all these curtained off areas?" I asked, having a feeling I already knew.

"These are our private rooms." He hesitated. "VIP guests can invite patrons to join them up here for a more *intimate* party of sorts." He shrugged and shook his head. I think he was nervous about how I would react. And I probably would've been mad if Jill hadn't planted her wicked idea in my head earlier tonight.

"Are any of them empty now, so we can have a more *intimate* party of our own?" I batted my lashes and let a slow grin play across my lips. Christian's chest expanded as he took a deep breath, a feral look settling on his face. In the next moment, he was pulling me into the private room at the end of the hall.

And that's when Jillian screamed.

CHAPTER NINE

(Rose)

I spun and ran back toward the room I'd seen Jill disappear into. As I reached for the curtain, Christian was in front of me, pushing me back.

"Let me by!" I screamed. "Jillian's in there with some strange guy!"

"It's my job, Rose. Let me do it." He had a serious look on his face and walked me back toward the railing.

Dax bound up the stairs in the next second, giving Christian a quick nod. "Let's go."

Squeezing both of my hands, Christian looked me straight in the eyes. "Stay here. I'll bring her right out to you."

I nodded and gripped the railing… hard. *Dammit.* I knew I should have followed her up here.

After some light rustling and low voices, Jillian appeared from behind the curtain with a napkin pressed to her neck.

I rushed to hug her. "Are you okay?"

"Yes, I'm fine. I broke a glass and a couple stray pieces flew into my neck." She pulled away the blood-soaked napkin revealing two small, bloody dots.

"Oh, thank God. I thought that strange guy was attacking you or something."

She laughed. "He's not strange, and he's no stranger. I've known Justin for a while now."

I jerked back. I should've felt relieved, but I didn't. Instead a layer of annoyance settled over me. "How do you know him? I've never seen him before. Does he go to our school?"

Dabbing at her neck again, she shook her head. "No. I met him at the gym. In the yoga class I take at night."

"Yoga? Since when do you take yoga? And what would a guy like that be doing in a yoga class?" I could tell by the look on Jill's face I'd crossed a line, but I didn't care.

"Picking up pretty girls of course," a smart-assed voice replied. I looked up to see *Justin* as he made his way out of the private room with Christian and Dax following closely behind. He was definitely Jill's type:

longer blond hair, blue eyes, great body. *Wow.* I guess yoga really does do a body good.

"Hi, I'm Justin." He extended his hand, which I did not take.

I'm not sure why I felt so pissed toward this guy, but I did. "I'm Rose, Jillian's best friend. So exactly how long have you two known each other?"

"About four months." Jillian's snapped.

I knew she thought I was being rude, but it was just too bad. "Huh. Four months, and I've heard nothing about you." I turned to stomp toward the stairs, but Jillian grabbed my arm.

"Hey, what's wrong with you? When you were outside with Christian, I ran into Justin. We danced, and then he invited me up here. We were having a good time, then I broke a glass and screamed. Next thing I know Christian and this brute," she flicked a thumb toward Dax, "come busting in. And now here you are being all shitty. What's up with that?"

I didn't have an explanation for her. I was relieved she was okay, but I also felt angry and annoyed. Right as my temper started to rise for the second time tonight, Christian eased up beside me and placed a calming hand on my lower back. It was exactly what I needed.

I looked at Jill who had gravitated toward Justin. Taking a moment to really process the scene, I could tell he was truly worried about her. He was holding her hand in one of his, and with the other, reached up and started massaging tiny circles at the back of her neck, beneath her curtain of hair.

I took a deep breath. "Look, I'm sorry. It's just when I saw you disappear with someone that I *thought* was a stranger, and then I heard you scream... it really scared me." Feeling embarrassed, I tried to play it off. "I guess Dad's over protectiveness is rubbing off on me." I couldn't tell her why I was really upset... I couldn't tell anyone.

"Why don't you and Justin join us so I can get to know him a little better?" I offered. After almost blowing it with Christian, and now with Jillian, I wasn't sure it was possible, but I really wanted to try to end tonight on a high note.

Just then, I caught Justin eyeing Christian who exchanged a quick look with Dax. "Thank you, but I should really be going." Justin kissed Jillian on the cheek and darted down the stairs. Now I really felt bad because I had just chased off my best friend's boy toy for the night. Can you say cockblock?

I started to ask Christian if we could head back downstairs when Dax nudged his shoulder. "Can I speak with you privately?"

"Sure," Christian replied.

Kissing me once more, Christian left a fuming Jill and I standing alone at the top of the stairs.

Awesome.

CHAPTER TEN

(Christian)

After kissing Rose, Dax and I ducked back into Justin's private room. It was the same one he always reserved for his visitors. Justin was part of the nearby clan that resided just east of Masen.

Evangeline had made it a point to let all the vampires in the area know they were welcome at The Rising Pit, as long as they followed her rules.

Rule 1: Don't feed in public.

Rule 2: Make each feeding pleasant for your guest.

Rule 3: Make sure your guest doesn't remember.

Rule 4: *Never* kill.

Simple enough. There had never been a problem with anyone following the rules. On average, there were only about six or seven vampires that visited per night, and since there were fifteen private rooms, that meant there was always a place available for them to feed.

Making their visitor's experience pleasurable was just as easy as making them forget. All they had to do was use the sedative that flows from their fangs; the instant they pierced a vein, they could program their desires into that sedative. Tonight, it was obvious Justin's sedative had worked in order to make Jillian believe she'd been cut by a stray piece of broken glass.

"That was close," Dax stated bluntly.

"Yeah, I know. I would have never imagined the one person Justin decided to feed on tonight would be Rose's best friend. What are the odds?"

"Actually, it seems the odds are pretty good. I scanned Justin and the best friend. She was telling the truth. Jillian and Justin do know each other; apparently, he feeds from her all the time. Yoga is the cover story if you hadn't guessed."

Damn. How was I supposed to keep Rose from learning my secret if she was going to be moving out soon, coming here more often, and had a best friend that was the chosen guest of one of our regular vamps? This really sucked.

"Justin honestly does like Jillian if that helps at all." Dax was trying to make me feel better, but it wasn't working.

Just as we finished cleaning, the curtains parted and Evangeline walked in. "Did we have a problem? I saw Rose and her friend outside."

"No. No problem." Dax kissed her on the cheek. "We were just cleaning up Justin's mess. From what I got from my scan, when things got a little hot and heavy between him and Jillian, she screamed in delight. Then, he heard Rose and Christian coming and decided to break the glass to use as his cover."

"That was quick thinking." Frown lines appeared on Evie's forehead, evidence that she was concentrating on something else. Suddenly her eyes widened and her head snapped in my direction. "How does Rose know Terrance?"

"What?" I was shocked, then realized she must be scanning the girls outside as we spoke.

"I'm scanning Jillian, and her memory of the evening is just as you described. She knows Justin from *yoga*. They were making out up here, then she broke a glass and sent pieces flying into her neck. What I don't understand is why I just saw an image of Terrance float through Rose's mind." Evie stared at me.

"I have no idea." A lump formed in my throat, then I remembered she'd been with me when Terrance came out of the woods the other night. "She did see him coming out of the woods."

Evie remained silent for a few more moments. "Right now, she's thinking of everyone she's met here: Dom, Tori, us, and though Terrance flashed through her mind just a moment ago, he's no longer present in her subconscious."

Relieved, I sat down on the couch. "I just wish we would get a sign of the new Sire already. I'm so sick of keeping my life from her. I want to tell her the truth."

Evie sat down beside me. "I know it's hard Christian, but until you have approval from the new Sire that the change will be made, you know you can't tell Rose about us."

I knew she was right, but I couldn't help thinking how much easier it would be if Rose knew about my family. I couldn't wait to start making plans with her, maybe even move in together. And the best part was, I'd finally be able to feed from her—with her permission, of course. But that wasn't going to happen any time soon. "Are we done here? I need to get back to Rose."

"Yes, we're done." Evie looked sympathetic as she took Dax's hand and headed toward the curtained exit. "I feel so bad for him," I heard her whisper.

"Don't feel bad for me Evie. I know it will all work out soon."

Suddenly, she whipped around and launched herself directly at me, grabbing me by my shirt as she slammed me down onto the couch.

"What the hell?" I yelled.

The curtains flew open, and I saw Rose and Jillian standing there, taking in the scene before them. I was lying on the couch as Evangeline hovered over me, both her hands wadded in the front of my shirt.

"What the hell's going on here?" Rose demanded.

Evangeline stared deeply into my eyes before smoothing the front of my shirt back in place. Then, she plastered a smile on her face. "Christian just saved me," she said as she righted herself. "My heel snapped and thankfully he broke my fall."

I looked at Evie and got the distinct feeling that something major had just happened between us. Unfortunately, I had no idea what it was. It was obvious, though, now was not the time to discuss it. She bent down and removed her shoe, which did in fact have a broken heel. After apologies and polite goodnights, she and Dax left the room.

Rose turned back to me with a skeptical look on her face. She had questioned my relationship with Evie when we'd first started dating, and I'd told her the truth then; that *she* was the only one for me and had nothing to worry about, and I was going to make sure she knew it again now. I was in love with her and only her. "Jillian, could you excuse us for a few minutes?"

$$* * * * *$$

(Rose)

Jillian took Christian's hint and left us alone. "What really happened in here, Christian?" I hated questioning him, but walking in here to find him sprawled underneath his gorgeous boss on the couch, definitely set off the jealousy bugs in my brain.

"Rose, I promise nothing strange happened. Dax and I were cleaning up the broken glass when Evie came in to check to make sure everything was okay. She tripped on something, and then the next thing I knew... boom; we landed on the couch."

I supposed that was believable enough. I mean Dax *had* been standing right there. "Alright. I believe you." I sat down on the couch and let him pull me close. It felt so amazing to be wrapped in his arms.

"Have I told you how sexy you look tonight?" he asked.

"No, you haven't."

"Then how about I show you instead?"

Christian's kiss was sweet at first, but deepened as he maneuvered me on top of him.

"I want you so much," I whispered against his lips.

"I want you too, Rose. More than you can possibly know. But we can't. Not here."

Disappointment fell heavy across my skin as we kissed for a few more minutes. I was ready to take our relationship to the next level, but understood.

Sitting us up, Christian apologized. "I'm so sorry, but I have to get back to work."

Righting my clothes, I stood up and followed him from the room.

He walked me back down to the bar, to where Jillian had reclaimed her seat. "I'll see you later." He smiled and squeezed my hand.

I glanced at Jillian—still holding a napkin to her neck—then down at my watch. "Actually, I think we better go."

Christian nodded, then leaned in for one last kiss. "Okay. Besides, you have your bracelet now, and can come back whenever you have the chance."

"True. But that'll still be only once a month until I'm able to move out."

His face dropped, reminding me he wasn't thrilled with the idea. But now was not the time to discuss it. Plus, soon enough, he would see things my way.

Everyone would.

CHAPTER ELEVEN

(Evie)

"Evie, what's wrong? You seem distracted," Dax asked.

"I'm going to talk to Terrance. I'm still feeling uneasy about seeing him in Rose's thoughts tonight. Of course I remember she saw him coming out of the woods recently, but I have a gut feeling there's more to it than that. I didn't mention it before, because I don't want to upset Christian."

"How in the world could Rose know Terrance?"

"I have no idea, but you can damn sure bet I'm going to find out." I turned and stomped toward my office to make use of my private entrance into the rising pit, leaving Dax to deal with the club's closing.

There were a number of things about tonight that had me feeling on edge. The strange image of Terrance in Rose's mind; the fact Rose's best friend ended up being Justin's chosen visitor; and the most shocking?– Christian having commented on something that I had *thought*, not said. I was so taken aback when it happened, I launched myself straight at him. The poor kid probably thought I was attacking him, but I wasn't. It's been almost ninety years since I lost my Siring ability, and if Christian was starting to hear people's thoughts, that meant that he was developing powers which was the first sign of a vampire being triggered to become a Sire. I realize I overacted, but the thought of Christian becoming a Sire jolted me. I just wish I'd had time to explain before Rose walked in that I was ecstatic, not angry. The thought of Christian become the next Sire of my line... How amazing would that be? But man-oh-man would I miss him when it was time for him to leave.

All new Sires were expected to leave their current clan in order to start their own. I would retain my powers and control over my clan, but if Christian truly was going to be the next Sire, I would lose someone that I loved very much. *Dang it*. I couldn't think about that right now.

As I made the trek into the pit, I kept going over what I'd glimpsed in Rose's head. Images of Dominique and Tori helping her at the bar, of Dax and Christian entering the private room together, and of myself sitting in my office. But then I had seen the flash of Terrance. It was so quick, that it gave me no way to pinpoint the specifics, and that's what really bothered me.

As I rounded the corner, I heard Terrance rattling his chains. I shouldn't have been surprised that he didn't like the idea of being alone with me. I may not look imposing or frightening to the naked eye, but since I was the one who decided if they lived or died, my clan couldn't help but fear me. Luckily, I had never been forced to kill anyone in my clan... yet.

I approached the cell which had no door, but instead a large square opening that led into the room. The walls were composed of gray cinderblocks and had several sets of chains mounted to them, as well as to the ceiling and the floor. I realized that this was the first time I'd ever had to use them. It made me sad.

"Terrance. How are you feeling tonight?" His eyes were locked on mine, radiating hatred. This wasn't a look I saw very often. After all, we were family, and there was very rarely a reason for discord among us.

"What do you want Evie?" Terrance's tone was laced with contempt, "You already had Dax scan me, remember?"

"Yes, I remember. And I know that you're hiding something. But I'm not here to talk about the girl in the woods. What I want to know about is Rose." I had hoped the abruptness of my question would shock him into revealing something right away, but no such luck. Instead, I was only picking up on our current conversation running through his head.

"Rose, who?"

"Rose Reynolds, Christian's girlfriend."

"Oh. The curvy blonde he's been dying to take a bite out of for months?" His tone was harsh and sarcastic.

"Christian loves her. He knows he can't feed from the one he loves without giving himself and his secret away. But what about you, Terrance? Do you love anything anymore?"

"Look at me, Evie. I think you know the answer to that." He was referring to his now permanently darkened appearance. It was obvious he no longer felt love for anything and wasn't going to drift back. He was practically forcing me to inflict the true death on him. Like he was asking for it.

"Are you ready? Or would you like to see Dax one last time?" I couldn't help the quiver in my voice. I knew I had no choice, but Terrance was like a son to Dax. Back when I had turned Terrance, Dax had made it a point to watch over his wife and children, ensuring they were safe and well taken care of before we moved on. That had sealed their friendship for centuries.

"No. What's the point? Just do it." Terrance went slack and lowered his head.

Our true death wasn't as horrific as it had been portrayed on TV or in any of the books people had read. In reality, it was quite simple. All I had to do was sink my fangs into Terrance's neck and program my sedative to carry the poison of death into his system—another power that resided only with the Sire. The poison would then spread through his veins, effectively paralyzing him as it hardened his body, eventually reaching his heart.

While the heart of a vampire no longer beat, it was still the main energy source for our afterlife. Once the poison reached his heart, it would harden and wither, and then he'd simply turned to dust. No mess, no fuss... just dust.

As I approached, I could feel the tension drain from his body. He knew that this was the end. I gently placed my hands on his shoulders and guided us both down onto our knees. I looked into his eyes and kissed him once on the cheek.

As I extended my fangs and lowered my head to his neck, I couldn't stop the tear that dripped from my chin and landed on Terrance's shoulder. He tensed as the evidence of my emotions ran down his bare arm. I felt a slight shudder move through him. *Finally.* When faced with the end of his existence, he started to show some emotion... and that's when I struck.

CHAPTER TWELVE

(Rose)

After my goodbye with Christian, Jillian and I climbed into her car and headed for home. "Did you end up having *any* fun tonight?" Jillian asked.

Not really. But I didn't want to tell her that; she'd think it was all her fault. "Sure, it was fun being able to hangout inside for once, and spending time with Christian is always great." I tried to sound convincing, but it didn't work.

"Then what were you guys fighting about earlier?" She looked at me with that *don't bullshit me* look on her face. The one that only a best friend could pull off.

"He wasn't thrilled when I announced that I'd be moving out soon." My voice had gone flat. I understood he worried so much because he loved me, but it was imperative that I got out of Dad's house as soon as possible. With everything that had happened, I just couldn't handle being there anymore.

"You'd think he'd be psyched that you're getting your own place. I mean, it's total freedom and you guys would get to see each other all the time. What's his problem?"

See, this is why I loved my best friend. She gets me.

"That's exactly what I was thinking. But when I told him and Evangeline, he freaked out and said he didn't like the idea of me living alone. Honestly, it still chaps my ass when I think about it. But… I know that once I have my place, he'll chill out and realize just how brilliant it is. We'll be together all the time. Together forever." I plastered on a cheeky grin.

Jillian remained quiet for the stretch of a few miles. "Actually, I was hoping we'd be getting a place together, but it sounds like you're setting up house for just you and Christian." Her voice rang with disappointment.

"Oh! Well, I guess I hadn't thought much about a roommate. And you don't graduate college for another year and a half." Jill hadn't taken the AP courses like I had, so even though she was older than me, she was only in the middle of her junior year. "Plus, I thought your plan was to keep mooching off your parents for as long as possible," I joked.

"My parents aren't as strict as your dad, and I'm already twenty-one. If I want to move out, I'm sure they will keep paying for college and everything as longs as I keep my grades up." She was defending her case well, but with what I had planned for my future... I really couldn't have a roommate.

"I don't know Jill. Won't it be weird to be there with Christian and I together so much?" I usually didn't mind talking to her about this kind of stuff. I mean we talked about sex all the time, but when it came to this, I really just wish she'd drop it.

"Um, haven't you ever heard of setting rules and using code? A tie on the doorknob, switching off days of the week, a certain colored hall light? Or, we could always just look for a place that had a great layout where the bedrooms were far apart. I'll be having Justin over too ya know!" *Wow... she was really picturing this happening.*

Snagging the opportunity to change the subject I said, "Tell me more about Justin. I can't believe you guys met at a yoga class. That's just so... strange."

"Why is it strange? I found the class when I was walking home one night after a volleyball game with Penny. We thought it looked fun, so we stopped in to grab a brochure, and as we were coming back out, we ran into Justin."

"So he doesn't actually take the class? He just lurks outside of it?" This just kept getting better and better.

"What is your problem with him? Is it because I didn't tell you that I'd met someone new?" Now, she was getting defensive. "Like I said, we met about four months ago, but we've only gone out a few times. I guess I just didn't want to say anything until I knew how I really felt about him. And, honestly, before tonight we hadn't even made out." Her cheeks were red and her breath was coming out in small, tight huffs.

"And so, after one make-out session, you're ready to invite him into your house and make it official?"

"Yeah. Actually I am." The look she gave me dared me to say anything else. Which I didn't.

We rode the rest of the way home in silence.

CHAPTER THIRTEEN

(Christian)

After feeding and closing the club for the night, we all started to make our way down to the pit. Dax and I told everyone what happened with Justin and Jillian, and their laughter and jokes weren't helping my mood.

All my vampire brothers and sisters thought it was hilarious that after 602 years, I went and fell in love with a human. So, anything that made my situation with Rose more difficult was like the punch line to the most hysterical joke to them.

They continued to tease me and laugh as we made our way to the bottom of the stairs. The circular enclosure, and top of our pit, settled in place with its customary boom. That's when we heard Terrance scream.

Dax glanced in my direction, his eyes wide and a panicked look on his face. He took off running, and we all rushed to follow.

With our preternatural vampire speed, we filled the opening outside the cell within seconds. Once there, we all shared a collective sigh.

Evie wasn't delivering the true death to Terrance, but was, instead, looming over him with both of her hands clasped on either side of his face. He screamed again just as Evie whipped back her head of jet-black hair.

I'd never seen anything like this before. I thought she was "making him sing," but he wasn't *singing*. Only screams broke his lips.

Dax move forward, preparing to enter the cell, when Evie let Terrance go. He hit the ground like a drunk who'd finally reached his limit. Dax caught Evie just as she started to do the same.

Her hair immediately drifted back to its natural, medium brown, and she held his eyes for a moment, then whispered, "There's a woman." In the next moment, she collapsed into his arms.

Dominique was the first to move. She helped Dax gather Evie then followed him to their room. Bobby, Tori, and I slowly made our way forward and could do nothing more than stare at Terrance lying on the floor, still in chains.

"So, who the fuck is this woman?" Tori's question broke the silence. It was laced with a touch of venom, as she and Terrance had been known to occasionally mess around.

"I don't know," I said.

"Looks like we'll have to wait until tomorrow to find out. The sun's almost up, and I'm barely going to make it to my room as it is." Bobby waved us off and headed down the hall.

We were your typical vampires. When the sun rose, we fell. Literally.

Even though the sun didn't burn us, once it rose in the sky, we were rendered comatose, not rising again until it set. It was a real pain in the ass.

Imagine if we got caught in a park or were walking along a road when the sun started to rise... you'd find tons of *dead* people lying all over the place until they *magically* got up once the sun went down. Not exactly the easiest thing to explain. So, for the protection of our species, every clan had a secure lair, like our pit. And, like good little boys and girls, we all made sure that we were tucked in our beds before the sun came up. No one liked waking up on a hard floor or in a ditch somewhere.

The moment my head hit the pillow, I shut my eyes and thought of Rose. This was my ritual every night. Since we didn't dream in our comatose state, whatever we thought of last would also be what we thought of first, and I loved that. Waking up to an image of Rose was pure heaven.

* * * * *

(Rose)

When I woke up and didn't see my twinkling stars, I panicked for a few seconds. I always did that when staying over at Jill's. It took me a few moments to realize where I was.

After our awkward ride home last night, we'd gotten over it in our usual way—sharing our customary bowl of ice cream before going to bed.

Today was Saturday, and since Dad wouldn't be home before 4 p.m., I thought I'd ask Jill to go look at apartments with me.

Yes. This was me trying to say I was sorry.

I still had no intention of rooming with her, but I would drop that bomb later. Right now, I just really wanted her with me while I scoped out my prospects. I was a little nervous, I guess.

The first neighborhood we drove to was only about ten minutes away from my house, and honestly, I wasn't sure I wanted to be that close to home. But it was a nice complex and was within walking distance of some really great shops and restaurants which added bonus points to my checklist. But as we drove up, I couldn't help but giggle. The sign read, "Tranquil Acres."

"What's so funny?" Jill asked.

"It sounds more like a retirement home than an apartment complex."

Jill laughed. "Yeah, but this one's is supposed to be one of the nicer ones in the area."

She was right, and even better, the business district would be a relatively short commute from here. Even though I didn't need money, since my mom's settlement would sustain me for most of my life, I was still planning on getting a job after college. Being close to where I planned to work just earned this place another bonus point.

As Jillian and I headed toward the main office, I noticed a swimming pool off to my left. It was oversized and had wonderful landscaping. I pause momentarily, having a severe case of déjà vu.

Suddenly, I found myself on the ground with Jillian hovering over me. My breath pushed out of me in rapid succession, causing me to hyperventilate. I was seriously close to a full-blown panic attack.

"Rose, my God, what's wrong?"

The complex manager was headed toward us, and I tried to calm myself, but I wasn't sure I could. This pool reminded me of the one that my mom used to give swimming lessons in, but that still didn't explain why this was happening to me now. My mom had been a swim instructor, and it wasn't like I hadn't been around pools since her death, but for some reason seeing this pool had me reliving more than I wanted to face.

"I'm so sorry." I repeatedly apologized to the complex manager, then raced back to Jill's car. I hated that I had made such a scene, but I really needed to get the hell out of here.

"What was that about?" Jill asked.

"I'm sorry, I freaked out. That pool must have reminded me of where my mom used to give swim lessons." My voice was shaky as my eyes filled with tears.

Jill leaned over and gave me an awkward hug in the car, "Oh, Rose. I'm sorry. Why'd you even put this one on your list then? Maybe we should mark off any complexes that have pools."

My voice caught on a sob. "I didn't realize something that simple could get to me so badly. Let's just get out of here."

I looked back and watched the pool fade into the distance as we drove off. I couldn't believe I'd had a panic attack because of a fucking swimming pool. But with everything that I had experienced with Mom during her lessons, I guess it shouldn't have come as that big of a surprise. Finding Mom being fed on by a vampire after one of her lessons was how I had come to learn they even existed in the first place.

CHAPTER FOURTEEN

(Christian)

I woke up and thought of Rose, just as planned. The image in my head was enough to start anyone's night out with a smile. But as I got dressed, a sense of dread slowly settled in my chest. I listened but couldn't hear anything out of the ordinary.

Maybe I was one of the first to rise. I hoped so, I couldn't wait to meet with Evie and see what all that craziness last night had been about. After showering and dressing for my night, I headed out to locate Evie and Dax to see what was on the agenda for the evening.

I rounded the corner at the end of the hall to find Dominique and Tori standing outside Evie and Dax's room with concerned looks on their faces.

"What's wrong?" I asked.

"Evie hasn't woken up," Dom replied.

Dax was sitting on the side of the bed, but as he got up and walked toward me, Evie's prone form was revealed. It looked like she was still comatose.

"Something's wrong," Dax stated. "She hasn't actually woken up, but I can hear her thinking in my head when I scan her. It's like she is aware, but she *can't* wake up. I keep getting glimpses of Terrance feeding from some woman in the dark, and for some reason, this *really* has Evie upset."

I wasn't sure why this would be so upsetting. Feeding in the dark wasn't exactly *unusual* behavior for any of us. None of us had ever killed anyone or been discovered, so the fact that this particular scene of Terrance feeding was so upsetting to Evie was definitely strange.

"Anyone have any ideas of who this woman could be?" Dax asked. "Has Terrance mentioned that he's been seeing anyone new lately?"

We all supplied a round of "Nos" as our individual answers. Just then Bobby joined us. "Why don't we just ask Terrance?" he suggested.

"I already have," Dax replied. "After I couldn't wake Evie, I went straight to his cell and questioned him about what happened last night. Needless to say, he wasn't very forthcoming. As I scanned him, all I got were images of Evie and him locked in the same embrace we all saw them in last night. It was like he was trying to only relive that moment. It just kept repeating in my head like a record."

Dominique shook her head, Tori started to bite her nails, and Bobby just swore "Well, shit."

I hated leaving things unsettled, but we had a club to open. "This is going to have to wait until tomorrow. We all need to head out to feed and get back in time to open the club," I stated.

Dax looked at me with a worried look on his face. Who could blame him? "I'm not leaving Evie. Christian, you're in charge of the club tonight, but come get me if there are any problems."

With our marching orders, we all scattered in different directions.

As I walked past Terrance's cell, I glanced inside to find him with his back to the opening. *Whatever.* It wasn't like I wanted to talk to him anyway.

"I know it was her. What the hell did she do to me?" I heard Terrance say. His voice was like a whisper on the wind.

"Who the fuck are you talking about?" I turned around to confront him.

He slowly spun around, a strange look plastered on his face, and just stood there... staring at me.

I asked him again, "Seriously, what are you talking about? And, who did what to you?"

This time, he took a couple of steps in my direction. "Can you hear what I'm thinking Christian?"

Frustrated he had the nerve to fuck with me like this, I tightened my fists, wanting nothing more than to enter his cell to beat his ass for some answers. But, since Evie had commanded us not to go near him, I literally couldn't touch him. Instead, I flipped him off and continued toward the stairs. *What an asshole.*

I'd never really liked Terrance anyway. Especially with the crap he'd been pulling lately. Now, it looked more and more like he'd done something to Evie while their minds were connected, and that was last straw. I was really over this guy.

* * * * *

(Evie)

Dammit, what the hell had Terrance done to me? I'm lying here trapped like a prisoner inside my own body. The last thing I remember was leaning in, pretending I was about to deliver the true death, and feeling his mental shields give way. That's when I struck. But instead of killing him, I tried again to make him sing about the root of why he'd permanently drifted dark. The second I found the image, his shields clamped back in place, and damn that hurt.

No one had ever been strong enough to do that to me before. But then again, it's not like I had to scan my people very often. Maybe my gifts were starting to fade, since it looked like Christian was close to becoming the new Sire—who the fuck knew. But, God, I really needed to wake up soon so we could figure out who that woman was, and why in the world Terrance was so afraid of her.

CHAPTER FIFTEEN

(Rose)

After my melt down at the apartments, Jillian drove me back to her house, and I cancelled all my other appointments for the day.

"Are you sure you're okay?"

"Yes. I'm fine."

And I was, it was just a little startling to realize how much I had blocked out about my mom. Apparently, I had gotten very good at hiding things... even from myself.

"Do you mind if I take a bath? I just need to be alone right now," I asked.

"Sure. Let me get you a towel." Jill headed toward the linen closet, glancing back repeatedly with a concerned look on her face.

There was no way I'd be able to explain why I was so freaked out, so she was just going to have to continue to think I was simply missing my mom. Which *was* true, but honestly, what I really needed to contemplate the most was how the hell Jillian had gotten mixed up with a vampire, and if I could use him to complete my original plan.

* * * * *

(Christian)

The club ran smoothly, even though we were all on edge. After closing, we all headed back to the pit and heard Dax's raised voice echoing from the end of the hall. "Tell me what you did to her!"

Shit. That didn't sound good. I guess Evie hadn't woken up. We all stopped and continued to listen from around the corner.

"I didn't *do* anything to her, I swear." Terrance sounded tired, but oddly enough, sincere. "I honestly thought she was going to deliver the true death, but instead she scanned me, trying to force me to *sing*. It hurt, and all I could do was scream. I wish she had just killed me instead."

My God, he sounded so sad.

"What happened to you, Terrance?" Dax asked, practically pleading. "Why can't you just tell me? We've been best friends for centuries. I've always known your darker appearance stems from the pain and sorrow you carry due to the loss of your family, but you never killed anyone and you've always drifted back... so what changed? And how the hell are you hiding it from us?"

"I'm not hiding anything. I don't know why you and Evie can't scan my thoughts. Honestly, I don't know what's happened to me."

The weird thing was... I actually believed him. Silence held for the next few seconds, then I motioned everyone around the corner.

"Everything okay?" Bobby asked.

"No. It's not okay. Evie is still comatose, but when I scan her, I can still hear her thoughts. I also keep getting the image of Terrance feeding from a woman in the dark. It should be no big deal, but it's really upsetting Evie. And Terrance won't tell me who the woman is or why Evie can't wake up." Dax sank to the floor in the hall, resting his back against the wall and placed his head in his hands.

I'd never seen him this distraught, but who could blame him? I knew he felt helpless—we all did.

"I told Dax I don't know why they can't scan my thoughts. I'm not purposely trying to hold anything back. I can remember a woman, but I don't know anything about her. Whenever I think of her, things just get fuzzy," Terrance said, sounding defeated from inside his cell.

I'd never heard of anything like this before, and I wondered if Evie had. Unless you'd gone through the ritual of being triggered and becoming a new Sire, no one else really knew a lot about the process or what went along with it. I was starting to wonder if her scanning ability had been weakened by the fact that she could no longer inflict *the change*. If Evie didn't wake up soon, I'd have no idea what we were going to do next.

Dax didn't seem to have a clue as to what was happening either. And from the looks of it, he was getting really pissed. Suddenly, he pushed himself up off the floor, and in a burst of speed, had Terrance by the throat. "I may not have the poison of true death, but I can still make you suffer."

I grabbed Dax by the arm and tried to ease his grip on Terrance. "Hey, hey, hey... I think we should all just clear our minds and calm down. *Wait*... Maybe that's it!

"Dax, you said that you can scan Evie's thoughts and see what's she's thinking, right?"

"Yeah? So?"

"Well, what if we used your scanning abilities to try to *communicate* with Evie. Since you're her consort, the bond you two share should not only allow you to scan her thoughts, but it should also let her scan yours as well."

Dax stared at me for a moment, and I couldn't tell if he thought I was crazy, or if he could see the brilliance of my plan. "Okay, so you're saying I should just think about how I want her to clear her mind and that should work?"

"Yes. Terrance said that when he thinks of this *woman*, his thoughts get all fuzzy. What if that's what's happening to Evie? Because she's so focused on this stranger, maybe that's why she can't wake up."

Everyone stared at me like I suddenly had three heads. I couldn't explain it, but I just knew this was the right thing to do, and there wasn't a moment to waste. "Come on. We at least have to try."

As everyone headed toward Evie and Dax's room, I heard Terrance whisper again, "What did she do to me?"

It was becoming glaringly obvious we needed to wake Evie up soon, and find out who this mystery woman was.

CHAPTER SIXTEEN

(Christian)

Dax sat down on the bed next to Evie while we all gathered around the door. He took her hand, closed his eyes, and lowered his head. I'd told him to focus on giving Evie a clear picture of letting go of her thoughts and releasing the image of Terrance and this woman out of her head.

After a few minutes, Dax opened his eyes. "I think it's working. When I scan her now, I can see that she is trying to focus on calming her thoughts and blanking out her mind. I think we should know any minute whether it's worked or not."

We all stood there holding our breath, anticipation so thick it coated the air. Nothing like this had ever happened to any of us before and honestly, I think we were all a little scared that Evie might never wake up. But right then Evie's eyelids fluttered. She was fighting to wake up. Thank God.

"Evie?" Dax pleaded. "Come on honey, I know you can do this. Come back to me. Come back to us all."

Dax was a big guy. He was muscular, had a buzz cut, and was easily the most intimidating of us all, but right now he sounded like a little kid who had lost his puppy. In my eyes it didn't make him any less of a man; it actually filled me with respect for him and the love that he carried for Evie. I felt the same way about Rose, and I knew that if anything like this ever happened to her, I would be acting the same way or worse.

Evie finally opened her eyes and took in Dax's face. She reached up and stroked his cheek. "Thank you, my love," she whispered. "How did you know that clearing my mind would work?"

"I didn't. It was Christian's idea." Dax scooped her up into his arms and started kissing the top of her head.

Evie stared at me with a look on her face that I couldn't quite describe. There was a hint of gratefulness, a hint of curiosity, and a hint of respect. I wanted to rush in and start asking questions, but just then Dominique spoke up. "Why don't we give these two some time alone? The sun is almost up and we'll all be out again soon, so let's just plan to meet back here first thing after rising. If that's okay with you, Evie?"

"Thank you, Dom. That would be great. I'll see you all after rising... and Christian, thank you."

I nodded my head and headed out the door toward my room. I couldn't wait until I had some alone time with Evie, because for some reason I had a feeling that there was more going on than just what had happened between her and Terrance. As a matter of fact, I still hadn't had the opportunity to ask her why the hell she launched herself at me back in the private room. So yeah, we definitely needed to talk.

After making my way back to my room, exhausted from the night's drama, I didn't even bother getting undressed. I just laid down on the bed and thought of Rose, letting the darkness claim me.

* * * * *

(Evie)

I watched Christian walk out my door as I relaxed into Dax's embrace. I had to figure out what all this meant. Not only did I need to get to the bottom of what was going on with Terrance, but I also needed to confirm if Christian really was the one being triggered to become the next Sire. It certainly appeared to be the case. He was able to hear my thoughts, and somehow, he'd mysteriously known that clearing my mind would work. I was actually starting to wonder what other traits he would start displaying. I tried to remember back to when I was triggered to become Sire, and these traits were definitely not things that had happened to me. But then again, thinking back that far was like trying to access ancient history.

Dax broke my train of thought as he twisted me around in his lap. "Are you truly okay Evie? I was worried sick and so mad that I almost tore Terrance limb from limb."

"I'm fine. Now that I'm awake, when I think about what happened, all I get is the image of Terrance and I locked in our embrace. For some reason I don't see the image of that woman. It's almost like it's now blocked from me."

"Terrance said that he isn't purposely hiding anything from us. That when he thinks back to the woman you mentioned things just become fuzzy."

"I don't know what's going on, Dax, but I'll admit I was scared, which really pisses me off. Nothing like that has ever happened to me before. Something strange is definitely going on, and we need to figure it out fast."

Dax hugged me tightly. "We'll figure it out Evie. I promise."

I didn't doubt him; I never did. Dax was the love of my life, and for a vampire, that's saying something. It had taken 327 years for me to find the perfect man to become my consort. It happened in 1162 A.D. when I was in Ireland. I had been on my way to find a boat to the Americas, and that's when I had first seen Dax.

He was working at the docks, and for the first time since becoming a vampire, I actually felt out of control. The pull that he had on me was like gravity. He was so beautiful: his sculpted body, his buzz cut brown hair, and those sparkling brown eyes had me postponing my trip just so I could stay and watch him.

I followed him for three days, but after several silent trips back and forth through the shadows, I knew he was the man I wanted to share eternity with. He was masculine, kind, and had a great sense of humor. But I didn't think I could bring myself to actually kill someone and force them into a life with me without them having a say at all. The next day, in a cruel twist of fate, my concern was eliminated for me.

There was an accident on the docks. One of the pulleys holding the ropes that were used to lift heavy containers onto the ship broke. I watched in horror as the large wooden crate headed straight for Dax. He didn't move fast enough and it landed on him, crushing his legs.

I didn't take time to think, but instead used my vampire speed and strength to toss the crate aside, scoop him up, and run until we were safely in the woods outside of town. All of which took about ten seconds.

Dax was of course in shock, but after explaining what I was and how by changing him I could save his legs, he agreed to become my vampire consort, and the rest is history.

CHAPTER SEVENTEEN

(Rose)

After bidding Jillian goodbye and thanking her parents for having me yet again, Dad and I headed home. We stopped for takeout on the way, and were now sitting in our living room, finishing our Saturday evening with Chinese food and small talk.

"Did you have fun with Jillian this weekend?"

I wasn't sure if Jill's parents told my dad we'd "gone to the movies" or not, but I didn't think so. He'd always been pretty good about trusting them to watch out for me, so I decided not to share this little tidbit. "Yeah, it was okay, we really didn't do much Friday night, but today Jill and I went looking at apartments."

The topic wasn't one he wanted to ever discuss, but that was just too bad. After Christian and my's little argument, I was still feeling jaded about the subject. It was time I stood up for myself, even if that meant having an argument with my dad.

Dad took a deep breath. "I know you turn twenty-one in April and then graduate in May. And I know I said that you could move out then. But Rose, don't you think it's still a little too soon, after everything that's happened?"

"I don't think so, Dad. I'm a responsible girl, and I know Mom would want us to move on with our lives, and that is exactly what I'm trying to do." I set my fork down, shifted in my chair, and met Dad's gaze. "I could have easily given up on everything when she died. And there were times when I thought I wanted to, but I didn't. Instead, I kept getting out of bed every morning, I kept going to school every day, and I kept getting good grades so I could get a good job after college, even though I don't need to. I want to live my life, Dad, and that involves me growing up and moving out."

The more I thought about Christian and my dad having a problem with this, the quicker my temper continued to rise. "And if I can be honest here, I'm feeling really stifled with how protective you've become. You just said it yourself; I'm going to be twenty-one soon, and I really don't feel like I should have to have a sleepover every time you head out of town." I shoved the chair back from the table and stood up, continuing my rant as I cleared the dishes away. "As a matter of fact, I want to buy a car of my own. I'm sick of being driven around by your guard dog for hire, or having to bum a ride with Jillian." I was on a roll.

I wasn't sure where this newfound strength was coming from, but I was happy to have found it. It felt good to get all this off my chest. Dad, on the other hand, was looking at me like I'd just lost my mind.

He sat there stunned for a few moments while I leaned back against the counter, crossing my arms over my chest. I felt like a badass for finally speaking up and was now trying to look the part. It didn't work.

"You know I've always been proud of how well you pulled yourself together after what happened." He pushed from the chair and stood up. "And I'm even prouder that you want to get a job after graduating instead of living off of your settlement money." He picked up his plate, his jaw flexing. "But that does *not* mean I will ever stop being your father. And with that comes the right to not only protect you from others, but also to protect you from yourself." He chucked his plate into the since with a loud crash. "I don't care how much you want your freedom, I just don't think you're ready to be out on your own yet."

My dad wasn't someone who showed anger very often, but clearly my little speech had pissed him off. "Honestly, Rose, I can't believe you are coming at me with this kind of attitude. We haven't even had a single conversation about me buying you a car, or you moving out, and the first time you want to talk about it, you act like this? Not the brightest move, kiddo."

"It looks like we are having a conversation about it right now! And I'm sorry if I have an attitude. I'm just trying to talk to you about my future, but for some reason you refuse to acknowledge that I have one! Plus, I don't need you to buy me a car, I can buy it myself!" Now I was the one who was pissed. "I'm so sick of you seeing me as nothing more than a sweet little girl who can't take care of herself."

Dad opened his mouth as if he was about to yell back at me, then shook his head, took a deep breath, and slowly walked in my direction. "Rose, I'm sorry." He placed both hands on my shoulders, "I just don't think I'll ever get past seeing you as my little girl. And you're right; you've been dealing with the brunt of the fear that I've been fighting since your mother's death, and it's not fair to you. How about on Monday I pick you up from school and we go car shopping? Then we can talk about this apartment idea of yours."

Wow. That was quite a turnaround. Not that I wasn't grateful for the change in his perspective, but I had a feeling things weren't going to go as smoothly as he was making them sound. "Okay," I said tentatively. "That sounds great." I tried to keep my voice steady and strong.

Dad hugged me and moved off to put away his left-over Chinese food. I started to do the same when I heard a knock at the front door. Dad's head snapped up from the table. "Are you expecting someone?"

"No, are you?"

"No, I'm not. Get upstairs right now and don't come out of your room, no matter what you hear." Dad's voice was clipped, serious, and once again panicked.

So much for making progress on his over protectiveness. For all we knew, it could just be a couple of Jehovah's witnesses, but he was acting like Satan was knocking at our front door.

CHAPTER EIGHTEEN

(Christian)

It seemed like everyone had risen at the same time today. After moving through our usual routines fairly quickly, we arrived outside Evie's door at practically the same time. It was pretty obvious we were all still concerned about what happened and wanted to see if Evie had risen tonight without any further complications.

Standing quietly outside, we heard Evie and Dax talking from within. *Thank God she was awake.*

"Hey! Quit messing around in there. You've got a crowd of concerned people waiting out here." Tori announced.

"Okay. Give us just a minute and we'll meet you guys upstairs," Evie called out.

Bobby wagged his eyebrows. "I bet it takes them more than a minute if you know what I mean."

Everyone started laughing as we headed down the hall. Finding Evie awake and okay had definitely lifted our spirits. As we filed past Terrance's cell, we found him sitting on the floor, back resting against the wall. He gave us all a weak smile, then said, "I take it Evie woke up?"

Everyone stopped and looked at me. I guess since I was the first vampire Evie created after siring Dax, it kind of put me higher up in our ranks, even though we didn't actually have ranks.

I gestured for everyone to head on up while I took a moment to answer Terrance and maybe ask a few questions of my own. "Yes, she woke up. We're heading upstairs to have a meeting about what happened."

"Would it be too much to ask for you to let me know how that goes?" Terrance sounded calm and collected. I supposed I would too if I was trying to get information out of someone.

"Yeah, I don't know about that. Plus, you know that's something only Evie can decide."

It took only a second for him to launch himself at me, rattling the chains until they pulled tight. His eyes were glued to mine and squinted slightly. I thought he was trying to attack me, so I landed a kick to his chest, sending him flying backwards into the concrete wall. "What the fuck do you think you're doing?" God... every time I got near this guy he did something else to piss me off.

Taking a moment to right himself, he stood with his back against the wall. "Huh. I guess I was wrong."

I started into the cell. "What are you talking about? Wrong about what?" I was so over this asshole. All I wanted to do was land a few more punches before he answered, but his next statement stopped me in my tracks.

"Wrong about the fact that you're going to become our new Sire." The deadpan look on his face was the only indication that he was serious.

"You really have gone crazy, haven't you?" I turned to walk away when I heard him call out, "You've read my mind before Christian, and you were just able to go against Evie's command. What do you think that means?"

Holy shit! I *had* just entered his cell against Evie's command. But me? Sire? I didn't think so. I hadn't shown any signs of developing powers, and Evie certainly hadn't reported it if she'd sensed I was the one being triggered. As for being able to enter the cell, I wondered if Evie's powers were truly fading? This could possibly have nothing to do with me, and was just another classic case of Terrance starting trouble, being his asshole self.

As I reached the top of the stairs and emerged from underneath the stage, I saw everyone sitting at one table, talking casually. Obviously, they hadn't noticed that Dax and Evie huddled just inside Evie's office.

The two must have used the direct passage that led to her office, and by the look of things, they weren't ready to get this meeting started just yet. Dax was frowning and Evie was shaking her head back and forth. I didn't think they were arguing, but it was pretty obvious they didn't agree about something.

"What did Terrance want?" Tori asked, pulling my attention away from the couple.

"Nothing really. He was just being an asshole. And he asked if we could tell him what happens in this meeting."

"Yeah, right. Like that's going to happen. No way will Evie keep him updated on what's going on. Especially when what happened to her was his fucking fault," Bobby snapped. It was clear he was having a hard time controlling his anger; his hair kept drifting from blond to brown and back again.

"Yeah, that's pretty much what I told him," I said.

Dax piped up, "I think we should deal with one thing at a time is all. Let's get to the bottom of what's happening with Terrance first, and then you can question Christian."

I turned around to ask what they would need to question me about, only to find that Dax and Evie were still inside her office. Evie looked up and met my eyes just as Dax started out the door.

Something strange was definitely happening here. All vampires had the ability to hone-in and hear things from a distance, but you usually had to make a conscious effort to do so. And right now... my hearing had just zoomed in on something without my control. By the look on Evie's face, she knew what had happened and was concerned about it.

Dax and Evie made their way over to the table and all the chatter quieted down. "I'll start by saying that I probably don't have the answers that you want, but I'll tell you everything I can remember," Evie stated. "First of all, I want you all to know that when I went down to talk to Terrance, I had no intention of delivering the true death, but when it became clear he wasn't going to willingly give me the answers I was looking for, I decided to let him think that his time was at an end. At the last moment, I felt his mental shields give way, and that's when I struck. I tried to make him sing, and as you are all aware, that didn't work out very good for either of us." Evie looked around, making eye contact with everyone. "I want you to know that I had no idea it would be so painful for Terrance. The last time I had to make someone sing, they were weakened mentally and physically afterwards, but there was no evidence of actual pain. With Terrance, however, you could tell by his screams that this wasn't the case."

I could tell this was upsetting for her. She sounded guilty and almost apologetic, even though she had nothing to be sorry for. Terrance had brought this on himself as far as I was concerned.

"The moment I penetrated his mind, I caught the image of him feeding off a woman in the dark. She was tall, thin, and had long, blonde hair from what I could tell. The moment that I locked on and tried to expand the image, Terrance's shield snapped into place, causing me a lot of pain, and then our connection was severed."

We all sat there in silence, none of us really knowing what to say. I had never heard of anything like this and from the quiver in Evie's voice, neither had she.

Bobby broke the silence. "Did you recognize the woman?"

"No. I did not. I was hoping I could have picked up on a name or something more specific, but as soon as the image started to sharpen, it was over, and I was being knocked out."

I stared at Evie and asked, "Terrance says whenever he thinks of that woman his thoughts go all fuzzy. Do you think that's the reason you were unable to wake up? Because of whatever weird effect this woman has on Terrance?"

"I've been thinking about that a lot, and it definitely seems like the most logical answer. But I just can't figure out how the woman could be affecting Terrance or me." Evie looked up at Dax and smiled sweetly. "I thought Terrance had started reveling in the kill and had figured out a way to hide things from us, but now I'm not so sure. I almost think he may be just as much a victim in this situation as the girl in the woods. I hope everyone can understand that I feel we need to keep Terrance around until we can figure all of this out."

Whether I was as convinced of Terrance's innocence or not, I knew it would make Dax feel better if Terrance ended up not being the bad guy we all thought he had become, and that made me happy. "Is there anyone you can contact to see if something like this has ever happened before?" I asked.

"Dax and I have discussed it and decided that I should contact my Sire. If something like this has ever been recorded, then I'm sure Balam will have heard about it. Now, let's go feed and get this club open. I know this situation has everyone on edge, but I'm fine now, so there's no need to worry."

I wasn't as convinced by Evie's pep talk as everyone else, but that was because of what I had accidentally heard her and Dax discussing. I was going to approach her about it, but then she and Dax started heading toward her office again. I could only assume she was going to make the call to her Sire now, and I certainly didn't want to delay that by any means. We needed to get some answers soon, so instead, I headed out to feed with the others.

We were usually able to charm a few people in the park nearby, taking only our fill, then making them forget. No harm, no foul. I, for one, couldn't stand the idea of hurting anyone, and it wasn't my fault that I required blood to survive. So, like most vampires, we fed only out of necessity and didn't hurt anyone in the process. We were almost complete opposites to the vampires of legend, but I wouldn't change a single thing. I was happy in this life, and I knew everyone else in our clan felt the same way—Terrance notwithstanding.

If Rose *was* eventually changed, I would be the happiest vampire alive. What a contradiction.

* * * * *

(Evie)

"Dammit, Dax! I know Christian heard us talking from inside the office. I'm telling you, he is displaying signs of becoming the next Sire. I need to talk to him about it."

"Evie, please. Let's get to the bottom of this thing with Terrance first. I'll will be just as happy as you if Christian is the one being triggered, but right now, you have to understand that I am a nervous wreck because of what happened to you. You have no idea what it was like sitting there next to you and not having a clue how to help. I thought I'd lost you, E." Dax pulled me close, his body trembling slightly.

He was right. The situation with Terrance needed to be our first priority. But for reasons I couldn't explain, I felt a strong sense of urgency about Christian becoming our new Sire, and I couldn't deny it had me on edge.

CHAPTER NINETEEN

(Rose)

As soon as Dad heard the knock at the door, he fell straight into panic mode. And for some reason, so did I. I was now listening for any noise that could identify our unexpected caller from behind my cracked bedroom door. So far, all I heard were jumbled voices.

After a few deep breaths, I started downstairs when I finally heard something... a female giggle. *What the fuck?*

As I rounded the corner, I got a good look at the intruder. It was a woman with long blonde hair in a pencil skirt and heels. And she had her hand on my dad's arm.

"Rose! It's okay honey. Please come here. I'd like you to meet someone." Dad's voice was high-pitched, and had a panicky sound to it.

As I walked toward them, my dad took a step back and the woman turned around to face me. She was really pretty and had a Barbie doll smile plastered on her face. "Hi, I'm Meredith." I shook her hand thinking, *and I why should care?*

"Honey, Meredith is one of my clients from Masen," Dad explained.

Why would one of my dad's clients be at our house on a Saturday night? I didn't think I liked where this was going. "Didn't you just finish your meeting in Masen last night, Dad?" I asked, all the while keeping my eyes plastered on Meredith's.

"Yes, actually I did, so this is quite a surprise." He looked at Meredith and then gestured toward the living room with his arm outstretched. "Why don't we have a seat in the living room and you can tell me to what do we owe this pleasure?" Meredith led the way, Dad followed, and I slunk in behind them.

Once we were all seated in the living room—Dad and Meredith on the couch, and I huddled in the recliner—Dad turned to Meredith. "So, what exactly are you doing here? Is there something wrong with the campaign we discussed?"

Okay, so maybe Dad's nervousness was work related. I still thought it was pretty damn odd that someone would just show up on our doorstep instead of calling to set up another meeting.

"Actually, after you left, the partners and I discussed your campaign, and we absolutely love it. So much, in fact, that we want to ask you to head up another campaign for a sub-company of ours. That's why I'm here. I was so excited to tell you the good news, I thought I'd just follow you back from Masen and deliver it in person," Meredith explained. "I have a friend in the area I'll be staying with and thought we could get together for lunch tomorrow to discuss the details."

She had such an excited buzz about her, and her smile was about to drive me nuts, so I took her story for what it was. Dad took a deep breath and visibly relaxed. "Well, that is fantastic news. I'd be honored to head up another campaign for you. And yes, lunch tomorrow sounds great." Dad grinned and looked in my direction. His smile faltered slightly as he took in my expression. I was pretty sure I wasn't sporting the most gracious look on my face. Whether I believed her story or not, for some reason I just didn't like this woman very much. Maybe it was because she looked so much like my mom

.

CHAPTER TWENTY

(Evie)

After Dax and I settled on the questions I needed to ask my Sire, I had requested to be left alone. I couldn't remember the last time I'd spoken to Balam. It had been so long ago that I'd been triggered and made a Sire, it truly felt like a completely different lifetime. And even though I considered Balam an old friend, I was still a bit nervous to actually be contacting him.

Usually, once a new Sire left their original clan to begin their own, there was no further contact between them. Not that it was forbidden, it just wasn't a necessity, and for whatever ancient reason, that's how things worked.

Traditionally, once a vampire was confirmed as the next triggered Sire, they were led through the history lessons about their kind. This included all the different new "powers" that came with being a Sire: the poison of true death, the sedative of eternal life, the scanning abilities, and the importance of choosing their consort. Once they received the guidelines on how to use each of these things, they would then go through the "Passing of Powers" ritual. This is where their Sire passed abilities onto them. They were then expected to leave their current clan, set up a new home location, and begin building a clan/family of their own.

The first vampire that they sired became their consort and shared in their scanning abilities. This was the most important, and the first thing a new Sire needed to do. They had to choose wisely, because once their consort was changed, they were eternally bound to them. If they died... so did the new Sire.

After choosing their consort, there was no limit to how many vampires they could create. The process of the change was pretty typical. The Sire bit the chosen person, and then injected them with the sedative of eternal life. The Sire would then feed from the person until they were dead. Once the new vampire had risen, the first thing they were made to do was drink from the Sire. That sealed the bond and completed the process. Once the bond was made, the new vampire then drifted to their "normal" coloring. Most people rose as light vampires, but like Terrance, if they carried sorrow and pain within them, they would mostly likely show signs of that by drifting to a darker color.

As I sat there recalling all the lessons that Balam had taught me, I started to feel a little more relaxed about contacting the man who had blessed me with eternal life, even though I hadn't spoken to him in over a thousand years.

After digging his number out of my archives, I took a deep breath and dialed.

"Hola, habla Balam."

I smiled. His accent still carried its Mayan heritage, and even though he could speak English, he chose to speak modern Spanish. To this day he continued to go by his real Mayan name, Balam. Just hearing his voice made me realize how much I'd missed him.

"Hello, Balam. It's Evangeline."

"Evangeline mi amor, no te he visto en mucho tiempo"

He knew I hadn't spoken Spanish for hundreds of years, but he was going to make me ask anyway. "Balam, you know I no longer speak Spanish, may I ask that we speak in English, Sire?" He was very formal when it came to titles and respect.

His only reaction to my request was a small *hmph* before continuing. "Yes of course, my darling. I was just saying it has been forever."

His voice was kind and immediately took me back to the villages of Chichen Itza. I wasn't originally from Yucatan, but when I was turned by Balam, he took me home to where his clan lived, being one of the original Mayan people. It was amazing, and his lair resided below the ruins and still did to this day.

"To what do I owe this pleasure?" Balam asked.

"I have a situation developing within my clan that I've never experienced before, and I need to ask you some questions." I figured there was no point in beating around the bush.

"What's the situation?"

"I have a vampire who has drifted permanently dark, which is unfortunate, but not unheard of. The problem is, when I tried to scan him to reveal the cause of his darkening, I was forced into unconsciousness and trapped there until I cleared my mind of the incident." Balam continued to listen as I explained further. "It was only then that I was able to wake. My vampire also reports that whenever he thinks of a particular woman, his thoughts get fuzzy."

Silence lingered for more time than I was comfortable with, but I knew Balam was processing the information. The man had a millennium of experience and history to sort through. I just hoped that something rang a bell.

"Have any of your other vampires drifted permanently dark, or is it just this one?" Balam's voice was calm, but serious.

"No. Just Terrance."

"And you say that his thoughts get *fuzzy* when he thinks of a particular woman, correct?"

"Yes. And I think due to our mental connection, whatever this woman has done to Terrance is why I was knocked out when I tried to scan him."

"Yes, I would suspect that is correct."

It seemed like he had an idea of what was happening, so I was more than happy to wait for his next question.

"Has Terrance shown any aggression toward the other vampires in your clan?"

"No. We have him chained up right now, and he's not exactly happy about it, but he hasn't tried to hurt any of us. Dax and I noticed about six months ago that he started having trouble drifting back after feeding and that he was becoming quiet and solitary. We kept an eye on him, making sure he fed with the others, and up until last week, he had never killed anyone before. But now, all that has changed, and he appears to have drifted permanently dark." I couldn't help the sadness in my voice. I truly didn't want to have to deliver the true death.

"Evangeline, even though as Sire you are immune, it is absolutely imperative that none of your other vampires get close to Terrance from now on. He is a danger to your clan."

"What? Why? He's chained up, and like I said, he hasn't shown any sign of aggression toward any of us." This was starting to confuse and scare me.

"Evangeline, please do as I say. I don't want any of your other vampires to become infected."

"Infected? What are you talking about?" This conversation was definitely taken a turn.

"Yes. Infected. I'm almost certain that the woman that Terrance encountered was in fact a zôt—or what you would refer to as a demon."

CHAPTER TWENTY-ONE

(Rose)

I watched Meredith scoot closer and closer to my dad as they made plans to meet for lunch the following day. I'd come up with a creative form of entertainment that allowed me to remain calm throughout the rest of her unexpected visit—repeatedly imagining myself flying across the room and strangling her to death. It was pretty fun.

Once she had finally left, I excused myself and headed straight to my room. I thought it would be best to avoid any conversations about her at that moment. You know the saying... if you can't say anything nice, don't say anything at all.

A few minutes later Dad knocked on my door. "Honey, are you alright?"

"I'm fine, Dad. I just want to go to sleep." I could tell he was considering pressing the issue, but thank God, he didn't.

"Okay, honey. Goodnight then. Oh, and Rose, I'd like you to go with me tomorrow. Meredith and I are meeting at the café in the business district for lunch, and I thought you could do some shopping while I met with her. Then afterwards, you and I could take in a movie together." Dad sounded so upbeat, and after our argument tonight, I really did want the chance to continue our conversation about getting a car and moving out.

"Okay Dad, sure thing. That sounds great." I would fake it for him, but I still didn't like the fact he was meeting *Barbie* for lunch.

* * * * *

(Jeremy/Dad)

Wow. What a surprise that had been. I couldn't believe Meredith followed me back from Masen, and straight to my house, no less. I had told her when we'd initially started dating, that she'd have to settle for only seeing me once a month during my overnight visits there. She said she understood why I couldn't bring her here to the house where Rose's mother had been killed, especially since she looked so much like her.

It was over a year ago when I first met Meredith, and even then, it had been a shock that she looked so much like my wife. If I was being honest with myself, though, the fact that she *did* resemble Loraine so much, probably contributed to why I'd been drawn to her to begin with. But once we began to spend some quality time together, I realized she was a wonderful person, and the fact that she furthered my career had nothing to do with it.

I didn't know how I was going to tell Rose about Meredith, so for now, I thought lunch and some casual conversation would be the perfect place to start.

* * * * *

(Rose)

After Dad and I made breakfast, we went online to search for what he thought would be a dependable brand of car for me. We figured we would narrow down our choices today, and when the car lots opened tomorrow, we wouldn't have to waste time running around from place to place.

"I really like the Ford Focus," Dad said for the hundredth time.

"I don't mind that one, I guess. Though the new Mercedes look hot," I giggled. I had never been a car person, so the fact that I even knew the name of a certain kind was pretty much a joke. I'd also never really been into brand names, so as far as I was concerned, it really didn't matter to me what I got, as long as I could call it my own.

It was about 11 a.m. when we shut the computer off and started to get ready. I wasn't exactly sure why Dad wanted me to go. I mean, I was all up for some shopping, but I really wasn't looking forward to seeing Meredith again. The fact that she looked so much like Mom totally creeped me out.

At 12:30 p.m., Dad's voice echoed up the stairs. "Rose? You ready to go?"

"Yep. Be right down."

As I rounded the bottom of the stairs and caught a glimpse at what he was wearing, I had to hold back a snicker. I expected him to be dressed in his usual business suit or his Sunday best. But instead, he had on a nice pair of stylish jeans, a white button up shirt that he'd left untucked, and his leather jacket that I hadn't seen in years. He'd also left a slight five o'clock shadow on his face. I guess he was trying to go for that scruffy, sexy older man look. But, oh my God, this was my dad. What the hell was he thinking? All of a sudden, it dawned on me. Meredith was more than just a client. And now it looked like I truly would have to kill her.

CHAPTER TWENTY-TWO

(Evie)

After hearing Balam's idea about what had happened to Terrance, I sat there in complete shock. I had no idea what to say or what to think. I had never believed in demons or whatever he had called them—zôts. So, after allowing myself a few moments to calm down, I listened even closer as he continued to explain.

The history lesson I received went back thousands of years, to the time when the Maya people were facing the threat of extinction. He explained that Yum Camil, the demon ruler in Xibalba, had sent forth his favored son, Camazotz, the demon bat-god, or blood-feeder, into the human realm. He had told him he needed to bite and infect as many humans as possible before the end, so that their bloodline would continue on. Because even as demons, they weren't going to escape the destruction that was quickly approaching their civilization.

Camazotz went into the world at his father's request. He bit and infected as many people as he could, transforming humans to be like him. This was the beginning of the vampire race.

I couldn't wrap my head around the fact that Balam was one of the direct descendants of the first vampires ever created.

Though Yum Camil and Camazotz were classified as demons, they weren't inherently evil, so when Camazotz infected the humans, it was the combination of his blood and the light within the human soul that manifested into the ability of drifting.

Balam continued to explain that after some time, the vampires that Camazotz was creating started having a bad reaction to the change.

Balam's theory was that Camazotz, in his effort to complete his father's mission, remained in the human realm for far too long. Being out of his natural environment for such an extended period of time had caused his blood to become contaminated.

Camazotz's contaminated blood had infected the new vampires, and right from the start they had drifted straight to dark. Soon after, they became violent and turned on their clan.

Once the fighting began, it became obvious that the dark vampires were passing their infection to the others. Because when a light vampire was bit, they too, drifted dark.

Soon the dark vampires started to outnumber the light ones, and the originals feared they were going to be overrun.

Camazotz then called upon his father to come aid him in what could only be described as a civil war amongst vampires. Yum Camil came to his son's aid and found that the only way to kill the darkened vampires was for him to bite them again, infecting them with a poison that only he, the ruler of Xibalba, possessed. Upon realizing this, Yum Camil chose a few light vampires, and through his Mayan magic, blessed each of them with the ability to reproduce his poison. These vampires became the first Sires who possessed the poison of true death.

After sending Camazotz back to Xibalba, Yum Camil and the newly created Sires fought to destroy all the darkened vampires. Once the dark ones were eliminated, Yum Camil conducted the first "Passing of Powers" ritual.

In order to bestow the Sires with the sedative of eternal life that was needed to create new vampires, he had to link minds with them. Linking minds with Yum Camil is what led the Sires to have the ability to scan. During this initial rite he also bestowed a time-limit on how long the Sires could hold their powers. This was to prevent a Sire's blood from becoming contaminated like Camazotz's had. He then taught the Sires how to perform the "Passing of Powers" ritual, and decreed that the Sires divide the remaining light vampires into clans and separate to the four corners of the world.

I thought this was where the lesson would stop, but Balam continued to explain the one key point that was relevant to my current situation.

He explained that once the Sires had separated, before returning to Xibalba, Yum Camil continued to infect humans with his *own* blood. Since he wasn't a blood-feeder by nature like his son, the humans weren't transformed into vampires. Instead, they remained human, but had demon blood flowing through their veins, becoming zôts. It was this line of humans that continued to exist throughout time, hiding their demon heritage from the world.

This was the only way that Yum Camil could guarantee that his bloodline would continue, since the humans his son had bitten ended up as a new species entirely. That had been an unforeseen twist to his plan. Balam had explained that Yum Camil hadn't meant for the humans he infected to be a threat to anyone, but that like any dying God, only wanted to meet his end knowing that some part of his race would live on.

Obviously, he'd taken into account how the two species, his demons and his son's vampires would interact. Who would have ever guessed that they would be like poison to one another?

Apparently, the woman Terrance bit six months ago was one of the demon descendants of Yum Camil. Her demon blood had infected him and was the reason behind his fuzzy thoughts and his now permanent darkness.

It was more important than ever to find out just who this woman was. And since the infection prevented me or Terrance from accessing any further information about her, I had no idea how we were going to do that.

Before ending our conversation, I asked Balam if there was any hope of saving Terrance. His answer had been just what I expected: not that he knew of. Dax was not going to be happy about all I had learned. And right now, I couldn't imagine facing all of them with this kind of news. How was I supposed to explain that all of our lives had just changed and that we were now being faced with demons?

Our feedings were going to have to become very strict and limited to only people we'd fed from before. Because now that it was clear that at least one family with demon blood resided in our area, who knew how many more could be out there? I just couldn't take the risk of any other member of my clan becoming infected.

By the time I finished my phone call, the club was in full swing. I found Dax talking to one of the members of the liquor board who had apparently stopped in to make an impromptu inspection. They seemed to be going through the checklist that the inspector was carrying with him. As the owner, I should have made an appearance and schmoozed the pencil pusher like I always did, but after everything that happened, I just didn't have the energy to deal with that tonight.

Just as I slid back inside my office, Christian appeared in the doorway.

"Evie, are you alright?" he asked.

I could tell he was nervous, and like the rest of them, probably wanting to know what I had learned. But with Dax and the rest of the clan occupied with their jobs, it was the perfect opportunity to have a conversation with Christian about his potential triggering. "I'm fine Christian, but please come in."

CHAPTER TWENTY-THREE

(Rose)

As we drove to the café, I just couldn't bring myself to question Dad about his relationship with Meredith. So instead, I sat there imagining all the expensive things I was going to buy with the credit card he'd given me, while he pretended to have a business meeting with his whore. Yes, I was that mad.

How in the hell could Dad continue to tell me that it was "too soon" to move on, when he apparently didn't have any trouble moving on from Mom's death whatsoever? The more and more I thought about this, the angrier I became. The rage inside of me was building at a steady pace, and I felt the tears threatening to spill.

"So, like I said, I figured you could do some shopping while Meredith and I have our meeting. I think I remember you mentioning that you needed some supplies for school and some new cookware to replace the things that I ruined at the house," Dad said with a chuckle. "I'll text you once we're done, and then you and I can go to see that new movie that came out. Sound good?"

I can't tell you how hard it was not to scream at him. It took everything I had to say, "Sure Dad. That'll be fine." I had to keep my head turned toward the window, because if I actually looked at him, I knew I would breakdown. But apparently, diverting my face wasn't enough to hide the waves of tension rolling off me.

"Is something wrong, Rose?" he asked.

Damn it, why can't he just let it drop? "Well, Dad, now that you mention it, I guess I'm not really looking forward to seeing Meredith again, since it's obvious that she is more to you than just a *business acquaintance*." I knew my voice carried a tinge of anger, and I didn't care.

A sigh escaped his lips, as he shook his head back and forth. "Rose, I'm so sorry. I had no intention of dating Meredith when we first met, but after getting to know her, we really hit it off, and spending time with her has truly helped me deal with my grief. I didn't say anything because I just didn't think you would understand." Guilt as thick as molasses dripped from his voice.

"Oh no, Dad, I understand just fine. You banging someone that looks just like Mom really helps lessen the blow that she's truly gone." Fuck being nice; I'd had enough of being kept in the dark.

"Rose Reynolds! You watch your mouth. How dare you say such a thing to me. I loved your mother with all my heart, and I would never disrespect her memory by using someone else as a substitute for what we had together. Yes, Meredith does have similar features to your mother's, but what's really important is that she makes me feel alive again, which is something I never thought would happen. Don't you dare think you are old enough to understand what I've gone through."

I was confused by his last comment, but didn't have time to dwell on it since we had just pulled up to the café. I threw open the door and bolted from car, "Enjoy your lunch, Dad. *Maybe* I'll see you at home?" I ran into the crowd before Dad even had a chance to shut off the car. I noticed Meredith sitting at one of the café tables as I ran by. She looked up, preparing to smile, but then got the most curious look on her face. I was extremely angry, and seeing the most vicious frown form on that bitch's face had only made it worse.

* * * * *

(Jeremy/Dad)

"Jeremy, what's happened?" Meredith asked as I approached the table.

"Rose knows about us, and it didn't go well," I explained.

Damn it. I hadn't wanted her to find out like this. I had hoped to have a successful business meeting with Meredith before things turned personal. I was planning to tell Meredith that I wanted to let Rose know about us, and then ask Rose to join us for dessert. That way, they could spend a little time getting to know each other before I shared the news. So much for that plan.

I had never seen Rose act that way before. She had always been so level-headed and such a good girl. I couldn't believe the venom that her words had carried.

"I should go after her." I started to panic, because I suddenly remembered her last words, *"Maybe I'll see you at home."* I had to find her before she did something stupid.

"Jeremy, I think you should just let her blow off some steam. She'll cool down after a while, and then we can go look for her. The fact that she doesn't have a car yet is definitely a good thing right now. She shouldn't be able to get too far," Meredith reasoned.

"I guess you're right." Resolved to let Rose cool down before we continued this *conversation*, I sat down and reached for Meredith's hand. "Thank you. I'm really glad that you're here."

* * * * *

(Rose)

Watching Dad reach for that bitch's hand made me want to scream. I had run into the nearest alley between two of the shops and propped myself up against the brick wall while I tried to catch my breath. Then, I peeked out to see how close behind me Dad was. But, to my surprise, he wasn't even following me. He had sat down with Meredith instead and then reached for her hand.

That was it. I'd had it. I'd been feeling guilty I was going to be moving out and leaving Dad all alone, but it was pretty obvious he already had someone to fill the void that Mom, and now I, would be leaving in his life. What a bastard.

CHAPTER TWENTY-FOUR

(Christian)

As I entered Evie's office, I could tell whatever she had learned from her Sire had left her shaken. Her hair had drifted a little darker and it looked like she had run her fingers through it a number of times. But I couldn't control my curiosity. "What did you find out from Balam?" I asked, taking a seat.

After she lowered herself into her chair, she closed her eyes, and took a deep breath. "I think it's best if I tell everyone together, after closing. Right now, there's something else I want to discuss with you."

Damn, I really wanted to get to the bottom of this, and waiting until closing to find out what Evie had learned was going to be torture. "Okay, what is it?"

"I'll cut right to the chase. I have reasons to believe that you are being triggered to become the new Sire." Even though she looked tired, the smile on her face indicated that for her, this was good news.

"Are you kidding me?" I shook my head back and forth. This was the second time someone had mentioned this to me.

"No, Christian. I'm not kidding you. And if I'm right, it will be a dream come true for me. From the moment that I found you on the Swedish island of Gotland, it was clear to me that you were a wonderful person." She paused, reflecting briefly. "It was actually a coincidence that Dax and I even stopped on your island. I remember we were travelling through the Baltic Sea and there was a problem with the ship. Once it docked, we decided it would be best if we explored the island to feed, rather than remain with the boat." She looked at me with such pride in her eyes. "It was the best decision we ever made."

Evie rose from her chair and continued to relive the story that brought her and Dax to find me. "I remember stumbling upon your little village and seeing all the hardworking people, and the sense of community. As we watched from afar, I told Dax that I only wanted to have a small clan so that we would always remain as close as the people we saw there."

"I've always wondered why you created so few vampires for your clan." I had never asked, mainly because I thought it would be rude, but apparently, she had gotten her wish. Our small clan had always been happy... until now.

"We watched your village for several days and fed only when someone would head to the stream for water. Dax had dug out a burrow that provided us safety while we slept, but then one day, we awoke to screams."

I knew the day she was referring to; it was the last and first day of my life.

"The crew of the boat had discovered your village. When we reached them, they had already started to plunder and pillage. I remember seeing you fighting so fiercely to protect that young girl. Dax and I fought off everyone we could while trying to not frighten your townsfolk, but by the time we reached you, you had been stabbed through." Evie had circled behind me and now rested her hands on my shoulders. "There was no way I could let you die. Not after seeing what a wonderful person you were. So helpful to your village, such a hard worker, and an amazing fighter. I knew in that instant you would become my son. My first vampire son."

Evie squeezed my shoulders, then made her way back around to sit behind her desk once more. "If you are, in fact, the one being triggered, I want you to know that I couldn't be happier or prouder."

I sat still, stunned silent for a moment. Not because of her speech, but because I hadn't thought of that day in so very long. It was going to take me a minute to shake the memories from my head. "I'm at a loss for words. Honestly, I feel like there has to be some mistake. I haven't shown any signs of being triggered and..." My words drifted off as I truly didn't know what else to say.

"Actually, you have been showing signs. Remember in the private room when I launched myself at you? It was because you had commented on something that I had *thought*—not said. I was so shocked and surprised I literally flew across the room to see if I had imagined things. But then we were interrupted and I couldn't explain."

I sat there dumbfounded as she continued. "Then, there's the fact that when I was trapped in the comatose state, you just happened to *know* what the right thing to do was. I actually think that's because you are developing the psychic ability called claircognizance, which means 'clear knowing'. Then, when you were outside the office tonight, you had the most quizzical look on your face so I scanned you and found that you had heard Dax and my conversation by accident. I can honestly say that I have never experienced any of these things myself, but it leads me to believe that you are in fact the one being triggered." Evie sat there just looking at me with a smile on her face.

I couldn't move. I sat there stunned, shaking my head in hopes of knocking my brain back into gear. "I just thought my hearing had been doing weird things. I have heard some people whisper a couple things, and then accidentally honed-in on your and Dax's conversation. And as far as the 'knowing'—I'm not sure how I knew how to help you when you were comatose. But really Evie, I don't see how that can equal me being triggered. I thought there were *specific* signs to look for." I was confused and a little nauseous. I just couldn't wrap my head around this. I couldn't possibly be the one.

"I have been wondering that too, so when I spoke to Balam, I asked him if all Sires show the same symptoms when they are triggered. He informed me that each Sire is different. It's the fact that you are starting to display *any* new powers that identifies you as the one being triggered. Now, as to what those powers might be, that's something that is individual to each vampire. The scanning ability, the sedative of eternal life, and the poison of true death are all things that are passed between Sires during the Passing of Powers ritual, but each Sire usually has an additional power or two that they develop during their triggering. When I was triggered, I actually developed the ability of telekinesis. I could move objects with my mind." Evie demonstrated by moving a stapler from one side of her desk to the other. "It is not something I use very often, and it's also something that only Dax and Balam know about."

I must have looked like a cartoon character with my mouth gaping open and my eyes bugged out of my head. I couldn't believe the shit that was happening lately. No way could I be the next Sire. And I couldn't believe she had never told us about her telekinesis. I also couldn't believe the amount of information and history that was being kept between the Sires. Now I was really curious as to what other secrets Evie would be sharing with us later tonight.

"Christian, are you okay?"

When I finally looked up and met Evie's eyes, I could tell that she was worried about me. And honestly, I didn't know if I was okay or not. This was just so much to process, and we hadn't even gotten to the situation with Terrance yet. I just wasn't sure if I could deal with this right now, and truth be told, I wasn't sure I wanted to become the next Sire, because the one thing I did know was that it meant I would have to leave the only family I had known for over 600 years. I couldn't imagine leaving my family or Rose. *Wait... Rose.* If I became the new Sire, I would be able to change Rose! No petitioning, no waiting, I would be able to change her myself, and then we could truly be together forever.

"Evie, if I am the one who's been triggered to become the next Sire, can you tell me how the consort bond works?" I couldn't hold back the excitement in my voice. This suddenly had the potential to become very good news.

"I know what you're thinking Christian, and yes, you would be able to choose Rose as your consort. But, that is a very important decision and one that isn't without consequences."

Just as I was about to push the subject, Dax opened the door and strolled inside to take the seat next to me. "Liquor board inspection is done. We're good." He looked between the two of us, probably noticing I was on edge. "Everything okay? You guys look a little tense."

"Everything is fine. I was just explaining to Christian that I believe he is the one being triggered to become the new Sire." Evie looked at him with a firm set to her chin.

Dax pushed out of the chair and started pacing. "Dammit, Evie! I thought we agreed to not bring this up until everything was settled with Terrance."

"If you recall my dear, I didn't agree to anything. I know you expressed that you thought it was for the best, but I never agreed to remain quiet. Plus, after what I have learned from Balam, I think it's necessary for Christian to understand what is happening to him. He may actually be of great use to us in figuring out what's going on with Terrance."

Great. This sounded ominous, and not something I really wanted to be involved in. Like I had said, Terrance was an asshole, and I didn't want anything to do with him.

Dax sighed, and the look he gave Evie wasn't exactly a loving one, but then he said, "Okay, Evie. Whatever you think is best." He quietly left the room, closing the door behind him.

"Why do you think I'll be able to help figure out what's going on with Terrance?" I really didn't care, but I thought it would be best if I knew exactly what Evie was expecting of me.

"I'm not sure yet, but I feel that if we can keep tabs on your developing powers, especially the claircognizance, it might be of use in his situation." Evie rose from her chair and I followed suit. She hugged me then held my shoulders tight and looked deeply into my eyes. "Everything will work out Christian, you'll see. Just please come to me if you experience any strange sensations or if you have questions about what's happening to you. Again, I can't tell you how proud I am."

As I headed for the door, I looked back at Evie and forced a smile onto my face. I wanted her to know that her pride in me was definitely something I appreciated, though I didn't share her sentiment that everything would work out. As a matter of fact, whether it was my new found *psychic ability* or not, I suddenly felt that things were going to get a lot worse.

CHAPTER TWENTY-FIVE

(Rose)

I couldn't stand to watch my dad sit there with that bitch for a second longer. Now that it was obvious there would be no shopping and no movie in my near future, I pulled out my cell phone and dialed Jillian. "Hey can you please come pick me up at the northwest corner of the business district? I have to get out of here, like NOW!"

Jillian started to question me about what was wrong, but I didn't have the patience to explain. After grasping my level of frustration, she agreed to come pick me up right away.

"I can't believe your dad is actually seeing someone and didn't even tell you about it." Her shock was genuine, but I was too mad to discuss it.

"Can we just not talk about it?" I asked. "I would love it if we could just go for a drive. I'll pay for the gas. I just need some time to get rid of this angry feeling before I can process any of this."

"You got it. Where do you wanna go?"

"I don't care. Let's just head east I guess." I really didn't have a specific destination in mind, but it was beautiful this time of year, and the idea of taking in a little of the countryside sounded just about perfect right now.

Jillian hummed along to the radio as we drove, and I stared out the window watching the trees go by. I kept thinking about all those overnight trips that Dad had made to Masen. It was pretty damn obvious he'd spent them with her, and I couldn't help but wonder how long it had been going on. It still pissed me off to think he had jumped into a relationship right after Mom had died, and I still didn't understand the statement he had made about me not knowing everything he'd gone through. What the hell was that supposed to mean?

I was lost in my thoughts, trying to process everything that had happened since Meredith's visit: the way she had scooted closer to Dad on the couch, seeing him in that ridiculous "hip" outfit that was obviously meant to impress her, and then watching her comfort him at the café. But what had really struck me as odd, was the strange, almost angry look that Meredith had given me as I ran by her table today.

I could understand I probably looked a bit distressed, but then wouldn't you think that she would have had a surprised or concerned look on her face instead of an angry one? What the hell did she have to be angry at me about? She was the one who was secretly sleeping with my dad, so if anyone had the right to be mad, it was me! This line of thinking wasn't helping me calm down, instead I was starting to get even more pissed off, but then a bump in the road jostled my attention back to the present.

"Hey, where are we?" I asked, not recognizing the road we were now traveling down.

"I turned off the highway a little ways back. It's almost dark and this is the town Justin is from. I thought that since we were this close, I'd drive through and check it out."

Jillian's answer surprised me. I'd forgotten all about her new vampire boyfriend. Of course, it hadn't surprised me that he'd made some sort of excuse to be unavailable until after dark.

Thinking about Justin pulled my thoughts back to my incident at the apartment complex. After having my melt down at that pool, all the images from my first encounter with a vampire had started to replay in my head.

It had been only about seven and a half months ago, right after I had started seeing Christian, when I had made plans with Mom to stay late after school in order to get some research done in the library. She was supposed to come pick me up after her swim lesson was over, but instead, she had called saying that her lesson was going to run late and that I should take the bus to meet her. She had given me the address of the training facility, and by the time I arrived, it was barely after dark.

As I approached the pool, I didn't hear anything, but instead saw thrashing waves in the pool. Once I looked closer, I saw my mom and a guy struggling underwater. Instead of throwing my bags to the ground and diving in like I should have, I completely froze. I couldn't move or scream, and after a moment, the waves in the water started to clear. What I saw next was enough to scare me into hiding. I ran back around the corner of the building and watched as the man climbed out of the pool carrying my mother in his arms with his mouth plastered to the side of her neck.

At first, I had thought, *"Holy shit, my mom is having an affair,"* but once I looked closer, I could tell he wasn't kissing the side of her neck, but that he had sharp teeth piercing her skin instead. I quickly realized what I had first thought were sensual kisses were actually long drags of sucking. This man was *drinking* from my mom.

I had sunk to the ground, not knowing what to do or think. I remembered feeling like I was going to pass out. But as I continued to watch, the man finally removed what could only be called fangs from my mom's neck. He then laid her on one of the chaises next to the pool and gently brushed the hair out of her eyes. She sat up with a smile on her face and waved as the man started to walk away. I was so relieved to see she was okay that I sucked in a quick breath. The man's head spun in my direction and he stared me down with intense, dark eyes.

After a moment, he crooked his finger at me, indicating for me to come to him. I was still frozen in fear and literally couldn't move. The next thing I knew he was standing right in front of me. Only a split-second had passed and I hadn't even seen him move, but there he was, dripping wet, towering over me with a cocky smirk on his face.

"Hi. You must be the daughter." His voice was deep and sexy, just like the rest of him. *What the fuck?* I couldn't believe the thoughts in my head, especially about the man who had just been holding my mother so intimately, but I couldn't deny reality. The guy appeared to be in his mid-thirties, with dark brown hair and eyes to match. He was tan and muscular, and probably about 6' 4". He looked like sex-on-a-stick.

"Yes, I'm her daughter. Who the hell are you?" Getting myself under control, I stood up to face him.

"I think the question you want to ask is 'What are you?', am I right?" He had a mocking glint in his eye, and that damn cocky grin was still plastered to his face.

"I'm not stupid. I know what you are." Whether I wanted to believe it or not, it was obvious that this *man* was... "You're a vampire."

His grin widened. "Are you scared?"

"Should I be?" I tried to bolster myself so the fear I was feeling wouldn't come across in my shaking voice.

He stared at me for a long time then gave a slight *hmph*. "No, beautiful, you have nothing to fear from me. One a night is all I can handle."

I hated that his *one* had been my mom, but I was damn glad he'd be leaving me alone. "Did you hurt her?" Now that I felt somewhat better, I had a shit-ton of questions that I was dying to ask. Well, maybe dying wasn't the right word to use.

"No, I didn't hurt her, and she won't remember anything about tonight," he explained. "What about you? Should I bite you and make you forget?" He seemed genuine in his question.

I tried not to shiver, despite the goose bumps on my arms. "No. I don't want to forget. Actually, I have a lot of questions I would love to ask you. I'm a history major, and I can't tell you what an amazing paper I could write with your help." Seriously, had I just asked a vampire to help me get a good grade on my history paper? So lame.

He turned around and watched Mom gather her things. "Why don't you meet me back here tomorrow night, and I'll answer some of your questions."

"Really? Or is this some kind of trick to get me here so I can be your meal of the day instead?" I was excited but not stupid. I wondered if crosses or stakes would actually work on this guy. Not that I'm Buffy, but a girl could try.

"No trick. I do, however, enjoy the taste of your mother's blood. It's different from any other I've ever experienced before. So, once you spend the evening with her and realize I'm telling the truth—that I didn't hurt her—as long as you agree I can still feed from your mom, I'll be willing to answer your questions. Is that something you can handle?" He extended his hand as if preparing to shake on a deal.

"Okay. But if Mom shows any signs of being hurt or acting weird, then you'll never see us here again." It was a lame threat because he could probably just follow us home or find us whenever he wanted, but I had to make sure he understood that if he had hurt my mom in any way, the deal was off.

"Deal." He shook my hand and then started to walk away. "Oh. One more thing. What's your name?"

"My name is Rose. What's yours?"

"Terrance. My name is Terrance."

CHAPTER TWENTY-SIX

(Christian)

After we finished closing the club, we all gathered around waiting for Evie to share what she had learned from Balam.

"What I have to tell you is going to come as quite a shock," she stated. "I'm not going to recount the entire history of the how's or why's, but what we've come to figure out is that a woman that Terrance fed from, the woman I saw in his thoughts, is a zôt—or what you would call a demon."

Gasps and curses filled the room. Dax collapsed into a chair and Evie placed a hand on his shoulder. "The zôt's blood is the reason behind his odd behavior. It acts like a poison and literally infects him. It's what is causing his memory loss and his thoughts to become fuzzy whenever he tries to think of her. Apparently, the demon's blood has something like a built-in protection feature. It is how they have kept themselves hidden throughout history. It's also what is causing him to drift permanently dark." The sadness in her voice was the first indication this was going to be a bad night.

"So, if this is an infection, is there any way to cure him?" Bobby asked.

"No, honey. Not that we know of." Evie's eyes filled with tears as she took a seat next to Dax.

"Okay. If this woman is a zôt, or demon, or whatever, but we can't figure out who she is because of the automatic brain-fuck her blood causes, then how the hell are we supposed to find her? I, for one, do not want to accidentally feed on some goddamn demon." Tori's hair was drifting from light red to a seriously deep maroon color. She was pissed and had never been one to hold back her feelings.

"Until we get to the bottom of this, I think it's for the best if we only feed from people we have previously fed from before since we know them to already be safe. I'm thinking that throughout the night we can each take a turn and invite a previous guest to one of the private rooms. This way we can remain safe inside the club and not risk running across another zôt while hunting outside. Just make sure when you feed from them you use your sedative to get them to come back again and again." She didn't look happy about this idea, but continued anyway. "Also... no one is to go near

Terrance from now on. Apparently, once an infected vampire permanently drifts dark, they can infect other vampires." She looked at me with a look on her face that could only be described as disheartened.

"I have faith that we will get to the bottom of this, but until we do, I'm not going to deliver the true death to Terrance. I want him around in case we find the woman. Maybe by some miracle, locating her can provide the answers we need, or perhaps even a cure we don't yet know about." She stood and with the command in her voice said once again, "No one is to go near Terrance from now on." Evie wasn't stupid, and I'm sure she realized we all planned to interrogate Terrance the first chance we got.

She must have been scanning us because the next thing she said was, "I am going to be questioning Terrance again, and explaining what we've learned. All of you are more than welcome to witness this."

As Evie and Dax headed toward her office, the rest of us just sat there in silence. Finally, Dom broke the tension. "Have any of you ever heard of anything like this? Of demons actually existing?"

"No. But I guess it shouldn't come as a huge surprise. I mean, who'd believe that vampires really existed either?" Bobby asked.

He was being way more relaxed about this than I was. I wish I could ask Evie some more questions, but figured we had better head down so we didn't miss her questioning Terrance again. "Come on. Let's get below and see what Terrance has to say about all this." I hit the switch to unlock the stage.

Once we were all downstairs and gathered outside of Terrance's cell, Evie stepped up to the opening and stopped. Obviously, she was serious about not getting close to him. "Terrance, I have some news as to what's happened to you."

"Oh, goody. Please share with the class." He was being sarcastic and had an almost menacing look on his face.

"You've been infected by demon blood." Evie's statement dropped like a bomb.

Terrance just looked at her, huffed, and shook his head. "Wow, is that the best you can do? I know you want to have a clear conscience when you deliver the true death, but making up bullshit reasons as to why you *have* to kill me is pretty fucking lame."

"Why is he acting like that?" Tori whispered.

Evie turned around and said in a low voice, "I think it has to do with the poison. It literally makes him act dark and then wipes the memories of it from him."

Turning around she continued, "First of all, I don't have to justify delivering the true death to you at all. You've drifted permanently dark, and you know that is grounds for immediate execution. Secondly, I wanted you to know what's happened to you, so that you would understand why you're having trouble remembering things and why your thoughts become fuzzy when you think of that woman. It's her that is the demon. She's the one who has infected you."

Terrance sat there with an angry look on his face. I didn't think he was buying what Evie was trying to explain, but then suddenly the lines on his face smoothed out and his eyes seemed to lighten just slightly. "Are you telling me this is real? That I'm infected with demon blood?"

"Yes, my friend. That is exactly what I'm telling you. We are hoping that once we find her, she can provide a cure." Evie's voice carried the hope we were all feeling.

"Oh, thank God. I just couldn't understand why I had lost it, but I guess now it all makes sense. I never even knew that demons really existed. How in the hell did I run across one?" Terrance seemed to almost be back to his old self, except that his hair remained completely black.

As Evie started to move into the cell, obviously feeling confident in Terrance's breakthrough, I suddenly got the sense that something was terribly wrong. I sprung into the cell, grabbing Evie just as Terrance lunged for her, pulling his chains tight. His eyes were again completely black to match his hair, and his lips were pulled back, revealing his fangs as he growled at us.

Dax was up in a flash and carrying Evie out of the cell. "Son of a bitch, Evie. What the hell are you doing? You're the one who said to stay away from him, and now we know why. He's lost it. He almost bit you."

"It's okay. I know what I'm doing." Evie wiggled free of Dax's arms. She took a moment to glance at everyone. "That, my dears, was a test. And you're right, Terrance has lost it. I wanted you to see why it's so important to stay away from him. He's completely lost to us now, and will try to manipulate anyone he gets close to him. I, however, am immune to his bite since I carry the poison of true death. Because of that, I can't be infected."

We all stood there, completely stunned. "You could have warned us." Dax said.

"No, I couldn't have. I wasn't sure it would work." Evie had a timid smile on her face as she shrugged her shoulders. Sometimes it was hard to remember that she was over twelve hundred years old.

We all turned and stared at Terrance, who was still baring his fangs and snapping at us. I couldn't believe how quickly he had deteriorated.

"I hope we can figure out who this woman is fast. I can't stand to see him like this," Dax said. The sad note in his voice mirrored the look on his face. He hung his head and started to walk off. "I'm going to bed."

Everyone else said their goodnights and headed toward their respective rooms until it was just Evie and myself standing outside the cell. "It happened again, didn't it? You *knew* something bad was going to happen when I entered the cell, didn't you?" Evie prodded as we started down the hall.

I guess I couldn't deny it any longer. "Yes. I got an overwhelming sense that something was wrong. But I just can't believe that I'm supposed to become your successor. It's completely unreal to me."

"It could have been anybody from the clan, Christian, but I'm glad it's you. You're going to make a wonderful Sire." Evie hugged me.

"How am I supposed to use any of these new skills to help figure out who this woman is? It's not like I can control it." I was feeling so unsure of myself and the things that were apparently now happening as part of my triggering. I had no idea what to do.

"The first thing I would suggest is that when the darkness claims you tonight, let your last thought be of your emerging powers. Concentrate on them and how they make you feel when they happen. Maybe that will trigger something in your subconscious." Evie touched my cheek then headed for her room.

I supposed anything was worth a try. Evie certainly had experience dealing with the subconscious, so maybe she was onto something. Though it was going to be strange to not have Rose be the last thing I thought of at night. However, the chance of an eternity with her was enough motivation for me to try anything. I wanted to be the best Sire and consort I could possibly be.

CHAPTER TWENTY-SEVEN

(Rose)

After Jillian explained this was where Justin was from, I couldn't help but wonder if he could be of any use to me. I had a surprise for Christian—not only was I going to be moving out soon, but I was also going to become a vampire just like him. Then we could be together forever.

I hadn't told Christian I knew vampires existed yet, because Terrance warned me revealing that knowledge could get us both killed. He also taught me I had to hide my thoughts around other vampires, making sure I only focused only on the events immediately happening around me. After spending time with him at the pool, I came to learn quite a lot about vampires and how they weren't the bad, evil villains of lore. Terrance had explained how every night they fed from only one person and only took their fill. Using their powers allowed them to make the feeding process an enjoyable act for both vampire and human, and it also let them compel the human so that they didn't remember anything about the exchange.

I grew more and more comfortable with Terrance feeding from my mom, and it amazed me how she didn't even care. She was never hurt or out of it in any way. There were times when I thought he may have taken too much blood, but she never seemed to show any signs of feeling sick or anemic, so I came to trust Terrance pretty quickly. Once he fed, he would use his sedative to put my mom to sleep for a short time, so he and I could continue to talk.

During our conversations, I admitted I had no idea that Christian was a vampire. When we started dating, I truly believed he slept all day because of his job. Only after meeting Terrance had everything become crystal clear. Once he confirmed he knew Christian and lived with him at the club, I asked him why I'd never seen him there when I came down to visit. He said it was because he always left the vicinity to feed, only returning when it was time for the club to open.

I continued to see Christian even after learning the truth, recalling how completely nerve-wracking our next date had been. I thought for sure it'd be impossible to hide my thoughts from Christian, but surprisingly enough, he never seemed to notice a thing.

After multiple conversations with Terrance, I finally worked up the nerve to asked the question I was dying to know the answer to. How did someone become a vampire? He explained the process, which really wasn't a surprise. The vampire bit and fed from the human until they drained them, and then the human fed from the vampire in return. They would then die and be reborn as a vampire in a matter of hours. And after a few weeks of contemplating it, I made up my mind. I was definitely in love with Christian and wanted to become like him, so we could be together forever, so I asked Terrance if he would change me, and he agreed.

He did, however, make it a point to explain that no one could know we knew each other, or what our plans were for my change, since this wasn't the usual way things were done. Apparently, the normal way for new vampires to be made was for the clan to vote on who they wanted to add to the *family*, but Terrance agreed to change me in secret, because he knew everyone would be happy and understood I wanted it to be a surprise.

But after making our plans, Mom had died. Initially, I thought Terrance had done it because of the bite marks on her neck, but quickly came to the conclusion that it couldn't have been him. He only ever fed from the at the pool.

After Mom's death, and once I'd been placed on lockdown by my dad, I never saw Terrance again. That is, until the night he emerged from the woods outside of the club. It had taken everything in me to not act surprised or let on that I knew him in any way. But since Christian and Evie never mentioned anything, I assumed I'd pulled it off. When I first saw him, though, I wanted so badly to confront him and ask if he knew what had happened to my mom, but I'd never gotten the chance.

Jillian hit the curb as she parked the car, once again shaking me out of my thoughts. "Sorry, I just thought we could grab a bite to eat. I'm starving," she said hesitantly.

"Okay. Yeah, I guess I could eat. Why don't you call Justin and see if he can come meet us?" I smiled and tried to sound like the supportive best friend.

After phoning Justin, Jillian and I walked into a nearby restaurant and grabbed a seat by the front window. Jill kept looking at me from over the top of her menu, questions shining clearly in her eyes. "Are you feeling better now?" she finally asked.

"I am. Thank you for getting me out of town. I just don't think I can deal with my dad right now. He has apparently been seeing this woman, Meredith, and it really took me by surprise. The worst part is, she looks a lot like my mom." I slumped a bit in my chair. I couldn't get over how much that bothered me. I think hanging out with Justin couldn't have come at a better time. I was ready, now more than ever, to leave this world behind. I really hoped he would agree to change me, now that Terrance wasn't an option.

I sat there contemplating how in the hell I was going to get Justin alone, when the vampire himself came strolling down the sidewalk. I watched him cross the street and head in our direction. Once Jill saw him, she knocked on the window to gain his attention. He smiled, waved, and sped toward the front door.

By the time he reached the table, Jillian was beaming. He leaned in and placed a gentle kiss on her lips. "What in the world inspired you two to head all the way out here?"

"Rose had a mental breakdown and needed to get out of town."

I shrugged. She always did love to throw me under the bus.

"I saw the sign for the turnoff and remembered you saying this was where you were from. Plus, I was getting hungry," Jillian confessed.

With a little chuckle Justin said, "Well, that was perfect timing, because I'm starting to get hungry too."

I almost spit my soda across the table at his obvious statement. Jill didn't have a clue about him, but it cracked me up to see how many people were mind-fucked by the vampires in our area. As the huff left my lungs, I shook my head slightly and looked right at Jill's neck and then back at him. I was trying to be obvious, and thought it worked, when Justin's eyes quickly widened before he squinted and stared right at me.

I nodded and then tilted my head to the side, exposing my neck to him. He smirked and casually licked the tip of one of his fangs. Jillian remained completely oblivious, flagging down the waiter with a huge smile on her face.

Justin turned toward Jillian and took her hand. I thought it was just a sweet gesture until he lifted her wrist to his mouth and bit down. I couldn't believe he was doing this in the middle of a restaurant, but suddenly, he released her hand and the tiny holes closed immediately, leaving no trace of a puncture behind. Jillian stood up and announced that she needed to use the restroom. It was obvious then that he'd used his powers to *suggest* she leave us alone.

Once she was gone, Justin turned toward me. "How do you know about me?" He didn't exactly sound mad but was definitely concerned.

"I met someone like you who taught me all about vampires. But don't even think about feeding on me or I'll tell Christian and he'll kill you." I wasn't sure I was safe with Justin like I'd been with Terrance, but I wasn't taking any chances.

"Not that I was planning on feeding on you, but what are you talking about? Christian can't kill me."

"I know that if a human tells anyone they're aware of vampires, it puts them and the vampire at risk of being killed." I wasn't sure why I had to explain this to him, and honestly, I didn't have time for small talk. There was only one question I needed to ask him. "I want to know if you'd be willing to change me. I'm completely in love with Christian and I want to surprise him by becoming a vampire so that we can spend eternity together. The vampire who was going to do it has recently disappeared," I continued in a rush.

Justin sat there, staring at me like I was completely crazy. I knew throwing this out there would be a shock, but Jillian would return soon, and I needed an answer. "Well? Will you change me or not?" I demanded.

A severe frown formed on his face as he slowly shook his head. "I don't understand. If a vampire has taught you all about us, then you should know that I *can't* change you. Only a Sire can inflict the change."

I sat there, dazed and confused. Terrance had never mentioned anything about a Sire, or that they were the only ones with the ability to create new vampires. Justin must be making excuses not to change me, and that pissed me off. He could have easily just said no. "Why are you making shit up? You could've just told me no. I can always ask another member of Christian's clan to do it."

"Rose, you don't understand. I'm not making shit up. I'm telling you the truth. Whoever taught you about us has fed you a line of bullshit. Was this person feeding off of you, too?"

"No. I found him feeding from my mom, and he liked the taste of her blood, so he agreed to teach me about your kind as long as he could continue to feed from her." I was so confused right now I couldn't sit still. "Let's get out of here." I flew out of my chair and headed back to the car.

Justin waited for Jill, then deposited her in the backseat after using more of his sedative to put her to sleep. Climbing into the driver's seat, he drove off down the street.

"Okay, so you're going to have to explain why you think I've been fed a line of bull. My friend has always been honest with me, so I don't understand why he'd lie about that."

"I'm not sure either, but I'll tell you anything you want to know. If some vampire has been manipulating you, then there is definitely something seriously wrong. And Rose, I think you need to tell Christian everything."

CHAPTER TWENTY-EIGHT

(Christian)

The moment I woke from my comatose sleep, I knew there was a serious problem within the clan. But I didn't expect it to be between Terrance and Tori.

Apparently, Evie's idea for me to concentrate on my developing powers while I slept had worked, because when I woke, the first thing I saw was a vision of Terrance sinking his fangs into Tori's neck.

I headed straight for Terrance's cell expecting the worst, but when I rounded the corner, what I saw was a surprise. Tori was actually walking toward Terrance's cell, but she hadn't reached it yet. I guess my *vision* was more of a premonition.

"Are you okay? What are you doing here?" I asked her.

"I'm going to ask Terrance a few questions of my own." The tone in her voice indicated she was not happy. "I want to know who this demon bitch is, and I plan to find out even if it takes a bit of *coercion*." The baseball bat she produced from behind her back totally caught me off guard.

I guess she was planning to beat the truth of out Terrance. But thinking back to my 'premonition', I knew it wasn't going to work. Terrance would end up burying his fangs in her neck. "Tori, you can't do this. Evie commanded us to stay away from him. I don't even know how you've made it this far, but there's no way I'm letting you put yourself at risk by entering that cell, so just forget it."

Seeing her tiny frame holding that bat was almost comical, but I knew better than to underestimate her. All vampires had preternatural speed and strength. I knew that if it came to me fighting her off, I would win, but I was sure she would put up a damn good fight.

Just as Tori stepped toward me, Evie and Dax rounded the corner at the end of the hall. "Tori, stop right there." Evie's command rang in my ears. Tori stopped midstride and remained frozen until Evie reached her.

"I commanded you to stay away from Terrance, so why did you think you'd actually get close enough to use that bat?" Evie didn't sound angry, but I could tell it wouldn't take much to push her in that direction.

"When I walked past his cell tonight on my way to Dom's room, I noticed I was able to get really close despite your command. So, I went back to my room, grabbed my bat, and was just coming to see if I could make him talk. Someone has to figure out what's going on." Tori's voice was rising and her hair and eyes had begun to drift dark.

She sounded so upset, and I couldn't blame her. I knew she and Terrance had previously been involved, but I think what was really upsetting her had more to do with the fact that we were trapped inside the club, feeding from the same people over and over.

Tori had been raised in a very strict household, and while Dominique had enjoyed the life of a '20s flapper, Tori had been stuck at home, caring for their parents and doing most of the chores. Once their parents had passed away, they lost their home, and Evie found the girls wandering the streets together. When Tori awakened from the change, the freedom that came with being a vampire set her heart to flight. She loved being outside, and I knew that's what she was missing the most.

"Honey, give me the bat. I know you want some answers and obviously think this is a good way to get them, but I promise you... you're wrong. Please don't risk yourself by doing something like this. Terrance *will* bite you, and then you'll be infected and will drift permanently dark. And you know what I'll be forced to do if that happens." Evie held out her hand to take the bat from Tori.

Tori handed it over, then took a couple more steps toward Terrance's cell. "Terrance, can't you tell us anything about this woman? We just want to help you. Please, just tell us," Tori pleaded.

Terrance sat there, glaring at us all, just like I knew he would. Evie reached out and placed a hand on Tori's shoulder, then hugged her tight as she melted into her embrace. As the two women walked off, Dax and I stood outside the cell, staring at Terrance.

"Not that I'm ungrateful, but why were you here trying to stop Tori?" Dax asked.

"When I woke this evening, the first thing I saw was an image of Terrance sinking his fangs into Tori's neck." I shrugged and started to make my way toward the stairs.

"So, I guess that Evie's right after all. You *are* the one being triggered as the next Sire. How do you feel about that?"

I wasn't sure and didn't really know what to say to Dax, but the stress of discussing it was immediately postponed as we reached the top of the stairs.

As I emerged from the rising pit, I looked up and found Rose standing in the club... right next to Justin.

CHAPTER TWENTY-NINE

(Rose)

After riding around with Justin, I learned that not only had Terrance lied to me, but that I had absolutely no way of becoming a vampire anytime soon. Apparently, it was common knowledge between the clans that Evangeline had lost her ability to inflict the change. They were waiting on the next Sire to be triggered, but until that happened, there was no way I could become a vampire.

Justin also informed me we would not be killed if I told Christian's clan the truth—that I knew vampires existed. He explained that the only time a vampire is killed is if they drifted permanently dark.

My brain was fuzzy from all this new information, but once I got it together, I told Justin about Terrance coming out of the woods, Christian's reaction to him, and how he'd had really black hair and eyes.

Justin convinced me to go with him to the club right then and there, so we could tell Evangeline everything and what Terrance had been up to. Since my plan to become a vampire and surprise Christian was ruined, I decided Justin was right; it was time for the truth. I was completely petrified, but for reason, I knew in my gut it was the right thing to do.

We arrived at The Rising Pit just before 8 p.m. The door was locked, but Justin knocked once and Evie opened it with a surprised look on her face, then escorted us inside.

"This is a surprise, Rose. I hadn't realized you knew Justin. And how in the world did you get away to come visit us on a Sunday night? I know your father is quite strict regarding your schedule."

She was probably wondering if Justin had bit me and brought me to the club so I quickly answered. "Actually Evangeline, Justin brought me here because I have something important to discuss with you and Christian." I tried to keep my voice level and my thoughts blank. I still wasn't going to let Evie poke around in my head, even if I was planning on revealing everything.

As we headed toward the office, Christian and Dax appeared from under the stage. The look on his face was one I'd never seen before. I couldn't tell if he was happy or mad, but from the rapid drifting of his hair from blond to brown and back again, I knew he was having a hard time controlling his emotions.

I stared at him openly, with my mouth gaping open, since I'd only learned about drifting during my car ride with Justin. It was obvious why Terrance never touched on that subject; it would have been apparent he was one of the bad ones.

"Rose, what on earth are you doing here with him?" Christian didn't sound mad, but he continued to drift as he made his way over to me.

"I have something I need to talk to you and Evangeline about. Can we please go into her office?" If I waited much longer to get this off my chest, I didn't think I was going to be able to do it.

Evangeline had already moved to hold the door open when Christian grabbed my hand and brought it to his lips. It felt so good to be near him, but also made my heart hurt. The devastating blow of realizing my plans to become his eternal love had been crushed was almost too much to bear.

"Rose, I'm going to wait in the car with Jillian if that's okay." Justin gave me a tight smile then eased his way back outside.

The way Christian was looking at us was freaking me out. "Christian, don't worry. There is nothing going on between me and Justin. Just come on... I'll explain everything."

He closed the door behind us as we entered Evie's office.

Instead of her usual, casual demeanor, Evangeline had her hip propped on the corner of her desk and a bleak look on her face. "Rose, I'd be happy to hear what this is about, so please, without further delay, would you be so kind as to put Christian and my anxiety to rest?"

"I don't really know how to start, so I guess I'll just state the obvious. I know that you all are vampires." I paused and hoped Justin was right— that Evangeline wouldn't kill me for knowing their secret.

Christian and Evie stared at each other for a few seconds before he turned and glared at me. "How? How do you know? And how long have you been lying to me?"

Shocked, his words hit me in the chest like a blow from a prizefighter. "I didn't lie to you. I just didn't tell you I knew what you were." I had hoped my confession would be a relief to him, but obviously it was not. "How and when I found out is the reason I'm here."

Christian looked at me like I was a complete stranger. I hoped that by sharing Terrance's deception he would see this as a good thing in the end.

"I found out vampires existed about seven and a half months ago. I was coming to meet my mom after one of her swim lessons and found a vampire feeding from her instead." I was so nervous to reveal who that vampire was, that in that instant, I didn't know if I could do this.

Evangeline moved off her desk and came to kneel in front of me. "Rose, just tell us everything that happened. I'm not angry with you and you are in no danger from anyone in my clan."

Even though I would have preferred some reassurance from Christian, I was thankful for Evangeline's words. "Thank you. I never meant to deceive anyone. I was just trying to surprise Christian by becoming a vampire, so we could be together forever."

Again, I was hoping my revelations would soften Christian's opinion of the situation, and from the look he gave me, it had worked... if only slightly. The emotions warring across his face were caught somewhere between love and complete disbelief. "How were you going do that Rose? Evie is the only one who can create new vampires."

"I know that now, thanks to Justin, but before I was told something different... by Terrance."

At that point Evangeline actually fell backwards, flat onto her ass. "I knew it!"

I continued in a rush, "I'm sorry I kept it from you, but he told me that if anyone found out we knew each other, or that I knew vampires existed at all, we would both be killed. I now know that isn't true. And as a matter of fact, I think everything he told me was a lie. I just don't understand why." I took a deep breath. "I'm so sorry I didn't come to you sooner."

Evangeline picked herself up off the floor and leaned against her desk. "Why don't you tell us exactly how you two met and everything he's told you about us?"

By the time I finished relaying all the lies and promises Terrance had fed me, Christian and Evangeline both looked completely devastated. Evie found it especially interesting Terrance's price for this information was that he be able to continue feeding from my mom.

"I'm sorry if you feel I've lied to you, but I swear I had no idea what he was telling me was a complete crock of shit. I only found out the truth of how things really worked tonight. I have Justin to thank for that."

Evangeline smiled. "Rose, I don't blame you. Terrance was manipulating you, and I have a pretty good idea as to why."

CHAPTER THIRTY

(Jeremy/Dad)

"I've called Jillian's house and her parents haven't seen either of them." I didn't know what I was going to do if I couldn't find Rose soon. I was so panicked about where she could be and all the bad things that could be happening to her, I was ready to call the cops. Thankfully, Meredith was here and trying her best to keep me calm. She made us some chamomile tea in an effort to settle my nerves and continued to remind me that Rose was a big girl. Something I'd refused to see for several months now.

"I just can't believe she ran off. I never imagined she would actually leave and not come home." It was only 9 p.m., but it was dark outside and with her last words ringing in my ears, *"Maybe I'll see you at home,"* I was regretting everything that had happened between us.

"Jeremy, I'm sure she's fine. It's obvious Jillian picked her up, and since her parents said she hasn't broken curfew yet, I'm sure they'll return soon. I know you're regretting what happened today, but I really do think everything will be okay."

"Thanks, Meredith. I know in my head that you're probably right, but it's convincing my heart that's the problem." I started to calm down a bit, then my phone started ringing in my hand.

"Hello? Rose?"

"No, Jeremy, it's Adrienne Case. I spoke to Jillian and wanted to let you know that the girls are fine. They just finished dinner with some friends and asked if Rose could spend the night. I told them that would be fine but wanted to let you know in case you wanted to come pick her up instead."

I sat there, relief flowing through my veins like warm whisky. I needed to tread carefully, but my first instinct was to rush over there, pick her up, and continue to explain about Meredith. But it was obvious, Rose needed more time to process everything. I was just be grateful Jillian had checked in with her parents.

I turned to find Meredith beaming at me. There was no *I told you so* look on her face—just genuine relief and caring. "Thank you, Adrienne. I think it will help Rose to cool down if she can spend the night there, so I appreciate the hospitality. Please let her know I will be by in the morning to pick her up."

"Sounds good, Jeremy. I'll let her know, and don't worry, I'm sure this will blow over soon. You two never fight and are as close as a father and daughter can be." Her response was exactly what I needed to hear.

I hung up the phone and took a deep breath, reveling in the fact my only daughter was safe. Turning to Meredith once more, I was struck with a new set of emotions. "Thank you for staying with me through all of this. I never realized how much having you here truly grounds me." I walked toward her, preparing to show her just how grateful I was. "Would you do me the pleasure of spending the night with me? Here in my home?"

Meredith smiled. "I thought you would never ask."

CHAPTER THIRTY-ONE

(Rose)

I'm not sure exactly how many times I almost passed out while listening to Evangeline explain what had happened to Terrance.

Infected by demon blood? How the hell was I supposed to process that? I thought I'd handled the fact that vampires existed pretty well, but demons... come on.

From what Evangeline said, it was obvious they thought my mom was the zôt that had infected Terrance. I actually think I threw up in my mouth a little at that revelation. All I wanted to do was run away.

"You have to be wrong! You have to be! There is no way my mom was a fucking demon!"

"Rose, please calm down. We'll figure this out." Christian knelt in front of me, rubbing his hands over my thighs.

I loved that he wanted to help, but I was nowhere close to being consolable. After lifting his hands from my legs, I pushed out of the chair and started to pace. "How am I supposed to calm down? You just told me you think my mom was a demon, but I'm telling you, there's no way it's true. She was just my mom. A normal, everyday, suburban mother who taught swim lessons for a living and took care of me and my dad."

"Rose, we initially thought the woman who infected Terrance had done so maliciously, but from what you're telling us, it seems like it was a simple side-effect from him accidentally encountering her demon blood."

At least Evangeline wasn't blaming my mother for what had happened, if what they were say *was* true.

"I know this will be hard to deal with, and I'm sorry for having to put you through this, but it's obvious Terrance is the one who killed your mother," Evangeline stated.

I sank down to the floor and let Christian wrap me in his arms. I'd seen this coming from a mile away, but it was still devastating. I just couldn't understand why he'd done it. Terrance had always treated my mom like something he cherished, so how could he end up killing her instead? Something didn't add up.

Once I regained my balance, and even though he was the obvious choice, I just couldn't believe Terrance had been the one to kill my mom.

"Honey, you have to face facts. Terrance was addicted to the taste of your mother's blood. You said so yourself—that he told you it was unlike anything he had ever tasted before. I'm sure as the poison spread, the need for her blood became more and more prominent. He probably just followed her home one night and lost control. Rose, I'm sorry, but you have to agree it makes perfect sense." Christian was right, it did make sense, and wrapped up my mom's death in a nice little bow. Mystery solved. "I guess you're right. But what I don't understand is why he didn't come back for me."

CHAPTER THIRTY-TWO

(Jeremy/Dad)

My night with Meredith had been a whirlwind of passion, but when I woke up to find her sprawled in my bed with her blonde hair spilling over my dead wife's pillow, it sent a jolt of shock straight through my heart. We'd spent the night together before, but it had always been at her apartment in Masen. So waking up here, in the bed I shared with my wife for years, was something I clearly wasn't ready for. I instantly had *major* regrets and a *major* change of heart.

"Meredith, I have to go pick up Rose. I'm sorry, but I'm going to have to ask you to leave." I knew it sounded rude, and I realized I was taking the coward's way out by using Rose as my excuse to get rid of her. But in reality, I just couldn't bring myself to look at the woman who reminded me of Loraine for a moment longer.

I don't really know what I was thinking by getting involved with her in the first place. Rose was right. I had obviously gravitated toward Meredith because of her looks and how she reminded me of Loraine, which at the time was a good thing. But now, it was obviously I'd just been using her to fill the gap the gap in my heart.

"I don't have to be back in Masen until tomorrow. Are you sure you don't want me to stick around? I could help explain things between us to Rose, if you'd like." I could see she was truly trying to be helpful, but I suddenly couldn't stand the thought of her being around my only daughter.

"No. Thank you. I really need to speak to Rose alone." I was already heading toward the shower as I took in the hurt expression on her face.

"Jeremy, is everything okay? Have I done something wrong?" Her voice was filled with trepidation.

"Of course not. I'm just anxious to pick up Rose and clear the air between us. I'm sorry if it offends you, but this is something I need to do alone." I was feeling frustrated at having to justify the fact that this was between my daughter and me. Yes, I knew it concerned her since she was part of the reason Rose ran off in the first place, but since our arrangement was quickly coming to an end, I just couldn't muster up the energy to make her feel better.

"Look, Meredith. I'm grateful for the time we've spent together, but after seeing Rose's reaction at the café, it's clear to me I've rushed into things. I think it would be best if we stopped seeing each other. I need to get things settled with Rose and truly figure out how I feel." I turned to continue my escape into the bathroom, but heard a crash.

A broken vase was shattered on the floor. "You have got to be kidding me!" Meredith shouted. "After everything I've gone through to be with you, you're going to let your daughter dictate how our relationship goes?" She was kneeling on the bed completely naked, her eyes glowing bright red.

CHAPTER THIRTY-THREE

(Rose)

"I'm not sure why Terrance didn't come back to kill you, Rose. It's a completely logical question, but one I'm not sure we'll be able to get an answer to." Evangeline explained the poison was keeping Terrance from focusing on any of the time he had spent with my mom. And now that he had drifted completely dark, she didn't think he'd be in a sharing mood, even if he could access the memories.

"Couldn't we at least try? Maybe if he sees me and realizes his deception is no longer a secret, he would open up about it." I couldn't imagine leaving here without some answers.

After hesitating briefly, Christian stood up and took my hand. "I'll take Rose down to question Terrance. I suggest you stay here and explain to everyone what's happening."

"I'm not sure that's a good idea. You saw how he launched himself at me last night, and I know he would have attacked Tori earlier too, if she had gotten any closer." Evangeline was clearly concerned Terrance was a threat to both Christian and me.

"We won't get close to the cell. Besides, he's still in chains and has nowhere to go. I think it's important I be the one to escort Rose to see him." Christian's eyes narrowed while he took in Evangeline's concerned expression. It was clear the two were having some sort of private communication.

"All right. Come straight back up through my office once you're done. And for God's sake, whatever happens, please make sure you stay out of his reach." Evangeline hugged me, then quickly exited her office, leaving Christian and me standing alone, still holding hands.

"I can't tell you how sorry I am this is happening to Terrance, and apparently it's all my mom's fault." It was still a hard pill to swallow, but obviously one I was going to have to get used to. There seemed to be no other explanation.

"Oh, Rose, none of this is your mother's fault. Not really. It seems to me Terrance just happened to cross paths with her at the pool. Honestly, it could have easily been any one of us." He gently lifted my face with the curve of his finger beneath my chin. "I don't blame your mother or you for anything that's happened. And to be honest, I'm thrilled to hear you wanted to become a vampire like me. The thought of spending eternity with you makes me happier than you can imagine." He bent down and kissed me softly.

I didn't have words to express how relieved I felt. When this whole fiasco had started, I wasn't sure he'd be willing to forgive me for keeping the truth from him. But now, with the everything revealed, we could both move forward with our lives. I threw my arms around his neck and increased the intensity of our kiss, but Christian pulled back.

"Come on. We need to get this over with before the club starts to get busy." Christian led me over to the book case behind Evangeline's desk and pushed a button underneath one of the shelves. The bookcase separated, revealing a staircase that led down into a white tiled hall. Once downstairs, Christian led me in the direction of Terrance's cell. I was nervous to see him again, especially now knowing everything I did. "Are you sure you're going to be up for this? You've experienced quite a few shocks tonight already." Christian stopped and rubbed his hands up and down my arms.

"Yes, I'll be fine. I have to do this." I was tougher than people gave me credit for, and I was about to prove it.

Rounding the end of the hall, Terrance's cell finally came into view. He was sitting on the floor with his back against the wall, his hands and feet still cuffed in chains. He looked up and caught sight of me and immediately jumped to his feet.

"Obviously you recognize Rose, and the fact that she's here in our pit should be a pretty good indication that your secret is out of the bag." Christian's voice was sharp, and obviously set Terrance on edge. With wide eyes, he frantically kept looking back and forth between the two of us.

"Terrance, why did you lie to me?" I guess if Christian was going to play the bad cop, I was the good cop. Not that I wanted to be, mind you. I would much rather be slamming my fists into his gorgeous face. Because seeing him again, knowing he'd played me for a fool this entire time, pissed me off more than I could explain. It felt like a rising tide of lava was preparing to explode from within me.

"I'm sorry, Rose. I think she somehow *made* me do it." Terrance sounded so... normal. I'd expected him to be foaming at the mouth, or maybe yelling and screaming. But instead, he sounded like his old self: the nice vampire that had opened up my little sheltered world to one of imaginary creatures and the possibility of eternal life.

"What are you saying? She made you lie to me, or that she made you kill her?" I refused to let him off the hook that easily.

As I waited for his response, Christian tilted his head, a curious look spreading across his face. I refused to discuss anything in front of Terrance, so I left it for later. "So, tell me. Exactly what did my mother make you do?"

"Your mother? What are you talking about?"

I guess it was true. Her demon blood did have a masking effect on Terrance's thoughts and memories.

Unable to control my rage a second longer, I took a step toward the cell. Christian grabbed my arm and shook his head.

"You know exactly what I'm talking about you son of a bitch. You fed from my mother and her demon blood infected you. Then you lied to me. Everything you told me about vampires was a complete load of shit. You never had any intention of changing me, since obviously—YOU CAN'T!" I was shaking by the time I was done and sunk back into Christian's arms.

After staring at me for a few seconds, Terrance shook his head and collapsed back down to the floor. "I did feed from your mother. And yes, I did lie to you. I lied to everyone. But you're wrong, Rose. Your mother wasn't a demon, and I didn't kill her... I loved her."

CHAPTER THIRTY-FOUR

(Rose)

After Terrance's revelation, Christian pulled me away from the cell. Probably because I was dangerously close to losing my temper again.

"Why are we leaving? We were just starting to get somewhere." I was desperate for more answers. Especially regarding my mom not being a demon and that he loved her. What the hell?

"I need to talk to Evie before we continue. There is something else going on here, and even though it's still unclear to me, I think it's important to let her know what Terrance said immediately."

We entered Evangeline's office through the bookcase, then waited for it to close before heading out into the club. It was pretty clear Christian thought what Terrance had said was somehow important, I just didn't understand why.

After pulling me through the crowd by my hand, Christian approached Dax. "Where's Evie?" Dax almost flinched at the stoic tone in Christian's voice.

"What's wrong?"

"I'm not sure, but I need to find her to discuss something, so where is she?"

"She's feeding upstairs." Dax looked at me as he said it, probably to gauge my reaction.

Christian nodded in Dax's direction, then pulled me up the stairs. "Do you want to wait outside?"

I raised my eyebrows. Obviously, it was going to take a little time for everyone to adjust that they didn't have to hide things from me anymore. "I watched Terrance feed from my mom plenty of times, so if it's okay with Evie, I'd like to come inside."

The look that filled Christian's eyes was full of love. "It makes me so happy to finally be able to share every aspect of my life with you." He leaned down and kissed me.

"I feel the exact same way." I kissed him back, trying to show him exactly how happy our newfound honesty made me. "I can't wait until all this is over and we can actually start seeing each other on a regular basis again." I knew right now wasn't the time to discuss it, but the idea of Christian spending the night and day with me in my new apartment was like a little slice of heaven.

"We'd better get in there to tell Evie what happened or else I'm going to drag you into one of these private rooms and finish what we started the last time I was here." I slid my hands down his chest and bit my lower lip in an effort to stop myself from kissing him again.

"You're right. But very soon, I *will* be getting you alone." His voice had that sexy, gravely quality that never failed to make me melt.

Christian stepped toward the curtained entrance and lightly called out, "Evie, may we enter? I have some news."

Silence reigned for only a split second. "Yes Christian. Please come in."

I was a little nervous to enter the room, but was pleasantly surprised to find Evie sitting on the velvet couch with her visitor's wrist pressed to her lips. She used a little handkerchief to dab the corners of her mouth as she pulled his arm away. It was all so civilized. So pleasant. And for the first time since learning of their existence, I actually wondered what it would be like to be fed from.

"What news do you have for me?" Evie asked. Her visitor stood up and silently exited the room, leaving the three of us alone.

"Terrance recognized Rose. And when she questioned him about her mom, he was able to focus on the memories and actually told us that she *wasn't* the demon and that he didn't kill her. Also, he was in love with her."

The confused look on Evie's face matched the jumbled thoughts currently rattling around in my head. I didn't see how this meant anything other than Terrance was still obviously lying to everyone.

"That is extremely interesting and disconcerting at the same time." Evie stood and started to pace the luxurious room.

"No offense, but what in the hell does that mean?" I was getting tired of feeling left in the dark.

"Whenever I question Terrance about the woman I see in his thoughts, the one he was feeding from, the images are always blocked or fuzzy. When you told us that Terrance had been feeding from your mom it just seemed clear that your mom was the demon. But now I'm not so sure. Because if she had been, he wouldn't have been able to focus on her or talk about her in any way."

"What? I still don't understand. You said that my mom was the demon and that feeding from her is what caused Terrance to drift dark and do the things he's been doing. Now you're saying that it wasn't my mom?" I'd be absolutely thrilled if it turned out my mom wasn't to blame, but it still didn't clear up all the questions as to who was responsible and how it was connected to her death.

"What exactly did Terrance say?" Evie returned to couch, sat down, and crossed her legs.

"He said, 'I did feed from your mother. And yes, I did lie to you. I lied to everyone. But you're wrong, Rose. Your mother wasn't a demon, and I didn't kill her... I loved her.'" Christian's verbatim account of what Terrance had told us seemed to leave Evie with even more to think about.

"There's something else." I turned to Christian, confused, since Terrance hadn't said anything else.

"What is it?" Evie asked.

"I think my new ability—the one you said I'm developing—somehow worked while we were with Terrance. I can't explain it, but for whatever reason, I just *know* that Rose's mother wasn't the demon. Terrance was telling the truth."

CHAPTER THIRTY-FIVE

(Jeremy/Dad)

I spun around to face Meredith's rage and swore her eyes were glowing red. But once I refocused, it was clear it had only been a play of light from the red vase she'd smashed on the floor. The sun was streaming in through the bedroom windows and had apparently hit the vase just right, lighting up her face in scary relief.

"Answer me! Are you seriously going to let your daughter control how you live your life?" She was clearly still upset but had sunken back down onto the bed, covering herself up with the sheets.

"I'm sorry if this is hard for you. But you have to understand, Rose *is* my life. She's my only family now, and I will always put her first." I tried to speak calmly in order to soften the blow, but I wasn't in the mood to coddle her. We were both adults and it wasn't like this was true love. I already had that once in my life, and I knew nothing else would ever come close again. "I'm going to get in the shower, and then I'm going to go pick up my daughter. You're more than welcome to wait until I leave and I'll walk you out, or you can just go and I'll call you later this week. It's up to you."

I heard her quiet sobs as I shut the bathroom door. I knew I should feel worse than I did, but the only thing I could concentrate on right now was getting to my daughter and apologizing for being such a terrible father.

* * * * *

(Meredith)

The moment Jeremy shut the bathroom door I tried to dry my tears. I couldn't believe this was happening. After everything I had gone through to be with him, one little hissy fit from his daughter ruins everything? I just couldn't allow it.

I got dressed and gathered my things. There was no way I was going to wait around so he could walk me out, carting me to the curb like a piece of trash. Screw that! I'd leave all right, but you could damn sure bet I'd be back soon.

* * * * *

(Jeremy/Dad)

Meredith was gone by the time I finished my shower and got dressed. I couldn't pretend I wasn't relieved. I really did need to get to Rose and make sure she was okay. I noticed I had missed a call from her, so I was hopeful that we would be able to work things out today. But with my anxiety ratcheted up, I just couldn't settle my thoughts. The urgent feeling to reach Rose was quickly climbing to an uncontrollable level.

As I rounded the corner, I saw Jillian's car in the Case's driveway. This was a good sign and definitely helped to relieve my stress. I parked and headed toward the front door, but just as I was reaching for the bell, the door opened and out walked Jillian.

"Good morning, Mr. Reynolds." She was dressed in her usual sporty attire and seemed bright-eyed and bushy-tailed. I expected to see Rose following closely behind, but instead Jillian shut the door and started toward her car.

"Jillian. Where's Rose?" So much for my stress levels staying in check.

"She actually took the bus to school this morning. She said to let you know she's not quite ready to talk, and that car shopping would have to wait. She did say that she'd see you at home tonight, though."

The words hit me hard.

I guess I shouldn't have been surprised, but the news of her heading to school to avoid me really hurt. I needed to tell her how sorry I was, and that I had called it off with Meredith, but obviously that would have to wait until tonight. "Well, thank you for the message, Jillian, I won't keep you."

I headed back to my car, wondering what I should do to fill my day. I rarely took days off from work. I was never sick, and since Loraine died, unless Rose was home, I didn't really enjoy being in the house alone. So, with the entire day to myself, I decided to head to the gym to clear my head. After pumping some iron, I should be a little less stressed and then maybe I'd go looking for Rose's new car on my own. Anything to pass the time.

CHAPTER THIRTY-SIX

(Rose)

Christian, Evangeline, and I were still sitting in the private room of The Rising Pit when Dax entered the room. "What's happened?"

Evie smiled at her consort and began to explain. "When Christian and Rose went to question Terrance, he didn't deny that he recognized her. He was also able to focus on Rose's mother and he admitted had, in fact, been feeding from her." Dax sank into the chaise opposite Christian as Evie continued. "Terrance told them that Rose's mom wasn't the demon."

"Do you believe him?" Dax asked.

"Thanks to Christian's new developing ability... yes, I do."

I hadn't had the chance to ask Christian what they were talking about yet. It sounded like a good thing and something that Evie was coming to rely on, so I decided to let it go. We definitely needed to deal with the bad stuff going on before we could get to the good.

"So, if Rose's mother wasn't the demon, then who was? And why were they having Terrance manipulate and lie to Rose?" Dax asked.

"I'm not sure. It could be that the two things aren't even related. Terrance could have fed from this demon, and then once he started to permanently drift, the lies and manipulation developed as a natural part of him going dark." Evie stood and made her way to take a seat at the end of Dax's chaise. "This could actually be good news for everyone. Not only is Rose's mother not the demon, but now we have a chance of finding this woman alive. That means, maybe we can still find a way to save Terrance." She leaned down and kissed Dax on the cheek.

We sat there in silence for a few moments, which allowed me to piece everything together in my head. Finally, I was left with just one question I just hadn't figured out. "I know you said you thought my mom was the demon because of the timing of everything: Terrance's feeding from her, her death, and his drifting. But if you've seen this woman in his thoughts, then shouldn't you have known that it wasn't my mom from the beginning?"

"Well no, Rose. Actually, it was quite the opposite. When you explained everything that had happened and described your mother's appearance, it made perfect sense. The woman I saw in Terrance's thoughts was just as you described: tall, thin, and with long, blonde hair."

It took me a moment to process what Evie had said. Tall, thin, and with long, blonde hair. *Holy shit!* "I can't believe this. I know who the demon is!" I jumped up and reached for my cell phone. I had to call my dad and warn him that the bitch he was seeing was actually a demon. "I just met my dad's new girlfriend, and you wouldn't believe how much she looks just like my mom." I was going to nail that bitch to the wall.

"Rose, come here." Christian grabbed my hand and guided me back down on the couch next to him. "Think about this for a minute. The only reason we thought it was your mother was because of all the other coincidences. This woman you are referring to could just be another person with blonde hair. It's most likely she has nothing to do with it."

I knew his words made sense, but for some reason, I could feel that I was on to something. "I don't know, Christian. It seems like a pretty big a coincidence she came into my dad's life right after my mom was killed, and around the same time Terrance drifted dark. I really do think there's a connection."

"We can't afford not to check it out," Evie said. "Rose, it's almost sunrise, so why don't you borrow Christian's car and head to school? See if you can use the library at the college to dig up anything on this Meredith woman. I had Justin take Jillian home and use his sedative to convince her and her parents to give your dad a cover story. If I were you, I would probably avoid seeing your dad until we get this figured out. I'll leave a key to the club for you with Dominique. Pick it up on your way out. That way you can come straight back here after school."

Evie stood and walked toward me. "I can't tell you how happy I am that you and Christian finally have things out in the open. Normally, he would have been required to keep our secret from you until the new Sire is chosen, but since you came to us, there are no rules that have been broken. I'm very happy for the two of you." She kissed my cheek then headed for the door with Dax following closely behind.

I never expected Evie to be so gracious in welcoming me. As a matter of fact, I thought she was going to rip my head off the second she heard I knew vampires existed.

I sat back down next to Christian, his hair and eyes drifting as soon as I scooted closer. I wasn't one hundred percent sure how this drifting thing worked yet, so I was unclear if something was wrong. "What is it?"

"It just makes me so angry that all of Terrance's lies have left you with such a violent and completely distorted vision of us." He ran his hand down the side of my arm.

"I know it will take some time for me to sort through all the lies, but I'm really glad I finally told you the truth. But this also means, I won't be surprising you by becoming a vampire any time soon." I reached up and touched his cheek. I couldn't wait to start my forever life with him, and it almost brought me to tears to think there was no way to make that happen now.

"I wouldn't be so sure about that." Christian's response had me confused, but filled me with hope at the same time.

"What do you mean?"

"Do you remember when Evie and I were talking about my 'new developing ability'? Well, Evie thinks I'm showing signs of being triggered. If it's true, that means I'm in line to become the next Sire."

Holy shit! I about fell off the couch. My boyfriend was going to be the next Sire, which meant... he could be the one to change me?

The coming morning just got a whole lot brighter.

CHAPTER THIRTY-SEVEN

(Rose)

I was so tired after being up for twenty-four hours, but there was no way I could sleep with the idea my dad's new girlfriend being the demon who infected Terrance running through my head. So, instead of heading home to catch a few hours of sleep, I went straight to the school like Evie had suggested.

Once there, I was happy to see Mr. Thompson assigned open study for his class today. He was notorious for doing that when it was close to graduation, in order to give the slackers time to ask questions and really buckle down. Luckily, I was ahead of the game when it came to my thesis, but Mr. Thompson didn't need to know that.

"Mr. Thompson, may I have a pass to the library for the rest of the day?"

"Of course." He scribbled out the pass, then whispered, "I wouldn't want one of my best students to not have her thesis completed on time." I smiled and thanked him, then bolted from class. I just hoped this wasn't a waste of time. I really did think Meredith was the one we were looking for, and if I had to spend an entire day digging for dirt on her, then that's exactly what I would do.

* * * * *

(Meredith)

The moment I crossed the bridge back into Masen, I headed straight for my apartment. I couldn't believe Jeremy had kicked me out and called things off between us.

There was no way I was letting that half-breed daughter of his ruin everything I had gone through to get to him.

I remembered the day he walked into my office over a year ago. Tall, confident, and gorgeous as hell. I sensed right off that he was a demon, but after spending a few hours in his presence, it was clear he had no idea.

I knew there were other demon bloodlines out there, but Jeremy was the first I'd ever run across. Which meant, I still had a shot of continuing my pure demon bloodline. The only thing I needed to do was get Mr. Reynolds into bed.

After a few business meetings I manipulated, Jeremy became the head of all of our marketing campaigns. That meant, he would be spending a lot of time here in Masen and a lot more time with me. And time was exactly what I needed if I was going to get him to cheat on his wife.

Everything had been going great during our business meetings. I had gotten to know him over long phone calls, video conferences, and of course the monthly, overnight meetings here in Masen. But the one thing I'd learned from all of our time spent together was that he loved his wife with all his heart. She was a swim instructor and they enjoyed a simple life, raising their daughter in their family home. How picture perfect. Too bad none of them knew the truth about themselves or the world around them.

It hadn't taken me long to find a vampire clan close to Jeremy's home. So, once I'd visited The Rising Pit and chose the vampire I wanted to do my dirty work, I offered myself up to be his visitor for the night. Terrance had been more than willing to escort me to one of the private rooms.

With his fangs set in my neck, he began to take long draws of my blood, and I could sense the moment my demon blood had started to infect him. After that, I had gone back a few times, knowing my blood would have caused his memories of me to be hazy. So, repeating the processes again and again, I made sure he was well on his way to drifting dark.

I learned of the old stories and demon histories from my mother, just as she had learned them from her mother, who had learned them from hers and so on and so on. But I wasn't completely sure this would work since there hadn't been a record of it in over 100,000 years. It was actually pretty rare there was anyone left who truly knew the demon/human bloodline even existed.

There were cases every now and again in the bigger clans where a vampire had accidentally bitten a demon while feeding and had drifted dark, but the cases were so few and far between, the vampires had no idea what had caused the odd events. Since they could never figure out why it happened, their "rule" was to deliver the true death to any vampires that had drifted permanently dark. It was so convenient. By killing their infected vampires, the clans were helping to keep our race hidden from the world without even knowing it.

I'd thought I could control Terrance, since he'd been infected with my blood. All I should have needed to do was give him a suggestion through the mind bond we shared, and he would do anything I asked, the poison conveniently wiping it from his memory.

Unfortunately, I never imagined he would fall in love with Loraine too. I guess I should have known something was off when he first reported her blood tasting different to him. He'd been more than willing to continue feeding from her, keeping her occupied while I'd arranged late night meetings with Jeremy. And when Rose discovered them, the easiest thing to do was to have him continue keeping them both busy by lying and feeding her fantasies of becoming a vampire. It had given me plenty of time to continue to lure Jeremy into my bed.

At first, I really didn't have any desire to actually kill Loraine, but once I noticed Terrance was close to completely drifting dark, I knew it was only a matter of time before his Sire delivered the true death. So, unless I got Jeremy to sleep with me before that happened, I was going to be forced to find another vampire to continue my charade. And with Rose now involved, I knew it would be easier to just get rid of Loraine altogether. Besides, I'd really grown fond of Jeremy and could see myself building a life with him instead of just a one-night stand. Plus, I wasn't even sure that I would get pregnant during our first encounter, and who knew if I'd ever convince him to sleep with me again. No, getting rid of Loraine was the only thing I could do.

At the time, I thought Terrance would of course be the one to do it. It could've easily been a "side-effect" of his drifting dark. No one would be surprised if he just happened to lose control while feeding from her. But with his emotions so deeply involved, I wasn't sure my mind bond would be strong enough to actually force him to kill the woman he loved. Plus, there was the problem of dealing with Rose. My initial thought had been for Terrance to just bite her and use his sedative to make her forget, but then I remembered she was half-demon. I had no idea if Rose's blood contained enough poison to give her control over Terrance, but I wasn't willing to risk it. No, it turned out I had to be the one to take care of things myself.

* * * * *

(Rose)

After digging for three hours, I found absolutely nothing incriminating on Meredith Karver. Besides discovering her last name, I hadn't run across anything else of use. I traced her family back to the southern area of New Mexico, but if what Evie had told me held true, then multiple demon families would have scattered across the world throughout history, so knowing where she came from really wasn't going to make much of a difference.

Completely out of ideas and with exhaustion setting in, I headed back to the club like Evie suggested. I wasn't ready to see my dad yet. I needed sleep, and figured I'd inform the clan my little research trip had been a complete waste of time once they all woke up.

Gathering up my books, I headed down the hall just as the bell rang. Carried along in the waves of people, I didn't really notice when Jillian slid up next to me.

"Hi!" she beamed.

She must have gotten enough sleep last night. Lucky bitch. "Hey, how are you?" I asked.

"I'm okay. Last night was fun, huh?" The look she was giving me was freaking me out. I knew Justin had given them some kind of cover story, but I hadn't exactly gotten all the details.

"Um, yeah... it was great!" I decided to stick vague answers.

"We should road trip more often. That delicious dinner we had with our friends... YUM! We are so going back to that restaurant. Actually, Mom said we could probably go back this weekend when you spend the night again. Anyway, I can't wait. Catch ya later!" She bounded off in a flurry of ponytail swishes and tennis shoe squeaks.

I assumed Justin had removed himself from the story last night which was fine by me. I really didn't want to have to start explaining things to Jillian too. Right now, I was utterly happy to leave her in a bubble of ignorance.

CHAPTER THIRTY-EIGHT

(Rose)

When I arrived at the club, I used the key Evie had given me to let myself in. It was so odd being here during the day, knowing everyone was below sleeping in the pit, including Christian.

It only took me a few seconds to find the button he'd used to open the bookcase in Evie's office. I figured if I was here and was going to be getting some sleep, I wanted to be doing it in my boyfriend's bed.

Thankfully, finding Christian's room had only taken me opening one wrong door. I'd found Bobby sprawled across his bed, fully clothed, thankfully. The next door I opened revealed Christian lying on his back in only a pair of snug fitting boxers and no shirt. The sight of him took my breath away.

I wasn't exactly sure how this would go, but since I assumed he really did mean *dead to the world,* I didn't think I would disturb him if I climbed into bed.

He wasn't cold or stiff like the movies say, so I maneuvered his arm out of the way and made room for myself to curl up next to him.

It felt so perfect to finally be resting in the arms of my boyfriend. It didn't matter that he was a vampire. Christian, and everyone in his clan for that matter, had always been completely nice to me, Terrance notwithstanding. They had never once made fun of me or showered me with pity because of what had happened. In truth, these vampires were nicer than most of the humans I knew, and I couldn't wait to become part of their clan.

I let these thoughts fill my head as I started to drift off to sleep. What better way to spend my dreaming hours than imagining myself as part of Christian's life forever?

* * * * *

(Christian)

The moment I started to rise, I knew something was different. As usual, the image in my head was of Rose, since she was the last thing I thought of before lying down. But this was different. It was like I could actually smell her.

The moment I broke through into consciousness, I realized Rose was actually here in my bed, snuggled up against me, sleeping softly. *My God, what did I do to deserve such a reward?*

This was how I wanted to wake for the rest of my existence: Rose's beautiful blonde hair, pouring over her shoulders and onto my arms. Her sweet scent filling my nose, her sexy body pressed into me just right. Damn, I had never wanted anything more than I wanted her in that moment.

I decided to follow my gut and reached around to smooth her hair away from her face. She started to stir as I kissed my way down her neck. "Good evening, angel."

"Mmmm. Good evening indeed." Her voice was sultry and smooth as honey as she started to wake. The way her body moved and curved as she twisted around to face me sent delicious shocks racing along my nerves. I was ready for her in an instant.

She must have felt my growing need. "Mmmm... this is exactly what I was just dreaming about," she said.

I was so on fire I couldn't even reply. I continued to kiss and caress my way down Rose's body, making sure to soak up every single inch as we peeled each other out of our remaining clothes.

"Are you sure we have time for this?" Rose asked.

As I looked up and met her heavy-lidded eyes, she must have taken in my darkened appearance, because a sexy smile spread across her mouth. One that made me ache to kiss her until we were both breathless.

"And here I thought it was a bad thing when you drifted dark." She giggled between kisses, while continuing to run her hands down my back.

With the level of emotion I was feeling right now, I was probably as dark as Terrance. But this kind of drifting had nothing to do with demons, or poison, but instead an intense desire and passion that stemmed from the love I felt for Rose.

"I love you, Rose. I love you with everything I am, which may not be much, but it's all yours." I knew that sounded stupid and sappy the moment it left my lips, but it was the truth. In that instant, I knew I'd give her everything and anything she wanted. I refused to live without her.

"I love you too, Christian. And I'm yours, now, and soon to be forever."

CHAPTER THIRTY-NINE

(Jeremy/Dad)

After spending the rest of the afternoon car shopping for Rose, I decided it wouldn't be right for me to pick out her first car, or try use it to smooth things over between us. I've never had to buy my daughters affection in the past, and I certainly wasn't going to start now.

After a quick shower, I made myself a sandwich and waited for Rose to come home from school.

I thought things would go pretty smoothly once I told her I'd broken things off with Meredith, but I wasn't stupid. I knew she felt betrayed that I'd kept my relationship a secret in the first place. And the even bigger hurdle was her protectiveness over her mother's memory. Who could blame her?

I'd never truly expected to start dating Meredith after Loraine's death, but while dealing with my grief she listened, consoled, made me laugh, and encouraged me to focus on Rose. I was truly grateful to her for helping me through the pain. Then one night, during my overnight meeting in Masen, she had expressed her feelings for me. I remember being a little surprised, but not really. She always seemed to have that glint in her eye; the one that makes it pretty clear to any man when a woman is interested in him. She told me that listening to me talk about Loraine and Rose had made her realize what a wonderful man I was, and that she couldn't deny her feelings for me. She also said if I felt she was being disrespectful of Loraine's memory, she would understand if I wanted to end things.

I should have been stronger. The truth was, as much as I liked Meredith as a person, it was because she reminded me of Loraine that I fell into her bed. Thinking back now, it had been wonderful and just what I needed at that time. I know that made me sound like a terrible person, but it was true. If I hadn't had Meredith to turn to during these past few months, I probably would have withered away, or even worse, been even more obsessive about Rose's life than I already was.

I knew Rose humored me by letting my driver take her and pick her up from school. And she was always such a sweet girl about following my insane rules when it came to her safety. If I was being honest with myself,

I knew it was only a matter of time before she snapped. I'm actually pretty surprised it took this long.

But now we could clear the slate and have a fresh start. I realized my overprotectiveness was only going to push her away, so it was time I let my little girl grow up. I needed to start a new life, too. I couldn't continue to fake my way through a relationship with a woman who looked like Loraine. It was time to move on.

* * * * *

(Meredith)

I had to figure out a way to get Jeremy back. Not only to continue my pure demon bloodline, but also because I'd truly fallen in love with him. I never met anyone so dedicated to his family. He was the perfect man: tall, dark, handsome, smart, sophisticated, and sexy. I absolutely refused to let him go. But how? How was I supposed to get around the fact he was now focused on his daughter and her feelings about our relationship? What a bunch of bullshit. The girl was almost twenty-one, and would very soon be staying twenty-one forever. I had to get back into Jeremy's life, because when Rose turned into a vampire, he was going to be devastated all over again. And just like before... I'd be there to pick up the pieces.

Who knew how long it would take for Rose to actually get accepted into the clan and changed, or what effect the change would have on her? Word on the street was that Evangeline couldn't sire anymore new vamps, and their new Sire hadn't been triggered yet. I supposed I could get rid of her the same way I did her mom. It hadn't really been all that hard when the time had come to finally do it.

Since I knew where Terrance met Rose and Loraine, I'd waited in the parking lot of the swim complex until he'd finished feeding, then used my mind bond with him to instruct Loraine to leave her bedroom at 2 a.m. Once everyone had gone their separate ways, I followed Loraine and Rose back to their house.

I only had to wait a few hours, then right before 2 a.m., I broke in. She was coming out of her room just as instructed. I figured I would use the recently closed puncture wounds Terrance had left to make it look like a vampire draining. Demons didn't have fangs like vampires, but our incisors were sharp enough that if we wanted to drink blood like our ancestors had, we definitely could. I remember my grandmother telling me that drinking human blood was not only the way of our demon ancestors, but that they'd believed it filled them with the essence of the person from whom they drank. I figured in this case, since I already looked enough like Loraine, it could only help me to ingest her essence while I eliminated her.

Once she had been drained, I left with the feeling I'd just come home. Whether it was her essence flowing through me, or the fact that I now knew that Jeremy and I would be building a life together, it had been euphoric. Getting rid of Loraine had been the best idea I had ever had.

But getting rid of Rose was a different story. I couldn't risk biting her since she was a half-demon. There was a chance her blood would allow her to take control over me, if I were to ingest it. And since she wasn't a vampire yet, I couldn't infect her with my poison like I had with Terrance. I honestly had no idea how I was going to make this work.

I knew she wouldn't willingly help me get back on Jeremy's good side, so I was going to have to come up with a different plan all together: one that would put me back in Jeremy's life and eliminate Rose's hold over him.

I'd already decided that infecting another vampire was too much trouble at this point, so the only option I had was to threaten Rose and turn her father against her. I thought about simply killing her in a more modern way, like shooting her, or a random stabbing at her college, but as much as I wanted her gone, I didn't want to risk starting a war with the local vampires. I knew that Rose's death would put them on the hunt, and with Terrance still alive, it would only be a matter of time before they found me out.

CHAPTER FORTY

(Rose)

After reveling in the best experience of my life, Christian and I laid in his bed, kissing and snuggling like two newlyweds.

"I wish we could stay like this all night and do that over and over again." I nipped little kisses along his jaw line. God, I just couldn't keep my hands or lips off of him. "You are the most delicious thing I have ever tasted."

He laughed. "That's something the vampire should be saying to you, not the other way around."

The smile on his face kept the comment light, but the reality of it hit me right away. "Do you want to feed from me?"

Christian started drifting the moment the words left my mouth. His hair got darker and his eyes started to lose their caramel swirl, and since everything I had learned about vampires had been completely wrong, I didn't know if I should start to panic or not. But then, my heart caught up with my head, and I realized Christian would never do anything to hurt me.

"I assume since you're drifting it means you're hungry?" I wasn't sure if I was making a mistake by talking about it so openly, but what the hell... I was tired of keeping secrets, especially if I was going to become a vampire soon, too.

"Yes, I'm hungry, and the thought of feeding from you is delectable and playing havoc with my brain... as well as other body parts." He sat up and scooted closer. "Before you knew I was a vampire, it was forbidden for me to feed from you because I was in love with you. When a vampire feeds from the one he loves, there is no sedative that can make you forget. So, if I were to have fed from you before, you would have immediately known I was a vampire, and revealing ourselves is something no clan permits."

"I guess it's a good thing I figured it out all on my own then, huh?" I smiled as he leaned in to kiss me. "So now that everything is out in the open you can feed from me without getting in trouble?"

"Yes." His voice was low and steady, but I could tell he was actually straining for control.

I loved having this much power over him. To know that it was me he loved and craved in so many ways was definitely a turn-on. So, with a surge of excitement burning like fire in my veins, I let the sheet drop back onto the bed, revealing my breasts as I tilted my head. "So go on then... feed."

* * * * *

(Christian)

It took every ounce of will power to stop myself from launching at Rose. With the memory of what we'd just done etched into my brain, and her beautiful breasts on display, plus the pumping of blood pounding in her veins... it was excruciating! But the moment I started to consider her offer, my "new ability" must have kicked in. Because not only did I know this wouldn't be the right time, but that it would, in fact, be a huge mistake. I didn't know why, and I didn't know how I was going to explain it to Rose, but I knew completely one hundred percent, I shouldn't feed from my girlfriend.

"Rose, I can't tell you how tempting you are right now, but we really don't have time for me to feed. I can hear Evie and the others starting to gather, and they know you are here. They're very anxious to hear what you found out. I'm sorry." I peeled myself from the bed and dressed in a flash of vampire speed. Now who was the one hiding things?

As we made our way up into the club, Rose seemed quiet. I'm sure it was because of my rejection, but there was nothing else I could do. I also knew I was going to have to tell Evie what had happened.

When we reached the top of the stairs and exited from underneath the stage, the smiles that greeted us were a good sign that everyone would be accepting Rose into the clan. "Look what the cat drug in," Tori teased.

Rose smiled and scooted tighter against my body. "Hi, everyone."

Evie moved toward us and reached out to hug Rose. "I can't tell you how it does my heart good to see you wake with Christian. And hopefully soon, we can make that a permanent thing."

Everyone gave their whoops and cat calls in agreement. I was so proud to have Rose on my arm.

"So, Rose, what did you find out about Meredith?" Evie motioned for all us to take a seat.

"Unfortunately, nothing. I found out her last name and that her family was originally from the southern part of New Mexico, but I don't see how either of those things is going to help us in any way."

I could tell Rose felt bad for not having more valuable information to share.

"Well, that's okay. I think we definitely need to keep an eye on her though, so I'm going to send for Renard and Loni. They are traveling in Europe at the moment, but I know they will be more than willing to cut their honeymoon short, once they find out the situation we're facing." Evie finished by telling Rose she could use the key to the club whenever she wanted, and now that she knew of our existence, she could join us when the club was open as well. Since we no longer had to hide our true selves from her, it would be easy to bite and sedate any law enforcement that would question her presence in the club.

As everyone headed off for opening, I pulled Rose close. "Are you going to be okay going home to face your dad? He's probably pretty worried about you by now."

"Yes. I should be fine. I'm going to call him on my way and make sure that demon bitch isn't going to be there. Maybe once we're alone, I can talk some sense into him." She rose up on her toes and kissed me goodbye. "Thanks for an amazing night. I love you, Christian."

"I love you too. Call me if you need anything. I can literally be there in flash." For some reason, I was reluctant to let her go.

CHAPTER FORTY-ONE

(Jeremy/Dad)

As five o'clock ticked by, I realized Rose wasn't coming straight home after school. I'd tried her phone, but there was no answer. I called Jillian's house, and as expected, everyone was out. I hoped Rose was with them and not somewhere on her own, but honestly, I knew better. I didn't think she was doing anything wrong, just taking more time to wrap her head around everything that had happened. But damn it... if she would only come home or pick up her phone, I could let her know there was nothing to be upset about. That Meredith and I were over.

I sat there stewing, pacing, cussing, and almost crying for another two hours before she called.

"Dad, I'll be home soon." She was safe and sounded fine, but it was obvious by the shake in her voice she was nervous. It made my heart tighten.

Throughout our entire lives, Rose and I had been extremely close. She wasn't exactly a daddy's girl—because she'd been equally close to her mother—but that was the beauty of it... we were the perfect family. Then Loraine was murdered, and even though Rose and I remained close, there was a distance her death put between us. I was coming to realize it was all my fault, but I didn't know how else to behave. Protecting my daughter was a primal instinct. But I shouldn't have been so overbearing. I just hope my realization wasn't coming too late.

"Okay, honey. I'll be waiting. See you soon." I tried to keep it light and not indicative of how upset I was.

By the time I heard a car pull up in the driveway, I'd practically worn a path into the carpet between the living room and the front door. When the car didn't pull off again, I realized this wasn't Jillian dropping her off, but was, in fact, Rose herself. I wondered if she'd gone to buy a car without me.

I swallowed the hurt. It was something I really wanted to do with her, and now her anger had robbed us of another father daughter moment, and there was nothing I could do. I supposed as long as the car was dependable, I'd have to let it go. But when I peeked out the window and saw a suped-up muscle car instead, I almost passed out. This was so unlike Rose, and I suddenly wasn't sure our conversation was going to go so well after all.

* * * * *

(Rose)

The entire time I was driving home, I tried to think of a reasonable excuse for my dad *not* to see Meredith. Besides the fact I thought she was a demon, everything else I came up with just made me sound like a spoiled brat, upset that her daddy had moved on with his life. Pretty ironic, since that's exactly what I'd been complaining about and trying to do for months.

The moment I pulled into our driveway, I stopped thinking about Meredith and Dad, and instead wondered how I was going to explain about Christian's car. Then again, I was so over this sweet, innocent white Rose persona everyone put on me, I was actually looking forward to telling the truth. Opening up to Christian and his clan had been so freeing, and now I had to be honest with dad.

As soon as I opened the door, I saw him sitting in the living room. I really didn't know how to start, or what I was supposed to say to convince him to not see that bitch ever again, but I had to start somewhere.

"Hey, Dad. I'm sorry I ran off after our fight. But you have to see how upsetting it was to realize that not only were you seeing someone new and keeping it from me, but that Meredith looks almost exactly like Mom. How did you think I was going to react?" I flopped down into the chair opposite him.

"Rose, I understand why you were upset, but I cannot excuse the way you behaved. We'll talk about my relationship with Meredith, but first, we're going to discuss where you've been and why there's a hot-rod sitting in my driveway." Dad seemed stern but not mad, so I guess it was time for the truth.

"It's my boyfriend's car. Remember, Christian? He was the boy I was seeing before you tried to turn me into a nun." My truth was coming out with a bite.

"I guess I hadn't realized you were still seeing him. I'm sorry."

Wow. Dad really did look sorry, and like he hadn't slept very well. I could tell there was something on his mind, and I really wasn't in the mood to drag this out.

"Why don't we just get this over with? I'm tired, and I have to study for an exam."

"Okay. Well, first of all you should know I broke things off with Meredith. There's no excuse for keeping our relationship hidden in the first place, but I wanted you to know that before I tried to explain anything else."

I couldn't believe this was happening. How perfect! Now I didn't have to play games in order to convince him to dump that bitch.

I sat back in the chair, feeling better than I had for days as Dad continued. "I met Meredith over a year ago, and while she does share certain traits with your mother, the two of them are nothing alike. Besides, you know how much I loved your mom. But when she passed, I didn't think it was fair to bombard you with the pain I was feeling, so I turned to Meredith instead. We were already friends through work, and she was so understanding. It really helped me process some of the emotions I was feeling as a man who had lost his spouse. Once I realized she had developed feelings for me, things did turn intimate." He took a deep breath and scooted to the edge of the couch. "I know there's no excuse for what I did. But Rose, I'm an adult, and to be honest, I don't have to justify my actions to you. I want you to understand that at the time, I did not think I was using Meredith to fill the hole your mother's death left within me. But now, looking back, it's exactly what happened."

Dad scooted back on the couch, all the air leaving his lungs in a big rush. It was obvious this was what he needed to get off his chest. I was so happy he called things off with Meredith, I really didn't need to hear any more. "Dad, I'm sorry for overreacting. You're right. You're an adult and you don't have to justify anything to me. I guess I just felt hurt by the fact that you thought you needed to keep it a secret in the first place. But with how much Meredith looked like Mom, I can understand it was a difficult position for you to be in." I walked over and sat down on the couch next to him and gave him a hug. "I love you, Dad. And I do want you to be happy, just not with a woman that looks like Mom. I honestly don't think it's good for you, or me."

"I love you too, Rose. And thanks for understanding adults can make mistakes too. Especially when our hearts are involved." Dad kissed the top of my head, then guided us up off the couch. "Let's head to bed. All this worrying and fretting has left me exhausted, and you said you have a test to study for, right?"

"I do. But one last thing. Are you okay with me having my freedom back? I really don't want to fight with you anymore." I tried to say it jokingly, but I was dead serious.

"Yes, honey. I'm okay with you having your freedom back. I'll let Dennis know tomorrow he'll no longer be driving you. But... I really do think we need to get you a car of your own. The thought of you zooming around in that thing out there completely terrifies me."

I laughed as I hugged him again. "Okay. Sounds good. Can we plan to go car shopping after you get off work tomorrow?"

"Absolutely. Sounds like a plan to me."

I didn't know what was going to happen with Meredith or with Christian and me, but it made me feel good to be back on good terms with Dad again.

Too bad it couldn't last.

CHAPTER FORTY-TWO

(Meredith)

It's about damn time. The moment I saw Jeremy's light go off and Rose's go on, it was finally time to move. I'd been waiting in my car for them to finish their little father daughter talk, in which I'm sure he told her he'd broken things off with me. But that was going to change very soon.

I made my way inside, breaking in the same way I had before, then snuck up stairs and headed straight for Rose's room. I could hear through the door, she was on the phone with someone, so I waited... and waited. *Damn.* Maybe I should have done this tomorrow morning instead, in case she screamed or put up a fight. Jeremy would be at work, and her boyfriend would be asleep, leaving her all alone.

With my head on straight and a better plan in place, I turned back toward the stairs... right as Rose's door opened.

* * * * *

(Rose)

I'd just gotten off the phone with Jillian when thought I heard my dad coming up the stairs. When I opened the door, what I found was a complete shock.

I stood there face-to-face with Meredith, literally frozen in terror. I couldn't move, even with all my instincts screaming at me to run. Even worse, when she looked at me, I swore her eyes flashed red.

"Don't panic," she whispered.

"Are you fucking kidding me? You break into my house and you're going to go with, *'don't panic'*? You're crazy!" I started to race back into my room, preparing to scream, but she caught my elbow just as I reached the door jam.

"We need to talk. Let's go downstairs so we don't wake Jeremy." She nodded her head toward the stairs as she tightened her grip on my arm.

I had no idea what this demon bitch was capable of, but I couldn't risk her hurting my dad. "Fine. But one wrong move, and I'm screaming my head off." I jerked my arm out of her grasp and pushed past her to make my way down the stairs. She may be a demon, but she didn't know I was onto her just yet, and I refused to ger her the satisfaction of scaring me in my own home.

Once we reached my dad's study, I ushered her in and shut the door behind us. "What are you doing in my house in the middle of the night? I should call the cops right now you crazy bitch." I wasn't sure how long I could keep up the tough girl act but hoped she would buy it long enough for me to dial Christian on my cell.

"I would watch your mouth if I was you, little girl." She took a step toward me, just as I hit send. "You have no idea who you're dealing with or what I'm capable of."

We continued to circle each other as I watched her eyes take on a red tint again. "Who are you? And why are you so interested in my dad?" I was hoping I could trick her into revealing she was, in fact, the demon, while Christian was listening on the phone. And it worked.

"From the look on your face and from the company you keep, I think you know exactly who I am. Or should I say... *what* I am." She had to feel like she had the upper hand, because she calmly sat down behind my dad's desk. "I'm a demon Rose; the very one in fact that infected your friend and killed your mother."

* * * * *

(Christian)

It was barely 8 p.m. when Rose's number flashed on my phone. I smiled and made my way to the end of the hall, so we could talk in peace. I hoped everything had gone all right with her father.

The moment I answered, I heard Rose's voice. "Who are you and why are you so interested in my dad?"

Damn it! Something was wrong. I instantly knew she was confronting Meredith, but I had no idea where they were.

The next thing I heard was Meredith's voice. "From the look on your face and from the company you keep, I think you know exactly who I am. Or should I say... *what* I am. I'm a demon Rose; the very one in fact that infected your friend and killed your mother."

Oh, shit. This was not good, but apparently my psychic ability had paid off again. By having Rose return to her dad, we now knew exactly who the demon was. Rose had been right, but now it sounded like she might pay for it with her life.

I heard a whoosh of air leave Rose's lungs. She must have fallen to the floor at Meredith's confession. "Why? Why did you kill my mom? And, is that why you're here? Did you break into my house again so you could kill me, too?"

Way to go, Rose.

With her location revealed, I raced toward her house. Arriving within minutes, it only took a moment to focus and pinpoint Rose and Meredith's voices coming from the main floor. I raced to the backdoor and silently made my way inside, then headed toward the of my life and the demon currently threatening her.

I heard Meredith say, "You *will* help me win back your father, or I'll tell him that you and your vampire friends were responsible for your mother's death."

How did she think that would work? I'm sure Mr. Reynolds would believe his daughter over his girlfriend. And talking about vampires would only cause him to think she was bat-shit crazy. But then she continued.

"Don't you remember, I can control a vampire once they bite me. All I'd have to do is force them to reveal themselves to your dad. He would have no choice but to believe me if he came face to face with a vampire, don't you think?"

Damn, I guess she had a point. How in the hell was I supposed to protect Rose when I couldn't bite Meredith without becoming infected? I knew nothing about how to defend against a demon. Oh well... guess it was time to learn.

The moment I opened the door to the office, I flew to Rose's side. Turning to Meredith, the first thing I noticed was her eyes glowing red. "How dare you interfere? This has nothing to do with your kind," she yelled.

"You involved my kind the second you infected Terrance. And there's no way in hell I'm letting you hurt Rose. I may not be able to bite you in order to kill you, but I can certainly rip you limb-from-limb. And trust me, now that we know your kind exists, my clan will make sure we destroy every single one of you. You're never going to use us or hurt anyone again."

I stared at Meredith's red eyes and considered just grabbing Rose and speeding away from the house. But since we had no idea why she was so interested in Rose's dad, I just couldn't leave him alone without knowing he'd be okay.

"I may not be as strong as you, but after I killed Rose's mom, I became a lot stronger than your average human. I'm sure it came from drinking in her essence like my ancestors used to do, and now... I think you'll find me a lot harder to kill." It sounded like she wasn't one-hundred percent sure of her abilities, but she certainly wasn't backing down either.

She launched herself across the room, grabbed Rose, and flew out the door. Damn, she definitely had some speed. I raced after her and caught up with them in the living room, but to my surprise, she wasn't hurting Rose, but instead was whispering something in her ear which left Rose completely limp with shock. I didn't have time to wonder what it was. I was too worried that any moment Meredith would snap Rose's neck.

In a flash of speed, I sped around and grabbed Meredith from behind, restraining her while I yelled to Rose, "Grab the poker from the fireplace. You're going to have to kill her. And hurry, I can't hold her for much longer."

* * * * *

(Meredith)

The moment Rose's vampire arrived, an idea formed in my head. I knew I wouldn't to be able to beat him in a fight, or out race him if I tried to run, so I'd use this opportunity to set them both up instead.

I heard Jeremy stirring upstairs, so I knew it would only be a matter of time before he came to find us all. When the moment was right, I grabbed Rose and sped toward the living room.

I hadn't lied to Christian. When I drank Loraine's blood, it definitely had an effect on me. I was so euphoric to feel her essence flow into me, but what I failed to share was that in addition to the euphoric feeling, it had also infused me with her actual life force.

After I killed her, I traveled to my grandmother's house to ask her about the old ways. She'd informed me that demons of old drank human blood to not only absorb their essence, but also to lengthened their lifespan. Through the drinking of blood, the ancient demons gained strength, speed, and the ability to defy death—they were becoming immortal. But their transformation hadn't been completed by the time they faced extinction, and the old ways were lost. Grandmother explained our line never consumed human blood, because it was uncertain how it would affect us.

I was now the first to risk it, and would be putting the myth to the test. I hoped by drinking Loraine's blood I would start to become immortal, or at least a little less destructible. Especially now, since Christian was threatening to kill me, or to hunt me down from this point forward. Honestly, what did I have to lose?

It would only be few seconds before Christian was on us again. I may have gained in speed and strength, but I would never be as fast as a vampire. So, as quickly as I could, I leaned in and whispered in Rose's ear. "You wanted to know why I was so interested in your dad? It's because he's a demon. And so are you."

I felt her go limp just as Christian entered the room. "If Christian finds out, his clan will kill you both," I finished.

Christian sped around behind me and held me in place as he instructed Rose to do exactly what I wanted her to do.

Jeremy was rounding the bottom of the stairs as Rose followed Christian's directions and grabbed the fireplace poker.

I steadied myself as she ran back in front of me and took aim with a rage-filled look on her face.

* * * * *

(Rose)

I couldn't believe what Meredith had whispered into my ear. Me and my dad were demons too? That was why she killed my mom?

Just as I started to scream in denial, Christian raced into the room and grabbed Meredith from behind. "Rose, grab the poker from the fireplace. You're going to have to kill her. And hurry, I can't hold her for much longer."

I could barely process the words, but the malicious smile that spread across Meredith's face was enough to propel me into motion.

I was so angry I could almost feel the heat radiating from my face. "I don't care if you're lying or not, I will not let you hurt my family again."

I never thought I'd be capable of murder, but the moment Meredith confessed to killing my mom, all I could think about was her demise. Taking a deep breath, I slammed the poker into her stomach, watching as she collapsed to the floor.

Then I heard my father scream.

CHAPTER FORTY-THREE

(Meredith)

I met Jeremy's eyes just as his daughter rammed the poker through my stomach. He gasped with shock then screamed.

I collapsed into a heap on the floor and laid as motionless as possible. The stab definitely hurt, and I'm sure it looked fatal to everyone in the room, but I could already tell it was starting to mend itself. I guess the theory of my demon immortality was proving true. I laid there, listening to my plan fall into place, as Jeremy screamed at his daughter.

I knew she wouldn't try to explain I was a demon, and that Christian was a vampire. My secret was safe until I decided to share it that Jeremy myself. So, right now, it just looked like his precious Rose was guilty of attempted murder. *Perfect!*

"What have you done? My God Rose, what have you done? You've killed her!" Jeremy repeated his panicked question as he made his way over to me.

"I... I'm sorry. I... Dad, she killed Mom." The truth dropped like a bomb, but Rose had no way to prove it, and I hoped Jeremy would see it as the excuse of a young, desperate girl.

"I don't understand! Tell me what happened, Rose. Tell me *exactly* what happened!" He was still screaming by the time he knelt down next to my body.

* * * * *

(Rose)

I had no idea what to say to my dad. There was no way to explain that Meredith was a demon, and that he and I were, too.

Christian stood still, watching me as Dad approached Meredith's body. I think he was trying to remain out of the way in case he needed to react in a hurry. But I wasn't sure what was going to happen next... until an idea formed in my head.

Since I was planning on becoming a vampire soon, this seemed like the perfect opportunity to make a clean break from my old life. I hated the idea of leaving Dad with this image of me, but since there was no way to explain what had truly happened here, I decided I didn't have much of a choice.

"Dad, I promise what I did was for the best. For you, for me, and whether you believe me or not, for Mom. I hope you don't call the cops on me, but I'll understand if you feel you have to."

I saw Christian shaking his head at me, trying to get my attention. When I looked at him, he licked his fangs and motioned to my dad. *Oh, no.* He was going to bite my dad and use his sedative, but I couldn't let that happen. According to Meredith my dad was a demon and would infect Christian if he bit him. How the hell was I supposed to get out of this? My eyes widened and I shook my head at Christian. I'd have to explain myself later, but was thankful he was following my lead.

Resolved to the fact that running was my best option, I moved to hug my dad. He was still kneeling above Meredith, shocked into silence with a panicked look on his face. I leaned down and hugged him tight. "I love you, Dad. Please don't ever forget that."

I couldn't stand to stay and hear his response. I knew he'd plead with me to stay, that we would figure everything out, but I'd made up my mind. It was time to start my life with Christian. I looked at him and nodded my head toward the front door. In an instant we were running for his car. We peeled out as soon as we were both inside, and by the time we hit the end of the block, an ambulance was already blaring down the street.

I buried my head in my hands and began to cry. I knew Christian probably thought that it was because I was leaving my father with the impression his daughter was a murderer, but in reality, it was because deep down, I knew Meredith was right. I was a demon, and if Christian found out, he and his clan would want to kill me.

My life was officially over.

* * * * *

(Meredith)

As I laid there listening to Rose break Jeremy's heart, I knew my plan had worked. Jeremy had seen his sweet, innocent daughter try to kill me, and now she and her boyfriend were on the run. I knew Evangeline would hide them, so I'd have to convince him not to press charges and just let her go. I already had an idea of how to do that, and if I was right, it would guarantee my spot back in Jeremy's life.

I wasn't sure when, or if, I would reveal our shared heritage to him, but I knew that my life was about to begin with the man I loved. Today had been a good day to die.

* * * * *

(Jeremy/Dad)

As I knelt next to Meredith, I was overwhelmed with emotion. All my feelings surging back in a rush. When I'd heard voices downstairs, I first thought that Rose had invited her boyfriend over to pick up his car, but then I'd heard Meredith's voice, and the sounds of violence.

As I raced around the corner, I couldn't believe what I was seeing. Rose's boyfriend had Meredith by the arms, holding her in place while my beautiful daughter stood ready to stab her with a poker.

I had screamed, and then watched in horror as Rose pierced my ex-girlfriend through the stomach. Meredith had collapsed to the ground, blood gushing from her wound.

I raced to her side, trying to process how my little girl could have done something so heinous, so criminal.

"I... I'm sorry. I... Dad, she killed Mom."

"I don't understand! Tell me what happened. Tell me *exactly* what happened!" I screamed.

What she said next will haunt me until my dying days. "Dad, I promise what I did was for the best. For you, for me, and whether you believe me or not, for Mom. I hope you don't call the cops on me, but I'll understand if you feel you have to."

I sat there completely stunned. I understood I was in shock, and couldn't get my brain to work, but I wanted to cry out and grab her as she hugged me. But instead, I was rooted in place, and in the next instant she was gone... my little girl was gone.

Suddenly, a breath escape from Meredith and my brain kicked back into gear. I jumped up and dialed 911, then immediately returned to her side. All my attention was focused on her as she slowly opened her eyes. *Thank God she wasn't dead.* I tried keeping her still as she started to say something. I couldn't quite make it out so I lowered my head, straining to hear what she was whispering. "Don't report Rose. Protect her."

I couldn't believe what I was hearing. Here was this woman bleeding to death in my home and she wanted to protect my daughter? The person who'd just tried to kill her? How did I ever think leaving her had been the right thing to do?

Before the EMTs made their way inside, I grabbed the fireplace poker and wiped it clean, then placed Meredith's hand on the handle. I made sure to meet Meredith's eyes, and nodded as I mouthed, "Thank you."

After stabilizing Meredith's vitals, the EMTs stopped the bleeding and bandaged her wound. While loading her into the ambulance they said the wound wasn't as bad as it looked. I climbed into behind them, holding Meredith's hand as we headed to the hospital.

The gleam in her eyes radiated such love, and I couldn't believe I'd almost ruined this relationship. "I'm so sorry." I hoped she understood I was apologizing for everything: for keeping her a secret from Rose, for me breaking up with her, and most of all, for my daughter attempting to kill her. I would gladly spend an eternity making it up to her if she'd let me.

"It's okay," she whispered. "I love you. It will all be okay."

Once we reached the hospital, the nurses started an IV and the cops arrived to begin their questioning. I made sure to remain close enough to Meredith so she could hear my responses. If we were all going to get out of this, we'd better have our stories straight.

With Meredith listening, I lied and told them we were having dinner and decided to follow it up with some dessert in front of the fireplace. And that when we started to move the equipment out of the way, that's when Meredith tripped and impaled herself on the poker.

My God, what was I doing? I hope this worked, because if it didn't, not only would my daughter go to jail for attempted murder, I would be right behind her for conspiracy. I couldn't believe this was happening. One wrong move and my life was over.

After running Meredith's fingerprints to verify my story, the cops ruled it an accident and thanked us for our time.

I dropped into the chair beside Meredith's bed, shaking with relief. She was starting to drop into unconsciousness from the pain medication in her IV drip, but before she fell asleep, I quickly leaned in and whispered, "I love you, too."

With one part of my life repaired, I tried to come up with a plan to go after Rose. Now that I knew she was still seeing Christian, obviously that's where I needed to start. It stung to know Rose had kept seeing him behind my back, but I couldn't deny the irony. If I hadn't been so crazed with keeping her safe, I might actually know more about this guy—like where he lived or who he really was. But instead, I knew nothing about the boy who just whisked my daughter away.

But that was going to change very soon.

CHAPTER FORTY-FOUR

(Rose)

By the time we reached The Rising Pit, my eyes were finally dry. I literally couldn't cry anymore. Just a few hours ago, everything had been so perfect. My dad had broken up with that demon bitch, I had finally gained back my freedom. We were even going to buy me a new car the following day.

But in a flash, everything had changed. I found out my mom had been murdered by a demon who was after my father, because apparently, he was a demon, too. And not only was I a demon as well, but now... I was also a murderer.

I hadn't thought twice about killing Meredith when Christian told me to do it. Not only did I want revenge for my mom, but also, I had to keep her from telling Christian I was a demon.

I had no idea how I knew it, but when Meredith admitted to killing my mother, the rage inside of me rose to the point that something physically had changed within me. It was like I could feel my DNA shifting. So, when she revealed my father and I were demons too, I knew she was telling the truth. I also knew what she said about Christian's clan was true as well. If they found out, they would kill me.

I had no idea how I was going to keep this secret, but then again, I'd been good at hiding my thoughts.

My God, that was it!

It was my demon blood that allowed me to hide my thoughts from Evie. Just like the affect Meredith's blood had on Terrance, keeping his thoughts protected and *fuzzy*. It all made sense now.

"Rose? Are you going to be okay?" Christian's question startled me out of my inner turmoil. With everything racing around in my head, all I could do was nod in response.

"I know what happened is something that's going to take some time to process. But you have to realize, you didn't have a choice. She killed your mom and could have hurt you or your dad. She infected Terrance and there was no way I could let her threaten anyone else in my family. Killing her was the right thing to do."

Christian shifted in his seat and took both of my hands in his. "We need to get you inside and tell Evie everything that's happened, but first I need to ask you a question. You know you can no longer go back to your old life, right? I'm sorry, but I won't let you be placed in a situation where you could go to jail. I love you, and I *never* want to live without you." He swallowed hard and cupped my cheek in his palm. "I will soon become the new Sire, and when I am, I want you to be my consort. If you agree, I'm sure Evie will let you stay here with us from now on. We can start our new life together right away."

Oh my, God. This was what I'd been dreaming of for so long, but how was this going to work now? I was a demon and Christian wanted me to become his consort. It was going to kill me to have to tell him I couldn't become a vampire anymore. That our forever could never be.

I was so scared and knew he was right… I'd never be able to go home again. Staying with the clan seemed like the best way to stay protected. They could bite and use their sedative on anyone that came looking for me, which made it the obvious choice—even if it wasn't for the reason Christian thought. "Yes. I would love to stay with you and the clan. Thank you, Christian. You're truly saving my life."

"You *are* my life Rose, and I'll gladly spend an eternity proving it."

He leaned over and kissed me. Soft, tender, and filled with emotion. The pain in my heart felt like I was the one with a poker through my chest. How could I live with the man I loved, while planning to lie to him every single day?

I guess I was about to learn *exactly* how to break a vampire's heart...

Tish Thawer

Roses & Thorns

A Rose Trilogy Short Story

Roses & Thorns

(A Rose Trilogy Short-Story)

***

A flash back to how Rose and Christian's whirlwind romance started, as they build the relationship that will see them through the difficult times ahead.

CHAPTER ONE

(Rose)

"Oh my god, that was the best concert EVER!" Penny yelled.

"I know, right? I've never screamed and danced so much in my life," Jillian added.

My friends and I had just left the Nine Inch Nails concert in Masen and were being driven home in one of my dad's company limos. It was Friday night and since we'd be off from school Monday as well, this was the perfect start to a long weekend. We didn't have a curfew, but since some of us still weren't twenty-one, and since there really wasn't anything fun to do at two in the morning, we were all headed back to Jillian's where we'd spend the night.

Suddenly, Jillian announced, "I've got to pee."

As the girls continued to giggle and drink more of the complementary soda—*Dad had made sure all alcohol had been removed*—I pushed the button for the intercom. "Excuse me. Is there somewhere we could stop to use the restroom? Apparently, it's an emergency."

After a moment's pause, our driver's voice came through the speaker. "Yes ma'am. There's a nightclub just up the road. It's the only place close by, so I'll stop there if that's okay?"

"Yes. Thank you. That'll be fine." Jillian was the only one in our group that was already twenty-one, so stopping at a nightclub wouldn't be a problem.

We drove for a few more miles and then coasted to a stop. As I looked out the tinted window, I saw the club's sign lit up in bright red lights. *The Rising Pit.*

One of the "car crew" got out and opened the side door. Jill hurriedly climbed out of the car and gave a little wave to the driver. "Thank you," she said, then followed him to the front door.

"I can't believe your dad set all this up, Rose. It's really cool. I haven't had this much fun in a long time. Thanks for inviting me," Penny said.

"You're welcome. I was really surprised when he told me we'd be going in one of the company limos. I hadn't realized at the time it would come with a babysitting crew, though," I joked.

I knew my dad would ensure the escorts kept an eye on us all night, and though I thought it would be a pain, it really hadn't bothered me in the least. They were all very nice, and one was pretty damn cute, too. The one who had just accompanied Jillian inside, actually.

I looked back to the club just as Jill and the cutie disappeared behind the door, then watched as a man stepped outside carrying a girl in his arms. He placed her on her feet, steadying her before letting go. It looked like she was crying. As he talked to her, she wiped the tears from her cheeks and then gave a quick nod of her head and smiled. Clearly, whatever the man had said was making her feel better. It was obvious the guy worked there, since he had a black t-shirt on with the club's name and logo on the front. I continued to watch, wondering what could have happened that left a club employee comforting a crying patron on the front steps, but the moment the man smiled, my curiosity was forgotten.

It was as if the heavens were highlighting my destiny for me. The clouds broke, and suddenly it wasn't just a "man" I was staring at... it was an angel. He was so gorgeous. Maybe about 6' 2", and solid muscle from the looks of him, but not bulky, just very athletic. Wide shoulders, broad chest, thin waist, and what I was sure would be strong, muscled legs. With the moonlight shining on him, I could see he had dark blond hair with golden highlights, cut short and sharp. I realized I was half-hanging out the open window of the limo, and sucked in a quick breath. That's when he suddenly turned and looked right at me. I thought I would die.

His eyes were so beautiful and mesmerizing. They were an amber color, a rich brown with golden highlights, mixing together like swirled caramel and honey. The intensity of his gaze was piercing. He was easily the most beautiful thing I'd ever seen.

Jill came barreling out of the nightclub with her escort closely in tow. We all started busting up laughing as we heard her say, "I only wanted a quick shot." I continued to stare at the gorgeous man as she started to make her way back to the limo, but as she walked past him, he reached out and tapped her gently on the shoulder. I continued to watch, jealousy filling my veins, as she stopped and started to speak to him. I couldn't imagine what they could possibly be talking about, but she kept glancing at the car and then back to him with a huge smile on her face. I'm sure she was trying to make sure we were all seeing that this beautiful man was paying attention to her. I loved Jill, but she could definitely be an attention whore sometimes. After a brief moment, I saw him hand her something and then he walked back inside. My angel was gone.

I settled myself back in the limo, trying not to let the stickiness of the leather seats on my bare legs elevate my frustration as I anxiously waited for my best friend to come brag about how this impossibly gorgeous guy had just asked her out or something. I tried to convince myself their conversation had only been about her using the facilities instead of being a paying customer, but I doubted that was really the case.

When Jill got in the car, she sat there for a moment with a cat-ate-the-mouse grin on her face that I wanted to smack off, but then she handed me a business card, and everything changed. I was confused and almost handed it back, but she just sat there smiling, so I quickly looked down and examined the shiny card. It had the club's logo on the front, which looked like a square hatch opening up with a bright red glow shining from within, and the club's name, *The Rising Pit*, printed above it. The moment I turned it over however, is the moment my life changed. The first thing I noticed was a handwritten note that started with my name. Now I was interested. It said, "Roses are red, but I'll be blue, if I'm denied the pleasure, of meeting you. ~ Christian."

I read it about three times before I looked up and saw Jill still smiling at me. She grabbed the card out of my hand and passed it to my friends. "He asked me your name and then scratched out that poem so fast that I could barely see his hand move. His number's on there too and he said for you to call him after dark in two days."

I was stunned into silence. I couldn't understand how this extraordinary man could possibly want to meet me. *Me!* Not that I wasn't thrilled, but suddenly I was so nervous. I didn't think I could survive two days without losing my mind. My thoughts drifted to the first thing a girl thinks of when preparing to meet her dream guy... what was I going to wear?

My friend's laughter and Jillian's question brought my attention back to the present. "Holy crap, Rose. Are you gonna call him?"

I thought for a moment then answered, "Hell yes, I'm gonna call him! He's frickin' gorgeous."

The girl's conversations quickly became background noise as I stared out the window. *Why would this incredible man want to meet me?* I couldn't help but wonder if calling a complete stranger was a monumental mistake. But, as the butterflies increased their pace in my stomach, I glanced out the window again and could have sworn I saw those golden-swirled eyes staring back at me from the reflection. *Hell yes I was going to call him.* And suddenly... two days seemed like an eternity.

CHAPTER TWO

(Rose)

I pulled the covers over my head and squinted my eyes against the sunlight blaring in from behind the curtains my mother had just yanked open.

"Rise and shine. We're going shopping." Mom's enthusiasm exhausted me. She was so upbeat all the time, and while I loved that about her, it was something that could also get old really fast. Especially when you'd planned to use Sunday to recuperate from a sleepless night spent with your friends after a rowdy concert. "Come on, Rose. I want to hit the sales at Kohl's before all the good stuff is gone. They've slashed prices on all their swim wear, and I'm in serious need of some new suits."

I watched her dark hair sway just below her shoulders as she bounced toward my closet.

"Alright, alright. But can you give me a few minutes to actually wake up?" Mom's cocked hip and the angle of her head as she spun around and threw a dress onto my bed was an indication that her answer was no. I narrowed my eyes at her as I jumped out of bed, grabbed the dress, and stomped into the bathroom.

Fumbling through a rushed version of my morning routine, I quickly combed through my long blonde hair and stuck a hat on my head. A little mineral powder on my cheeks and some tinted lip gloss was going to be the extent of my makeup efforts this morning. I emerged dressed and ready to go in just a few minutes.

As I made my way downstairs, I heard a commotion in the kitchen. I suddenly wished I had taken longer to get ready. Mom and Dad were saying their goodbyes for the morning, but from the way his hands were grabbing at her and the intensity of their kiss, you'd think we were leaving for a yearlong safari in Africa, instead of an afternoon of shopping a few miles away.

I cleared my throat as I slipped on my flip-flops. "Okay, I'm ready."

Mom broke off their passionate kiss and backed out of Dad's embrace with a huge smile on her face. "Okay, let's hit it." She gave Dad a little wave as we headed out the door. It must have been her who initiated their dramatic goodbye scene, because Dad just stood there, frozen in place, then started laughing.

I shook my head and grabbed my purse from the hook next to the wooden credenza by the door. "Bye Dad, catch ya later!"

"Bye, honey. Try to keep your mother's spending in check for me, will ya?" he hollered out the door.

I knew he was kidding because he never did anything to "keep my mother in check." My parents loved each other so much, and they both had successful careers, so money wasn't really a big deal. It's not like we were super-rich, but we didn't have to worry about overspending on a sale at Kohl's, that was for sure.

"So, what else are we doing today besides shopping for swimsuits?" I asked.

"Well, I thought we could get some lunch and you could tell me all about your concert. I talked to Adrienne this morning and she said you guys were all pretty excited when you arrived at her house."

"Yes, we had a really good time. The concert was great."

I only debated a moment before deciding to tell her about Christian too. Mom and I have always had a really close relationship.

"But even more exciting, is the guy I met on the way home."

"Oh, really?" Her coy smile was the first indication this shopping trip was actually just a recognizance mission. She must have found the business card in my laundry already.

"Yes. If you don't already know, his name is Christian, and he works at The Rising Pit. As a matter of fact, I'm supposed to call him tonight."

She giggled as we turned the corner and headed toward the end of the shopping district which housed the best little breakfast café. "Yes, I found the business card in your things when I was cleaning up this morning, and that's why I thought we could buy you something nice to wear for your date." She glanced in my direction, probably to see if I was mad that she had 'cleaned' my things, but I wasn't. Like I said, there wasn't much I hid from my parents.

"That sounds great. Didn't you just love his little poem?" I asked.

"Yes, it reminded me of when your dad and I first met and the romantic thing he did to win my attention."

"Aha... is that why you practically attacked him before we left this morning? Were you reminiscing?" I laughed as I watched Mom shake her head. Obviously, I'd pin-pointed the reason for her behavior.

"Yes!" she declared with a hint of shyness in her voice.

"Well, I think it's cute. I can only hope that when I meet 'the one', we'll be as in love as Dad and you are."

At the mention of *love*, Mom's tone turned serious. "I wish that for you too, Rose. Follow your heart, but just be careful. That's the best advice I can give. You're not a child anymore, and the fact you'll be graduating college this year only adds to the pressure of growing up, but I hope you take the time to really live. Enjoy your life. Meeting new boys and having fun is something I want for you, but I'm also your mom, and that means I worry about you at the same time."

"Don't worry, Mom. I'm going to call him after dark like he asked, and then hopefully he'll invite me down to meet him... in a public place. So, will I be able to borrow the car?"

"Yes, that'll be fine."

"Okay, thanks. I really do hope he invites me down. For some reason, I feel like he's going to be a *really* great guy."

"Well, I hope you're right. Now how about some breakfast? I'm starving."

"Sounds good." As a matter of fact, *everything* was sounding good. Mom was on board with me meeting Christian for the first time, she and Dad were perfectly happy as usual, and I'd be graduating college early this year. So yeah, everything was perfect. Now I just hoped that things would stay that way.

CHAPTER THREE

(Christian)

Long blonde hair, beautiful blue eyes, and a mouth I was dying to kiss were the first things that entered my mind as I awoke for the night.

Being a vampire came with a few neat tricks, and this was one of them. Whatever our last thought was before we fell asleep, was also the first thing we thought of when we woke up. For the last two days I had made it a point to think of Rose.

Two nights ago, I'd carried Sari out of the club, trying to sooth her broken heart. As I sat her on her feet, I was met with the most delectable scent drifting on the wind. Wanting to be a gentleman, I focused on Sari and tried to explain that Bobby wasn't trying to be mean, but that she needed to understand he was a free spirit and she was just going to have to accept that if she wanted to remain a part of his life. But what I'd truly wanted to do was search the area and envelop myself in what or whoever was the cause of that delicious smell.

As Sari wiped her tears, I smiled at her and was met with the sound of someone taking a quick breath. *There.* There she was. The most beautiful woman I had ever laid eyes on was practically hanging out the window of a limo. She looked like an angel sent straight from heaven.

Just then, I caught a whiff of the same smell as a couple started to walk past me. I could tell that they'd been in the car with my mystery woman. Without thinking I reached out and tapped the girl on the shoulder. The guy walked a few paces on and then stopped to wait for her, so I thought I'd better make it quick. "Excuse me, but could you tell me the name of the blonde woman looking out the window of your car?"

After smiling wildly, she answered, "Yes. Her name is Rose." My informant continued to look back and forth between me and the girl, her heartbeat racing.

I reached for my wallet and took out one of my business cards, then scratched an impromptu poem on the back of it, adding my phone number at the bottom. "Could you please give her this for me and ask if she'd call me after dark in two days?"

"Um... sure, I guess," she replied.

The anxious feeling in my chest had me turning and quickly heading back into the club.

Two days had passed, and this was the night I hoped my dream girl would be calling. I had taken the evenings in between to talk to my Sire, Evangeline, and let her know I'd found someone I was interested in and would hopefully be seeing very soon. I didn't need her permission, but since we weren't allowed to tell humans of our existence, I needed everyone to be aware someone new might be coming around. Evie was happy to hear it. Her exact words were, "Oh Christian, I'm so happy you've finally found someone you want to share your life with." She then proceeded to tear up and gave me a series of smothering hugs as she beamed with pride.

I'd never really had a serious relationship since becoming a vampire. I fed out of necessity and never hurt anyone while doing it, since we all have a sedative that flows from our fangs to make the feedings pleasurable, but even more importantly... forgettable. It's how we can exist in the human world; we have the means to make them forget.

But ever since seeing Rose leaning out of that limo, the thought of a relationship was exactly what I had in mind. I couldn't explain why I was so drawn to this particular woman, but I knew from the moment I caught her scent on the wind, there was something special about her. The way it had taken every ounce of my strength to not dart over and crush my lips to hers, had definitely caught me off guard. She smelled like innocence and sweetness: like fresh cotton and sweet tarts, and sunshine and rain, all mixed together. I felt as if I was already in love. I knew how dramatic that sounded, but after being alive for six hundred and two years, there was no denying I'd found someone special.

I left the mirror and walked back toward my closet, discarding yet another shirt on the bed. For some reason, even the simplest things like choosing my clothes and what cologne I would wear, were suddenly daunting tasks. I'd essentially dressed the same for centuries, always making it a point to adapt to the current styles. And since there was literally nothing I could do to change my appearance, picking the right clothes seemed oddly important. But... not as important as the need to attend to my drifting.

Drifting was something that happened to vampires when they experienced any kind of strong emotion. If they were hungry, angry, or aroused, their physical appearance actually drifted darker and then back to normal once the emotions had passed. It was something that made it easy to tell who was experiencing heightened emotions in the vampire community, but obviously it was something we had to hide from the humans. How would anyone explain their hair and eyes changing colors? You simply couldn't.

If I fed and kept my emotions tightly reigned in, I should be able to avoid drifting in front of Rose. So, after dressing in dark navy jeans, a light blue cotton button-up, and a nice pair of hiking boots, I headed out to quench my thirst and prepare to meet the girl of my dreams. If she called, that is.

CHAPTER FOUR

(Rose)

After finishing breakfast, Mom and I headed to Kohl's to look for her swimsuits and an outfit for my date. Well, hopefully I would have a date tonight. I wasn't sure what my plans were going to include since I hadn't actually made the call yet. But I was confident that Christian and I would be seeing each other soon, even if it wasn't actually tonight.

"What kind of outfit are you looking for?" Mom asked.

"I'm not really sure. A dress, I guess. Something casual, but not too boring. But nothing too over-the-top either." I didn't want to come off as trying too hard, but I wanted to show off my curves at the same time.

I watched as she slid dress after dress to the side of the rack, flinging the hangers like they had personally offended her. Finally, her perusing stopped and she held up a calf-length, strapless sundress. "How about this one?"

It was light turquoise with a simple print on it. The material was a rayon blend and should flow just right, hanging perfectly along my curves. It was perfect. I had a pair of tan wedges that would go great with it, and I could wear the choker I'd bought recently as well. "That's the one!"

Once we'd paid for our things, Mom and I headed to the pool. She was a swim instructor and worked at the local training facility. I knew Mom wanted to give her new suits a test run, and since it wasn't time for the sun to go down yet, I actually welcomed the distraction. Anything to keep my mind off making the call that would hopefully be the beginning of something wonderful.

When we entered the large square foyer, Mom waved to the attendant who stood behind the counter. This area of the complex was surrounded by glass and full of light. "Hi, Andrew. We're gonna take a few laps in the indoor pool today, if that's alright. We'll be out before the next open swim session starts."

"Sure thing, Mrs. Reynolds. Open swim doesn't start until six p.m., so you're good to go," he replied.

We both smiled and then made our way downstairs to the locker room. As I sat on one of the wooden benches, I began to wonder what it would be like to meet the man I would end up marrying. Yes, I had high hopes for tonight. "So, Mom... how exactly did you and Dad meet? I'm assuming it wasn't by him handing you a card outside a nightclub." I shrugged my shoulders, feeling a little shy about the topic as we continued to undress.

"Well, no. No poems by the roadside, but he was pretty darn romantic. I was on the swim team for my high school, and he was at one of the meets. I remember after my first race, which I won," she said with a proud smile, "a friend told me she'd seen this guy checking me out and cheering me on, even though we were competing against his school." As Mom put her things in the locker, she continued the story. "I remember looking for him in the direction my friend had pointed, but didn't see anyone matching her description. But about an hour later, when the meet had ended, I was heading to the bus when I saw a guy standing next to the sidewalk with a bouquet of fake flowers, waving me over."

"Wait—Dad brought you *fake* flowers?" I laughed as I pulled on one of her new suits. It was nice being able to share clothes with your mom.

"Yes. But don't judge. It was the best he could do on short notice. Anyway.... the closer I got, I realized he was really cute. When he told me he'd run to the art room to try and make something creative, but all he'd found were those fake flowers instead, my heart melted." She giggled as she finished getting dressed. "How sweet was it that he even tried to get me anything? At that time, most guys would have just flipped their collars and pulled a James Dean, trying to look cool and assuming I'd worship the ground they walk on. But your dad was different. He made an effort that got my attention, and that's what really impressed me."

"Oh my, God. That is so cheesy, but definitely thoughtful."

"I know! I told you he was a romantic. We started dating that month, and have been together ever since. We were each other's high school sweethearts."

I thought about Mom's story as I shuffled my feet along the damp, cold hall that led from the locker room out to the pool. I couldn't imagine being with someone for that long and still being in love, but suddenly it sounded like a pretty amazing goal to have. I didn't know what would happen with Christian, but in this moment, I actually felt like my heart was opening, and I realized that I was truly ready to find love for the first time in my life.

I'd had plenty of boyfriends in the past, but I could admit I hadn't been particularly serious or very open in my relationships. I didn't have a sad story as to why, other than the fact that I'd always been highly motivated to succeed. Starting junior year of high school, I had signed up for AP classes, so when I went into college, I actually entered as a junior, having attained two years worth of college credits already. This meant I'd be graduating early, exactly as planned. I'd always been passionate about setting goals and meeting them, and was pretty proud I'd be accomplishing that. But it wasn't without long hours and hard work, and as you can imagine, that put boys on the backburner.

"So, tell me more about Christian. What does he look like?" Mom's question brought me back to the present.

"Oh, man. He's gorgeous. Tall, blond-highlighted hair, toned but not overly muscular. Um... I'd say he just about perfect." I stared out the skylight as I floated on my back in the pool. "His eyes are like caramel swirled with honey. And he has a really sweet, gentlemanly demeanor."

"You got all that from seeing him out the window?" She tried not to sound skeptical, but I could tell she was probably worried I was getting my hopes up.

"Yes, I did. I can't explain it, but when I watched him help that girl, it made my heart melt. And Jill said he was really sweet when he spoke to her too."

"Well, just keep it casual and don't talk about stuff that's too serious on the first date. And no messing around."

"Really, Mom? You think I'd just jump in bed with some guy on the first date?" Actually, imagining how gorgeous Christian was, that didn't sound like a bad plan at all.

CHAPTER FIVE

(Christian)

After heading up the spiral staircase that led from our secure lair below, I was met in the club with jeers and smiles. My vampire brothers and sisters had already started giving me crap about seeing a new girl.

"So... where you gonna take *Rose* on your first date?" Bobby asked.

Bobby the DJ here at the club, was also my best friend.

"I'm not sure," I replied, "since she hasn't even called yet." I was getting nervous she might not call at all. I'd thought about running into town to track her down, but I'd really rather not come off as the stalker-type right from the get-go.

"Well, if she *does* call, where are you gonna take her?"

I laughed. He just wouldn't let it go. "I'll probably take her to dinner and then walk around town. Is that acceptable enough for you?" No way was I going to tell him I already had everything arranged, including reservations and a surprise after dinner in the park.

"No. That is not acceptable. You need to show her a good time, and by that, I mean a *GOOD TIME!*" Everyone started laughing as we watched Bobby gyrate his hips around and around.

"Well, you can forget that. You know I would never be so bold on a first date." I realized I sounded like an old stick-in-the-mud, but I didn't care. I would never expect a woman to "put out," as they say, on the first date or even on the twenty-first date. I was old-fashioned and refused to let myself fall into the modern way of "hooking-up" like Bobby had.

Just as I was about to say these exact words, my cell phone rang. Everyone went quiet. The anticipation in the air was palpable.

Butterflies took flight in my gut as I answered the phone. "Hello?"

CHAPTER SIX

(Rose)

Once Mom and I finished our workout, we got dressed and headed back to the house. Dad had spent the day doing yard work, and was now ready for a late lunch. I left them to it and headed for my room, wanting some time alone before I started to get ready.

I smiled as I hung my new dress from the hook on the back of my door, smoothing the material under my hands. After gathering all the accessories I wanted to wear it with, I laid down on my bed and stared at the blank ceiling. I needed to relax a little and process everything.

Here I was getting ready to call a complete stranger that I *saw*, not met, outside of a nightclub alongside the road. Suddenly my stomach was in knots. What if I was making a huge mistake?

I must have fallen asleep while contemplating everything because I suddenly found myself being woken up by my mom. "Rose. Wake up, sleepy head. It's almost dark. Did I wear you out in the pool today?" She sat down on the edge of the bed and gave my shoulder a little shake to make sure I was awake.

"Yeah... I guess. I was just laying here staring at the ceiling and thinking about tonight. I guess I dozed off." I pushed up on my elbows, and once my eyes finally adjusted to the changing light, I found my mom staring at the ceiling. "What are you thinking about?" I asked her.

"Well, I'm thinking we should paint your ceiling black."

"What? Why on earth would you want to do that?" I was giggling by the time I fully sat upright.

"You'll see. But tomorrow, after you've debriefed me about how this date with Christian goes, we're starting a project." She winked and casually strolled out of my room.

Oh yes, my date with Christian. Despite my earlier butterflies, I was still excited to see where this would go. I slung the covers back, jumped out of bed, and bounced toward the bathroom. I was going to have to hurry to get ready in time, since I'd fallen asleep. I wanted to be dressed when I called, in case he did actually want to meet up tonight.

After adding little extra glittery eye-shadow to my normal makeup routine, I slipped on my dress, necklace, and shoes and was ready in record time. I just needed to give my straight hair a slight curl on the ends, and then I'd be ready to make the call. Checking the full-length mirror on the back of my bathroom door one last time, I nodded, satisfied with my appearance. *Stop stalling*, I thought to myself. It was time to do this.

I walked across the room, the soft carpet cushioning my steps, and grabbed his business card from the top of my dresser. After making my way to the bed, I sat down and took a few deep breaths, then dialed his number. He answered after only two rings. "Hello?"

"Hi, Christian. This is Rose. Rose Reynolds. You had asked my friend to have me call you tonight." Suddenly, I felt like a complete dumbass. What if he didn't remember seeing me or giving Jillian his business card at all? *Oh my, God.* This was mortifying.

I was seriously on the verge of hanging up when he responded, "Hi, Rose. I'm so glad you called. I wasn't sure if you would be or not, seeing the unusual circumstances of our first encounter."

Oh, thank goodness, he did remember. "Yes, I'm sorry I was unable to get out and actually meet you that night, but I was thrilled to get your note. It was very sweet."

"I'm glad you liked it. It was the best I could do on short notice." He laughed, then I heard a door close in the background. I could now hear the wind whistling through the phone, so I assumed he just left his house. "Speaking of short notice, I wondered if I could actually see you tonight? No pressure though, I'll understand if you're unavailable."

"Honestly, I had hoped for the same thing. Did you want me to come down there or did you have other plans?" *Yes!* This was going exactly as I wanted.

"I'd be more than happy to come pick you up, or you could just meet me at the restaurant. I thought we could have dinner at the steak house on the corner of Elm and 3rd. I've heard it's very good."

"Yes, that sounds perfect. I'll meet you there in say... twenty minutes?"

"Sounds great. I'll wait for you outside. And Rose... I really am thrilled you called."

I ducked my head, as if he could see my gushing smile. "Me too. I'll see you soon."

CHAPTER SEVEN

(Christian)

As soon as I hung up the phone, I tried to escape without seeing my vampire family again, but no such luck. Bobby and Dominique had followed me outside when I left the club to talk to Rose.

"So, the steak house on Elm and 3rd, huh?" Dominique teased.

God, I really didn't have time to deal with their shit. "Yes. The steak house on Elm and 3rd," I answered dryly. "I figured I could get a rare steak and force my way through it. I want a chance to really talk to this girl and thought dinner would be the best way to start. Do you have a different opinion?"

Shaking his head and holding up his hands in a *we-give-up* sort of way, Bobby answered for her. "No, no... that sounds like a great plan. Just don't be surprised if you see all of us peeking in the window from across the street." He and Dominique busted up laughing as they headed back inside.

Sighing heavily, I climbed in my '67 Mercury Comet Caliente and hoped he was only kidding. As the engine rumble to life, I realized I didn't drive this car as much as I would like to. There was just no need. My vampire speed could get me most places in a matter of seconds, but it sure felt nice and normal to actually be driving somewhere instead. And what was waiting for me at my destination made the trip even more enjoyable.

I sped onto the interstate toward Seela, the little town where Rose lived. I couldn't wait to meet her. As a matter of fact, I was so caught up in thinking about how to make a good first impression, I almost missed my turn off. Screeching the tires, I made the adjustment just in time and headed toward the section of town that now seemed like the most important place on Earth.

As soon as I parked the car, it took everything I had not to race across the street. Instead, I forced myself to calmly walk toward the restaurant and our predetermined meeting place. The butterflies in my stomach were going wild. An indication of how anxious and nervous I really was. It'd been ages since I'd been out on a real date, but there was no time to worry about that ... here she was.

She was just as gorgeous as I remembered, though her hair had a little more curl to it than last time. And my God, those legs… they were as sexy as I'd imagined. I watched her lock her car and walk in my direction and suddenly realized keeping my drifting in check tonight was going to be an exercise in sheer willpower.

She was smiling as she hopped up onto the curb right in front of me. "Hi!"

My first instinct was to grab her and race away to somewhere private and sink my fangs into her neck. She was so sexy and smelled so good.

"Hello. It's nice to actually meet you, Rose." I held out my hand, hoping she'd take it. She did.

"It's nice to meet you, too."

Her smile was mesmerizing. So much so, I could barely think straight. "Um… are you ready to go in for dinner?" *Ugh… what a stupid question!* I turned toward the restaurant, praying I wouldn't blow this.

"Absolutely. Let's go." She was so confidence as she led me inside, which immediately put me at ease. I'd been around some extremely confident people in my six-hundred and two years old, but none had ever commanded my attention like this woman.

I think I was in love.

CHAPTER EIGHT

(Rose)

I was so excited Christian had actually wanted to meet for dinner that I raced downstairs after hanging up the phone, grabbed my purse, and headed straight for the car. Just as I was about to open the side door to the garage, Mom's voice rang out from the back door. "I take it your plans with Christian are a go?"

"Yep. We're having dinner here in town. I'll be home later. Love you!"

"I love you too. And Rose, have fun, but be careful and call me if you need anything."

As I backed out of the driveway, I gave one final wave to Mom and Dad, who had now joined her at the back door. They stood there watching me with smiles on their faces as he wrapped her in his arms. It made me so happy to see how in love they still were after all these years. I hoped someday I'd find that same kind of love, and suddenly, I was feeling the pressure of tonight's date.

I saw him the moment I rounded the corner. He had just stepped up onto the curb in front of the restaurant. I hoped I wouldn't screw up my parallel parking. I took a few deep breaths and pulled my car to a halt. I didn't want to seem like a nervous Nelly, sitting there trying to get myself together for too long, so I forced myself out of the car right away and locked the door. I noticed him watching me as I walked across the street, and put as much swagger into my stride as I could without looking like a runway model trying to work it too hard.

"Hi!" I said as I bounced up beside him.

"Hello. It's nice to actually meet you, Rose."

Damn, he has a sexy voice. An uncontrollable smile spread across my face as I took the hand he offered. "It's nice to meet you, too."

"Um... are you ready to go in for dinner?" he asked.

"Absolutely. Let's go." He hesitated for a moment, and I found myself grinning from ear to ear. I took the lead and quickly pulled him into the restaurant before I embarrassed myself. The hostess took in an eye full of

Christian before meeting my gaze, but who could blame her? He truly was drop-dead gorgeous.

"Table for two, under Christian," he said. That's when I noticed he wasn't even giving the hostess a single glance. His eyes were focused completed on me.

I smile wide and pressed my tongue to my teeth, letting out a slight giggle. I actually hated girls that giggled in the presence of a guy, but oh my God, *this* guy… He had me wanting to run through fields of daisies laughing like a lunatic. I was that ridiculously happy.

One of the hostesses led us to our booth, which was perfectly situated in the quiet part of the restaurant. I thanked her and slid into my seat. Christian smiled and thanked her as well, receiving a beaming smile in return along with a, *"Let me know if you need absolutely anything"* parting comment, to which he didn't even respond.

"Would you like some wine?" he asked.

"I would love some, except that it might get us thrown in jail."

"Why would it get us thrown in jail? Are you a violent drunk who'd trash the place?" he teased.

"No, but I'm only twenty years old. Thanks for the offer though." I smiled back at him as he set the wine menu off to the side.

"Oh, well that explains it. Sorry. I shouldn't have assumed. It just feels like I already know you, so I didn't think to ask your age."

"It's okay. But now that you know how old I am, it's your turn to share. How are old are you?"

"Yes, of course. Formal introductions. My name is Christian Royce, and I'm twenty-four years old. As you already know, I work at The Rising Pit. I'm their head of security."

"Cool. Well, I'm Rose Reynolds, and I'm a senior at Seela State University."

"Nice. What's your major?"

"History."

"What a coincidence. History is my favorite subject."

His dazzling smile and the sparkle in his eyes were so damn distracting, I didn't even care if what he was saying was true or not. Maybe he was just trying to score points. Either way, I was hooked.

"I have to tell you, Rose, I'm a little nervous. I haven't been on a date in over five years." *More like fifty.* "And you are the first girl I've ever taken to dinner."

"Really? Where did you take your other dates? The racetrack?" I tried to make light of the situation, but internally, I was doing a happy dance. I liked that he hadn't dated anyone in five years, but suddenly wondered if there was something wrong with him. "If you don't mind me asking, why haven't you dated anyone in five years?" *Please have a good answer.*

"No, I don't mind you asking at all. I guess you could say I'm pretty old fashioned and not in the habit of 'hooking-up', and everyone I've encountered wasn't exactly what I'd consider 'relationship material'. So, I've only had brief, non-serious acquaintances while I kept my eye out for the perfect girl." He winked as he picked up the menu. *Definitely a good answer.*

I couldn't help but bite my lip in an effort to keep the biggest, goofiest grin from taking over my face. "So, I guess you're saying that you asked me out because you think I'm *relationship material?*" I hoped I wasn't digging a hole for myself. Mom had warned me not to talk about too serious of stuff on our first date, but Christian wasn't the only one who felt like we'd known each other forever. I was so comfortable talking to him, and even the vibe he gave off was one of genuine kindness. So, needless to say, I was really liking how things were going so far.

"Yes. That's exactly what I'm saying. When I saw you looking out that window, you were so beautiful. I just couldn't stop myself from asking you out. I would have come over, but I was on duty and had to get back inside. I just hoped that you would call, and I can't tell you how happy it made me when you did."

The waitress arrived asking if we were ready to order. Christian ordered a rare steak—*eeeww,* and I ordered the garlic shrimp fettuccine. After passing her the menus, we just sat quietly for a few moments staring at each other. I don't think I ever felt so connected and excited about anyone before.

CHAPTER NINE

(Christian)

After Rose and I got past the informatory part of our conversation—which included me giving her the fake last name I often used and my estimated age—we ordered, then sat there staring at one another. She was the most beautiful thing I'd ever laid eyes on, and the moment I caught the scent of her excitement, had me digging my nails into my thighs in an effort to keep from drifting.

I would love nothing more than to bed this gorgeous woman tonight, but since that was never going to happen, I thought it best to change the subject... quick.

"So, tell me more about yourself. What does your family do?"

I listened as Rose talked lovingly about her mother and father, sharing stories from her youth which painted the picture of a perfect family. Our conversation continued to flow as we both enjoyed our meals, even though it was a bit of a struggle getting the raw steak down. It had been so long since I'd had to fake my way through an actual meal, but all-in-all, things were going great.

"I wondered if you would like to take a walk with me after dinner? I have something I'd like to show you just around the corner."

"Sure. That sounds great."

As I laid the money for the bill and tip on the table, I made sure I was in complete control before reaching for Rose's hand. Again, she didn't hesitate to take mine in return. We walked out of the restaurant like a couple who'd been dating for a while. It was wonderful, and perfect.

"I thought we could walk around the block and head to the festival in the park that's going on tonight."

"Oh, that's right. The movie festival. I love those. I wonder what's playing?"

I already knew what was playing. And as cliché as it was, I was interested to see what her reaction would be. "I believe it's Dracula."

"Awesome! That's one of my favorites."

Damn, this just keeps getting better and better.

We strolled around the block, casually chatting about the town and how she'd lived here her whole life. When we reached the park, we wove our way through the crowd and settled on a bench toward the back under one of the red maple trees. "Will this be okay? Can you see the screen from here?" I asked.

"Yes. It's perfect." With that, she slid closer, and I put my arm around her shoulders.

It was a simple thing, and felt so easy. We sat in silence and watched the rest of Dracula under the full moon.

"I can't tell you how great this night has been for me." I tried not to sound like a complete lame-ass, but it was the truth. I hadn't experienced this kind of emotion in a long time, and I was pretty impressed with myself for keeping my drifting at bay throughout the evening. But... all that changed when she turned to face me, slipping her hand around my neck, and leaning in to place her lips on mine.

I closed my eyes after making sure hers were closed first, and let the sensation of her soft lips penetrate my brain. I knew anyone walking by would see the previously blond guy suddenly sitting here now with dark brown hair, but honestly... I didn't care.

Since Rose had initiated the kiss, I let her control the intensity. It was sweet and gentle, but had the makings of something that could turn fierce in a heartbeat. I never wanted it to end. When she pulled back, I used all my willpower to blank out my emotions, making sure she found me drifted back to normal.

"That was for a perfect evening." She smiled shyly and ducked her head, then reached for her purse and started to stand.

I wanted so badly pull her back down onto my lap and kiss her senseless, but didn't want to risk ruining anything by being too aggressive. Besides, that just wasn't me. "You're right... tonight has been perfect. So, I was wondering if you'd be open to making plans for later this week?" *Please say yes.*

"I'd love nothing more."

CHAPTER TEN

(Rose)

Once Christian and I parted ways after sharing a few more delicious kisses, I couldn't wait to get home to talk to Mom. I had to see if the feelings I was experiencing were the same she felt after meeting Dad. Because honestly, I don't think I'd *ever* felt this way before.

I knew it had been bold of me to lean in and kiss him first, but I just couldn't resist. The whole evening had been so amazing, and while sitting there in his arms at the park, I really did have the overwhelming feeling that we'd been together for years. So... I did it. I leaned in and gently placed my lips to his, and it was incredible.

As I pulled the car into the garage, I noticed a warm light radiating from the den window. *Yes, Mom's still awake.* After tiptoeing in my open-toed shoes through the dew-covered grass, I opened the back door and put my things down just as Mom stuck her head into the kitchen.

"So... how was it?"

"Heaven. It was absolute heaven. Mom, he's sooooo nice, and gorgeous, and it felt like we'd known each other forever. I can't even explain it." I continued to gush as we headed back toward the den. I flopped down onto the sofa, and met my mom's smile with one of my own. "I can honestly say I've never been this happy in my entire life."

"Well, that's saying a lot, because as your mother, I can remember plenty of times you've been extremely happy." She continued to smile as she made her way to join me on the couch. "I'm so thrilled you feel there's a connection there, but just be careful. Don't get your hopes up too high. Everyone puts their best foot forward on a first date, but I say, until you've hit the three-month mark, you don't really know who a person is."

"Well, we've already made plans to see each other again later this week. And if things continue to go like this... not only will we reach the three-month mark, but I could see making three years, easy!"

Her eyes widened briefly, then a gentle, loving look settled on her face. "Rose, that's great. I'm truly happy for you, but again, please don't rush into anything, okay?"

"I promise I'll be careful. But for the first time in a long time, Christian has given me something else to be excited about besides school. It feels good. But don't worry, it's not like we're gonna rush off and get married or anything." I pushed up from the couch and began to make my way out of the den. "I love you, Mom. I'm gonna head to bed and hopefully have some juicy dreams about Christian."

She cupped her hands over her ears and shook her head. "TMI, TMI." Smiling as she followed me out of the den, she continued, "Alright. Sleep well, but tomorrow be ready to work. We're starting that project in your room, remember?"

"Are you seriously going to paint my ceiling black?"

"Yes. Yes, I am. It's for a specific purpose, so keep your eye rolls to a minimum and wait and see what I have planned. You're going to love it, I'm sure."

Laughing, I waved my hand over my head and headed upstairs. I wasn't kidding about wanting to have some good dreams about Christian, but what I truly wanted to do was get to my room, change into my pjs, crawl into bed, and give Christian a call. Our date may have been over, but he'd made sure to tell me, that due to his work schedule, he literally stayed up all night. So, we'd made plans for me to call him as soon as I got settled at home. And since there was no way I'd be getting him out of my head anytime soon, I figured I'd spend the rest of my night talking to the man of my dreams.

CHAPTER ELEVEN

(Rose)

After spending a couple of hours talking to Christian, I finally reached the point of exhaustion. He must have heard it in my voice because he said, "I can tell you're getting tired. Why don't you lay down and get some rest? I'll call you after dark tomorrow. During the day, I'm dead to the world. Goodnight, Rose. Sweet dreams."

And oh boy, did I have some sweet dreams. Christian and I in Paris looking at the lights of the Eifel tower. Christian and I kissing outside of a Scottish castle. Christian and I riding in a gondola in Venice. I didn't want to leave this glorious dreamscape, but with Mom rummaging around outside my bedroom door, my fanciful dreams were quickly put to an end. As I gradually woke up, all I could think about was seeing Christian again.

"Good morning," Mom announced as she cracked open my door. I sat up, propping myself up on the pillow and watched as she dragged in a bunch of supplies. Black paint, rollers, drop-cloths, and a large bag from the metaphysical store in town. Now I was getting nervous. Mom's project was about to hit full-swing.

"So, we're really doing this?"

"Yes ma'am. But painting the ceiling's not all!"

"Oh goody... there's more." I rolled my eyes and gave her a goofy grin. "Would you like to elaborate?"

"Of course." After setting down her supplies, she spun in a circle, her arms held out wide. "We're going to create a nighttime wonderland."

As I watched her turn around with her beautiful smile and sparkling eyes, I knew I couldn't say no. I loved when Mom got one of her crafty ideas, but I wasn't exactly following what she had in mind. "Want to elaborate... *more*?"

She took a seat on my bed. "We're going to paint your ceiling black, then hang these beautiful crystals from it." She dug out a handful of stars and moons in all sizes and colors and laid them across my bed. "It will be beautiful, and you'll feel like you're sleeping under the twinkling stars every night," she continued with a spark of wonder in her voice.

I lifted one of the crystals in my hand and let in dangle in the sunlight. The rainbow it cast onto my wall was stunning, but I wasn't convinced it would have the same effect at night. But knowing my mom like I did, there would be no stopping her. "Cool idea. Let me get dressed and we can get started."

"I'll head down and make us some breakfast first, okay?" She breezed out of my bedroom, not waiting for a reply.

As I slogged toward my bathroom, I noticed the little red light on my cell was blinking. I had a message. The butterflies started to stir again as I grabbed my phone and read Christian's text.

"Thinking of you. Talk to you soon. Have a good day at school tomorrow, and call me as soon as the sun goes down. Love, Christian."

Love, Christian.

I can't tell you how long I stared at that phrase. Suddenly energized, I threw on my artsy coveralls and pulled my hair up into a ponytail, then jogged down the stairs. "Smells good, Mom."

"I made cinnamon toast, bacon, and eggs." She smiled as she sat the plate in front of me and then grabbed one of her own, piled high with the same yummy goodness. "So, I heard you on the phone last night. Just couldn't get enough of Christian from your date, I take it?"

I wiggled my eyebrows as I took a bite out of my toast.

She laughed and shook her head. "Oh, young love. I remember it well."

We continued talking about boys and the gushy feelings they gave us, then headed back to my room once breakfast was done.

It took most of the day to paint the ceiling. Not because it was a particularly large room, but because we sucked at painting. I kept hitting the walls and having to do touch-ups, and even though Mom was in awesome shape, we had to take a lot of breaks because our arms kept getting tired from working the brush above our heads. Eventually, we finished and decided to head out for a late lunch while the paint dried. So, after we both showered and attempted to wash off all the black specks that decorated our hair and skin, we drove to our favorite local pizza place.

As we were seated in our booth, I heard a familiar voice. "Hey guys, can we join you?" Jillian and her mom Adrienne were walking toward us.

"Absolutely," my mom answered.

Jillian and I had been best friends since we were little. She had moved here from Arizona when she was six, and we'd become best friends on her first day of school. We'd grown up together, enjoying the same things until the end of junior high. That's when I became extremely focused on my school work, and she became a volleyball queen. We'd remained best friends and had always supported each other in everything we did, and right now, I couldn't wait to tell her about my date with Christian.

"I was so glad when you called, Loraine. Jillian and I were just watching movies to pass the day, and this was a great reason to take a break and get out of the house," Adrienne said.

"Of course. I figured if we were going to be enjoying pizza and talking boys, you two should join us."

I hadn't known Mom had called them, but it didn't surprise me. She knew me so well. So, for the next hour and a half, I gushed to my best friend and her mom about the amazing guy I'd just met, and how I couldn't wait for our next date. They "oohhhed" and "aaahhhed" at all the romantic details, and loved the idea of watching a movie in the park while being wrapped in his arms. "He sounds just about perfect," Adrienne said.

"He is. I'm almost sure of it." I laughed and continued to answer her questions with a huge smile on my face, but suddenly noticed Jill was being quieter than usual. I didn't ask her about it because I didn't want to upset or embarrass her. Besides, I figured she was just a little jealous of all my "Christian talk." She was used to being the center of attention, so instead of talking more about Christian, I directed the conversation to Mom and Adrienne and began to stuff myself with pizza.

"Well, I think our paint should be dry by now. It was nice to seeing you guys." Mom waved goodbye and slid out of the booth.

Feeling a little disappointed at Jill's reaction, all I said was "Bye," and then followed Mom out of the restaurant. We drove home in silence and then headed back up to my room to finish our project without conversation.

"Okay, are you ready to starting hanging your moons and stars?" Mom's tone was casual, but I could tell there was something else on her mind.

"Did you notice how Jill got all quiet when I kept talking about Christian?"

Sighing, Mom stopped spreading the crystals on my bed, and just looked at me. "Yes, I did. I think she was a little jealous. Are you okay?"

"Yes and no. I guess I expected her to be happier for me. I don't want anything to come between me and Jill, but I'm not going to stop seeing Christian because she's feeling insecure or upset, that for once, she's not the center of attention."

A loving smile spread across Mom's face as she stood up and hugged me. "When you choose a man over your best friend, it can be a scary thing. But, it is also the first sign that it may, in fact, be the start of a serious relationship."

I melted against her and felt a sting of tears threatening to spill, so I closed my eyes. "Thanks, Mom. I love Jillian, but for the first time in my life, I feel like everything else needs to come second, including her. I'm falling hard for Christian, and thanks for not making me feel silly about it."

"You're welcome, sweetie, and I'm so happy for you. Now let's make some magic." She pulled away from our hug and brushed her thumb gently over my cheek before moving toward my dresser to grab a sack full of small silver hooks. "You stand on your bed, and I'll hand you a hook. Just screw them in, and I'll give you a crystal."

It took us over an hour to get all of them strung up, which ended up being perfect timing, as the sun had finally gone down. "Are you ready for this? It's going to be amazing," Mom said.

I wasn't convinced, but as soon as I lay down on my bed, Mom opened the curtains to let the moonlight flow in, and I was speechless. She'd been right. I was amazed as I watched the beautiful little stars and moons twinkle and spin right here in my very own room. "Oh, Mom. It's beautiful." I lunged off the bed and into her arms. "I love it. I absolutely love it."

"I'm so glad. And, I love you, too. I'm so proud of the woman you're becoming, and I feel like this is just the start of some pretty magical things headed your way."

"I think you're right."

CHAPTER TWELVE

(Christian)

After my initial date with Rose, I spent the next couple of days trying to avoid all the jokes and teasing from my family. They thought it was hilarious I'd fallen for a human. When Bobby approached with a smirk on his face, I braced myself for yet another jab. "So, tonight's the first night you're gonna see Rose again, right?"

"Yes. Why?"

"Oh, no reason. I just wondered what you were planning to do for round two." Bobby puckered his lips and put his hands behind his head as he wound his hips around and around.

"You've really got to get some new moves." I shoved past him and headed toward Evie's office.

"Oh, I can show you some new moves if you need some help," Bobby yelled as I slammed the door.

I took a seat and smiled at Evie. "I need to warn you, I might beat the shit out of Bobby later."

Evie laughed and offered me a glass of dark red blood. "Well, just don't make a mess of the carpet."

I shook my head and politely declined. I couldn't stand drinking blood from a glass. Even if it was heated up, it just didn't taste the same. Plus, I never knew which donor Evie was currently using for her supply, and I didn't like *not* knowing where my food had come from. "I've invited Rose down tonight to come see me during my break. I told her I didn't have much time off work, and that we'd have to work around my schedule. I wanted to appear as if I have a normal job and responsibilities. Is that alright?"

"Of course. That's fine. But you know you can come and go as you please. You don't have to pretend your boss is a complete tyrant who won't give you a day off." She smiled as she set the glass back down on her desk.

"I know, but since Rose isn't twenty-one, and I'm really not ready for her to meet everyone just yet, I thought this would be a good compromise. I suppose I could continue to see her outside of here, but I don't want her feeling as though I'm hiding my work from her. This way we still get to see each other, and her curiosity is satisfied."

"That sounds reasonable, but you know we are all going to want to meet her sooner rather than later. Maybe I'll host a company mixer for just employees and their guests next month. How does that sound?"

I could tell she was chomping at the bit to meet Rose. Hell, they all were. "That sounds fine. And thanks for not rushing me, Evie."

I stood as she gracefully made her way around the desk and enveloped me in a hug. "You were my first son, Christian, and I'm beyond happy for you. Take all the time you need."

Just as I left Evie's office, I received Rose's text. "I'm almost there."

I'd told her to text me when she was close so I could meet her outside. I didn't want her running into anyone without my protection. I knew all the vampires who came to The Rising Pit were decent people and would never hurt Rose, but I wasn't willing to take that chance. Besides, the thought of someone else sinking their fangs into her, threatened to send me into a fighting rage.

As normal vampires, we couldn't kill each other. Only our Sire had the poison of true death. But, because of our super-strength and speed, our fights tended to be epic. It was rare for vampires to fight amongst themselves, though, and the only time it happened was usually over territory, which sometimes included humans. As archaic as it seemed, I definitely felt I had a claim to Rose. In my mind... she was mine. And I was hers.

I watched her pull into the parking lot, my veins sizzling with anticipation. Our first date had been perfect, and the conversation we had later that night had only solidified my feelings for her. But since this was the first time seeing each other since, I was feeling a little apprehensive about how things would go. Especially since in the back of my mind, all I could see was my vampire family rushing out of the club's door and bombarding us with questions and embarrassing the crap out of me.

"Hi, gorgeous." She threw her arms around my neck and kissed me gently.

"Well, hello to you too, beautiful." I knew I was smiling like an idiot, but the fact she seemed just as excited to see me as I was her, only made me want to smile more. "How was your trip down? Did you have any trouble finding the place?"

"Nope. Your directions were perfect, just like you."

As she started to close her eyes and lean in for another kiss, I lifted her off the ground and spun us around. The sound of her laughter was sweet music to my ears. "Since you're not twenty-one, we can't go inside the club, so do you mind if we just hang out in my car?" I knew it sounded lame, but I wanted to get her inside before another vampire in the area picked up her scent and came to check things out.

"Sure, that sounds great."

I felt more relaxed once we were sitting in my car, so I reached out to hold her hand. It was phenomenal being able to touch her again, and to be able to talk face to face. We spent the next fifteen minutes talking about random things, like how long I had worked here, and whether I liked it or not. She asked if the weird hours bothered me, and if I ever thought about doing something else. I hated lying to her about such stupid little details, but I didn't have a choice. Only when she seemed to drift off into her own thoughts did I worry my lies weren't convincing enough. Then, suddenly she leaned forward and kissed me, and this time with a little more heat.

"I'm sorry. I love talking to you, but watching your mouth move is a little distracting." She smiled shyly, but I could tell from the heat in her eyes and the sudden rise in excitement, she really didn't want to listen to any more of my stories.

I studied the planes of her beautiful face: the luscious contour of her lips, the mesmerizing sparkle of her light blue eyes, and the smooth perfection of her long blonde hair. Then I too was suddenly done with small talk. Leaning in, I threaded my fingers into her hair and pulled her lips to mine. The kiss only lasted a few seconds before she broke away and climbed into the backseat. I wanted to laugh. Not because she was being funny or silly, but because I was so happy, my undead heart felt like it was going to explode. She was so confident and secure in her sexuality, and obviously knew what she wanted. But we wouldn't be going all the way in the backseat of my car. I wouldn't do that to her. She deserved better. But even the thought of being intimate with Rose had me worried my drifting was going to be a *huge* problem tonight.

"Sorry. Does this make you uncomfortable?" she asked.

This time I did laugh as I climbed into the backseat to join her. "You're asking a guy if making out with a beautiful girl in the backseat of his car makes him uncomfortable? Um... no. It makes me the luckiest man in the world."

Her smile not only lit up the backseat of my car, but also my heart. With a serious look on her face, she continued, "I don't expect us to jump straight into the sack, but the connection I feel with you is unexplainable. I know this will sound weird, but it's almost as if there's something magical about it. I don't know... like I said, I can't explain it. This is only our second date, but for me it feels like we've known each other forever. I just hope that doesn't freak you out."

I took her hands in mine and looked deep into her eyes. "Rose, you don't have to worry about doing anything that is going to freak me out. I'm sure most people wouldn't understand it, but I feel exactly the same way. You're right, there is something magical when it comes to the way I feel about you. It's like we were together in another life or something. Everything with you is so easy and natural, and I love how confident you are. A lot of people have a tendency to deny what's happening to them, but I'm glad we can both accept our feelings and not be afraid of them."

I caught her as she threw herself into my arms, hugging me as though her life depended on it. "Christian, you make me feel so comfortable and safe. I can honestly say this is the first time I've ever felt *ready* to start a relationship." She pulled away from the hug and with a teasing glint in her eyes. "And I have to admit, I've never been as turned with anyone as I am with you."

Those were the last words spoken between us for quite some time—our bodies and mouths being otherwise occupied. The feel of Rose in my arms and the intensity of our kisses was something I'd never experienced before. I was thankful there weren't any lights in this part of the parking lot, because if there had been, then I'm sure she would have seen my drifted appearance. Instead, our eyes were closed or it was just so dark that she really couldn't tell the difference. I truly was the luckiest guy in the world.

* * * * *

From that day on, Rose and my relationship only grew. She would come visit me during my breaks at least a couple times a week, and I'd take her on real dates as often as I could, using the excuse of needing to wait for my paycheck to do something special. I loved how normal everything was progressing. We'd decided we weren't going to sleep with each other until the time was right, because as intense as our feelings were, just talking and exploring each other was the perfect way to justify those feelings without throwing sex into the equation. Plus, if we were to actually have sex, I didn't think I would be able to control my urge to bite her, and that would expose my secret.

CHAPTER THIRTEEN

(Rose)

Christian and I had been seeing each other for about a month and a half now. I would almost venture to say that we were in love, even though neither of us had said it yet. We weren't having sex, but I was happy with that decision. It made our conversations and the times we spent together much more real. Our relationship wasn't about sex, though if our make-out sessions were any indication, our sex life was going to be amazing when it finally did begin.

But tonight, I had other plans. While spending all of my extra time with Christian was certainly wonderful, it was definitely taking its toll. I was dreadfully behind in all of my classes, and I had a paper due this week. I refused to let all my hard work go down the drain just because of a guy. So, I bit the bullet and told Christian I couldn't come down because I'd made plans with Mom to stay late after school in order to get some research done. She was working late, conducting a class at the swim complex, and agreed to pick me up when she was done.

I was walking out of the library when my phone rang. "Hi, honey. Look I'm sorry, but this session is running late. I need you to take the bus over to meet me here instead. Is that going to be okay?"

"Sure, Mom. No problem. Just give me the address again." I quickly rummaged through my bag to grab a piece of paper and a pen to jot down the address. "Okay, got it. Looks like I should be there just after dark."

"Perfect. Just head around to the outdoor pool when you arrive. Thanks, honey. I'll see you soon."

The bus ride went pretty fast, and I arrived just after dark as expected. The huge complex at night was a little freaky, so by the time I made my way around to the outdoor pool, my nerves were shot.

"Mom?" I called out. There was no answer, but I saw movement in the pool. I slowly walked toward the edge, then froze immediately. My mom and some guy were struggling underwater.

I'd never been faced with an emergency situation, so even though I wasn't proud of it, I completely panicked. I couldn't move or scream until the moment the waves in the water started to clear.

What I saw was enough to scare me into motion. I ran back around the corner of the building and hid, while the man climbed out of the pool carrying my mother in his arms. His mouth plastered to the side of her neck.

Holy shit! Was my mom having an affair? My legs gave out, dropping me to the ground. I turned cold as ice, terrified to move. As I looked closer, I could tell he wasn't kissing the side of her neck, but instead had sharp teeth which piercing her instead.

What I first thought were sensual kisses were actually long drags of sucking, and that when thought hit me: *My God, a vampire is drinking from my mom.*

I quietly watched, not knowing what to do or think. I felt like I was going to pass out. At first, I was so scared and feared this monster was hurting my mom, tears instantly filled my eyes. But suddenly, my anger trumped the fear, and I looked around for anything made of wood I could slam into this asshole's heart. I wanted to scream when the man removed what could only be called fangs from my mom's neck. But then, he laid her on one of the chaises next to the pool and gently brushed the hair out of her eyes. The kindness in his actions left me dazed and confused. Mom sat up with a smile on her face and waved as the man started to walk away. I was so relieved she was okay, I sucked in a quick breath. The man's head spun in my direction, staring me down with a pair of dark, intense eyes.

He crooked his finger at me, indicating for me to come to him, but I was still frozen in fear and literally couldn't move. The next thing I knew, he was standing right in front of me. Only a split-second had passed, but there he was, dripping wet, towering over me with a cocky smirk on his face.

"Hi. You must be the daughter." His voice was deep and sexy, just like the rest of him. I knew my thoughts were inappropriate, but I couldn't deny reality. The guy appeared to be in his mid-thirties, with dark brown hair and eyes to match. He was tan and muscular, and probably about 6' 4". He looked like sex-on-a-stick.

"Yes, I'm her daughter. Who the hell are you?" I'd finally gotten myself under control enough to face him. This was definitely going to be a workout for my acting skills, though, because I was still scared to death.

"I think the question you want to ask is, 'What are you?', am I right?" He had a mocking glint in his eye, and that damn cocky grin was still plastered to his face.

"I'm not stupid. I know what you are. You're a vampire."

His grin widened. "Are you scared?"

"Should I be?" I tried to bolster myself so the fear I was feeling wouldn't come across in my shaking voice.

He stared at me a while. "No, beautiful, you have nothing to fear from me. One a night is all I can handle."

I hated that his *one* had been my mom, but I was damn glad he would be leaving me alone. "Did you hurt her?" Now that I felt somewhat safe, I had a shit-ton of questions I was dying to ask him. Well, maybe dying wasn't the right word to use.

"No, I didn't hurt her, and she won't remember anything about tonight," he explained. "What about you? Should I bite you and make you forget too?" He seemed genuine in his question.

I tried not to shiver as goose bumps spread up my arms. "No. I don't want to forget. Actually, I have a lot of questions I would love to ask you." I don't know why, maybe it was the brain-numbing fear or the years I'd spent researching as a history major, but in that moment the strangest thought occurred. *What an amazing paper I could write with his help.* Seriously... Was I debating on asking a vampire to help me get a good grade on my history paper? He'd probably kill me for being so lame.

He turned around and watch Mom gather up her things. "Why don't you meet me back here tomorrow night, and I'll answer some of your questions?"

"Really? Or is this some kind of trick to get me here so I can be your meal of the day instead?" I was excited but not stupid. I wondered if crosses or stakes would actually work on this guy. Not that I'm Buffy, but a girl could try.

"No trick. I do, however, enjoy the taste of your mother's blood. It's different than any other I've ever experienced. So, once you spend the evening with her and realize I didn't hurt her in any way... as long as I can continue to feed on your mom, I'll be willing to answer your questions. Is that something that you can handle?" He extended his hand as if preparing to shake on a deal.

"Okay. But if Mom shows any signs of being hurt or acting weird, you'll never see us here again." It was a lame threat because he could probably just follow us home or find us whenever he wanted, but I had to make sure he understood that if he had hurt my mom in any way, the deal was off.

"Deal." He shook my hand and then started to walk away. "Oh. One more thing. What's your name?"

"My name is Rose. What's yours?"

"Terrance. My name is Terrance."

CHAPTER FOURTEEN

(Rose)

Once I got Mom home, I offered to cook. Dad had a work meeting tonight that included dinner, so it was just going to be the two of us. All throughout our meal I watched her so closely I thought my eyes were going to pop out of my head. She seemed perfectly fine and acted as though everything was normal.

Normal? What a joke.

With all the vampire lore I studied in history, and with a new movie or book popping up every other week, I, like the rest of society, had become desensitized. I wasn't sure if that was a good thing or a bad thing, but since I hadn't run away screaming at the top of my lungs, I think it was a good thing. For just having discovered vampires were real, I thought I was handling it pretty damn well.

After dinner, I climbed into bed with Mom under the premise of watching a movie just so I could keep an eye on her. She really did seem totally fine. Even the puncture wounds where Terrance bite her had healed over, which was definitely something I was going to ask about.

As planned, I met Terrance back at the pool the following night. Mom didn't know I was there as stayed hidden and kept my eyes on the pool.

Terrance and I sat down with our backs against the brick wall and started talking. It was all so surreal. He explained how vampires weren't the bad, evil villains of lore, and how every night they only fed from one person, and only took their fill. He told me their powers let them make the feeding process enjoyable for both the vampire and human, and also that it allowed them to compel the humans so they didn't remember anything afterwards. He said these "powers" came from a sedative that flowed from their fangs. *How cool.*

Everything was going great, but I couldn't help the dreadful feelings of uncertainty when he finally asked if he could go feed from my mom. Yes, she had been fine the night before, so it wasn't like he'd lied to me. Plus, I didn't want to back out on our deal and make him so angry he decided to kill us both instead.

He told me to stay behind the building, so I did.

Mom waved at him as soon as she saw him walking toward her, then started back toward the pool. But he shook his head and gestured for her to take a seat on the chaise instead, and she did so instantly.

I watched as he made his way around the back of the chair and sat down gently beside her. It took everything in me not to run over and beg him to stop, but in the next instant, Terrance sunk his fangs into my mom's neck and began to drink. I covered my mouth to hold in my scream and immediately looked away.

He was done in a minute or so, and laid Mom back on the chaise like last time. But instead of her getting up to gather her things, she stayed completely still. I started to panic and ran toward them. "What did you do? You said you wouldn't hurt her."

"I didn't hurt her. I used my sedative to make her sleep for a while so we could finish our conversation. I thought you might have more questions."

"Oh, okay." He was right. I did have a lot more questions. The first being, why did my mom recognize him like they were friends?

"The first time I fed on her, I used my sedative to make her think I was one of her swim students. Since I don't have to breathe underwater, I sometimes submerge us in case anyone walks by. I'm able to control the flow of blood with my sedative so there's no mess, and if anyone see us while we're underwater, I'll have time to stop feeding and make it look like we were just doing some underwater training. And before you freak out, I always make sure she's never under for too long."

Freak out? What a fucking understatement.

Terrance spent the next half hour talking me out of a panic by explaining a few more specifics that came with being a vampire. Like how the puncture wounds close because of their sedative. Apparently, it's "programmable" and can not only be used for memory stuff, but also for pleasure and healing as well. And he explained that vampires didn't burn in the sun, but fell into a deep sleep at its rising instead, along with a lot of other interesting facts.

When Mom started to wake, Terrance said goodbye and asked if I'd like to meet again tomorrow. After pondering whether I should come just to keep an eye on Mom, I decided I needed some time to process everything and told him no… that'd I'd meet him again in a couple more days. At this point, I felt confident he wouldn't hurt her. After all, she was his meal of choice, and didn't seem to mind. Terrance was always a gentleman, and besides, I had a date with Christian tomorrow night.

CHAPTER FIFTEEN

(Rose)

Mom never showed any negative signs from Terrance's feeding, and went about her days as usual. I decided I should do the same.

School was normal, but I couldn't seem to focus. *Gee, I wonder why?*

I kept thinking about everything Terrance had told me. It was so hard to wrap my head around the fact that he was an honest to God vampire, yet he seemed so normal. As soon as the final bell rang, I headed toward the restroom to freshen up for my date. At this point, most of our 'dates' were spent in the back seat of his car, but trust me... I wasn't complaining. We talked about anything and everything, but inevitably, ended up in each other's arms, and there was no other place I'd rather be.

A bunch of girls in sportswear and ponytails busted into the restroom, rousing me out of my love-dazed thoughts. I spotted Jillian amongst the crowd and suddenly felt nervous. Not only did I feel guilty for not spending much time with my best friend lately, but also because we never really talked about what happened at the pizza place.

"Hey, Jill. You heading to practice?"

"Sure thing. What are you up to? I haven't seen you much lately... I miss you." She threw her arms around me, which made me feel tons better.

"I miss you too. I've just been hanging out with Christian, and working out with Mom at the pool a lot." No way could I tell her about Terrance—the *other* guy I was meeting after dark.

"Okay, well, have fun with Christian. I've gotta go kick some ass on the court!" Her whole team whooped and hollered as they bounced out of the restroom, leaving me to stare at myself in the mirror, wondering how dense I could possibly be.

Thinking about meeting Terrance after dark had me putting two-and-two together. How interesting Christian and I could never meet unless it was after dark as well? He was also the only person I ever met who ate everything practically rare bleeding on the plate. *Holy shit!* I think I was dating a vampire.

He had to be, and I knew one sure fire way to find out. I grabbed my cell and dialed Christian's number.

"Hello?"

"Hi, Christian. I'm calling to let you know I'm going to be a little late tonight. I got held up at school and still need to grab a bite to eat before heading down." I didn't want to cancel all together, but first... it looked like I'd be meeting Terrance tonight after all.

After dumping all my makeup back into my purse, I made a beeline for the car. Mom let me take it to school today since I'd be leaving straight for my date. This detour was unexpected, but one I needed to make.

I drove straight to the swim complex and found Terrance waiting in the shadow beyond the pool while Mom finished her last lesson of the day. I stood behind the corner of the building and waved him over the moment he noticed me. He was at my side in two seconds with a worried look on his face.

"Rose, is everything alright? You look upset and your heart is racing."

"I have to ask you something, and I want the truth. Do you know a vampire named Christian Royce?"

I knew the answer from the look on his face.

Terrance took my hand and guided me to the ground. "Yes. I know Christian. Royce is the last name he uses in the human world, but we really don't have last names once we're turned. We are both part of the same clan and live at The Rising Pit. How did you meet him?"

It took a few deep breaths before I could respond. "I've been dating him for the last month and a half. Why have I never seen you there?"

"I choose not to feed in the vicinity, and prefer to come into town instead. Christian has always fed close to home," Terrance explained.

Wow! The jealous feelings racing through me at the thought of Christian touching another person, sent my mind reeling. Despite him being a vampire, I couldn't imagine him with anyone else. I was also certain he would never hurt anyone, so I really couldn't be angry at him for feeding on humans in order to survive. He couldn't help what he was.

It took a few more moments to process, but suddenly, I was excited to tell him he didn't have to keep it a secret any longer. "Well, I guess it will be a big surprise for him tonight when I tell him I know what he is."

"No. You can't!" Terrance shot to his feet. "If you reveal you know vampires exist, you could get us both killed."

I sat there stunned as he went on to explain I'd need to hide my thoughts around other vampires too, making sure I only focused on the events happening around me. It seemed like an impossible task, but I needed to know how keeping this secret was going to affect Christian and my relationship before I made any rash decisions. So, following Terrance's advice, I planned to guard my thoughts as best I could and keep this revelation to myself.

On my way down to the club, I had a series of panic attacks and almost turned the car around multiple times. I was so nerve-wracked, I thought for sure I'd blow it. But apparently, I was pretty good at hiding things from people, because Christian didn't notice a thing.

Our date went off without a hitch, and the fact that I knew he was a vampire only heightened my emotions. He didn't act or feel any differently, which confirmed not only would I *not* be breaking up with him, but that I wanted to spend eternity with him. Talk about a life changing revelation.

I didn't see Terrance for a couple of days. I needed time to think about everything that had happened, and the decision I was considering. Once I had made up my mind, I met with Terrance and finally asked the question that I was dying to know. "So how exactly does someone become a vampire?"

"Well, it's pretty standard stuff, really. A vampire bites and feeds on a human until they've been fully drained, then the human feeds from the vampire in return. The human dies and is then reborn as a vampire in a matter of hours."

Standard indeed. No big surprises there. So, after a few more weeks of contemplating and finally admitting I was, in fact, in love with Christian and that those feelings weren't ever going to change, I had made up my mind I wanted to become like him so we could be together forever. I asked Terrance if he would be willing to change me, and he agreed.

"Okay, but here's the deal. No one can know we know each other or that I'm going to change you. This isn't the usual way these types of things happen, and by not following the rules, that puts us both in a lot of danger."

"Then what is the normal way? If there's a right way to do this without breaking any rules, I'll do it. I just want to keep it a secret from Christian. I want it to be a surprise."

"There is no other way. I told you we're in serious danger for you even *knowing* vampires exist. It's not like you can just walk in and ask everyone to take a vote. Traditionally, when a vampire wants to add someone to our clan, the whole clan has to vote on it so everyone has a say as to whom they want added to the family. But don't worry, as long as you can keep it a secret, I know everyone will be happy after the fact. I may be in trouble at first, but I'll deal with it."

With that settled, I had a plan in place. I would graduate college and move out of my childhood home first, then he would change me and I would surprise Christian with the fact that we could be together forever.

I couldn't wait.

CHAPTER SIXTEEN

(Rose)

Life went back to normal after my decision was made. Normal, but better. Everything now held a newfound excitement for me. My dates with Christian sparked such internal happiness, knowing we'd soon be together forever. I was on cloud nine whenever we were together. He finally expressed his love for me as well, and continued to display it in the most traditional ways: flowers, love notes, jewelry, etc., and constantly told me he never wanted to live without me. I loved hearing that, because in just under a year, he'd be getting his wish.

Tonight's date had been especially great. Christian told me his boss, Evangeline, was hosting a company mixer and all the employees were supposed to bring dates.

Though he never let on, this was obviously a way for him to introduce me to his clan, and I couldn't be more excited. If he wanted me to meet them, that meant at some point he was probably planning to have them vote as to whether I could become one of them or not—just like Terrance explained.

"Absolutely, I would love to meet everyone you work with." I accepted the invitation then kissed him goodnight, as it was really getting late. By the time I reached the house, it was after two in the morning, and I hoped I wouldn't wake Mom and Dad.

The moment I turned the corner at the end of my street, my vision filled with blaring red and blue lights. It only took a couple seconds for me to realize that the ambulance and cop cars were centered around my house.

Oh no!

I had no idea what was happening, but my first thought was of Dad. *I hope he didn't have a heart-attack.* He always worked so hard, and lately he'd had to attend a lot more meetings out of town.

I parked the car down the street and ran toward the house as fast as I could. I tried talking to the first policeman I saw. "What's happened?"

"Miss, you need to get back in your car and head on home," the cop politely stated.

"This is my home!" I screamed.

"Rose!" My dad's voice rang out, and my heart dropped. If he was running toward me, then something must have happened to Mom.

From the tear streaks coating his face, I knew it was bad. I stopped in my tracks halfway across the lawn and froze. By the time he reached me, everything had gone silent. It was like my ears were suddenly filled with cotton, and the whole world dropped into slow-motion.

Dad grabbed me and wrapped me in his arms and we fell to the ground. "Rose. She's gone. Your Mother is gone," he sobbed.

The dew on the grass was cold, but it wasn't what caused my goose bumps—it was the utter terror of what he'd just said. There had to be a mistake. I'd just talked to Mom early tonight when I told her I was going to be later than usual. There was no way she could be dead.

"Sir, if you and your daughter would come with us, we have a few questions for you," the same officer said. We were led into the house and instructed to take a seat in the living room.

I was so lost in my head, I didn't even hear the police as they started asking my dad questions. But once I regained a small amount of focus, it became clear someone had broken into our house and killed my mom when she came out of her room and spotted them. Dad said he hadn't heard anything, but that when he woke up and found the bed empty, he'd got up to check on Mom and found her in the hallway, just outside their bedroom. He said it looked like she'd just passed out, since there wasn't any blood, but when he tried to wake her, he realized she wasn't breathing and called 9-1-1.

Apparently when the ambulance arrived and began examining the body, they'd found two small puncture wounds on her neck, and requested my dad's permission to do an autopsy to pinpoint the cause of death.

Two small puncture wounds on her neck? My, God, no... Terrance.

That son of a bitch, no good vampire followed my mom home and killed. *Oh my, God!* What if he turned her?

I took a few deep breaths, trying to stay calm in front of the police and dad, and soon realized my train of thought didn't make any sense. If Terrance *had* turned my mom, her body wouldn't be here. He would have taken her with him so they could complete the process. No, this wasn't right. Plus, Terrance had always treated my mom like something he cherished, so why would he kill her? Something wasn't adding up, but I knew Terrance couldn't have been the one who killed my mom.

I continued to ponder all the possibilities, but soon heard the police rule it a "freak accident" as they finished up their interrogation and began to clear the scene.

My attention was suddenly snapped into focus as I saw my mom's body being wheeled out the front door in a body bag. My dad quickly grabbed me and forced me to look away.

Mom's life was over, and so was mine. How was I supposed to live without her? As the tears started to flow and the authorities finally left us alone, I sank into my dad's embrace. As devastated as I was, listening to him cry over the loss of his wife was what pained my heart the most.

After that night, everything changed. My dad took a sabbatical from work and pulled me out of school while we tried to work through our grief. He made funeral arrangements and had meetings with lawyers and insurance people all while insisting I stayed glued to his side.

It quickly became clear that Mom's death had turned Dad into a scared, over-protective father. The only time I was able to grieve on my own was when it was time for bed or when I used the restroom. He wouldn't let me see Christian anymore, and since I practically never left the house without him, I never saw Terrance again either. It had only been a month, but there was no end in sight to what I officially called my "lockdown." God, I missed my mom so much.

The only thing that made me happy was thinking about Christian. We talked on the phone as much as we could, and as harsh as it sounded, the fact that we would never have to go through something like this made me happy. I was beyond devastated my mom was dead... but I was going to live forever.

Tish Thawer

"Tish Thawer crafts a
seductive vampire tale with
her eloquent writing style
and keen sense of romance
that simply entrances!"

— Romancing the Darkside

Doubt blooms...
Someone bleeds...
Change is coming...
time to take heed.

Blood of a
Red Rose

∞ Book Two of The Rose Trilogy ∞

Blood of a Red Rose
(Book Two of The Rose Trilogy)

***

Rose's eyes close, and the darkness sets in.
How can I live with my lover as a friend?

CHAPTER ONE

(Rose)

Killing my dad's ex-girlfriend and living with Christian's vampire clan had been the best decision I'd ever made. I was able to spend my nights with the love of my life, and fill my days finishing my college courses online while they slept. I'd graduated on time and had now passed my twenty-first birthday. The only downfall... I really missed my dad.

"Rose, are you okay?" It wasn't Christian's question that startled me; it was, once again, the shock of how beautiful he was, and that I was a part of his everyday life now. My dreams had come true. He was my angel on Earth.

My mouth started to water as my eyes scanned him from top to bottom. He was standing there with a towel wrapped around his waist. Fresh from the shower, his light blond-highlighted hair was wet, and his caramel eyes sparkled with golden rays that could've been straight from the sun. He was so perfect, and damn did he have the most gorgeous body— one I'd become very familiar with over the past four months. All things considered, I was a very lucky girl.

I pushed off our bed and wrapped my arms around him. "I was just thinking about everything that's happened. Mom, Terrance, Meredith, my dad. I... I just can't believe how much everything has changed."

He pulled out of my hug, kissed me on the lips, then looked deeply into my eyes. "I know, baby, but now you're living and working here full-time, and once I become the new Sire, I'll change you. Then we can truly start planning our *very* long future together."

I plastered a smile on my face, and hoped Christian bought it. Becoming a vampire was no longer an option for me. Not after I learned I was part demon and that my blood would infect him, just like Meredith's had infected Terrance. I couldn't do that to Christian. Besides, the clan already vowed to hunt and kill any demons in the area. *Sucks to be me.*

Over the past four months I hadn't stopped thinking about Meredith's revelation that Dad and I were both demons. It was the reason she had gone after my mom. She wanted my dad all to herself. It was pretty obvious Dad didn't have a clue, and that was a problem. I had no idea how I was going to learn about our heritage, since I'd killed the only demon I ever encountered.

So many hurdles now made it impossible for me to become Christian's consort. Yet out of necessity to remain hidden and safe, I was still living here with the clan. Evie had put me to work at the club, so I actually had a real job and wasn't just a burden to them. I'd always been good with numbers and was now in charge of keeping the books. Not that books were even necessary, since they could easily bite and use their sedative to manipulate anyone who questioned them, like the liquor board or the IRS. But it was actually easier and more in-line with the clan's morals to run this business on the up-and-up, and I certainly wasn't complaining... I finally had a job.

When I'd first arrived, Justin and Christian set me straight about the vampire facts Terrance had lied to me about. I'd learned vampires were actually really great people and nothing like how the history books or fables of old portrayed them. They only fed out of necessity, and always used the sedative that flowed from their fangs to make sure it never hurt their prey. They could make the humans do and think whatever they wanted, but always made it a pleasant experience for them before wiping their memories of the event. It's how vampires remained hidden from the world for centuries.

Almost a year ago, when I first found out vampires existed, I'd hoped to surprise Christian by going through the change and becoming a vampire myself, so we could be together forever. But since Terrance was the one who was supposed to change me, everything he'd told me had been a lie. He was under Meredith's influence at the time, suffering from the poison of her demon blood. There had never been a way for him to make me a vampire as promised; that was something only a Sire could do. As I walked into the bathroom, I called over my shoulder, "Do you have any idea when you'll become the new Sire?" *Please let it be a long time.*

"I'm not sure. My abilities are increasing, but I think Evie wants to wait and see what other *talents* I develop before we do the Passing of Powers ritual. Honestly, I'm not even sure I'm really the one being triggered. It could all just be a big mistake."

Hope blossomed in my chest as I stared at myself in the foggy bathroom mirror. "What happens if it's not you?"

"I guess we just wait until someone else starts to show signs of being triggered."

Please let it not be him. The longer I had until a new Sire was triggered, the longer I had to figure out all this demon crap. One day very soon I was going to have to face my dad and get some answers. I didn't *think* he knew, but what if I was wrong and he'd known all along?

"I'm gonna hit the shower, but when I'm done... there's something I want to talk to you about."

CHAPTER TWO

(Jeremy)

Today was the day I was going to find my little girl. I just knew it.

After her attack on Meredith, she and that boyfriend of hers, *Christian*, had gone into hiding. It hadn't taken me long to remember where he worked, but when I went to see the owner and asked if she'd seen them, the answer I'd gotten was, of course, no. I didn't believe her.

I'd thought about going to the police and asking them to get a search warrant, but since Meredith didn't press any charges and Rose was over eighteen, there really wasn't anything I could do except continue to look on my own. Besides, involving the police could be detrimental to us all since we'd covered up what had really happened that night.

I did find out from her college that she completed her courses online and graduated on time, but they were unable to divulge any information as to where the computer's IP address was originating from without police involvement. Again, another dead end.

But today, I just had a feeling I was in for a lucky break. I had to take a trip back to Seela to go over some business accounts with my boss. After Meredith's recovery, I'd sold my home and moved to Masen to live with her. The decision wasn't easy, but it had been the best choice after my wife's death and Rose's attack on Meredith. I just couldn't stay in the home that carried all those horrible memories. It had been the place where I'd spent the happiest times of my life, but now it was a constant reminder of everything I'd lost.

So, after moving in with Meredith, we'd been blissfully happy for four months now. Her recovery had been almost miraculous according to the doctors. That type of injury usually would have been life-threatening, but Meredith was left with barely a scratch. She'd shocked all the therapists with how quickly she regained full mobility, too. We both had recently returned to work.

I was lucky enough to have moved my office to Masen, and instead of having to travel here every month or so, now I traveled back to Seela instead. Today was one of those days.

"Do you have everything?" Meredith bustled around the desk, gathering all the loose papers I had spread across it.

"Yes, honey. I have everything. I don't need those right now; they're for a different campaign." I was the Vice President of D&L Marketing and was headed to a meeting with my boss to go over my latest proposal.

"Alright. I'll just stack them here then." She always made it a habit to keep my desk tidy for me. I wasn't sure if it was because she was just curious, or a neat freak who was still getting used to my presence in her life. I'd tried to ask her about it once, and her response was, *"Don't be silly. You're my destiny, and I love having you here with me."*

I was slowly starting to share her sentiment, but our relationship was something of a conundrum. I'd originally met Meredith when my wife, Loraine, was still alive, and the shock of how much the two looked alike had been intense: long blonde hair, a tall athletic body, and a killer smile. Then Loraine had died, and Meredith had really been there for me and we'd started dating.

I knew it was awkward to be dating a woman that reminded me of my dead wife, but at the time, it was exactly what I needed to help me deal with the pain. Unfortunately, when Rose found out, I was suddenly forced to look at the relationship in a whole new light. One that cast it as something not quite as bright and brilliant as I had made it out to be.

I tried to break it off with Meredith, but then the whole situation with Rose attacking her happened. Her choosing not to press charges, but instead protecting my daughter and me... Well, that made me fall for her all over again.

"Are you going back to look for Rose at that club tonight?" Meredith asked, rousing me out of my stroll down memory lane.

"I was thinking about it. The owner said she hadn't seen either one of them since that night, but I don't believe her. I might just sit outside in my car and watch instead. Maybe that way I'll see something they weren't expecting me to." I wiggled my eyebrows, trying to relay how sneaky and brilliant I thought my plan was.

"Well, just be careful. And call me when you get there. At least if I'm talking to you on the phone, I won't be worried something bad is happening to you." She straightened my tie, then wound her hands around the back of my neck and pulled me into a passionate kiss. "I just got you back, and I never want to lose you again."

The feeling of Meredith's lips on mine, and the sensual feel of her curves pressed against me, had the potential to make me very late. This woman intoxicated me, and I was so grateful to have her in my life during this difficult time. I had to force myself out the door and into the garage, waving goodbye from the car as I pulled out of the driveway.

The trip to Seela from Masen took about two hours, so that would give me plenty of time to think over my plan for tonight. The business meeting was going to be a breeze, same old same old, but a stakeout was something new to me. I certainly hoped it would lead me to Rose, because as happy as Meredith and I were... I missed my baby girl.

* * * * *

(Meredith)

As soon as Jeremy drove away, I grabbed the phone and dialed. "Have you had anymore reports of Rose and her vampire at The Rising Pit? Are they still there?"

"Yes, ma'am. According to our people, they're still there. Rose is now working for Evangeline as her bookkeeper."

Our people. I liked the sound of that. I came from a long line of human/demon descendants, but until recently, I'd only associated with my own family. But after some searching, I'd begun to find more demons in the area and discreetly organized a few meetings to pull the families together. It was tricky since we'd spent our entire lives in hiding, but it was slowly working and was nice to finally connect with people like me. With *demons* like me.

When I'd met Jeremy, he didn't have a clue he was a demon, and still didn't. I wasn't sure if I was going to tell him or not. I was afraid if he found out the truth about me, let alone himself, he'd start to question everything about our relationship again. And that was something I couldn't permit. Not after finally getting everything I'd worked so hard for.

When I discovered Jeremy was a demon, I'd made it my mission to seduce him in order to become pregnant and continue my pure demon bloodline. But I never expected to fall in love. Once I had, the only way to secure my life with him was to kill the one person who stood in my way... his wife. And now, having successfully separated Rose from her father, we'd finally been able to start our life together. So, no, I wouldn't tell him that he was a demon. At least not yet.

Besides, I wanted to spend more time with the other demons I'd met first, to see how they lived their lives, and what stories of our histories they knew. A lot of demons were like Jeremy, clueless about their heritage, but every week, more and more of them were coming out of the woodwork and attending our little get-togethers. It was comforting. Especially since I knew it wouldn't be long until Rose and her boyfriend found out I was still alive. I knew they would all after me, and I'd have to be prepared. And the more demon "friends" I had, the better.

"I'm coming over. I have something I want to talk to you about."

CHAPTER THREE

(Christian)

Once again, I woke up realizing I was the luckiest vampire in the world. Rolling over in bed to find the love of my life, Rose, sleeping peacefully beside me was like waking up in heaven every night.

After gently brushing the hair out of her eyes, I leaned in and placed a light kiss on her cheek before tiptoeing into our bathroom to shower. I needed to talk to Rose tonight. I wasn't looking forward to what I had to tell her, so I was happy for this brief time to myself to collect my thoughts.

After showering, I wrapped the towel around my waist and slowly crept back into the bedroom in case she was still sleeping. She wasn't. Instead, I found her lying in bed with her hands tangled in her hair and a worried look on her face.

"Rose, are you okay?"

She sat up and a warm smile spread across her face, looking at me from top to bottom. If I hadn't been concerned over what she was what bothering her, I would have dropped the towel and proceeded to start our evening off in a much more delightful way. But, with a crease to her brow, she pushed off our bed and wrapped her arms around me. "I was just thinking about everything that's happened. Mom, Terrance, Meredith, my dad. I... I just can't believe how much everything has changed."

I pulled back from the hug to press my lips to her, then made sure to look her straight in the eye. I wanted her to know she didn't have anything to worry about ever again. "I know, baby, but now you're living and working here full-time, and once I become the new Sire, I'll change you and then we'll truly be able to start planning our *very* long future together."

When I'd started to show signs of being triggered as the next Sire, I was completely skeptical. Actually... I was still pretty skeptical. I wasn't truly convinced what was happening to me really meant I was the one, but in moments like these, I hoped it was true. Only a Sire had the ability to create another vampire, and the idea of being the one to turn Rose and to have her join me as my consort was almost euphoric.

She smiled then headed toward the bathroom. As I walked toward my closet, I heard her ask, "Do you have any idea when you'll become the new Sire?"

I was happy to hear the question because it meant we were both thinking about the same thing. "I'm not sure. My abilities are increasing, but I think Evie wants to wait and see what other *talents* I develop before we do the Passing of Powers ritual. Honestly, I'm not even sure I'm really the one being triggered. It could all just be a big mistake." I didn't feel the need to hide my insecurities from Rose. We'd been through so much together, and I knew we'd face this together too.

"What happens if it's not you?" she called back.

After pulling on my jeans and slipping into a navy t-shirt, I shrugged. "I guess we just wait until someone else starts to show signs of being triggered."

I heard the water for the shower turn on and then Rose said, "I'm gonna hit the shower, but when I'm done... there's something I want to talk to you about."

I mulled over her words as I finished getting dressed, wondering what it could be. I knew what I needed to tell her wasn't going to be easy for her to hear, but I thought it was something she needed to know, and hoped it would bring her some closure.

I was a little nervous, though, about how she'd react to the fact that Evie had sent Renard and Loni to spy on her father. Especially since what they found out would come as a pretty big shock. Jeremy, Rose's dad, had sold their family home and moved away. I knew it was going to be devastating for Rose to hear, but she had a right to know.

After her attack on Meredith, Rose and I went into hiding here at The Rising Pit. A few weeks after the incident, however, Jeremy had come to the club looking for us. Evie turned him away, telling him she hadn't seen either of us since that night. He hadn't been back since.

At the time Evie suggested one of us bite him and use our sedative to make him forget, but Rose panicked at the idea. She'd said no matter how bad the memories her father had of her were, she just couldn't live with the idea that he wouldn't remember her at all. Evie tried to convince her we could wipe just the memories of Meredith and the attack, but Rose was adamant. She insisted he needed to remember those things so he would be more willing to let her go.

Apparently, her plan worked because he'd moved away completely, leaving the memories of what happened and any hopes of finding his daughter behind. I guess he realized his *innocent* Rose was now a grown woman, and there was nothing he could do but move on.

It was a hard situation for everyone, and this conversation wasn't one I was looking forward to.

* * * * *

(Rose)

As I lathered my hair with my favorite honey and oat shampoo, I contemplated the best way to tell Christian I wanted to go see my Dad. I knew he'd probably say no—that it was too risky—but honestly, I didn't care. It wasn't like he or any of his clan could stop me if I really wanted to go. I would just wait until they were all comatose during the day, and head out on my own.

I wasn't sure what I'd say to my dad or how I would breach the demon subject, but I had to try. I needed to know why no one ever came after me for killing Meredith. Not that I wasn't happy about the fact, just confused. I needed to know once and for all if I was going to have to stay hidden forever.

I emerged from the bathroom in my terrycloth robe, towel drying my hair and found Christian pacing. "I've been thinking about it, and I want to go see my Dad." There. I'd said it. He stopped in his tracks and stared at me. Then his hair and eyes started to drift.

"Did you hear me? I said I want to go see my dad."

"I heard you. But I have something I need to tell you."

"I don't care if you think it's a bad idea. He's my dad, and it's been four months since everything happened. If the cops haven't showed up yet, then I doubt they will. I need to know what he told them, and I need to know if he's okay." I stomped back into the bathroom, threw my wet towel over the shower door, then took a seat and started doing my makeup.

Christian entered the bathroom and stood behind me, placing his hands gently on my shoulders. I stopped applying my mascara and looked at him through the reflection in the mirror. "I didn't say it was a bad idea, but I have something to tell you which pertains to your dad that I think you need to hear first."

I pushed out of the seat and spun around, balancing against the counter. "What? What do you need to tell me about my dad?" My grip tightened on the dressing table behind me, turning my knuckles white.

"Rose, your dad has moved. He sold the house and moved away."

CHAPTER FOUR

(Rose)

It took me a moment to catch my breath. I'd heard what Christian said, but it wasn't registering in my brain. There was no way my dad would have sold our home and moved away. I was born there, and every memory of my childhood revolved around us and that house.

"When? When did he move?" I couldn't get a grip on whether I was pissed or sad.

"We're not sure. Evie sent Renard and Loni to check on him a few weeks ago, and they found the house with a sold sign in the yard and no one there."

I pushed off from my perch and began to walk out of the bathroom. Christian reached out to grab my arm, but I quickly yanked it away. "Don't!"

Guess that settled it... I was pissed.

"How dare you keep this from me! Evie sent them to check on him *weeks* ago, and you're just now telling me?"

"I was going to tell you, but Evie wanted to try to gather more information, like where he moved to." Christian rushed to explain as he followed me out into the bedroom. "Unfortunately, we haven't found any forwarding address. Renard reported yesterday he thinks your dad still works for the same place, even though most of his office has been cleared out too."

I flopped down on the bed. I didn't trust my legs to keep me upright for much longer. As Christian continued speaking, I felt my head shaking *no* as if I was having an out of body experience. "If we could look around during the day it would be easier. We could use our sedative to force someone to tell us the information, but at night, running across someone who knew your dad has proven difficult." He knelt down in front of me and took my hands in his. "I'm sorry, Rose. I wasn't trying to keep it from you, I just wanted there to be more I could tell you when the time came."

I sat in silence and stared into Christian's eyes. They were drifting from caramel to dark brown and back again, along with his hair. It was obvious this was truly upsetting to him as well.

"I don't know what to say. I'm sad but also really mad. Can I just have some time alone?"

"Sure. But Rose, please know that I'm so sorry. Sorry for not telling you before, and sorry it happened in the first place." He kissed my hands, placed them back in my lap, and then strolled out of the room, shutting the door behind him.

I sat there stunned, thinking back to when my dad had come looking for me shortly after I'd gone into hiding. It'd made me feel good to know that after everything, he still wanted me in his life.

At the time, Evie suggested they bite him and make him forget everything, but I just couldn't allow that to happen. Not for the obvious reasons I gave them of course, but because if they bit him, they'd become infected with his demon blood. Skating around that had been a little tricky, but I finally convinced them. Instead, Evie just told him she hadn't seen Christian or I since that night.

It hurt to know my ruse had worked so well. That Dad had really given up on me. I knew I had no right to feel hurt by his actions; in his eyes I was a murderer and a runaway. Why did I expect him to care? This was exactly what I hoped would happen. But at the time, I also thought I'd becoming a vampire soon and would need to cut all ties because of it. Instead, that dream had been shattered too. My heart still hurt over losing my mom, and now being faced with having to live a mortal life without Christian or my father... I suddenly felt very alone.

I curled up on the bed, drew the covers around me, and did the only thing I could do: cry myself back to sleep.

* * * * *

(Christian)

As I walked down the white tiled hall of our secure lair, I realized I wasn't ready to face everyone just yet. Usually, once everyone awoke for the night, we'd all meet upstairs and head out together to feed before opening the club for business. But tonight... I just couldn't deal with everyone questioning my bad mood. I hadn't stopped drifting yet, so they'd immediately know something was wrong. Rose and I had been so happy since she moved in, and honestly, I was feeling a little embarrassed to admit we seemed to be having our first real fight.

So, instead of heading for the spiral staircase that led up into the club, I took the turn at the end of the hall which led to the area where the blood bags were kept. I would have to make do with cold blood tonight if I wanted to avoid everyone for a little longer.

"Hey, what are you doing down here?" Bobby asked as I entered the room.

So much for that plan. "Nothing. What are you doing here?"

"It's my turn to give Terrance his pity meal."

Evie had stocked the room with blood bags the night after Terrance had been chained up. Even though he had done some pretty bad things, she would never let him starve, so each night we took turns taking him his blood.

I turned around and started to head back to my room, but felt Bobby follow me out the door. "So, for real. What *are* you doing down here? I can tell you're upset. Did Rose stop putting out?" He chuckled, which was normal for Bobby—making light of every situation.

It didn't surprise me he picked up on the fact I was upset. He would have known even if I hadn't been drifting. Best friends always had a way of telling when something was wrong. Bobby and I had been best friends since the moment I'd saved him and petitioned that he be turned.

It was 1613, and we were in England to attend the marriage festivities of Frederick the Fifth and Princess Elizabeth, which included performances of six of Shakespeare's plays. Bobby had been one of the actors.

After one of the shows, the actors were drinking and apparently there'd been a scuffle and Bobby ended up getting shot through the chest. I'd been out walking, looking for someone to feed on, when I'd smelled the blood. They'd dumped his body in the river on the edge of the grounds. He was barely alive, but just enough that Evangeline was able to save him. We'd been best friends ever since.

"I just told Rose about her dad moving, and she didn't take it very well."

I prepared myself for his snide comment, but for once it didn't come. Our footsteps echoed in the hall as we continued to walk in silence toward Terrance's cell.

We didn't bother to stop and chat; Bobby just tossed the blood bag into Terrance's lap and kept walking, but then I heard something that stopped me dead in my tracks. *"I swear I'm gonna kill that bitch."*

Thankfully, I could now tell the difference when my *skills* flared up, allowing me to hear someone's thoughts. Before I just thought they'd been whispering something under their breath, but this was definitely one of Terrance's thoughts, and if it was about Rose—

"What did you just think? You swear you're gonna kill who? I promise you Terrance, if you are talking about Rose, I'll have Evie kill you tonight!"

He sat there staring at me while the muscle in his jaw ticked at an annoying pace. "I wasn't thinking about Rose. I was thinking about Meredith. The demon bitch who did this to me."

Bobby looked at me with a frown on his face. I was stunned into silence. This shouldn't be possible. Meredith's blood had infected Terrance, causing all memories of her to become fuzzy, ultimately hiding her involvement, even to him. He'd never been able to think clearly about her before, and shouldn't be able to think about her now, let alone contemplate killing her. Something was happening to him.

As I looked closer, I noticed his hair wasn't quite as dark and his eyes seemed slightly lighter too. *My god, could he actually be drifting back?* "Bobby, go get Evie. Now!"

CHAPTER FIVE

(Rose)

I woke up in Christian's bed... *our* bed, and immediately wanted to be somewhere else. I was shocked at the intensity of my feelings. Being with Christian had been all I'd wanted for the past year. But now, I just felt so stifled. I knew it was stemming from finding out about Dad selling our family home, but learning that had apparently opened a floodgate of emotions which were threatening to overwhelm me.

Maybe I could find Dad and smooth things over with him so we could live together again. Or maybe Jillian and I could get that apartment together like she wanted. I just knew that since becoming a vampire was no longer an option, I needed to come up with a new plan. It would take some time to figure out, but luckily time was on my side. As Christian had pointed out, their clan was in transition. They currently didn't have a Sire who could change me, and right now, that was a very good thing.

Christian wasn't even sure if he was truly the next in-line, but regardless of who the new Sire ended up being, it wouldn't matter. I'd never become a vampire, and I wasn't sure how I was going to convince Christian to let me go without telling him the truth.

However... the fight we just had presented me with a pretty good opportunity.

As much as it hurt me to do it, I would continue to act betrayed that he didn't tell me about my father sooner and slowly begin to pull away. But first, I had to find my dad. I needed to know if I was a wanted fugitive and how he really felt about everything that had happened. Maybe after leaving The Rising Pit, I could move back in with him and things could go back to normal. The problem was, I now had no idea where to begin my search.

My self-pity party continued as I got up to finish getting ready. I was just so mad, hurt, and confused. A year ago, I had a plan that would allow me to live forever with the man I loved, and now, everything was ruined. I pulled on a pair of jeans, a purple tank top, and slid into my flip-flops before flopping back down on the bed.

Grabbing my new cell phone, I prepared to dial Jillian. It was a risk, but it also seemed like the most logical thing to do. My parents had been friends with her parents for so long, and I didn't think my dad would have left town without telling them where he went.

"Jillian? It's Rose. Please don't hang up." I was happy she picked up at all since she wouldn't have recognized my new number. Christian had insisted I get a new phone when we'd gone into hiding.

"Hang up? Are you fucking kidding me? I've been worried sick about you! Where the hell are you?"

I almost burst out crying at the sound of her voice and the fact that she was worried about me. I wasn't sure how any of my friends would feel about me since I'd disappeared. "I'm sorry, I can't tell you where I am, but please know I'm okay. How are you? How have things been since I... left?"

"Oh my god, Rose, it's been crazy. First, you just disappear off the face of the earth, and then your dad up and sells your house to move to Masen and live with that woman. It's just been crazy. My parents are freaking out."

"Wait. What? Masen? What woman?"

"That Meredith bitch he was seeing. After you left, they moved to Masen together. Are you saying you haven't even talked to your dad this whole time?"

Oh God, no. She can't be alive and still with my dad. I dropped the phone and started to hyperventilate. This couldn't be happening. How the hell could she still be alive?

Jillian's voice echoed out of the speaker. "Rose, are you still there? Rose?"

Once the adrenaline kicked in, I grabbed my phone again. "Jillian, you can't tell anyone I called, okay?"

"What? Why? Rose, why can't you tell me what's going on? Your dad has been looking for you, and I miss you too. Where are you?"

With this new development, it was so important no one knew I'd contacted Jillian that I did the unthinkable... I threatened my best friend. "Jillian, I'm not kidding. You can't tell anyone I called. If you do, I'll kill you!"

Her loud exhale told me how offended she was, but right now I didn't care. I knew it made me seem like a real asshole, and possibly a psycho, but I couldn't risk anyone finding out I'd contacted her. They'd start poking around again, looking for me, and that was something I couldn't risk. Besides, the urgency I felt to get to Christian and tell him that we still had a demon problem to deal with, left me with no time to explain. Jillian was just going to have to continue to think I'd lost my mind.

I didn't wait for her response; I simply hung up and headed for the door. I couldn't believe Meredith was still alive and now had my dad within her reach 24/7.

CHAPTER SIX

(Meredith)

It didn't take me long to reach Damien's house. He only lived about ten miles away. He was the first demon I ran across after starting my search. He and his family had lived in the area for seventy-five years, and he told me I was the first demon outside their immediate family they'd ever met. We became fast friends. He was single and about the same age as Jeremy and I. He spent a lot of time with his cousins and started bringing them to our meetings. At this point, we had about twenty demons who showed up to our meetings on a regular basis. I was hoping that number would continue to grow.

As we made our way to the living room, he asked, "Hey, so what did you need to talk to me about that couldn't wait until this week's meeting?"

"I wanted to see how familiar you are with some of the ancient ways. I have something I want to share with the group, but wanted to run it by you first." I sat on the thread bare couch and waited for his response.

I could tell by the way he puffed up his chest he felt privileged that I'd chosen to share this information with him before anyone else. I didn't care how he felt as long as he was willing to do what I wanted. It wasn't because I met him first that I chose to share this information with him, but instead because after a little background check, he wasn't exactly the upstanding citizen he led everyone to believe. I was pretty sure he was a power hungry demon who'd revel in increasing his powers. Time to test my theory.

"My abuela use to tell me some pretty freaky stories. Why? What exactly did you want to know?" he asked.

"Well, did you know our demon ancestors actually drank human blood?"

"Yeah. She told me that and how they thought it would extend their life because they were ingesting another person's essence or some crazy shit like that."

Time to drop the bombshell. "It's not crazy shit. It works. It's happened to me."

His eyes grew to the size of saucers, but at least he didn't run away.

"I was injured recently, and because I chose to drink human blood to test the theory of our ancestors, I healed almost instantly." I waited to gauge his response before continuing. He was still staring at me but the glint in his eye was enough to tell me he was interested in what I had to say. "I also found that by drinking human blood, I gained inhuman amounts of strength."

Suddenly serious, he stood. "Show me."

I stood up from the couch, then picked it up with one hand.

"Believe me?"

The evil grin that spread across Damien's face was the last piece of confirmation I needed. I knew I'd picked the right guy. "Yes. Now who do we have to kill to get some fresh human blood?" He rubbed his hands together maniacally.

"That's exactly the question I hoped you'd ask."

We spent the next two hours going over everything I'd learned from my experience with the vampires and from killing Loraine. We talked about who else he thought would be willing to join us in enhancing our demon powers and our new quest for immortal life. He didn't have a clue about the vampires, but was now excited to start drinking human blood so he would be ready to take them on.

My plan was going perfectly. My recruiting had officially begun.

＊ ＊ ＊ ＊ ＊

(Jeremy)

My afternoon meeting flew by. It was now dusk and I was headed to The Rising Pit. I still had a gut feeling I'd catch a lucky break tonight. It'd been too long since I'd seen my daughter. When the accident happened, everything had been so chaotic. I hadn't been in my right mind and just sat there watching as she ran out of my life. But now that Meredith had recovered and we'd become settled in our new life together, it was time I found out exactly why Rose had attacked her in the first place.

Whenever I asked Meredith to give me details about that night, she would only say her memories were too foggy and that she couldn't say for sure. All she recalled was that she'd come over late to talk to me and had apparently startled Rose and Christian who seemed to be fighting. When she tried to step in, Rose went ballistic, yelling things about Meredith killing her mom and other ridiculous stuff.

That didn't sound like my Rose, but I saw her attack Meredith with my own two eyes and watched as she fled with her boyfriend. At this point, I wasn't really sure what to believe.

I eased my Lexus into the farthest parking spot I could find. It was in the very back corner of the club's lot and didn't have any lights surrounding it. So far, I was pretty pleased with my sleuthing skills.

I sat there for about twenty minutes before the club's front door opened and out walked Evangeline with a few members of her staff, but unfortunately, neither Rose nor Christian were amongst them. I blew out a frustrated breath, only to have all of them snap their heads in my direction. I knew they couldn't see me way back here, but I unconsciously slouched down in my seat. It felt as if they were looking right at me. I watched as Evangeline whispered something to one of the guys, sending him back into the club as the rest of them headed off in a different direction. It was all so odd.

I checked my watch and realized I'd only have another thirty minutes before I needed to hit the road to make it home in time for dinner. It looked like my lucky break wasn't going to happen after all.

CHAPTER SEVEN

(Rose)

The moment I entered the hallway I heard voices in the direction of Terrance's cell. I picked up my pace, anxious to see what the commotion was about, but especially because I was desperate to reach Christian and tell him that Meredith was still alive.

"Are you sure he's remembering her and not just going off the things he's heard us saying?" I heard Evie ask.

"No, he seems to be remembering specific things about her. I've been able to pick up on certain thoughts and they really are about Meredith," Christian replied.

I grabbed Christian's arm and spun him toward me. The worried look on his face had me holding my tongue.

"Terrance has started to remember things about Meredith. Somehow the thoughts are breaking through and he's really pissed about how she manipulated him," Christian blurted out. "I heard some of his internal thoughts when I was walking by earlier, and it appears he's starting to drift back. We're just trying to figure out how any of this is even possible."

"Well, I know one person we could talk to to find out." Everyone looked at me as if I'd sprouted another head. "Meredith. I just found out she's still alive."

Christian's mouth dropped open and Evie stumbled back a step, while Terrance just let out a roar that sent goose bumps racing up my arms. They were right... he did sound pissed.

"I'll kill that bitch for what she did to me. She caused me to lose the one and only thing I've cared about in over three-hundred years!" His chains rattled as he strained against them.

"How do you know this?" Evie asked.

I took a shaky breath, then answered. "I called Jillian. She told me my dad sold our house and moved to Masen to live with Meredith. Apparently, being a demon has some perks."

"I can't believe this. If she's still out there, then what's going to stop her from coming after Rose, or from infecting another vampire in the area to do her dirty work? We have to find her and kill her!" Christian was drifting so fast it was making me dizzy. Everyone else's emotions were starting to show as well. Seeing Evie with dark hair and an angry look on her face had me making a mental note to never piss her off.

"How are we going to kill her if she has super-healing abilities and lord knows what else? We know nothing about the demons except that they're really strong and fast, and we can't bite them because we'll become infected. We're flying blind here." Bobby, for once, was the voice of reason as he piped up from behind the group.

Evie's hair and eyes evened out as she stepped into the center of our little crowd. "Alright. Everyone just sit tight. Terrance, I'm sorry, but even though you're showing signs of breaking through whatever hold Meredith had on you, we just don't know enough to let you out yet. Christian, you and Rose stay here. I won't chance you running into Meredith until we come up with a plan. The rest of us need to go out and feed, but once the club's open tonight, I'm going to call Balam again to see if he can provide more information."

Terrance slid down to the floor, his head banging into the wall as the rest of the clan headed for the stairs.

"Do you want to go up and order some food?" Christian asked.

"Sure." I reached for his hand but immediately regretted it when a smile spread across his face. I couldn't let him think we were making up. Even with this new development, things hadn't changed for me. I was going to have to stick to my guns.

I pulled my hand out of his and started up the stairs, trying to think of a way to handle all of this. Currently... I was coming up blank.

Sounding defeated, Christian asked, "What would you like for dinner, Rose?"

"Chinese sounds fine."

After emerging from below the stage, I sat down at one of the tables as Evie, Dax, Bobby, Tori, and Dom left the club to go feed, while Renard and Loni both took seats at the bar. Christian pulled out his cell to place our order when Bobby suddenly walked back through the door. Using his vampire speed, he was at Renard and Loni's side in a split second.

"Excuse me a second, I need to see what's going on." Christian made his way over to them, while I sat still, straining to hear what was happening. I wondered what drama was unfolding now?

I hadn't really gotten to know much about the couple yet, except that Renard was originally from England and that's where they'd taken their honeymoon so he could show his cute American wife all the places he frequented as a human.

They both had a punk-rock look about them. Renard's hair was a dirty blond, smooth yet spiky at the same time. Loni had a short, edgy cut of blonde hair that was tipped in black. No one was sure why her hair had drifted like that once she was turned, but Evie assumed it was because she witnessed her sister being killed when she was a little girl. By the time she was went through the change, it was a distant memory, but Evie thought it was possible the scar it left still remained buried deep within her psyche. All I knew was that she was really sweet and pretty badass. She was the only female security guard on the staff. Now with Meredith being back in the picture, I was really glad they were both here to watch Christian's back.

* * * * *

(Christian)

"What's going on?" I asked.

"We just caught Rose's dad staked out in his car at the back of the parking lot. Evie wants Renard and Loni to follow him back to Masen so we can find out where Meredith is. It's a pretty lucky break. What are the odds he'd show up tonight after all this time?"

"Yeah, a lucky break." I knew I'd started drifting again as I walked back to Rose. How was I going to tell her that her dad was just outside and expect her not to go to him?

"So, what's up? What was that all about?" she asked.

"Let me order you some dinner first, and then we can talk about everything." I needed to allow as much time to pass as possible so hopefully her father would be long gone by the time I broke the news.

She crossed her arms and sat back in her chair. "Alright. But I'm not sure how much there is to talk about. It's obvious now why no one ever came after me for killing Meredith—because I didn't kill her. And as far as my dad's concerned, he made his choice to leave behind all memories of me and my mother to go be with her, so I don't see there's really anything to talk about at all." The tears shining in Rose's eyes broke my heart, and my will.

"I actually think there's a lot we need to talk about. Like how Meredith could somehow be controlling him like she was controlling Terrance. She could have forced him to sell the house and move to Masen with her; we really don't know. Until Evie gets some more information from Balam, I think we should just stay out of sight and off her radar, and unfortunately that means no more phone calls. But Rose, you should know, your dad still loves you and hasn't stopped looking for you. He hasn't left you behind. As a matter of fact, he was just sitting outside in his car probably hoping to catch a glimpse of you."

I knew I'd said the wrong thing when she stood up so fast her chair slammed to the floor. "Christian! My dad was just here and you didn't tell me?"

"Rose, please. I literally *just* found out."

It was clear she was too mad to hear anything else. She continued her rant without skipping a beat. "And how dare you try to tell me who I can or can't call? It's a damn good thing I did call Jillian, otherwise we wouldn't even know about Meredith!" She stomped toward the stairs but stopped before heading down. "Your whole clan is the same way. You all think you have the best ideas about what to do, but really... you guys don't have a clue about what's happening around here or how to handle any of it!"

I slammed my fist into the table, shredding it to splinters. Bobby, Renard, and Loni's heads were swiveling between me and a retreating Rose. So much for keeping our fight under wraps. This whole situation was out of control, and as much as I wanted to race after Rose and try to smooth things over, I couldn't... because she was right. We didn't have a clue what to do next. So, until Evie had more information and told us what the plan was, I'd just have to give Rose some space to cool off.

I was so tired of disappointing her.

CHAPTER EIGHT

(Meredith)

Damien and I were crouched around a homeless man in the alley behind the Salvation Army. The stench of sweat and garbage was almost too much for me to handle. But, I'd been so happy with the success of our conversation, we'd decided to put our theory to the test right away.

I'd gone over the plan again and again on our way over, and Damien was content with letting me start the process. I sunk my teeth into the man's neck, and with only a little pressure, had my first taste of warm blood since I'd killed Loraine. It was heaven. My body was filled with a rush of strength and my heart picked up its pace as the man's essence filled my soul.

"Enough, Meredith. My turn," Damien demanded. I was so caught up in the sensation I didn't realize I'd fed longer than expected.

"I'm sorry, you're right. Here." I tossed him the man's body and watched as he sank his teeth in the already open wounds on his neck. I was pleased but surprised he didn't show any signs of hesitation.

Watching the actual process and the effect human blood had on him was astonishing. It was almost as if Damien grew taller and wider right before me. The flare of red in his eyes signaled just how much he was enjoying the effects of the blood.

Breathing heavily and with crimson coating his mouth, Damien pulled away from the man and dropped his dead body to the ground. "It's working. I can feel it happening just like you said."

"I told you; you can trust me. Now that we know how to get stronger and extend our lives, I think it's time we started to look for others who'd do the same. Because once the vampires in Seela find out I'm still alive, they're going to come after me. The more demons we have ready to fight, the better our chances will be."

"I know a handful of people in my family that may be willing to join us, but the majority will be appalled by what we're doing."

I thought for a moment, then asked, "What if we don't tell them? What if we put some blood in the drinks at the next meeting, and little by little, feed them the essence that will make them all stronger? Once they realize they are being affected, they won't want to stop."

His sly smile told me he agreed with my plan. "You're brilliant. And gorgeous." In the next second I was being slammed against the hard brick wall. "I want you, Meredith. I want you right here, right now." I knew he was reacting to the high of the human blood in our veins, but I loved Jeremy and I wanted him to be the father of my baby... not Damien.

"Damien, back off!" I shoved him off of me and straightened my shirt. I was stronger than him and wasn't worried about stopping his advance. "I'm flattered, but there's no way I'm sleeping with you, and if you pull that shit again, I'll have your balls on a platter before you can blink. I need someone I can count on as my second, not someone whose emotions and feelings are going be an issue. Can I count on you, or should I start looking for someone else?"

"I'm sorry. I think I'm just overwhelmed by the blood in my system. Please accept my apology. Of course, you can count on me." He lowered his head and followed me out of the dark alley and back to the car.

"Good. I have to get home, but let's meet tomorrow night again, so we can gather more 'donors' to prepare for the next meeting."

A gluttonous smile spread across his face. "That sounds perfect!"

* * * * *

(Jeremy)

I wasn't sure, but I thought I was being followed as I headed back toward Masen. The blue SUV had been on me since I'd left The Rising Pit.

Evangeline and the rest of her crew—minus the guy who disappeared back inside—hadn't come back before I left. But as I pulled onto the freeway and pointed my car toward home, this truck had been behind me.

I thought maybe I was being paranoid, so during the two-hour drive from Seela to Masen, I tested my theory. I changed lanes, sped up and slowed down, and finally began to relax when I no longer saw the truck in my rearview mirror. I pulled out my cell to give Meredith a heads up I was almost home. "Hi, honey, I'm almost to the edge of town. Did you eat already or do I need to pick something up for us?"

"I would love some pizza if you're up for it. I can call Giovanni's and have it ready for pickup if you'd like."

Hearing her voice settled my nerves. After striking out on my stakeout, the idea of a romantic evening with Meredith was just what I needed. "Pizza and wine. That sounds perfect, babe. I'll be there in thirty minutes."

CHAPTER NINE

(Evie)

Once Renard and Loni were on their way to Masen to gather intel on Jeremy and Meredith, Dax and the others opened the club as I settled in my office and prepared to call my Sire once again.

I asked Christian to join me so he could relay the details of exactly what happened with Terrance if necessary.

Balam answered on the second ring, obviously recognizing my number from the caller id. "Evangeline. What's wrong? I didn't expect to hear from you again so soon."

"I'm sorry to bother you again, Sire, but our situation is far from over, and there have been some developments causing even more confusion."

"What developments, jovencita?" It was hard for him not to speak in his native tongue, but he knew I'd stopped speaking Spanish a very long time ago. But still, he couldn't resist calling me by the nickname he'd labeled me with so long ago... *young one.*

A small burst of laughter escaped me at the oddity of being called that. Me, a twelve-hundred-year-old vampire. But it did solidify just how ancient Balam truly was. I hoped being one of the original Maya people would lend itself to him possessing some more valuable information.

"The demon is still alive and my vampire son, Terrance, has shown signs of drifting back to normal. I was hoping you might have an idea as to how that's even possible. I know the rule is to deliver the true death to any vampire who's drifted permanently dark, but if he's drifting back, I think we need to make an exception to the rule." The speed of my explanation was apparently enough of a trigger for Balam to understand how panicked I truly was.

"Evangeline, calm down. After we last spoke, I contacted the other elders and we've discussed your situation at length. I think you're right; ending Terrance would be a mistake. He's the first vampire to ever go through something like this and come out of it alive. Our lack of information in the past has led to some unfortunate deaths, but now that we know demons are responsible for the few cases in which vampires drifted permanently dark, this is the perfect opportunity to study Terrance and his reactions, and maybe find a solution to the problem with his help."

Relieved, I closed my eyes and took a deep breath as I sunk into my leather chair. I was so happy Terrance would be allowed to live. Christian remained seated on the opposite side of my desk, watching me intently as he listened with his heightened hearing as Balam continued.

"I think one of the reasons Terrance has started drifting back is due to the lack of demon blood being introduced into his system. He hasn't fed from the demon in months, so it would make sense that her blood would work its way out of his system. Our rule of delivering the true death was something that Yum Camil established before my time and has always prompted us to end our affected brethren before they ever had a chance to recover."

If Balam was right, this would mean Terrance should soon drift back to normal and fully become part of our clan once more. But my hopes were dashed as Balam spoke again.

"Evie, you still aren't going to be able to let Terrance free. Even though the demon blood no longer poisons his system, we're not sure how the mind bond that was forged will be affected. Just because he's not feeding from her doesn't mean she couldn't still have the ability to control him."

Dammit! That was really bad news. Christian's eyes and hair were almost black as he shook his head. I knew how upset he was and exactly what he was thinking. Killing her, and every other demon we could find, was going to be our only choice.

"Balam, do you and the elders have any ideas on how we kill a demon?"

Silence hung in the air for a moment. "Let me contact the elders once more, and I will call you in a couple of days. The stories of our origins and that of the ancient demon culture are scarce, but I'm sure through our combined knowledge we'll be able to pinpoint the details you'll need to bring this nightmare to an end."

I thanked my Sire and hung up the phone. This was going to be a long couple of days.

"Do you think they have a chance of uncovering the information we need to destroy her?" The skepticism in Christian's voice proved he didn't think so.

"I'm not sure. We're facing something new for the first time in all of vampire history, and that means there are a lot of unknowns. Even Balam has never been through something like this. But I trust him to do everything he can to help us find the answer." With that, I pushed out of my chair and headed to find Dax. I knew my consort would want to know everything I'd just learned. Christian's hand on my shoulder stopped me just as I reached the door.

"Rose and I had a fight. She's mad at me for not telling her about her dad moving when we first found out. And now, with Meredith being alive, I think she's even more determined to contact her dad to find out what's going on. She's lost faith that we'll be able to control the situation, and I think she's losing faith in our relationship too. I don't know what to do."

The crestfallen look on his face had my heart breaking. This was Christian's first serious relationship in six-hundred years. "I'm so sorry, Christian, but try to understand. Rose has lost her entire family, and is now being forced to live with a bunch of vampires who can only interact with her at night. She must be feeling pretty alone, and then to find out we've been keeping things from her... you have to see how upsetting that could be."

"I do. But I wished I'd told her sooner. You said you wanted to gain more information first, and at the time, I agreed with you. But now, I think that might have been a mistake. We're going to have to trust her more. Especially since, once I become the new Sire she'll be my consort forever. I don't want any animosity between us right from the start."

"You're right. We do need to trust her more, but keep in mind, Christian, she's still human. Their emotions can make them do irrational things."

"Like run straight into the waiting arms of a demon because she misses her dad?" Christian asked.

"Exactly. And honestly, you do realize we have no way of stopping her from leaving during the day, don't you? Unless you plan to bite her and use your sedative, there's no other way to keep tabs on her while we sleep."

"I thought about that. And while I promised not to bite her, I could enlist someone else. And even though it will push her further away if she ever found out, I feel like she's leaving me no choice. I'm so terrified of what Meredith will do to her if she gets the chance. And Rose's fear for her father's safety is likely to push her straight into Meredith's grasp."

"Take tonight and think things over. If you want to use a human to guard her during the day, I know the perfect one. Just let me know what you decide."

* * * * *

(Christian)

I left Evie's office and took a trip around the club—for once doing my job instead of focusing on Rose. Well, almost. I needed time to think on how best to approach Rose with my apology... and my demands.

There was no way I could risk her running to her father only to fall prey to Meredith's scheme... whatever it was. I knew before I even reached the upper level of the club, I was going to take Evie up on her offer. I had to have someone who'd be able to watch over Rose while I was comatose. I would bite this human and program my sedative to turn him into her bodyguard. He would keep tabs on her, and if necessary, do anything and everything to protect her. People get body guards all the time...right?

CHAPTER TEN

(Rose)

I slammed the door to our room so hard I thought it would fly off its hinges. I couldn't believe my dad was just here and they'd all kept it from me. What harm could it have done for me to see him if he was alone? I hadn't killed Meredith, so it wasn't like I needed to worry about being chased by the cops any more, and talking to my dad might give us a better idea about what was happening with her. Then again, maybe Christian was right. Maybe she was controlling my dad like she controlled Terrance. Who knew? And even if she wasn't controlling him, I'm sure she was probably keeping tabs on him as a way to find and kill me.

I threw myself onto the bed and buried my face in my pillow. The familiar scent and texture had my eyes filling with tears. It was the pink pillow I'd had in my old room. The pillow my mom and I picked out together after our painting project all those months ago. *Months?* It felt like years.

Shortly after Christian and I had gone into hiding, I was so sad about having to leave my home, I longed for something to remind me of my old life. So, Christian, without Evie's knowledge, snuck back into my house and grabbed some of my clothes and a few small things that wouldn't be missed, including my pillow. He hadn't run into my dad or anyone else, and I was so grateful to have some of my things, I never even considered the risk.

Yes, we'd thought Meredith was dead at the time, but he could have run into her. If he'd bitten her, he would have drifted dark and been under her control, just like Terrance... which was the same thing that would happen if he bit me.

God, this was such a nightmare.

I sat up, resolute in my decision. I would put an end to this here and now. I grabbed the box of my things stashed under the bed and found my special stationery and pen. I'd write Christian a letter, telling him it was over. I had to get out of this situation while I had a good reason, and right now, with how mad I was and all the "fighting" we'd been doing, it was the perfect time.

I'd just finished my letter when I heard footsteps outside the door. I watched as the knob slowly turned and Christian called out, "Rose, are you in there?"

I quickly crumpled the paper, threw it into the box, and pushed the whole thing back under the bed. I simply wasn't ready to give it to him just yet. I needed to know what he and Evie found out from Balam, and I figured I could always rewrite it and give it to him later. Or possibly leave it on the bed during the day while he slept, taking the coward's way out.

"I'm here."

His head was hanging low as he made his way to join me on the bed. "I'm sorry."

I sat in silence, considering the best way to handle this. I couldn't forgive him like I wanted to, throwing my arms around his neck and kissing him until we ended up having make-up sex. No, I had to keep my shields in place. He had to believe I was still mad, or else he'd dig for the real reason I was leaving. A reason I could never reveal.

"I hate fighting with you, Rose. Can we please talk this through? I already explained I didn't tell you about your dad moving because Evie wanted to gather more information first, but I admit that was a mistake. And about what just happened upstairs, I honestly just found out about your dad being here right before I told you, I swear."

"I believe you. But Christian, the problem is... I'm starting to feel like a prisoner here. I should've been happy to find out I'm not a wanted murderer, but instead, I still have to remain here, hidden and scared, because the woman I *tried* to kill is still alive and wants me dead. I love you, and I appreciate Evie taking me in and everyone accepting me, but I miss my friends and my dad. This whole situation has been twisted around, and I'm just not sure if staying here is the right thing for me anymore."

The shocked on his face was enough to make me want to take everything back. I hated hurting him. But if things went back to the way there were, he'd think I was still planning to become his consort, and that was something that could never happen. At least this way, I was protecting him from being *truly* hurt.

"Rose, I know you're mad, and I certainly don't want you to feel like a prisoner here, but you have to understand we need you to remain under wraps for your own safety. I wish I was the new Sire already so I could just change you into a vampire, and then we wouldn't have to worry about any of this anymore. Meredith couldn't hurt you once you were like me."

I pushed off the bed and spun around to face him. "How can you say that? You guys are in more danger from Meredith than I am. If you bite her, you'll become infected. And then she can control you. Have you forgotten that? At least with me, the *human*, all she can do is kill me. I'd rather be dead than controlled."

"Dammit, Rose!" Christian flew across the room and had me by the arms in the next second. "No, I haven't forgotten any of what's happened, but don't you dare say stuff like that. Don't you dare say you'd rather be dead! I can't bear to hear it." He released me and ran his hand through his rapidly drifting hair. "I know vampires can't bite her, but soon, we'll have the information we need to kill her. If you were a vampire, you'd be strong enough to stand against her. That's all I meant."

I hated putting him through this. I almost meant what I'd said. I'd rather be dead, if only to avoid causing him pain. "Christian, I'm sorry this is hard to hear, but I'm going to reach out to my dad and find out what's going on very soon. There's really nothing you can do to stop me, and it upsets me to think you'd even want to try. Don't you want to know what's going on with Meredith?"

Christian was breathing heavy and he hadn't stopped drifting, but I didn't expect the menace in his voice when he said, "Evie already sent Renard and Loni to check things out with your dad and the demon. We should know their whereabouts by tomorrow. But Rose... you're wrong if you think there's nothing I can do to stop you."

CHAPTER ELEVEN

(Meredith)

After spending a perfect evening with Jeremy, eating pizza, drinking wine, and making love, I took the next day off from work, faking a cold. I had too much to do to prepare for the next demon meeting.

Damien and I were going to meet in an hour to check out the prospects for tonight's bloodletting. He'd been disappointed when I told him we wouldn't be able to continue drinking and draining our victims to death. No, we had to start draining and storing it so it could be introduced to the other demons at the meetings as planned, though killing the *donors* was still the ultimate end to the process.

"I'll be there in an hour. Are the workers still in the area?" I asked.

"Yes. They're taking a lunch break now, but once the horn sounds, they branch off again and head to their designated areas. There's one section way in the back and only two workers are assigned there. It's perfect."

"I'll decide if it's perfect once I'm there. I'm leaving now."

Damien had found what he thought was the perfect place to obtain some of our victims. There was a local logging facility outside of town that had recently hired a large crew of temporary employees. He figured it would be the ideal situation since there were so many new faces; it was likely that no one would miss the men we took.

Honestly, I didn't care if they were missed or not, as long as I got what I needed and we didn't leave any evidence behind. I wasn't stupid and had recently bought a bundle of gloves so our fingerprints wouldn't be found in the area. We'd have to knock these men out and transport them to a secure location before draining them.

When Damien first told me his plan, I looked up the area on the computer and found an abandoned hunting shack just a quarter mile from the location. I figured with my demon speed, it wouldn't take me long to transport the men there to meet their death. I had everything we needed to make it look like they wandered off and met their end by way of a wild animal. I was sure we could make this work.

As I gathered the last of my supplies and stuffed them in my oversized purse, I glanced out the kitchen window and noticed a blue SUV parked across the street. I couldn't recall if it had been there last night, but I'd lived here long enough to notice a strange car in the vicinity. I looked closer but didn't see anyone in the vehicle, so I made a mental note to check and see if it was still there later tonight.

I eased into my BMW, excited about starting this next phase of my plan, and sped toward my meeting with Damien.

* * * * *

(Renard)

It didn't take long for Jeremy to notice he was being tailed, so I backed off and let him think he lost us. Evie had been very specific with her instructions. We were to follow him and find out where he and Meredith lived, but were not to engage either one of them.

After tailing him to some pizza joint and the liquor store, we finally watched him pull his Lexus into the garage of an old brownstone off of 29th Street. It was a nice neighborhood; the streets were lined with tall trees and the lawns were manicured to a perfect green. We parked across the street and flew from the car to the shadowed area within the park that sat slightly to the east of their residence.

After feeding from a couple who'd been strolling in the park, I made sure the street was clear before Loni and I crept toward the house. We took care to remain as stealthy as possible, since we were still unsure of the extent of Meredith's demon powers. There was no need for us to worry though, as we found them occupied and distracted. From what we were seeing, it looked like Rose's father was enjoying being with the demon *very* much.

We spent the night watching the house from the car. After their romantic evening, they went to bed like any normal couple. We used our enhanced hearing to listen as Meredith washed her face while Jeremy brushed his teeth, then they slid into bed and slept until their alarm woke them at 5 a.m.

The sun had yet to rise, but knowing it would happen soon, we had to find a place to hide. Evie asked us to stay for another night to see if we could catch a break of any kind, so that meant we'd be comatose somewhere for the entire today.

"What about the hotel around the block? We wouldn't even have to move the car, we could just run there and check in," Loni suggested. She hated being in the car.

We'd recently returned from our honeymoon in Europe, where we'd trekked across the region during the night, hiding and sleeping in hotel rooms with "Do Not Disturb" signs hung from the doors during the day. It had apparently become our "thing."

"Sure thing, crumpet. Sounds like a good idea. We'll leave the car here so we don't lose our spot. Let me just grab our things out of the boot and we'll knock off." We climbed out of the car, and I took note of how soon the sun would be up. It was something built-in to our vampire DNA. We had less than two hours before the sun rendered us comatose, so we started walking down the sidewalk toward the hotel. After a few steps, I took one last look back at the brownstone and saw Jeremy looking out their bedroom window from the second story. *Bloody hell.* We were busted.

My gut instinct was to grab Loni, and with our vampire speed, get the hell out of dodge. But I didn't want to give Jeremy any more fodder to fuel his assumptions. So instead, I reached out for Loni's hand and hoped it looked like we were just a young couple out for a stroll. *At five in the morning... yeah right.*

I didn't risk turning around again, and in just a few minutes we reached the hotel, checked in, and hung the Do Not Disturb sign on the door. With the locks in place, Loni headed for the loo to take a bath, and I dialed Evie to check in one last time before nodding off.

"I think Jeremy saw us."

"Don't worry. Your recent absence is something that will work in our favor. Neither Jeremy or Meredith have seen you or Loni here before. Get some rest, but as soon as you wake, head back to the car and see if you can find out anything that could be of help to us."

"Roger that. Goodnight, Evie."

"Goodnight, Renard."

CHAPTER TWELVE

(Christian)

After Rose's and my fight, I left our room again, slamming the door in my wake. I was so mad at the way she was acting. It had been really hard to hear she was feeling like a prisoner here. How could being with the person you love feel like a prison? I loved her beyond measure. So much so, I recently gotten a tattoo to demonstrate the very fact.

It was three words done in Slavic runes: Truly, Madly, Deeply. It was located on my upper right shoulder-blade and was meant to describe how I lived and loved. I loved Rose with all my heart, but I was starting to question if she still felt the same.

I understood finding out Meredith was alive changed the situation for her... for us all, really. It had been good news Rose wasn't a wanted criminal, but I knew she feared for her father's safety again. What I didn't understand was why this had changed things between us.

"Hey. Can I talk to you?"

I hadn't realized I was in front of Terrance's cell until he'd called out.

"What do you want to talk about?" I leaned against the opening of his cell and watched as he paced what little distance he could while still chained to the wall.

"Have you found out where that demon bitch is yet?"

"Evie has Renard and Loni checking it out. They're supposed to be back tomorrow night."

"I'm going to kill her, Christian. Just find out where she is and let me out of here, and all our problems will be over. I'll make her pay for what she did to Loraine and me."

I remembered Terrance expressing his feelings for Loraine when Rose and I had questioned him months ago. But none of us had talked about it since.

"Did you really love her?" I asked.

"Yes." Exhaling, he stopped his angry pacing and leaned his back against the cell's cinderblock wall. "She was honestly the first person I loved since losing my family and being turned." His shoulders sagged and his head dropped, and I realized I was starting to feel sorry for him.

"Well, as soon as we learn how to kill her, I'll let you know. But honestly, I'm not sure Evie will let you out, even though you're obviously drifting back. She won't risk Meredith still having control you. This may be a fight you're going to have to sit out."

His chains rattled as he started drifting and pacing again. "She killed Loraine and messed with my mind! Made me lie to everyone I cared about and to Rose. She has to be stopped, and I want revenge for Loraine. I loved her, Christian. I really did."

"Then you and Rose have a common goal."

It was in that moment I realized I wouldn't be biting a human to guard Rose during the day. She needed to meet with her dad and start planning revenge for her mother. She hadn't killed Meredith the first time, but with all of our help... she wouldn't fail again.

"Hang in there, Terrance. I'll let you know what we find out."

CHAPTER THIRTEEN

(Meredith)

"I'm impressed." The logging site Damien scouted out really was ideal. Merry little men hustled around doing their manly work, yet in the last designated area of the site, there were only two workers far removed from the rest of the crew. "Let's go check out the hunting shack and get everything set up, then we'll head back down here just before quitting time."

"Okay, boss. Sounds good. Let me grab the stuff from my truck."

I watched Damien gather his supplies as I did the same. We were parked far enough from the work site, along a lone dirt road, that if anyone happened to stumble upon our vehicles, they would most likely think they belonged to a couple of hikers exploring the woods.

"Do you have everything?" I asked.

"Si. Do you need me to carry anything for you?"

"No. Let's just get this over with. I want to have everything set up before sundown, so when the final horn of the day blows, we can just grab them and go."

The excitement on his face was clear. He couldn't wait to kill these men and get another taste of fresh human blood.

"Do you think if we moved this week's meeting up to tonight, all of your cousins would be able to attend?" I asked.

"I think so. But why do you want to move it up? So, the blood will be fresher?"

"Actually, it's because I saw a strange car outside my house this afternoon before I left. I think the vampires have found me, and I need to get our people ready to fight as soon as possible."

"Are you sure it's the vampires?"

"No, but I won't risk it. I'm going to check the car out tonight when I return home, but I think it's better to be safe than sorry. Call your cousins and tell them the meeting's been bumped up."

"You got it."

*****

(Jeremy)

As the squawk of my morning alarm penetrated my ears, I slowly started to wake. But suddenly, the alarm wasn't the only noise piercing the silence. A car door slammed outside my bedroom window, followed by the chirp of its alarm being set.

This was usually a quiet neighborhood, and not many people were out the door before me. So, sluggishly, I made my way to the window and looked outside. The moment I noticed the young couple walking down the street, my weary eyes popped open and my paranoia revved into high gear. The car they left parked across the street looked exactly like the one from last night—the one that had been following me.

The young man glanced back at the car and then met my eyes for a split second. He wasn't anyone I recognized, and neither he nor his girlfriend looked menacing, just out of place. They resembled what I'd describe as a couple of European grunge pop stars. At least that's how Rose described some of the bands she used to listen to.

Rose. I missed my girl so much, and now having this couple show up here, a couple I was sure had followed me from The Rising Pit... I had to get back there and continue my search.

Maybe this weekend I would take Meredith out for a night on the town. A night that would include dancing at the club. When I'd been there looking for Rose, it seemed like a really nice place, and hopefully, if I could spend a little time inside, I might just discover the clues I needed to find my daughter.

Dinner, dancing, and some detective work sounded like the perfect weekend to me.

*****

(Damien)

I was so happy Meredith was pleased with my plan. I'd remembered this logging site from when my cousin had been one of their part-time workers a few months back. It was notorious for always having different workers constantly coming and going. Once I'd scouted the area, I figured the far back parcel would be the perfect place to snag some blood donors.

I gathered my 'set-up' supplies: some drugs, needles, pipes, etc., and the tubs we were going to be draining the blood into, then headed over to Meredith.

She was so beautiful. Her long blonde hair and that tight little ass. I'd blamed my reaction in the alley on the blood high I'd been experiencing, but really, it was because I'd wanted her from the moment we met.

I worked on the east side of town as a construction manager, and very rarely had a need to travel into the city. But on that particular day, I was headed downtown to drop off some building permits, and that's where I'd first laid eyes on Meredith.

She and Jeremy were having lunch at one of the outdoor cafés that littered the downtown area. The moment I laid eyes on her my body reacted. Desire flowed through my veins like hot lava. Not only was she sexy, but the red flare in her eyes had me assuming both she and Jeremy were demons. *Finally, another female demon that wasn't related to me.*

After gaining control, I'd walked past the lovebirds and went about my business, but on my way back out she'd been sitting alone and waved me over.

We started talking and she explained she realized I was a demon when my eyes flared as I walked by the table earlier. I guess I hadn't hidden my reaction to her as well as I thought. She told me Jeremy was still in the dark about his heritage, but that she was planning to set up a group where demons could get together and discuss their ancestry. She was happy to hear I had a large, extended family I thought would like to attend.

"Do you have everything?" she asked, pulling my attention back to the present.

"Yes. Do you need me to carry anything for you?"

"No. Let's just get this over with. I want to have everything set up before sundown, so when the final horn of the day blows, we can just grab them and go."

She was so strong and in control, which was fucking sexy. I couldn't wait to see how she handled herself tonight. How she would use her demon strength and speed to take care of business.

I wasn't sure if I would be able to control my lust for her a second time.

CHAPTER FOURTEEN

(Rose)

I felt the tears soaking my face before I even realized I was crying again. I'd been so shocked when Christian stormed out of our room after our second fight of the day.

What had he meant when he said I was wrong if I thought he couldn't stop me? He better not be thinking of biting me and using his sedative on me or else this whole charade would be over in a heartbeat.

As things stood right now, it wouldn't be too far of a stretch for people to think I'd walked away after finding out Christian had been keeping things from me. That was a "typical" reason people broke up all the time. The problem was... I loved him, and I wished I didn't have to leave, not to mention I had nowhere to go.

I couldn't return to my house, and I couldn't go after my dad since Meredith was there waiting for me. I didn't think she was controlling him, even though I couldn't tell Christian and his clan that. They'd wonder how I knew or what made me so sure. The fact that he was a demon would be the first clue, but I wasn't even sure that was an accurate assumption.

A knock at the door startled me. I wiped the tears from my face and crossed the room, opening the door to see Evie's smiling face.

"May I come in?" she asked.

"Sure."

"Thank you. Do you mind if we sit and talk for a moment?"

"Sure." I sounded like a broken record. I wasn't sure what Evie would have to talk to me about, and I really wasn't in the mood for another speech about how much Christian loved me. I knew he loved me, but unfortunately that didn't matter anymore.

"I wanted to talk to you about Terrance." Evie sat on the edge of the bed, and I slowly eased down beside her, slightly shocked.

"Okay. What about him?"

"I'd like to talk about the time you spent with him while your mother was alive."

Oh, hell no. This was not something I wanted to get into with Evie. When I explained all those months ago that Terrance had been the first vampire I'd met, I told them while everything he said had been a lie, he'd never hurt my mom. What else could she possibly want to know?

"Specifically, I want to talk about Terrance's relationship with your mother. You said he was always very gentle with her, but do you truly believe that he loved her?"

"Um... I'm not sure. Like I said before, he never hurt her and always treated her like she was special to him, but being in love with her? I just don't know. Why does it matter? My mom's gone, and even if he did love her, she loved my dad... not Terrance," I stated definitely.

"I know that, Rose. Please understand, I'm not trying to insinuate they were having an affair, but Terrance has claimed he wants vengeance on Meredith for killing your mom... the woman he loved."

I was suddenly on my feet. "What? He wants to go after Meredith to avenge my mom?"

"Yes, that's what he said."

"Well, isn't that a good thing? That he's remembering and wanting to go after her?"

"Yes, I'm very happy he's showing signs of drifting back, and that his memories are returning. But what I'm concerned about is that he may be using his feelings for your mother as an excuse to get released, when reality, he could be following Meredith's commands without our knowledge. That's why I'm asking your opinion. Looking back, do you think he was *truly* in love with your mother?"

I thought about my response, knowing what I'd say could make a difference in Terrance's release. But if he was willing to go after the person who killed my mom, I thought the risk was well worth it. "Yes. Thinking back to their interactions, I could definitely see he was probably in love with her."

"Alright. Thank you, Rose. I have a lot to think about, but just know that as soon as I hear from Balam, I'll call a meeting to discuss our plans to go after Meredith, and I want you to be there. No more secrets, I promise."

"Thank you, Evie. That means a lot to me."

I watched as she gracefully made her way out the door and thought to myself... *no more secrets? Yeah, right.*

* * * * *

(Christian)

As I rounded the corner at the end of the hall, I saw Evie knocking on Rose's and my door. She rarely entered our private rooms, so I was more than curious about her presence here.

I watched as Rose answered the door and then Evie disappeared inside. I thought now was as good a time as any to practice my newly developing skills, so I eased up to the door and flattened myself against the outside wall.

I'd never tried to use my *super-hearing* on purpose before, so I was unsure of how to even begin. But remembering the advice Evie had given me, I began to relax and concentrated on exactly what I wanted to do.

I took four deep breaths and imagined my ears opening up to let the outside thoughts around me filter in. Then I heard Evie asking, *"...but do you truly believe that he loved her?"*

I remained calm and listened as Evie continued to talk to Rose about Terrance and his feelings for her mother. But it didn't take long to realize I couldn't hear anything Rose was thinking in response. All the thoughts rapidly drifted away, and I was left with nothing but my irritation.

Why did Rose still feel like she had to hide her thoughts around us? I knew that was exactly what she was doing, because she'd explained Terrance had once informed her it was necessary. At the time though, she didn't know that only Evie and Dax were capable of scanning, and they only saw the thoughts of what you were immediately thinking. We explained all of this to her, and I thought she trusted us enough to no longer feel it was necessary. *Guess I was wrong.*

I supposed I couldn't blame her for not wanting Evie to know what she was thinking at the moment. I'm sure her head was spinning having to contemplate another man besides her father being in love with her mom. Under those circumstances, I would probably want to keep those thoughts private too.

I let go of my frustration and waited for Evie to emerge from our room. I wanted to ask her why she thought questioning Rose about this was necessary.

She didn't seem surprised to find me waiting outside. "I heard you approach and was scanning you as you tried to use your new ability. I take it you couldn't hear any of Rose's thoughts either?"

"No. But I'm sure it's just a habit of hers at this point. I was thinking about trying with her again later. I'm hoping if I can get my ability to work around her, it might give me a clue as to what she's planning and an idea of how to smooth things over between us."

"Alright. Just let me know if you're successful. And to answer your internal question, I'm debating releasing Terrance against Balam's judgment. I have a theory I want to put to the test, and Rose's thoughts about his feelings for her mother may prove important."

"What's your theory?"

"I'm not ready to discuss it yet, but once I have all the puzzle pieces in place, you'll be one of the first to know. Now why don't you give Rose some time alone and accompany me upstairs. There's something else I'd like to talk to you about."

As much as I wanted to enter our room and apologize to Rose yet again, I didn't think it would help at the moment. So, following Evie's suggestion, I left Rose alone and trailed behind her as we made our way back up to her office through her private entrance from the pit.

"Have a seat," Evie said, extending an arm in the direction of the couch along the far wall of her office.

Her formality suddenly had me nervous.

"What's up?"

"I'd like to discuss you becoming the next Sire. I know I said I'd like to wait to see what other powers you developed first, but honestly, with the situation we're facing, I'd like to perform the Passing of Powers ritual soon. I think it's important to make you a Sire right away."

My gut tightened, and I knew I'd begun to drift at her statement. This was such a huge step. For Evie, for me, and especially for Rose. It meant we wouldn't have to wait any longer for her to become a vampire and my consort. I was immediately overjoyed at the thought.

"There's one more thing," Evie continued. "I know it's traditional for a new Sire to take his consort and relocate, beginning their new life somewhere else, but in this case... I'd like you to remain with our clan."

I'd always assumed it was mandatory that the new Sire leave their old clan behind, so I was thrilled to receive Evie's offer. Leaving my family had always been the one thing I considered a downfall to becoming the next Sire.

"I'd love for me and Rose to stay here with the clan, but isn't that against the rules?"

"I've thought about it, and while leaving your old clan is *traditional* for a new Sire, I don't think it's ever truly been mandatory. I believe it was just a tradition that'd been passed down from Sire to Sire, clan to clan. Regardless, I think it's time we tested the theory, because the real reason I want to speed up this process, is so that when we finally face the demons, we'll have two Sires here instead of just one. We'll deal with whatever conflicts arise after this situation is resolved. Agreed?"

"Agreed. When do you want to do the ritual?"

"Right now."

CHAPTER FIFTEEN

(Rose)

After Evie left our room, I paced around aimlessly trying to gain control of the chaos in my mind. I couldn't believe Terrance had truly loved my mom. When he'd said all things those months ago, I hadn't really processed it at the time. Being faced with the demon who'd killed my mom had been a pretty big distraction. But now, I wasn't sure if it bothered me or was something I should be thankful for. I suppose the time they spent together was even safer and more pleasant for Mom, considering he did love her. God, I couldn't think about this right now.

I headed up to the club through Evie's private entrance, since coming up from under the stage while the club was in full swing wasn't allowed for obvious reasons. As the bookcase opened into her office, I saw her and Christian sitting on the couch against the far wall. "Excuse me, I didn't mean to interrupt. I'm just going to go blow off some steam on the dance floor if that's alright?"

"I'll be out to find you shortly," Christian replied stiffly.

I didn't respond, but instead walked out into the fray of happy people, bumping and grinding to the sultry beat filling the air.

I headed to the bar and plopped down on a stool where Tori and Dominique were working their usual magic. They made really good tips and had a loyal customer base since they were such great bartenders. I'd gotten to know them better while staying her, and they were both down to earth, kind hearted, and really funny. I'd spent more time with Dom though, because every chance she got, Tori would leave the club. Dom explained it was because she didn't get out of the house much when she was human, so now, she just really loved being outdoors.

I could relate.

I knew I wouldn't be allowed to go outside, especially at night when it was more likely I could run into trouble, but man... I really needed to get away. Find somewhere private and just think.

A light went off in my head. *Private.* The private rooms upstairs were used as feeding rooms for the visiting vampires, but if I could find an empty one, maybe I could finally get some time alone. Plus, I really wasn't looking forward to Christian "finding me shortly." I wasn't ready to have to put up my walls again. It was getting so hard not to fall into his arms and cry my eyes out. Especially since he explained everything. But this was for his own good, and I loved him too much to let anything ever happen to him. Besides, I knew as the years passed, he'd eventually get over me and move on.

Tears flooded my eyes at the thought, and I pushed off my stool, making my way through the crowd. Once I climbed the stairs to the second floor, I started toward the farthest room at the end of the hall, but didn't get far.

Someone grabbed me.

* * * * *

(Christian)

"Now? You want to make me the new Sire right now?"

"Yes. I think the sooner the better. I've told Dax my plan but no one else knows. I think it will be to our advantage to keep it a secret."

"So even if I become the Sire now, you want me to wait to change Rose?"

"I'm sorry, but yes. I think it would be to our benefit if the demons still think we don't have an active Sire to create new vampires. Plus, I feel whatever information Balam provides in regards to killing them, it will truly be to our advantage having two Sires instead of one. The element of surprise will be on our side."

I considered Evie's plan. It was a good one, I was just extremely nervous. I didn't think this day would be upon us for quite some time, and I wasn't sure I could keep it from Rose. "Alright, but even if I can't change Rose yet, I still want to tell her it's done. I don't want to keep any more secrets from her."

"That's fine. But please make sure she understands the necessity of keeping it secret. I don't even want the rest of the clan to know until I'm ready. I won't risk one of them becoming infected by accident and having this knowledge to share with our enemies."

"Alright. I'm ready. Should we go downstairs?"

Evie looked at the door and the lock slammed into place. I always forget about her telekinesis. "We'll be undisturbed. Let's begin."

"What do I need to do?" I asked, unsure of my part in all of this.

"Nothing. It's actually a very quick process. I will perform the ritual and say the words, then everything else happens internally. You'll feel a rush of additional strength as the poison of true death and the sedative of eternal life flow into you. Are you ready to begin?"

I shifted slightly on the couch, rubbing my sweaty palms against my jeans. "What if I'm not really the one being triggered? What if this clairaudient power is something else completely?" I couldn't help but share my insecurities. I was afraid of not being the one, and I didn't want Evie to attempt the ritual if it wasn't meant to be me.

"Christian, your clairaudience is just another psychic power which allows you to hear the unspoken. There is no doubt you're the one. Now please, trust me."

"Okay, Evie. I do."

She instructed me to lie down and stood over me with her hands extended. She explained she would be reading my energy and only when it was time to "pass the powers" would she be biting me. I closed my eyes and listened as she began.

Her voice carried the Sire command as she chanted, "I call on my ancestors, join me now. Flow through me as Christian completes this vow. The new Sire, he is triggered to be. Now let my powers flow from me."

In the next instant she'd shoved my head to the side and sunk her fangs into my neck. My body arched off the couch as warm liquid flowed into my veins. It felt similar to being turned, but a hundred times more intense.

I was bombarded by a variety of colors layering my mind. I saw sparkling yellow as the sedative of eternal life spread throughout my body. Then flashes of green blinded me as the poison of true death settled deep within my heart. It felt as if these powers were filling up special compartments within me, and the strength they carried with them was truly a blessing from the gods. The last thing to happen was the scanning ability snapping into place.

As soon as Evie released me, I bolted off the couch and grabbed my head. The noise was too much to bear. I assumed this was an unforeseen side-effect of the scanning ability combining with my clairaudience. But whatever it was, it sucked.

I was suddenly overwhelmed with the loud noises of everything and everyone in the vicinity. The club's music, people calling out their orders to Dom and Tori. Pieces of conversation rang through my head like a cacophony of squawking birds, and then I heard the one thing that overshadowed all the rest... Rose's scream.

CHAPTER SIXTEEN

(Renard)

After spending the day comatose in the hotel, Loni and I awoke with the sun's disappearance and immediately started making our plans for the night.

"Do you think Jeremy knows who we are? Are we in trouble here?" Loni asked.

"No, poppet, we don't need to worry. Jeremy isn't a threat. Even if he was daft enough to attack us, we could easily rectify the situation and make him forget. No, I'm not worried about him. But we do have to worry about Meredith. We need to see what she's up to. My suggestion for tonight is to feed in the park again, but then we need to move the car and keep watch from a different location. Hopefully, she'll make a move that'll shed some light on her powers or possibly her intentions."

"Alright, my love. Sounds like a plan." Loni kissed me, long and deep, and if we didn't need to rush to move our car from its present location, I would have sank back down onto the bed and relived some of the other fond memories from our honeymoon.

* * * * *

(Meredith)

Snagging the two workers had gone just as planned. As the horn signaled the end of their day, we knocked them out and rush them to the abandoned hunting shack.

I could tell Damien was having a hard time keeping his desire to drink from these humans in check. But after I told him he could have a small sip to begin the draining process, his mood quickly improved.

"I can't believe how quickly the changes take effect. I can feel my strength increase almost immediately." He made his point by slamming his fist through the solid log wall.

"What the hell are you doing?" I dropped the human I was holding and flew to within an inch of his face. "We've taken care to set this whole scene, and you think slamming a hole through the wall isn't going to raise a few questions?"

"Who cares? If anyone did track this scene back to us, I'd kill them. Problem solved."

"Problem solved? Problem solved?" My rage was boiling over, and I was sure my eyes were glowing red. I slammed him against the wall he'd just put the hole in. He may have just gained a boost in strength, but there was no way he could compare to me. "You listen to me, you blood-hungry asshole. I will not let you put everything I'm working toward in jeopardy by leaving a trail of bodies across this city. What we're doing has to be kept on the down low. I can't risk the vampire's finding out."

He pushed off the wall, shrugging out of my grasp. I let him go. "Fine. I'm sorry. I won't kill anyone without your *permission*." He paced the room, looking at the bodies on the floor, and after a deep breath continued, sounding remorseful. "I'll fix the hole. I have a sledgehammer in my truck we could leave here as evidence. I'll wipe it down, so all we'll have to do is put one of these guys' prints on it and we should be in the clear. A sledgehammer could easily put a hole like that through a wall this old."

For being as hot-headed as he was just moments ago, his plan actually had merit. I was pretty sure it would work. "Okay. Hurry and go get the hammer. I'll finish draining these two and make sure all the animal scratches and drugs are in place."

"Okay. And Meredith, I really am sorry."

I gave him a quick nod and watched as he sped out the door. It was becoming apparent I would have to monitor his blood intake. This whole situation was an unknown for both of us, but it was obvious that drinking human blood affected different people in different ways.

I became euphoric after drinking Loraine's blood, but I hadn't gone insane or power hungry. And I couldn't risk having a loose cannon as my second in command. If he ever pushed my boundaries, though, he'd find out that only a stronger demon could kill another demon—and I'd be making sure I remained the strongest of them all.

With this exact plan in mind, I pulled out the extra bag I'd brought and began siphoning off some extra blood for my personal stores, taking a moment to have a small taste. The warm blood flowed down my throat and filled me again with strength and joy. I was truly becoming immortal.

Damien returned just as I'd finished draining the second body. He swallowed hard as he saw the last drop of blood hit the container. I began our cleanup and removed all the IV equipment from our victims, then staged their bodies like we'd planned, adding the sledgehammer as the final touch.

"It looks good. Really believable," Damien said.

"Yes it does. The claw marks, blood, and fur certainly give it that wild feel we need." I laughed as we carried out the containers of blood and the rest of our supplies. "Did you get a hold of your family? Are they going to be able to make tonight's meeting?"

"Yes. They will all be there, though only a few are aware of what's happening. I told you a few of them would be down with drinking blood, but I've instructed them not to say anything to the others. We should be able to spike the drinks as planned and everyone will begin gaining strength and speed by the end of the night."

"Thank you, Damien. I appreciate your help. Now we just have to keep that temper of yours in check. No more blood for you tonight, okay?"

"I agree. I think I've reached my limit for today."

Watching his jaw twitch had me questioning his statement. I wasn't convinced I wouldn't have a problem with him at tonight's meeting. Maybe, I better start looking for someone else to replace him now. I'd have to pay special attention to everyone's reaction to the blood tonight. Perhaps one of his relatives would have a little more self-control.

Once we reached our vehicles and stowed our bounty, I explained the plan for tonight's meeting. "I'm going to run home and change, then I'll meet you at the conference hall. I want to get there around 7:45 p.m., so we'll be able to set up and spike the drinks in advance."

"Sounds good. I have to run home too, and then I'll meet you there. Should I bring a bottle of champagne so we can toast the beginning of your army?"

I knew he was teasing, but it didn't sound like a bad idea. After tonight, the vampires wouldn't stand a chance.

CHAPTER SEVENTEEN

(Rose)

The moment I was grabbed, I started screaming and dug my heels into the floor. Suddenly, a set of fangs pierced the side of my neck, and I was pulled into one of the private rooms.

Oh shit! This could not be happening. Who in the world would risk Christian's anger by biting me? It had to be a vampire from outside of town. Someone who didn't know who I was.

He must have used his sedative to quiet my screams, because in the next second I was completely calm... on the outside. Once my thoughts cleared, allowing me to focus on the nightmare this was going to become, my internal panic really set in.

I tried to pull away, but the vampire's fangs sunk deeper as he held me tight from behind. *Fuck!* I couldn't believe this was happening. I assumed in a few minutes my demon blood would start infecting whoever this vampire was. How the hell was I supposed to explain why this vampire drifted dark after biting me? My situation just went from bad to worse.

I didn't have any idea if it would work, but I knew I'd better try something fast. I wasn't even sure *how* to do it, but I focused on my anger and tried to release my demon side. Maybe I could forge a mind bond and force this asshole to stop.

Thankfully, I must have done something right, because all of a sudden, I felt the connection of the mind bond snap into place, and I could almost see what was happening through *his* eyes. I projected the thoughts I wanted him to feel, adding a verbal command for good measure. *Stop NOW!*

The vampire went rigid behind me and his fangs withdrew immediately. Luckily, I could feel and see through our connection that he used his sedative to heal the wounds in my neck. The instant his fangs slid free, the puncture marks closed, and it looked as if they never even existed.

I immediately spun around and shoved the vampire with all my strength. He let out a little *humph* as he landed on the red velvet couch. I didn't recognize him, but that didn't mean much since the only other vampire in the area I knew besides Christian's clan, was Justin. He was a handsome guy with a decent build, and he wore a black leather jacket. His hair was short and blond, but I knew that would change at any moment.

"Who are you? What's your name?" I nudged his mind so he didn't have any choice but to respond.

"My name is Kennedy."

"Where are you from?"

"Florida."

"What are you doing here, and how did you find out about The Rising Pit?" I had to speed this up, because like I assumed, his hair and eyes had already begun to drift dark.

"I was on vacation and visiting some friends outside of Masen. They told me about the club, and I thought I'd check it out before heading back home."

The guilt was building inside of me. Just because this vampire had made the mistake of biting *me*, he was going to lose all sense of right and wrong and possibly end up facing the true death. It sucked, but I had to face the hard reality... I couldn't allow him to leave. Letting him go, knowing he'd drift darker and darker and start hurting innocent people was just not an option.

"Okay, Kennedy. You're going to sit here and not move until someone comes to find you. Do you understand?"

"Sit here and not move. Yes, I understand."

"And you aren't going to remember anything about biting me or what I looked like either. Got it?"

"Yes. I don't remember you."

Wow. This mind bond thing could prove really useful. I just wished I had more time to test out my demon powers. Unfortunately, right now was not that time. I had to get as far away from this scene as possible, and fast.

I parted the velvet curtains a fraction of an inch and peeked outside. The coast was clear, so I rushed from the room and ran down the stairs into the bathroom. The moment I was inside, I nudged the door open a crack, watching what would happen next.

It didn't take long before I saw Christian, Evie, and Dax heading toward the stairs. The moment they hit the second floor, I shot across the dance floor and into Evie's office. I found the button on the bookshelf that opened the secret door to her private entrance into the pit, and made my way back to my room in a hurry.

I thought the best thing for me to do was pretend that once I finished dancing, I used the restroom, then headed back down here to get some rest. I just hoped no one saw me upstairs, or I could kiss that story goodbye.

* * * * *

(Christian)

After Rose's scream penetrate the chaos inside my mind, I was able to focus and regain my bearings.

"Christian, what's wrong?" The panicked look on Evie's face confirmed this wasn't a normal reaction to the Passing of Powers ritual.

"My head is splitting, and I can hear everything... including Rose's scream. She's in trouble."

I shoved off the couch and flew toward the door. As much as I wanted to dash straight upstairs, I knew I couldn't. Not with all the human patrons filling the club tonight.

As Evie and I wove our way through the crowd at a normal pace, I noticed her motion for Dax to join us. The three of us quickly made our way to the stairs to the private rooms. I knew this was where Rose's scream originated from. I wondered if becoming Sire heightened all my abilities, including my claircognizance? Right now, though, all the questions would have to wait. I needed to find Rose.

After reaching the private room that held her scent, I threw open the velvet curtains to find a young male vampire sitting on the couch alone.

"Who are you and what are you doing here?" Evie demanded.

"My name is Kennedy, and I'm just sitting here. Is that a crime?"

Dax took a step forward, his hair drifting slightly from blond to light brown.

Talking like that to a Sire, let alone his consort, was a really bad idea.

Suddenly, Kennedy launched himself at Dax and the two of them went crashing into the table, followed by the chairs and walls.

"Enough!" Evie's voice still held her Sire's command, and even though Kennedy wasn't a part of our clan, vampires had no choice but to obey a Sire when in their presence.

The two froze, hands still wrapped around each other's necks. I decided this was a good time to test my Sire's voice as well, since Dax already knew we'd completed the ritual. "Kennedy, sit down and don't move."

He did exactly as instructed.

Excellent. It worked.

The vampire eyed me as he slowly moved back toward the couch. That was when I noticed his eyes and hair were both drifting darker by the second. *Oh, no!* "Evie, we got a problem."

"What is it, Christian? What are you sensing?"

"Nothing. That's the problem. I can hear tiny whispers, but they're becoming distorted and fuzzy. And look at him... he's starting to drift dark. I think we have a demon in the club."

CHAPTER EIGHTEEN

(Renard)

Once Loni and I moved our car to a new spot around the corner, we took a few moments to feed in the park before checking to see if anyone was home at Jeremy and Meredith's.

After verifying no one was there, we launched ourselves into the nearest tree to secure a good position from which to spy on them for the night. It was a bloody good thing it was mid-summer and the trees were in full bloom, because if it'd been winter and the trees were sparse, I didn't think Loni and I would've made very convincing monkeys.

"This is perfect. I can see right into their living room and bedroom windows. Now all we have to do is wait," Loni said.

I glanced at my watch and assumed we wouldn't have to wait too long before someone made an appearance. It was 7:02 p.m., and even if Jeremy had made another trip to Masen for the day, he should be returning home at any moment. However, to my surprise and satisfaction, it was Meredith who arrived home first.

Loni and I watched as she parked on the street instead of pulling into the garage. Her rushed pace and the fact that she left her car running was a clear indication she was still on the move. Good news for us.

We remained hidden in the tree as Meredith burst from her home in a flash of speed that rivaled any vampire's. She'd changed clothes and was obviously in a big hurry to get somewhere, which was going to be a problem since our car was currently parked around the corner.

"Looks like we'll be following on foot," I said.

"Fantastic!" The giddiness in Loni's voice reminded me how much she loved running free through the night. Maybe this wouldn't be such a boring assignment after all.

* * * * *

(Jeremy)

As I drove home, I thought about my plan for the weekend and was excited to fill Meredith in. But just as I rounded the corner at the end of the block, I saw Meredith speeding away from our townhome. Suddenly, there was a blur of motion in the park across the street but my ringing cell phone quickly diverted my attention.

"Hi, honey. I'm just pulling into the drive. Where are you speeding off to?"

"My meeting this week has been pushed up to tonight. I shouldn't be too late though. How was your day?"

"It was pretty good. Nothing too exciting, but I do have some plans for this weekend I'm excited to share with you."

"Oooohhh... exciting plans, I like the sound of that. What are they?"

"I was hoping we could go out for dinner and dancing... at The Rising Pit."

Silence filled the line so I looked at my phone as I exited the car. Maybe I'd hit the mute button by mistake. "Mer? Did you hear me?"

"Yes. I heard you. But Jeremy, I think this is something we need to talk about first."

Hmmm. I thought she'd be more excited to have an evening out, especially since she'd been so busy with work and with the new group she'd been chairing lately. And honestly, I wasn't sure what there was to talk about. She knew I'd wanted to go back to the club since I'd struck out the first time, not to mention my failure again last night.

As I made my way inside, I could feel my frustration levels start to rise... literally. I was starting to sweat as I felt a flush of heat spread across my face. "Alright. I guess we'll talk about it when you get home."

I didn't wait for a response. I cut off our call, and threw my phone onto the counter along with my keys. For some reason, this was really pissing me off. I couldn't understand why she'd want to stop me from looking for Rose. Not after she'd been the one to protect her in the first place.

By the time I pounded up the stairs, I was fuming mad, which was not a good thing. I couldn't afford to lose my temper again, because lately... something strange had been happening when I did.

* * * * *

(Damien)

After a change of clothes, I headed over to the warehouse where I'd stashed the body of the woman I'd hid earlier in the day. I knew Meredith wouldn't approve, but I couldn't help it. The taste of human blood was now my new drug of choice. I'd had my fair share of others in the past, but none surpassed the high that fresh blood gave me.

The feeling of strength and power that flowed into me every time I tasted the sweetness of human blood was enough to have me salivating before I even entered the warehouse.

I made my way to the back of the abandoned building and found my donor in the same spot as I'd left her. She was pale, most likely from the blood loss I'd inflicted earlier, but other than that—and the puncture wounds visible on her neck—she looked perfectly fine.

She was propped up against the metal wall, sitting on the concrete floor with her knees drawn up to her chest. Her long, baggy dress was draped over her knees and hung loosely to the ground. It was the same mousy brown color as her hair. I couldn't tell she if she was sleeping or passed out, so I approached quietly. As I lifted her slack head, she began to wake.

I'd taken care to gag her earlier so I wouldn't have to hear her high-pitched screams again. Once she finally came to and realized her situation hadn't changed, the fear radiating from her made my skin tingle. Tears filled her eyes and she continually shook her head back and forth as a whimpering sound escaped from beneath the rag in her mouth.

I knew I wouldn't be able to show restraint this time, since only a small amount of blood had almost sent me into a frenzy only a short while ago. Unable to wait any longer I sunk my teeth into the same spots I'd created before.

The sweet taste of ecstasy flowed down my throat and filled my body with an enormous dose of strength.

I didn't care what Meredith said; I wouldn't be limiting my blood intake anytime soon. Besides, it would only prove to benefit her in the end. When we finally faced these vampires, I'd be just as strong as her, and together we would decimate them.

CHAPTER NINETEEN

(Christian)

Dax didn't have any problems taking our new prisoner through the club, since I'd used my Sire command to instruct Kennedy to follow without trouble. Once we reached the office, Evie and I remained behind as Dax took him below to get him chained up.

"How the hell are we supposed to tell who's a demon and who's not?" I asked.

"I don't know, Christian. Our scanning ability won't work on a demon because of their built-in mental blocks. And I won't risk ending up unconscious like before."

I paced the office, trying to come up with a plan that would weed out the demon in our midst. Unfortunately, I was drawing a blank. We couldn't scan it, we couldn't bite it, and if the demon was anything like Meredith, it would be almost as strong and as fast as we were. This was quickly shaping up to be a lose-lose situation.

I watched as Evie lowered herself onto the couch. I could tell she was upset from her drifting appearance, and it was obvious she was deep in thought. Suddenly, her head snapped up. "I wonder if the fact that we originated from Camazotz, and demons originated from his father Yum Camil, somehow puts them higher up in the hierarchy of things."

Evie had a point. It would make sense that the race created by the demon god, the *father* of our creator, would be stronger and have more powers and built-in defenses, leaving vampires second best.

I was just about to sink into the couch and embrace the hopelessness I was starting to feel, when suddenly, once again thanks to my claircognizance, I simply *knew* what we needed to do. "Alright. Let's close down the club and get everyone out of here. Hopefully, by dispersing the crowd we can prevent anyone else from biting the demon tonight... whoever it is. Then we just have to wait until the demon's blood leaves Kennedy's system and he should start to drift back like Terrance did. Once that happens, we'll be able to find out who the demon was that he bit."

"That sounds like a reasonable plan. And hopefully, we'll hear back from Balam tomorrow and finally gain some insight on exactly how to combat these beasts."

Evie stood and hugged me tightly. "See, Christian. You're going to make a wonderful Sire."

I watched her walk out of the office and start the evacuation of the club. It made me happy to know she had such confidence in me, but at the moment, I didn't feel like a wonderful Sire. I felt like a complete loser. I was so distraught over how all of this would affect my clan, I'd almost forgotten what had started this whole situation... Rose's scream.

I raced toward the bookcase and hit the button to Evie's secret door. I was so overwhelmed with concern for Rose's, I feared if anyone had hurt her, I'd end up killing every single person in this club, regardless if they were a demon or not.

* * * * *

(Rose)

I heard footsteps and voices in the hall, followed by the rattling of chains. I didn't have to look to know they were chaining up Kennedy at the opposite end of Terrance's cell. There was only one holding cell in the pit, but it was big enough to house three prisoners at once. *Two down, one to go.*

Though if Terrance continued to drift back, the prisoner count would soon be back to one. *Oh, crap!*

If Terrance was drifting back because Meredith's blood had left his system, that meant unless I found a way to slip Kennedy my blood on a continual basis, he'd start to drift back too.

Looks like I'd be finding a way to leave here sooner rather than later. But not before talking to Christian, apparently, because in a blur of speed he flew into our room, and I suddenly found myself nestled tightly against his chest.

"Oh my god, Rose. I'm so glad you're okay." He continued to hold me close as his breathing returned to a steady pace.

I slowly pulled out of his hug and eased myself down onto the bed. "Christian, what's wrong? Why wouldn't I be okay?"

The puzzled look on his face had me sweating bullets. I didn't know if sticking to my story was a good idea at this point or not. I decided to see what he said next before incriminating myself with a lie that could possibly blow up in my face.

"I heard you scream. And I just left a private room where we located a vampire that we think drank from a demon. The room was covered with your scent."

Dammit! Time to put my acting skills to the test. "You're kidding me! A demon? Here?" I've never detested myself more than I did right now.

"Yes. We think so, but since there's no sure way to tell, we had to chain the vampire up, and we'll be waiting until he drifts back to get the exact identity of the demon that he bit."

I didn't know what to say or do. I felt the walls closing in on me, and all I wanted to do was run. But run where? I still had nowhere to go that wouldn't lead back to my dad and Meredith. If I went to Jillian's, her parents would notify my dad for sure. Actually, if I showed up on any of my old friends' doorsteps, I was sure my dad and Meredith would be on the scene within hours. I thought of going to stay with Justin's clan, but there was no way that would work either. They would notify Evie and Christian, which certainly wouldn't end well.

Maybe I should just leave the state completely. Start over somewhere new. Somewhere I didn't know the local vampires or demons, and live my life like a normal human girl again.

"Rose. Why were you in that room? And what are you thinking about?" Christian's voice was layered with suspicion, and I thought I'd been busted without even saying a word.

"Everything. Nothing. I guess I'm just in shock thinking about all of this." My vague answer must have been enough to trigger his protective side, because he sat down on the bed next to me and gathered me in his arms once more. Thankfully, he ignored the fact I hadn't answered the first part of his question.

"I know things have been tense between us, but Rose, you have to know I would never let anything happen to you. I love you so much, and I'll do anything to protect you."

Tears filled my eyes, and I couldn't help but sink into his embrace. I'd missed this so much. Being held by the man I loved, and feeling how perfectly we fit together. Knowing he was strong and that I had nothing to fear as long as I was with him. This was every girl's dream. Too bad it was currently my nightmare. Before I had a chance to pull away and put the necessary distance between us once again, his next statement left me reeling.

"I have something important I need to tell you. Only Evie, Dax and I know, but once I tell you, you have to keep it a secret. Not even the others can know about it." He took a deep breath and placed both hands on my shoulders, pulling away only enough to look me in the eyes. "Evie and I completed the Passing of Powers ritual earlier tonight... I'm now officially the new Sire."

CHAPTER TWENTY

(Meredith)

I didn't know how I was going to get out of accompanying Jeremy to that damn club. It was obvious by the abrupt end to our call that I'd pissed him off, but that was too bad. I wasn't willing to risk my life by walking into the enemy's lair, just so he could go searching for that half-breed daughter of his.

I took a few deep breaths to clear my mind, and prepared myself for tonight's meeting. Everything else, including Jeremy's "exciting plans" were going to have to wait.

It was 7:40 p.m. and apparently, I'd arrived before Damien. I hurried to gather the containers of blood and the rest of the supplies for tonight's festivities while trying to contain my annoyance he wasn't already here to help.

The conference hall was a large facility on the bottom floor of an office building that had been closed down last year. The owners kept the bottom level open and used it to book meetings, conferences, wedding receptions or whatever else would pay the bills while they negotiated with investors as to what to do with the place. It worked perfectly for me, because there was never a worry of any uninvited guests showing up to our meetings.

I set up the tables, taking extra care to cover them with the nice tablecloths I'd brought along. I wanted to make sure our food and *drink* station was extra appealing tonight. After placing four large crystal bowls, the cups, and the utensils along the long table, I finally began mixing the punch. I couldn't help but giggle. This punch was definitely going to pack a "punch." Pun intended.

Just as I finished putting the last dose of blood into the mix, I heard Damien's truck pull up outside. Glancing at my watch, I breathed a sigh of relief. Even though he was running slightly late, he'd still arrived before 8:00 p.m., which gave us a half an hour to go over the plan once more.

He seemed a little disheveled as he came running through the door. Breathing hard he said, "Sorry, boss. I got held up." He finished tucking in his shirt and straightening his tie, and it made me wonder if by "held up" he meant "having sex." Not that I cared.

"No problem. We still have plenty of time to go over things before everyone starts to arrive. But first, take these containers and put them back in the trunk of my car."

I checked my reflection in the mirror hanging on one of the walls while I waited for him to return. My hair was shiny and smooth, and my eyes sparkled with the life essence that flowed through my veins. Anyone looking at me who didn't know the true cause of my glowing, might mistakenly think I was pregnant, which would be amazing! Could I be pregnant, though? I hadn't even considered the possibility until just now.

"Okay. We're all good. Let's go over the plan again." Damien's eyes roamed my profile, lingering on the shape of my ass a little too long. That served as the perfect motivator to snap my attention back to the situation at hand. I'd have to ponder motherhood at another time.

"Alright. We're going to treat this just like any other meeting. We'll start by welcoming everyone, making sure to introduce anyone who is new. Then I'll talk about our heritage for a bit and what a blessing it is to finally have a demon community that can actually come together... etc., etc. Then, we'll invite them to enjoy the food and drink while they mingle."

"Sounds simple enough."

"It may sound simple, but that's when things could get difficult. Once they start to ingest the blood, it *shouldn't* affect them in a noticeable way since it's just a small amount, but obviously since every demon reacts differently to it, we have no way of knowing what their reactions will be. What I need you to do is help me monitor everyone in case somebody starts to show signs of the blood's effects."

"No problem. Since most of them are my family any way, it should be easy enough to tell if someone's acting unusual. But for the few who actually know what's going on, can I have them gather in the other room so we can talk to them, and see if they feel anything different?"

"That's a great idea. As everyone arrives, just let those few know that once they start drinking the punch to nonchalantly head toward the first alcove on the right. We can meet them there and question them like you suggested."

I glanced at my watch and felt a rush of energy run through me. It was almost time for people to start arriving. Damien grabbed two glasses and scooped up some of the blood mixture. "Cheers. To the army."

I lifted my glass to his as the smile spread across my face. "To the army."

* * * * *

(Renard)

We followed Meredith's car by using our vampire speed to hop from shadow to shadow. It took around thirty-five to forty minutes before she parked outside an empty building and headed toward the ground floor.

We stayed hidden for another couple of minutes before moving into the shadows that hugged the east corner of the building. From there we were able to see through one of the small windows into what looked like a large meeting facility.

Meredith was busy setting up tables and a small spread of food. But what really drew our interest were the two large containers of blood we saw her haul inside that were now being split between four large punch bowls. Loni and I smelled the blood the moment she pulled them from the boot of her car.

We watched in silence for only a few minutes before an old blue Ford pulled up and parked next to Meredith's car. Our hiding place was apparently perfect because the Hispanic man walking into the building showed no indication of noticing our presence.

As soon as he entered the building, Loni and I focused our vampire hearing to listen in on their conversation. It started off pretty normal until Meredith got to the part about how she was going to talk about their demon heritage and how grateful she was that they now had a community of demons who could get together to discuss their history. *Bloody hell.* Evie was not going to be happy about this.

We continued to listen only to be stunned further. Apparently, it was Meredith's plan to trick these other demons into ingesting human blood in order to increase their demon powers, and based on what we'd just heard, she was doing it in order to create a demon army.

"This situation just went from a seven to a ten-plus on the 'we're fucked' scale," Loni whispered. I don't think I'd ever seen her this upset. Her hair and eyes had drifted completely black.

"You've got that right, love. We need to get back to The Rising Pit and report this to Evie right away."

We took off at lightning speed to retrieve our car from its present location. The information we now possessed needed to be reported as soon as possible, but I couldn't risk leaving the car behind since the plates were registered to Dax and The Rising Pit.

Once we were safely inside the car and headed back toward Masen, I pulled out my cell and dialed Evie.

"Hello?"

"Evie. We're headed back now and you aren't going to believe what we found out."

Her heavy sigh was the only indication she wasn't looking forward to our news. And who could blame her? This truly had the potential to send the vampire community into a panic. Demon armies... bugger me.

"Alright. When you arrive, come straight to my office and fill me in. I should be done dealing with our current crisis by then. Once I have all the information, I'll gather everyone together and deliver the news without having to repeat myself. Be safe and we'll see you two soon."

She didn't even give me the chance to ask what the "current crisis" was before hanging up the phone.

"Well, that didn't sound good." Loni's deadpan tone mimicked the sinking feeling in my gut. I looked over at my beautiful wife and her gorgeous hazel eyes, and suddenly wished we had never returned from honeymoon in England.

CHAPTER TWENTY-ONE

(Jeremy)

After my infuriating conversation with Meredith, I decided to take a shower in order to *literally* cool off. That was just one of the odd things that had started happening every time I'd gotten angry lately; my body temperature would rise, and I'd start sweating like crazy. It was like a volcano was building inside of me, just waiting to explode. The other strange thing... my eyes seemed to get red flecks in them whenever I was about to blow my top.

These reactions, however, weren't the only things confusing me. It was the fact I'd been getting angry so easily to begin with, and so much more often than usual. I didn't understand where these feelings were coming from, because I'd never really been an *angry* kind of guy.

But looking back, that probably had more to do with Loraine than myself. She was always the cheerful, bubbly, and calming one in our relationship, which in turn, kept me blissfully happy. I wasn't sure why my relationship with Meredith didn't bring me the same joy, but I suppose it boiled down to the fact that Loraine was my true soul mate. *God, I miss her.*

I turned on the shower and let the steam build. I still wasn't sure what I was going to say to Meredith, but thankfully, I was already feeling calmer—something that always happened whenever I thought of Loraine.

I smiled and shook my head then stepped into the shower and let the hot water pour over me, washing my irritation down the drain.

* * * * *

(Loraine)

I hovered in my ghostly form above Jeremy as he entered the shower. I longed to be able touch him once again. I tried, but as usual, I watched as my hand misted through his shoulder.

The first time I'd materialized in this spirit form had been a little disorienting. I'd opened my eyes and found myself white and wispy, just like you'd imagine a ghost to be. I was staring down at Rose as she cried, curled up on her and Christian's bed deep beneath The Rising Pit.

It felt as if a million tiny sparks of energy were being fused back together to once again form my body. In the next moment, my mind was flooded with memories. Memories of my life, and my death.

I suddenly knew things, like the fact Christian was a vampire, and that my husband and daughter both had demon blood running through their veins. I knew *everything*. I guessed it was the gods' way of getting me up to speed.

I'd rushed to Rose and tried to wrap her in my arms, but my hands only misted through her body. I felt a sense of grief for not being able to hold my only daughter, but was still happy for this chance to even see her again.

I watched Rose's tear-filled shudders calm until she was finally able to fall asleep. In that instant, I knew why I was here.

When I was alive, I discovered at a very young age, my mere presence had the ability to calm those around me. I'd always considered it a psychic "gift" of some sort. Though I couldn't manipulate people's emotions, all I had to do was enter a room and they would physically and mentally relax. I knew, without a doubt, that's why I was here—to be the calming presence in my daughter's life once more.

Since I'd been gone, her demon side had started to rise to the surface, and so had Jeremy's. Now, I was getting pulled back into my ghostly form whenever either of them was extremely mad, or when they were specifically thinking of me. The time in between my visits, however, was still a mystery. Once I'd disintegrate or disappear, there was just nothing... nothing until the next time I formed. No memories of the time in between, but full awareness of everything that had transpired while I was gone.

As I looked down at Jeremy while he relaxed in the shower, I knew he'd been upset about Meredith's reaction to his plan to visit The Rising Pit. A plan that would help him track down our daughter, providing a little peace for them both. I wish I could figure out how to actually help, or affect things from my ghostly state, but so far, I hadn't been able to. I could only hover, watch, and let my calming energy do its job for the people I loved. I guess that would have to be enough.

CHAPTER TWENTY-TWO

(Rose)

I sucked in a breath as my heart pounded louder and louder. I was stunned into silence as I processed Christian's big announcement. Talk about panic at the disco. I knew exactly what this meant. He was going to want to change me... soon. I almost expected him to launch across the bed and sink his teeth into my neck, turning me on the spot. I couldn't believe he was officially the new Sire. And I couldn't believe they completed the ritual without telling anyone else.

"I don't know what to say. How is this even possible? You weren't even sure it was really you who was being triggered." I was trying to stay calm and get as much information as I could, but I couldn't deny my urge to run screaming for the door. I didn't know how much longer I was going to be able to deal with all of this.

"I shared my concerns with Evie, but she assured me there was no doubt that it was me. She decided to perform the ritual right away and keep things a secret, so when the time comes to face the demons, the element of surprise and the fact they'll be facing two Sires instead of just one, will be to our advantage."

I could definitely see her point. It would be an awesome *surprise* for the demons to face, but I was still panicking at the fact that my timeframe for leaving Christian had just been bumped up again.

"Aren't you happy for me, Rose? For us? Once this nightmare is over, I'll be able to turn you and we can complete the consort ceremony."

I visibly relaxed when I heard the words *"once this nightmare is over."* Maybe I had more time than I thought.

"Evie doesn't want me to change you right away, as that would pretty much give away our surprise."

Oh, thank God. "I can understand that. And of course I'm happy for you... for us." I stood up and wrapped my arms around him, but made it a point not to linger too long. But as I started to pull away, he grabbed my hips, holding me in place.

"If it was up to me, I'd change you tonight. I can't wait for you to become my consort. The idea of spending eternity with you makes me happier than I can say."

He crushed his lips to mine and our tongues danced their familiar dance. I thought about how all of this—all of my hopes and dreams—would soon be coming to an end, and I couldn't force myself to pull away. Instead, I resigned to selfishly allow myself one last time with the man I loved.

The feel of his lips on mine and the sensation his roaming hands created on my skin, had me tingling in all the right places and my stomach fluttering like it was our first time. He ran his hands up my back, then weaved them through my hair as I worked the buttons on his shirt.

Shoving the piece of clothing off his shoulders and onto the ground, I broke our kiss and moved my lips to his neck. The flutter of his pulse under my tongue announced how much he enjoyed my attention there. I lingered briefly until his hands moved to grab my breasts. Squeezing them slightly, he had me arching into his touch.

He groaned as I kissed my way down his chest, moving my hands to his belt. I sat back down on the bed, putting me in the perfect position. Once his belt was loose, I begun to unzip his pants. I raised my eyes to find him drifting rapidly and looking at me with intense desire. He then tossed his head back in anticipation of the act to come.

That's when we heard a knock on the door.

"Dammit! What is it?" Christian cussed.

"I'm sorry to bother you, but Evie's asked that we all join her upstairs right away," Tori hesitantly announced.

The look on Christian's face was enough to scare anyone, but I knew he was only angry because he was just as desperate to be with me as I was with him.

I reached out and ran my hand down his arm. "It's okay. Let's go find out what's going on, and we can continue this later." I grabbed his shirt from the floor as he zipped up his pants and fastened his belt.

"All I know is that this better be *seriously* important, or I'm going to have Evie's ass."

Turned out... it was.

We made our way upstairs and gathered around the now empty club, waiting for Evie to begin.

"Sorry for interrupting everyone's evening, but Renard and Loni have just returned with news."

Apparently, they'd driven like a bat out of hell and made it home in record time. I was suddenly very happy Tori had interrupted us, because there was no way I was going to miss what Renard and Loni had to say.

"I gathered all of us here so that I wouldn't have to repeat myself. Our problem with the demons is much more serious than we ever anticipated. Meredith is secretly creating an army of blood drinking demons. An army that will soon be as strong and fast as she is."

The gasps and four-letter words that flew around the room, combined with the kaleidoscope of drifting hair and eyes was almost a funny sight. But there was nothing funny about this new development. The situation had been bad enough when it was just Meredith, but now... an army of demons? This was truly becoming a nightmare.

"Did they hear what her actual plans were? Did she say anything about my dad?" I asked.

Renard spoke up. "No, she didn't go into details about her plans, just that she was creating this army. And no, she didn't mention your dad, but we did see him. He seemed perfectly fine and happy. Sorry, Rose."

I was grateful for his apology because I had to admit, it would have been a lot easier for me to swallow if Dad had somehow been forced to go with her, but instead it sounded like he was happy to be there, which really sucked.

Evie continued, "We also had an incident here tonight. A vampire visiting from Florida bit a demon while in the club. We didn't catch the demon, but we have the vampire chained in the cell below. Once he starts to drift back, we should be able to learn who the demon was."

This time everyone's reaction was more depressed than angry. I think they all assumed Meredith had planted a demon here on purpose, and it didn't take much to realize things around here were about to change.

I'd recently overheard Evie talking to Christian about having the clan only feed from blood bags until they caught up with Meredith, and now with this new development, I was sure she'd be implementing this new rule tonight. The clan wasn't going to be happy.

"Tomorrow, I will be sending Bobby and Dom back to the hospital to gather more blood bags. We are going to have to restrict ourselves to drinking from them until we can put a stop to these demons. I will not risk one of you becoming infected and falling prey to their mind bond," Evie stated.

I knew it.

"Have you heard back from Balam yet?" Loni asked.

"No. I'm expecting his call tonight. Sunrise is still hours away, so once I receive his call, I'll gather you all again." Evie dismissed everyone and then she and Dax headed into her office, while everyone else moved to the bar to talk with Renard and Loni.

Just as I started to make my way to join them, Christian grabbed my hand and motioned me in the other direction with a nod of his head.

"I need to get out of here. How about we go back downstairs and continue what we started?"

I knew if I said no, he'd be confused, but I was already starting to feel guilty for allowing myself to give in earlier. As much as I wanted to fall back into bed with Christian and let him make love to me until the sun started to rise, I just couldn't. It wasn't fair to him.

"I'm sorry, Christian, but hearing about my dad has kind of ruined the mood. Plus, I want to ask Renard some more questions about what else they found out."

He gave me a small smile and nodded his head in understanding. "Alright. Well, I still need to get out of here, so I'm going to head back down. Come find me when you get your answers." He kissed me then started down the stairs, disappearing under the stage.

I walked toward the clan and scooted onto the red leather bar stool next to Renard. "I'm sorry to bug you, but you said that you saw my dad, right? Did he really seem okay?"

"Yes, we saw him and Meredith in their townhome. He seemed perfectly fine, and then the next day he woke up and started getting ready for work. Nothing seemed unusual or off with him at all," Renard explained.

"Thank you. I suppose that's good to hear." I wasn't sure what other information I expected, but I wished there was more they could've told me. Like maybe whether or not he seemed sad, or if they thought he was thinking about me at all. I knew it was silly, but I still felt like asking them. Then, one pertinent question did strike me. "Do you think he's aware of what Meredith's doing?"

"No, I don't think so. She went to this meeting alone and had a different guy there that seemed to be helping her."

Now this was information I could work with. If I could get a hold of my dad and convince him Meredith was up to something shady, maybe he'd leave her without ever getting involved in this whole demon mess. Maybe I could convince him that she was cheating on him with whoever this other guy was.

Now I had a plan.

CHAPTER TWENTY-THREE

(Christian)

I couldn't stand to be upstairs a minute longer. Not with all the voices in my head. As I sat there listening to Evie explain what Renard and Loni had found, I started to hear everyone's inner thoughts. I wasn't scanning them, but I think my clairaudient ability was on overload.

I could hear their panic at Evie's announcement. Dom was questioning whether she should take Tori and just run away. Bobby was giving himself a pep talk about how we could "take these demon fuckers out." And Renard and Loni were reliving everything they'd discovered and their conversation regarding what they thought they should do once shit hit the fan.

I didn't want to be hearing any of it. For one, it was confusing and was making my head hurt. And two, because it pissed me off to think anyone in my clan would even think about ditching Evie and the rest of us at the first sign of trouble. I knew they were all scared, and this was something we'd never faced before, but damn it... you don't just run off and leave your clan behind.

As I reached my room, I tried to gain some control over my new abilities. But the instant I entered and caught Rose's lingering scent, my mind once again shifted to her. I wished I could've convinced her to come back downstairs with me.

I understood she needed to talk to Renard about her dad and knew she still wanted to reach out to him. But I was getting desperate for us to have some time to ourselves. Desperate to be happy again, like we were before.

I walked over to my desk and pulled out a piece of old tattered stationery and decided to put my thoughts to words. I'd never been shy about expressing my feelings to Rose, but I needed another outlet to show her how much I still loved her, even if things were chaotic at the moment.

As I concentrated on Rose and thought of the words I wanted to write, I started hearing a whisper in my mind. It sounded like a female voice calling Rose's name. "Rose. Rose?" I looked around and found nothing out of place. So, after pouring my heart out on paper, I finished my letter and put it back in my desk for safe keeping. I then made my way over to the bed and laid down. It was time to do some meditating and get a grip on these voices... whoever they were.

* * * * *

(Loraine)

Once again, I felt myself being pulled back into my ghostly form. But when I opened my eyes and found myself in Rose and Christian's room, Rose nowhere in sight. I started to panic. "Rose. Rose?" I called out, knowing she couldn't hear me, but I didn't understand how I could be here if she wasn't.

I quickly noticed Christian sitting at his desk. He turned around and examined the room, looking straight in my direction.

Suddenly, I was filled with the knowledge he was now the Sire and gifted with extraordinary psychic powers. I floated over to him and looked down at what he was writing. It was a love letter to Rose. It must have been his thoughts of her, combined with his psychic abilities that pulled me into form. *How interesting.*

I continued to watch as he finished his letter and returned it to a box within his desk. Then he laid down on his bed and began to drift into what I recognized as a meditative state. Since I had no control over when I appeared and disappeared, I was stuck watching as he began his deep breathing and relaxation techniques.

Within moments, I felt a chill brush across me. Since I was a ghost, I wasn't sure how that was even possible. Suddenly, Christian opened his eyes and looked directly at me. "Loraine?"

I think if I still had the ability to faint, there would have been a shiny ghost currently laid out on the floor. "Christian. You can see me?"

"Yes. And apparently hear you, too."

I was so excited I could finally communicate with someone, that I flew up to the ceiling and spun around. I hoped this meant that soon I'd be able to talk to Rose and Jeremy again too. What a blessing this was.

"Not that I'm not happy to have someone to talk to, but how are you able to see me and hear me when no one else can?" I asked.

"I'm sure it has to do with my heightened abilities now that I'm..."

His sentence trailed off, and I realized he didn't know the amount of information I'd obtained since being dead. He probably wasn't even sure if I knew what he truly was.

"It's okay. I know everything. You're a vampire and the new Sire, your clan is preparing to face the demon bitch who killed me, and you love my daughter more than you've ever loved anything in all of your six-hundred-plus years." Suddenly, I was the one leaving out information. I was well aware that the vampires didn't know about Rose and Jeremy's demon side, and I also knew it wasn't time for that information to be shared.

"Yes. That's right. Now how exactly is it that you're here on this plane?"

"I'm not sure. It only started happening recently. I was first pulled into this very room while Rose was crying on the bed. I believe her grief, combined with her thinking specifically about me, pulled my energy to her. I was able to use *my* psychic gift to calm her. I've visited Jeremy too, and had the same effect on him. There seems to be a pattern; they have to be either very angry or thinking specifically about me, then I appear, and my ability soothes them."

"Rose never mentioned you had a psychic ability. Did she know about it?"

"No. Neither did Jeremy. But it wasn't something I had to activate or try to use on people; it was just something that happened whenever I walked into a room. People who were upset would calm, and anyone feeling fearful seemed to relax when I was around."

"Damn. That's a handy ability to have. I wish I'd developed *that* during my triggering."

By now Christian had pushed off the bed and was walking in my direction. I didn't feel the need to move, as I knew he'd just pass right through me. Surprised again, he bumped into my arm as he made to step around me.

"Whoa. That's never happened before. Every time I try to touch Jeremy or Rose, my hand just mists through them."

"This whole situation just keeps getting stranger and stranger. I know I'm the new Sire, but honestly, I don't have a clue what to do about any of this. And all I really care about is getting things back to normal with Rose. You probably know this already, but we've been fighting a bit, and there's been some real tension building between us. I just wish there was something I could do to make her happy again."

As I floated over to the vampire who loved my daughter, I thought of the perfect thing to help get these two back on track. Because regardless of Rose's plans, I somehow *knew* it was vital that she and Christian remain together. I assumed this was more cosmic information the gods felt I needed to know. So, I laid a hand on Christian's shoulder, still amazed I was able do so, and told him what he needed to do.

CHAPTER TWENTY-FOUR

(Rose)

Talking to Renard hadn't taken long, but I still wasn't ready to head downstairs to find Christian. I'd already made up my mind not to be selfish and allow more intimacy between us, so I'd wandered around for the next few hours talking and dancing and wasting time with Dominique, Tori, and Loni.

Currently we were upstairs in one of the private rooms talking about how Loni had been turned into a vampire.

"I met Renard when he was visiting Hollywood. I was working at Grauman's Chinese Theatre, and he came in doing the tourist thing. He was this cool European guy with spiky hair. He was so hot I wanted to jump him that first night. From then on, we spent every night together for two weeks straight. Of course, at the time, I had no idea he was a vampire. He told me he had to spend his days with his family, but that his nights were mine." Loni giggled and continued to reminisce.

"After spending those two weeks with him, I found out he wasn't just a pretty face, but that he was also really smart and shared my love of architecture. By the end of his vacation, I'd completely fallen in love with him and him with me. He petitioned Evie to change me and she agreed. He told me what he was and that if I accepted to join his clan, we could be together forever. And so I did. That was about eighty-six years ago."

It amazed me after that long, she still gushed about him like they had just met. But I suppose for a vampire, eighty-six years really was just a drop in the bucket when it came to forever. I almost asked why they waited so long to formally wed, but I didn't want to be rude. Plus, I was suddenly depressed because this perfect dream of spending an eternity with the man you loved had almost been mine as well.

I excused myself and headed back downstairs. As I reached the main floor, Evie came out of her office and looked around the club. "Rose, can you please go downstairs and ask Christian to join me in my office?"

"Sure, Evie."

I ran down the spiral staircase and descended into the pit, wondering what Evie wanted to talk to Christian about now. Hopefully she'd heard from Balam and would soon be sharing the news with us all.

When I reached the door to our bedroom, I listened for a moment before turning the knob and walking inside. The lights were off, and I couldn't see a thing. It was dead quiet. But suddenly there was a click, and the entire room was lit up with sparkling moons and stars hanging from a black ceiling.

I fell to my knees and started to cry as I stared up into a replica of my old room.

"I hope you like it. I wanted to do something special to show you how much I love you."

"Oh, Christian." I could barely speak as I was wracked with emotion. The sight of this had me missing my mom and falling in love with Christian all over again. I looked up at him sitting on the bed, and saw him looking at something off to the side.

I flew into his arms. "I love it. I can't tell you how much I love it."

"I'm so glad. When I got the idea a few hours ago, I snuck upstairs through Evie's office and out of the club to go grab everything. They aren't the original ones from your house, but it's all I could do in a rush."

"It's perfect. Perfectly perfect." I couldn't stop crying as I buried my head in his chest. He kissed my hair and continued to hold me tight. I thought I heard him whisper thank you to someone, but wasn't sure, as I couldn't hear much over the sound of my sobs.

Once I was able to get myself under control, I looked around at all of his hard work. He must have used his vampire speed to paint the ceiling because there were little splashes of black paint on the walls where it had splattered from his rushed brush strokes. The crystals were just like the old ones in my room, and they were sparkling in the artificial moonlight that Christian rigged to shine on them from a new lamp in the corner.

"Christian, I'm sorry for being so distant and angry lately. It's just with everything that's been happening, I've been really sad and emotional. Even though I love you with all my heart, I still miss my mom and dad and my friends. And then when you told me about my dad moving and the other stuff, I just felt angry and betrayed. I know it wasn't your intention to keep things from me, but it's how I felt at the time. Can we just start over, please? I hate fighting with you, and I don't ever want to be without you."

Talk about a one-eighty. I knew it was a big risk to change my plans of leaving, but honestly, I didn't care. No matter what happened, I couldn't leave Christian. He was truly the love of my life, and whatever we faced, we'd face it together. Now and forever... however long that ended up being. It was worth it. *He* was worth it.

His passionate kiss was all the answer I needed. I started to fall into his arms when I remembered the reason I'd come to find him in the first place. I jumped up from the bed, wiped my face, and pulled myself together. "Wait. Evie sent me to get you. She wants you to come up to her office."

He stood up, grabbed my hand, and kissed me once more. "Alright. Let's go see what Evie has to say. I think we're about to find out exactly how to put an end to Meredith and her fledgling army."

CHAPTER TWENTY-FIVE

(Meredith)

All the demons arrived for the meeting right on time. After welcoming everyone, we'd had a great time talking about our heritage and all the stories that had been passed down through the generations of our different families. I tried to hide my impatience and I thought I did a pretty good job, but Damien on the other hand was having a hard time keeping his excitement under control. Twice I had to ask him to join me again as he kept wandering over to the tables.

Finally, I announced, "Everyone, thank you for coming. Now please help yourselves to the wonderful spread we have for your enjoyment tonight."

Damien nodded to each of his relatives that were aware of what was really going on. All of them grabbed a glass and filled it with the punch without hesitation, and after slamming back the drink, headed toward the alcove as planned.

Damien waited for a few minutes before following them. I stayed to mingle with the others who were unaware, monitoring them as they continued to chat, make their plates, and pour their drinks. Once everyone had started to sip from their glasses, I slipped out to check on Damien and the others. "How's it going in here?"

"Good. They've each reported they can feel the effects of the blood, but it's very subtle. Like they've just chugged an entire energy drink," Damien explained.

"Perfect. We don't want an overwhelming reaction from anyone tonight, so that's good news. I'm going back out to monitor the rest. Let me know if anyone starts to show signs of aggression."

"Sure thing, boss."

As I re-entered the main hall, I watched everyone mill around, working off their nervous energy. The boost they were experiencing from the blood seemed to be the perfect dose. Everyone was happy and seemed to be enjoying how they felt, whether they understood the reason behind it or not. No one was acting strangely or showing any signs of ill side effects... yet. Most of them were still on their first cup of punch. I wondered if we would need to worry once they started having seconds and thirds. Only time would tell.

I watched as Damien and his pack of relatives headed back to the table for refills. I motioned for them to take some food too, so they wouldn't look suspicious. After filling their plates and glasses, they once again headed back to the alcove. I joined them after a few more minutes of mingling.

"Any changes?" I asked.

"Yes and no. They still feel like it's just a nice boost of energy, but we've tested the effects and watch this."

He motioned to one of his cousins, who picked up a metal folding chair and proceeded to fold the leg in half. It seemed the blood was having a greater effect after all.

"Great. But that needs to be it for tonight. No more tests, and no more refills. Understand?"

"No problem," Damien replied.

The rest of the men nodded their agreement as I headed back out of the room. But as I rounded the corner and took a final glance back at Damien, the angry look on his face had me nervous.

I think I was going to have to address these reactions of his sooner rather than later.

* * * * *

(Jeremy)

After my shower, I felt so relaxed I decided to not even broach the subject of going back to the club with Meredith once she got home. She said she wouldn't be late, but it was already eleven o'clock, and I hadn't heard from her yet. Usually, her meetings only lasted an hour and she was home by 10 p.m., so I decided to grab a beer from the fridge and watch TV in bed while I waited up for her.

I still planned on heading to The Rising Pit at some point in the near future, but instead of involving Meredith, I'd just do it on my own. Rose was my daughter and there wasn't anything or anyone who was going to stand in my way when it came to finding her.

Just as I sank into bed and flipped on the TV, my cell phone vibrated on my nightstand. I picked it up and answered it.

"Hi, honey. It's me. Sorry I'm running late. We had a larger crowd than usual tonight and the clean-up is taking me longer than expected," Meredith explained.

"No problem, babe. I'm just drinking a beer and waiting for you to bring your sexy ass home and join me in bed."

"Mmmm. That's all I needed to hear. I'll be out of here in five."

I chuckled as I tossed the phone back onto the table. Once I found my daughter, my life would be perfect once again.

I eased down against my feather pillow and a sense of calm settled over me. I wasn't much of a drinker, but apparently a beer after a hot shower was the remedy needed to ease my stress.

* * * * *

(Loraine)

Once Christian thanked me for my help, I watched as he enveloped my crying daughter in his arms, then I felt myself starting to disappear. But this time it was different.

I didn't completely disintegrate, but instead, felt like I was traveling at light speed. In the next second I was hovering over Jeremy as he laid in his bed with a beer in hand.

I hated to admit it, but he looked content. I knew I'd never truly have my family back, and all I wanted was for them to be happy. But the thought of Jeremy being happy with the woman who killed me was too much to bear.

I wished I could figure out how to appear and disappear whenever I wanted, because staring down at my husband, knowing he was lying there waiting for my killer to join him in bed, had me begging the gods to take this power away.

CHAPTER TWENTY-SIX

(Rose)

As we made our way to Evie's office, I asked Christian if he wanted me to wait outside, so they could talk in private. His answer was no.

Now sitting on the couch in Evie's office, we waited for Dax to join us.

"I assume Christian has shared the good news with you," Evie said with a smile on her face.

"Yes, he did. I'm so happy for him, but I understand we need to wait to change me, and that you don't want me to tell anyone else."

"Thank you for understanding. I just can't risk any of the clan accidentally biting one of Meredith's demons and having that knowledge to share."

Dax entered the office from behind Evie's bookshelf and took a seat in the chair next to the couch. "Terrance and the prisoner have been fed. I couldn't get any more information from Kennedy. His thoughts still remain fuzzy, but Terrance requested that we keep him posted on what we find out from Balam."

"I'm still debating on what we should do with Terrance. I have a theory and a plan in mind, but I need a little more time before deciding for sure," Evie stated.

She stood from behind her desk and walked around to join us, taking a seat in the remaining chair. "I did hear from Balam tonight, and what he explained was quite overwhelming. I'm not sure I've even had enough time to wrap my head around it myself, but here goes.

"After Balam and the elders completed their research, their theory is that since vampires came from Camazotz and demons came from Yum Camil, only a hybrid—a demon *and* vampire—will be able to kill an immortal demon. Which Meredith and her army are quickly becoming.

"Apparently, a stronger demon can kill another demon, but since Meredith is currently the strongest demon in existence—and the original Mayan demons were wiped out eons ago—the elders conclude combining the two races is the only chance we'd have at killing an immortal demon."

Conversation erupted as the three of them tried to riddle out exactly how a vampire was supposed to bite and turn a demon without becoming infected by their blood. This theory was sounding like an extreme long shot.

"Obviously, our first problem is locating a demon. And secondly, how in the hell am I supposed to bite one and drain one to the point of death, without becoming overtaken by the poison in their blood? Then, what happens if I *am* successful, and they rise with the ability to control me? This whole thing sounds completely fucked." Christian was frantically pacing and running a hand through his now jet-black hair.

It was definitely going to take some serious brainstorming to figure out *exactly* how to make something like this work. But in the end, for some reason, I was confident we'd be successful. I just needed to do a little research first, then it appeared I had a confession to make.

* * * * *

(Meredith)

After almost two hours of mingling and chatting with everyone here, I was extremely pleased with how tonight had gone. No one had showed any signs of aggression from drinking the blood-spiked punch, but everyone seemed to unknowingly enjoy its effects.

I'd begun to clean up and was almost finished when I looked at my watch and noticed it was already getting close to eleven o'clock at night. I picked up my cell and dialed Jeremy to let him know I was running late.

"Hello."

"Hi, honey. It's me. Sorry I'm running late. We had a larger crowd than usual tonight and the clean-up is taking me longer than expected."

"No problem, babe. I'm just drinking a beer and waiting for you to bring your sexy ass home and join me in bed."

"Mmmm. That's all I needed to hear. I'll be out of here in five."

God, I really did love that man. Hearing his voice and imagining him lying naked in bed waiting for me had my thoughts drifting back to earlier tonight. I looked down at my stomach and rubbed a protective hand across it. *I wonder if I really am pregnant?* It would be my dream come true, but at the same time, I wasn't sure now was the best timing.

The vampires hadn't come looking for me yet, but I knew it would only be a matter of time before they did. And even though I wasn't planning on being the one to initiate any fighting, I wasn't going to stop forming my army. What was that old saying... the best defense is a good offense? Well, that was the plan: create my army and prepare to defend myself and my kind.

As I finished my cleanup, I noticed one last thing I needed to take care of. The chair with the bent leg had found its way out of the alcove and was stacked with the others. I shook my head and grabbed the chair, wondering if all of this was such a good idea after all.

I knew as long as I kept drinking my fill of human blood on a regular basis, I didn't have to worry about any of these boys surpassing me in strength and posing a threat, but I did have to worry about their egos and stupidity. I was going to have to meet with Damien again very soon to make sure he'd be able to keep his cousins in line. Because if he couldn't... I would.

CHAPTER TWENTY-SEVEN

(Damien)

After the meeting was over, I told Meredith I'd like to leave with my cousins in order to keep an eye on them, instead of staying to help her clean up as usual. She thought it was a good idea, waved goodbye, and said she'd give me a call tomorrow.

I was pleased with how the guys were handling the effects of the blood in their systems. But, after the boss put down her foot about no more tests earlier, we hadn't been able to find out if everyone in the group had increased in strength, or if it was just Raúl. So, I decided, to hell with her rules and we were currently heading to the warehouse to conduct some tests on our own.

I disposed of the woman's body after I finished with her earlier, so that was no longer a concern. Besides, I didn't want to introduce them to killing and feeding directly from a person just yet. I couldn't risk any of my cousins becoming frenzied and growing stronger than me. Instead, we were just here to test the limits of our newfound strength.

"This is fucking amazing. I'd heard the stories of our ancestors drinking human blood, but honestly, I thought it was a crock of shit. Just fairy tales that fed into the Mayan sacrifices and stuff like that. I had no idea it was true and could have this kind of effect on us," Raúl said.

"I was pretty shocked when Meredith first introduced me to it as well. She's the first of our kind to figure it out and begin the process of turning immortal."

"She's pretty fucking hot, cuz. Have you tapped that yet?" Juan never was known for his tact, so his crass statement didn't surprise me.

"No, Juan. I haven't, but trust me... I plan to." Their laughter and catcalls rang throughout the warehouse as we made our way inside.

Thinking about how much I wanted Meredith had me ready to demonstrate just how strong I'd become. Strong enough to take out her lame-ass boyfriend, Jeremy, that was for sure. The dip-shit demon who didn't even know what he was. What a joke.

* * * * *

(Terrance)

Watching my new cell-mate drain his blood bag had me jonesing to get the hell out of here. I did not play well with others. Especially a strange vampire who'd drifted dark and was already demonstrating signs of aggression.

He was pleasant enough when Dax first brought him in and secured his chains. But it didn't take long before he started bucking, growling, and baring his teeth at me. It was like watching a rabid dog throw a hissy fit.

Since I was able to focus on Meredith and everything she'd made me do, I knew all of her blood had finally left my body. I wasn't sure why Evie was still holding me here. I wanted to ask the question, but already felt bad enough over everything I'd put them through and didn't want to be an ass by pressing the matter. I knew she'd let me out sooner or later. I just hoped it was sooner.

I leaned back against the cinderblock wall as I closed my eyes and did the only thing that brought me peace. Thinking about Loraine.

The memories of her were the only thing that had gotten me through this situation. Once my thoughts had started to clear, I focused on her beautiful face and how her laugh used to make me feel. It was truly a miracle despite Meredith's manipulations, I'd genuinely fallen in love with her.

She never knew how I felt. She loved her husband, and therefore I chose to keep my feelings to myself. It was so easy and relaxed when we were together, and even though I knew she'd never reciprocate my feelings, it didn't diminish what I felt for her. There were times I wouldn't even feed from her, but we would just sit and talk instead. I knew if anyone heard me expressing these tender emotions, they would think I was being manipulated again, but it wasn't that. It was just Loraine and how she'd made me feel.

As I sat thinking about our time together, I felt a cool breeze brush past me as I relaxed into my memories. It almost felt as if she was here with me. I laughed at the stupidity of my thoughts. But in my own defense, sitting in a cell, chained to a wall, while listening to an infected vampire rant and rave... it was definitely a situation that lent itself to fantasizing about the woman I loved.

* * * * *

(Loraine)

After my plea to the gods, I felt myself start to disintegrate again. Thankfully, I was sent whisking through space and escaped Jeremy's bedroom before Meredith came home.

When I felt my ghostly form solidify once again, I opened my eyes and received a surprise. I was in the basement cell of The Rising Pit with Terrance.

I quickly looked around for Rose or Christian, but only saw Terrance and... *Kennedy?* Yes, there was the information I needed. His name was Kennedy, and he was a vampire who was infected with demon blood... Rose's blood. *Oh crap.*

I settled down next to Terrance, and received more information. Apparently, I was called here by the vampire who loved me.

CHAPTER TWENTY-EIGHT

(Jeremy)

After waiting up for Meredith and welcoming her into our bed as planned, we spent the night in each other's arms and the thought of going back to The Rising Pit never crossed my mind again... until this morning.

I decided it was something I was going to do on my own. I wasn't sure why Meredith was against going to the club, but I didn't want to pressure her to go with me if she didn't want to. And if I was being honest with myself, I didn't really want to hear why she thought it was a bad idea.

I kissed her goodbye as I threw my suitcase into the backseat of my car. I was once again headed to Seela for another business meeting that would keep me overnight. *How convenient.*

I made the normal pit-stops on my way out of town: the cleaners, the Coffee Hut, and the Donut Mill, then spend the rest of the drive thinking about what I'd say to Rose if I was lucky enough to find her.

Obviously, we'd have talk about the accident and why she'd practically gone off the deep end and attacked Meredith. But we'd also have to discuss what was going to happen next.

Since I'd sold the old house and moved in with Meredith, I honestly didn't see my twenty-one-year-old daughter wanting to live with me and the woman she attacked. It would be a dream for Rose to come back to me, but I had to be realistic. It was never going to happen. But, as long as I knew she was okay and that we'd be staying in contact, I supposed it was time to let my little girl go.

Halfway into my trip, my cell phone rang, showing a number I didn't recognize.

"Hello. This is Jeremy."

The line was silent. I looked down at the display to make sure I hadn't dropped the call, but it still showed as active. "Hello?" I didn't hear any breathing or background noise at all.

"Hello? Is anyone there?" Again, silence. But, just as I was about to press the end button, I heard, "Dad. It's me... Rose."

Tears filled my eyes and I eased my car onto the shoulder. "Rose? Honey, is that really you?"

"Yeah, Dad. It's me. Are you alone?"

"Oh, baby, it's so good to hear your voice. And yes, I'm alone. I'm in my car. Where are you? I'm actually headed back to Seela today."

"That's great. I'm still in Seela. Is there any way you could meet me somewhere today?"

"Of course! Just tell me when and where."

* * * * *

(Rose)

After listening to Christian, Evie, and Dax argue about the finer points of creating a vampire-demon hybrid for the past two hours, I finally decided to call it a night. Once Christian joined me back in our room, he delivered the disappointing news they were no closer to figuring anything out than they were before.

I had so many things to figure out on my own, and the first bit of research involved my dad. I warned Christian I was going to be reaching out to him soon. I just hadn't clarified I'd be doing it tomorrow. I'd call Dad in the morning and see if I could arrange a meeting during the day, while Christian and the clan slept. I didn't think I'd anything to worry about from Meredith, because I was going to make sure Dad would be coming alone.

I snuggled up next to Christian just before he went comatose. I figured I'd better get a few hours of sleep before putting my plan in motion. Just the thought of seeing my dad was exhausting. Exciting, but exhausting. I knew he'd have tons of questions, and to be perfectly honest, I didn't know how I was going to answer any of them. The one thing I did know? Things were about to change.

* * * * *

(Christian)

I couldn't believe I'd just become the new Sire, only to be faced with an impossible situation. What Balam and the elders had come up with as our *"best chance"* was absolutely ludicrous. I was pissed at the prospect of having to bite a demon and risk permanently drifting dark, but the real problem came from the damn mind bond they were able to forge. How could we risk a Sire, *any* Sire, ending up under the control of a demon? It simply wasn't going to work. We'd have to find another way.

I knew my hair and eyes were most likely still drifting even as I reached my room, but seeing Rose lying in there with her long blonde hair splayed over my pillow had me relaxing instantly. I should have followed her out of Evie's office and spent time finishing what we'd started earlier, but I couldn't. I had to stay behind and continue to talk circles about what we should do.

As I laid down next to Rose, I informed her we hadn't gotten any closer to finding a solution to the problem, then I opened my arms to her, letting her snuggle close.

I wasn't going to let this new problem take the enjoyment out of simple things like this—holding the woman I loved as I fell comatose. No matter how bad things seemed, all I had to do was put my arms around her and everything was right in my world once more.

CHAPTER TWENTY-NINE

(Evie)

"I think we have something else to consider here. We know that once the demon blood works its way out of your system, you'll drift back to normal, just like Terrance. And until then, we'll keep you locked up so you won't be a risk."

I was trying to explain to Christian the risk of Balam's plan might be minimal, if we planned ahead. Our only hope of destroying a demon was to create a hybrid, and that was exactly what we needed to do. Was it going to be tricky? Sure. But what other choice did we have? Balam explained since the old demon gods were no longer present in our world, this was our best chance.

"I understand you're nervous, and of course, it's not going to be easy. But at least now we have a group of demons to choose from. We'll just follow Renard back to where Meredith conducted her meeting and abscond with one of her little members. By the time she misses anyone, it will be too late."

"Evie, it's not that simple. Whether it's my clairsentient ability or something else, I just *know* that won't work. There's something we're missing, and until I get a clear picture of what that is, I'm not going to be biting anyone." Christian's statement held the slightest hint of his Sire's command.

As frustrating as all of this was, I was extremely proud of how well he was adjusting, and how powerful a new Sire he was going to be.

"You're right, Christian. We can't rush into anything. The sun is almost up, so let's plan to continue this conversation tomorrow. When you wake, I'd like you to meet me at the cell. We need to see if you can gather any more information from Kennedy, and find out if he's started to drift back yet."

"You think the demon blood has already left his system?" Dax asked.

"Yes, I do. Terrance was feeding from Meredith repeatedly for months, but Kennedy had only a small taste, so if the timing proves accurate, he should be drifting back by tomorrow night."

"Alright, Evie. I'll meet you there. Goodnight."

I watched Christian exit my office, then turned to face Dax. He was still sitting in the chair, gnawing on a plastic toothpick as his hair drifted from dark blond to the deepest brown. "I don't like this, Evie. None of it seems right. How can creating a hybrid demon really help us? Seems to me, we'd be playing into our own demise."

"I've considered that too, but I have to trust Balam. If he and the elders think this is our best shot, I really don't see any other option. Meredith may not have started anything yet, but it sure as hell seems like she's getting ready to. I won't let her and her army start infecting the vampires in the area. I'll do whatever it takes to protect our clan and our race."

Dax removed the toothpick from his mouth and slowly stood up from the chair. "I know you want to protect us all, but Evie, it's really not up to you anymore. It's Christian's job now, and like he said, he's not going to bite anyone until *he* figures things out. All we can do now is just support him, okay?"

I leaned into his embrace and rested my head on his shoulder. He was right, of course. I still held the status of Sire within my clan, but Christian was the true leader now. I just hoped with all of his abilities, he was able to figure out what piece of the puzzle we were missing, and soon.

* * * * *

(Rose)

I woke up just after 9 a.m., slid out from under Christian's arm, and proceeded to get dressed. I didn't have to worry about waking anyone up, as they were all comatose and would remain so until the sun went down.

As I showered and did my makeup, the butterflies in my stomach started doing flip-flops. I knew I'd need to make the call soon, or I'd risk missing Dad. If he still worked his same schedule, he was usually in the office by ten.

Even though I knew there was no risk of being interrupted, I decided to head upstairs into the club so I could truly be alone. I was nervous but excited to finally be reaching out. I glanced at the red numbers of the digital clock hanging above the bar—9:36 a.m. I picked up my phone and dialed.

"Hello. This is Jeremy."

Tears immediately started streaming down my cheeks at the sound of his voice. I couldn't say anything due to the huge lump taking up residence in the middle of my throat.

"Hello?" he repeated. "Hello? Is anyone there?"

With my emotions finally under control, I swallowed hard and said, "Dad. It's me... Rose."

The line was silent for a moment as I heard what sounded like a car slowing down. "Rose? Honey, is that really you?"

"Yeah, Dad. It's me. Are you alone?"

"Oh, baby, it's so good to hear your voice. And yes, I'm alone. I'm in my car. Where are you? I'm actually headed back to Seela today."

"That's great. I'm still in Seela. Is there any way you could meet me somewhere today?"

"Of course! Just tell me when and where."

"How about the park around the corner from that steak house on Elm and 3rd?"

It was the park Christian and I had watched a screening of Dracula on our first date. I hadn't thought about that night in so long, but it still made me giggle.

"That sounds great. I need to make a couple calls to cancel some meetings today, but I can be there in an hour."

"Wait. You can't call anyone! Dad, no one can know about this... especially Meredith."

The line went dead once again, and I was worried I'd made a mistake by bringing her up. But I couldn't risk any of her little peons knowing where I was. "Dad, I'm serious. If you don't promise not to call anyone and come alone, you can forget it. I won't come unless you keep it a secret."

After a heavy sigh, he said, "Alright. I'll head straight there and not call anyone. But Rose, I hope you're planning to explain all of this odd behavior."

"I am, Dad. But whether you'll believe me or not is a whole different story."

An hour later, I wiped my sweaty palms on my jeans for the umpteenth time as I stood nervously behind a large maple tree watching for my dad's car. I'd driven Christian's Mercury and parked it around the corner. I didn't want Dad or anyone else seeing it, linking me back to The Rising Pit. As far as he knew, Evie still hadn't seen Christian or me since the night of the accident, and that's exactly how I wanted to leave it, in case this meeting didn't go as I hoped.

The second I saw his car, I wanted to run. Run away or run into his arms, I wasn't sure. I was so nervous, because deep down, I didn't think he'd be listening to a single thing I had to say, which could prove to be a problem. He'd probably want to grab me and head to the nearest insane asylum.

As he approached the bench, I stepped out from behind the tree. He froze in place, tilted his head, then opened his arms to me.

I went running.

"Dad!"

"Rose, my baby girl. Are you alright?"

"Yes. I'm fine." I pulled out of our embrace and took his hand, then led him over to the bench.

He sat there quietly for a few moments just staring at me. "Rose, I've been so worried about you." He hugged me again, and this time, I didn't pull away. He stroked my hair and rocked me back and forth like I was a baby in his arms. I felt precious to him once again.

"Where have you been? I looked for you everywhere but didn't have any luck."

"Dad, I'm not going to tell you that. I love you, and I just need you to know I really am okay."

He leaned back, and the red sparks that flashed through his eyes were enough to send me into a full-blown panic attack. *Holy shit!* What if my dad *was* being controlled by Meredith? What if she'd started to feed him human blood to trigger his demon DNA? Shit, this could be really bad. What the hell had I been thinking?

"Rose, as angry as that makes me, I'm trying to respect the fact that you're a grown woman and don't need my protection. But I just don't understand why you can't tell me where you're staying. What's with all the secrecy?"

The red sparks left his eyes and he seemed to relax once more. As much as I wanted to head for the hills, I knew now might be my only chance to try to explain everything and maybe get some answers.

"Okay, Dad. I'll explain everything, but you have to promise to keep an open mind. I'm not crazy, and if you push me, I can prove everything I'm saying, but I'd rather you not force me to."

There. I thought that was a pretty good way to start the conversation.

Dad settled into his seat, getting as comfortable as you could on a park bench, then began to listen to my wild tale of vampires and demons.

CHAPTER THIRTY

(Loraine)

The moment I materialized and found both Rose and Jeremy sitting in a park, my heart started to break. Seeing my family together had tears running down my ghostly cheeks. I would have given anything to be able to communicate with them, but as usual I couldn't. Christian was still the only one who could see and hear me for some reason.

As I moved to hover around the back of the bench, I saw Jeremy's eyes flare red at whatever Rose just said. I let my hand mist through his shoulder and sensed him immediately relax. I knew my calming energy was going to be in high demand here today, because Rose was about to drop some major bombshells. I listened as she relayed the story of the vampires and demons to her dad.

She proceeded to tell him that his new girlfriend was in fact the demon who killed me, and that both he and Rose were demons too. Despite the skeptical looks that continually swept across Jeremy's face, he kept quiet and allowed Rose to finish her explanation. I was so thankful my calming ability still worked even from beyond the grave.

Rose continued to explain what happened the night she attacked Meredith, and how the bitch was now trying to build an army to fight against the vampires.

* * * * *

(Rose)

"I don't know what to say. I'm trying to wrap my head around this, but demons and vampires—it's just so unbelievable," Dad said.

"Dad, I told you I could prove it if you need me to, but I hoped you'd just trust me instead. Meredith is a demon and so are we. She killed Mom and wants me dead too, so she can have you all to herself. Did you really never have a clue about what you are?"

"What I am? What I am is your father and someone who goes to work every day to provide a good life for his family. I'm just a normal guy!"

"A normal guy? Is that why just minutes ago you had red sparks shooting through your eyes?"

That must have been the perfect thing to say, because in the next second he scooted closer and grabbed both of my hands. "You noticed my eyes flaring red?"

"Yes. When you got mad. It's a typical demon trait."

"Oh, my God. I thought I'd been imagining things. Lately, I seem to get angry a lot easier, and when I am mad, my eyes flare red and my temperature starts to rise."

He sagged further onto the bench. I was worried he was going to passing out. I knew this was a lot for him to take in—not only learning that vampires and demons were real, but learning that his daughter who'd been missing for months, was smack dab in the middle of it—Yeah, I might be close to passing out too.

"Dad, you have to get away from her. If she hasn't started slipping you blood yet, I'm sure it's only going to be a matter of time. I don't want you to end up under her control and a part of her stupid demon army. The vampires will have no choice but to destroy you if you do."

"I assume the vampires you're talking about are Christian and his *family*. I'm not stupid, Rose, and I know that's where you've been staying. I suppose I should be grateful to the owner for keeping you safe."

"Yes. I'm staying with Christian and his clan. We are in the process of figuring out how to fight the demons. I want you to come back with me. I know Evie would let you hide with us. You don't even have to go back to Masen. We could just go back to the club right now."

We sat in silence for what seemed like minutes. I didn't have anything else to say, and I knew Dad needed some time to let all this sink in. I hated that our first conversation after being apart for months was about demons and vampires, instead of how much I missed him and how happy I was to see him. But with the situation escalating like it was, it was something I couldn't avoid.

"Rose. I love you, and I'm trying here, I really am. But I can't just walk away from Meredith without at least confronting her about all this. I want to believe you, but at the same time, I don't. I can't stand the thought that I've soiled your mother's memory by falling in love with the woman who killed her. And if what you're saying really is true, then I *need* to face Meredith and bring things to an end once and for all.

"No! Dad, you can't. If she finds out you know about her and that you're aware of your heritage, she could hurt you, or even kill you. Especially when you tell her you're leaving. No. Please just come with me." I frantically grabbed a hold of his arms, but he shook me off.

"I can't, baby girl. Facing her is a risk I have to take. I know you said you can prove everything to me, but I need this... I need to prove it to myself. I'll call you later tonight."

I sat with tears running down my face as my dad kissed the top of my head, then walked off, back toward his car. *What have I done?*

I thought by telling him everything I could convince him to come with me so he would be safe. But instead, here I sat, watching him walk off to meet his death.

CHAPTER THIRTY-ONE

(Christian)

When I woke, even though Rose was the first thing to enter my mind, she was nowhere in sight. I assumed she'd already headed upstairs to spend some of her day out in the sun. I worried about her being outside alone, but I couldn't blame her for wanting to take advantage of it while she could. Becoming a vampire and never having that opportunity again was something she'd soon be facing.

I dressed in a hurry and headed to meet Evie outside of the cell as planned. I assumed she'd want me to see if I could obtain the identity of the demon Kennedy had bitten, but when I rounded the corner, I knew something major was going on. From the looks of things, I wouldn't be getting any information from our prisoner today... or possibly ever.

Everyone was gathered outside of the cell, including Terrance.

"What's going on? And no offense, man... but why is Terrance out of his chains?" I asked.

"Terrance has drifted back to normal, and I no longer fear Meredith's control over him. Plus... look at Kennedy," Evie deadpanned.

I glanced into the cell to find Kennedy foaming at the mouth, straining against his chains so hard they were beginning to dig into his skin. He hadn't started to drift back as Evie assumed, and now I suddenly realized the seriousness of the situation.

"How is it that Terrance has drifted back but Kennedy hasn't?"

"That's the question, isn't it? There's something about what happened to Terrance that's different from what's happening to Kennedy. Terrance was never like that, even when he drifted to his darkest point," Evie replied.

She was right. There was something special about Terrance's recovery that we weren't understanding. And we'd better figure it out fast, because if Kennedy didn't start to show signs of improvement soon, we'd be forced to deliver the true death.

"Let's all go upstairs. I have a lot of information to share with you and we need to talk this out as a group," Evie directed.

We all climbed the spiral staircase and emerged from under the stage only to find Rose sitting on the floor by the front door crying her eyes out.

I rushed to her side and wrapped her in my arms. "Baby, what's wrong? Are you hurt?"

"No," she sobbed. "But I did something stupid, and I think my dad could die because of it."

Everybody slowly took seats at sporadic tables around the club. It looked like tonight was shaping up to be full of questions and confessions. "What did you do, Rose? What's happening with your dad?"

"I went to meet him today, and I told him about Meredith and the war that's coming between the demons and vampires. I told him she killed Mom, and that that was the reason I attacked her. I hoped he'd come back here with me to stay safe, but he said he needed to confront Meredith and put an end to things."

She threw herself fully into my arms, and I tried to absorb the shakes now wracking her entire body. "Oh, Christian. What have I done? I just wanted him to come here with me to be safe, and now she's probably going to kill him when he tries to leave her. I'm so stupid. I should have listened to you. I'm so sorry."

I looked up to find everyone in the club staring at us with concerned looks on their faces. But the face I most wanted to see wasn't there.

I concentrated and called out with my mind. *"Loraine? Rose needs you."*

As soon as I opened my eyes, her ghostly form was hovering over us, laying a misty hand on Rose's back. *"There, there, baby girl. Everything will be alright,"* I heard her say.

"Are you sure? Is there any way you can go make sure Jeremy will be safe?" I asked the question in my mind, and thankfully she seemed to hear me because she nodded and disappeared.

Her presence did the trick because Rose sat up and wiped the tears from her face, then spoke to the entire clan. "I'm very sorry for not listening to Christian and Evie's advice. I hope I haven't made things worse by telling my dad of your existence, but I didn't think there was any other way to explain what happened. I understand if you no longer wish me to be part of your clan."

Evie stood and made her way over to us. She took Rose's hands and helped her to her feet. "Rose, we all understand your need to keep your dad safe. But please understand, the safety of my clan comes first, which I already consider you a part of. So, while I'm not mad at you, I do expect you to follow our requests. We wouldn't ask these things of you if they weren't important."

I wanted to grab Rose and speed out of the club and into the night. I knew Evie had every right to say those things to her, but I couldn't help feeling like I needed to protect Rose from her reprimand. "Baby, we'll talk about this later. But I'm sure your dad will be okay. Can you trust me when I tell you, I *know* things will work out?"

"Yes, Christian. I trust you," Rose answered.

We took seats at the table with Renard and Loni, and waited for Evie to begin her long explanation of what we'd learned from Balam.

The conversation went just as expected; everyone yelling and arguing about how we were so screwed since we didn't have a Sire to create a hybrid. Or whether that would even work or not.

I kept watching Evie, expecting her to let everyone in on our secret, but she didn't. When the arguments died down, we finally got to the part of the discussion I was currently most interested in: trying to figure out how Terrance had drifted back. It was becoming apparent that wasn't normally how things worked.

"I have a theory about how Terrance was able to drift back after being infected," Evie announced. "I briefly spoke to Terrance and Rose about it, and it seems like the only *logical* explanation to this illogical situation."

Everyone looked back and forth between Terrance and Rose, confusion lighting their faces. Even I wonder what the two of them had to do with this.

"While Terrance was under Meredith's control, he somehow fell in love with Rose's mother, Loraine. I think that being in love and still retaining access to those feelings throughout his infection is the real reason he's been able to drift back."

Everyone's shocked reactions floated through the air. Once again, I'd forgotten Terrance had admitted to being in love with Loraine. It made perfect sense though. Love was a human emotion: one that kept the light in our souls alive. That light must be the key factor in beating back the demon infection. *Love...* I guess it really does conquer all.

"I don't think it's enough to have the demon blood clear out of your system alone. I think you have to have that spark of love still touching your soul in order to be brought back to the light," Evie finished.

Terrance smiled at Rose, and she smiled back. I'm sure it was still awkward for her to know someone other than her father had been in love with her mom. But it seemed to be a good thing in the end. Loraine's influence really did touch everyone she was around, and I hoped right now she was using her ability to keep Jeremy safe.

CHAPTER THIRTY-TWO

(Jeremy)

Seeing Rose had been wonderful and terrible at the same time. I was so happy she was safe, but everything she told me left me so very confused. I didn't know what to do.

According to her, I'd been sleeping with the woman who killed Loraine, and my little girl and I were both demons. I would have never believed her story except that she knew about the red sparks that flared in my eyes whenever I got angry. I'd known all along something strange was happening, but admitting I was a demon was a pretty big pill to swallow.

I cancelled my business meetings and headed back toward Masen. I had to confront Meredith about all of this, even if it was going to be the death of me. At this point I truly didn't care whether I lived or died. How could I? I was so disgusted with myself for falling in love with the woman who killed my wife. I knew Rose was going to be fine on her own, so really... what did it matter how any of this turned out for me?

All the way home, I thought about the best way to approach Meredith, but when I reached our house, I didn't have to ponder any longer. There was a blue Ford truck parked in our driveway, so I decided to leave the car on the street and sneak my way into the house through the back door.

I immediately heard noises coming from the garage. When I cracked opened the door, I was hit with a coppery smell that made my stomach roll.

It was blood. I was sure of it.

As quietly as I could, I inched the door open to get a better look.

Suddenly, I wished I was at The Rising Pit with my daughter and her vampire friends, because what I saw had me scared to death. Meredith was standing behind a man with her teeth sunk deep into his neck. Blood was gushing from the wound and down the front of his shirt. His eyes were wide with shock as she continued to gulp down his blood.

I was frozen in place, unable to breathe or move. If this was what being a demon meant, I wanted nothing to do with it. And I certainly wanted nothing to do with her.

When I couldn't stand it any longer, I started to retreat as silently as I could. Apparently, I wasn't silent enough, because the door flew open and Meredith stood in front of me, blood dripping down her mouth onto the tiled kitchen floor.

"Jeremy!" She quickly wiped the blood away using the sleeve of her shirt. "What are you doing home? Oh my, God, Jeremy please, let me explain. I can explain everything."

Here I stood, scared to death, but it sounded like Meredith was just as terrified as I was.

"I don't want to hear anything you have to say. I know everything, and I'm leaving."

"No. Please don't go. You have to let me explain." Tears were running down her face.

"Explain what? That we're demons and you kept it from me? Explain that you killed my wife in order to be with me? Explain that you purposely ran my daughter off so you could have me all to yourself? What the fuck is left to explain, Meredith?" I was sure my eyes were pure red, and I didn't care. I let the anger build, for once not worrying about what happened when it did.

"Yes, I've lied to you. I knew from the moment I met you that you were a demon. I was so thrilled to have finally found someone like me that I did the unthinkable. I never expected to fall in love with you, but once I had, I couldn't live without you." She'd fallen to her knees as tears continued to stream down her face.

"I love you so much, and I'm so sorry for everything I've done. Please, Jeremy, you can't leave me!"

"Watch me." I began to storm upstairs to gather my things when she said the one thing that stopped me in my tracks.

"Please. You don't understand. You can't leave me... I'm pregnant."

* * * * *

(Meredith)

Earlier today, after Jeremy left for yet another business trip, I called Damien to invite him over. I wanted to know exactly how the rest of his evening had gone once he'd left the meeting with his cousins. I hadn't heard any suspicious new reports except for that of a missing woman, so I was optimistic they hadn't gone off on a killing spree after all.

It was one o'clock in the afternoon when I finally heard Damien's truck pull up to the house.

I invited him in and we sat down to enjoy the small lunch I'd prepared. "So, how did last night go? Any problems with your cousins?"

"No. No problems at all." He kept his head bent toward his plate.

"So, no side effects or problems with aggression?"

He picked up his sandwich and took a bite, shaking his head as he mumbled, "Nope."

I wasn't buying it. I cocked my head to the side and asked, "Alright. What really happened? You're never this quiet when it comes to the effects of the blood, so spill. What aren't you telling me?"

I knew I'd busted him when his shoulders dropped and he let out a long sigh. *Dammit.* My morning had been going so well, and I didn't want anything to ruin it now. I was going to be pissed if I had to go clean up some horrible mess of dead bodies somewhere.

"We didn't do anything wrong, I swear. We just went to an old warehouse and tested out everyone's strength. Raúl was able to bend the chair at the meeting but none of the others got to demonstrate their new abilities, so we just ran some tests of our own."

I sighed. That was a relief. I could handle boys being boys, but if they started leaving a trail of bodies, I'd be putting an end to Damien and his cousins fast. "Alright. No more tests without me being there. And definitely no feeding on the side. I think last night went really well, and doling out the blood in small amounts seems to be the way to go."

Even though he nodded his head and smiled in agreement, the look in his eyes had me wondering if I already had a problem with my second in command. If he was feeding on the side, that meant he could soon be as strong as me, and that was something I couldn't allow. "When's the last time you had any blood?"

"Last night at the party. Same as the others," he responded.

I squinted and tried to focus on his pulse to see if it was racing, which was a telltale sign of lying. And of course... it was. "Why are you lying to me?"

I flew from the chair and had my hands around his throat a second later. I drug him out into the garage and threw him across it. He slammed into the metal cabinet, putting a dent in it. *Shit.* How would I explain that to Jeremy?

"What the fuck, Meredith? Why does it matter if I have a little sip on the side once in a while? Are you worried I'll become more powerful than you?"

I knew in an instant I'd have to end Damien. Not only was he not following my directions, it was obvious by his statement that he was planning to overthrow me. "You'll never be as powerful as I am. Especially now that I'm pregnant with Jeremy's child."

Damien's eyes went wide.

It was true. I was officially pregnant. I really had been glowing and feeling more powerful, so I'd taken a test just this morning and confirmed the reason why. I was having Jeremy's baby.

The howl Damien let out as he stood up from the garage floor was loud enough to shake the walls. "No! No fucking way will I let you carry that lame-ass demon's baby. What the fuck do you see in him, Meredith? He doesn't even know who he is. I'll kill him the second I see him and then you and I can be together like we should be. Two powerful demons ruling together as one."

I flew across the garage, his words ringing in my ears. "*I'll kill him the second I see him.*" I struck so fast, Damien had no idea what was happening. With my teeth buried deep in his neck, I began to drink him dry. I wouldn't have to worry about a mind bond being forged, because he wouldn't be walking away from this.

No one threatens Jeremy and my happiness and lives to tell about it.

CHAPTER THIRTY-THREE

(Meredith)

As I stood there sucking the blood from Damien's neck, I heard a small noise at the door. I looked up to see Jeremy slowly turning away. *Oh God, no!*

I ran to the door. "Jeremy!" I wiped the blood from my mouth in a desperate attempt to salvage an appearance of normalcy, then pleaded, "What are you doing home? Oh my, God. Jeremy please. Let me explain. I can explain everything."

He stood frozen for a moment, then said the words that unhinged my heart. "I don't want to hear anything you have to say. I know everything, and I'm leaving."

"No. Please don't go. You have to let me explain." Tears poured down my face, and I fell to the floor as I listened to him yell at me.

"Explain what? That we're demons and you kept it from me? Explain that you killed my wife in order to be with me? Explain that you purposely ran my daughter off so you could have me all to yourself? What the fuck is left to explain, Meredith?"

I wanted to crawl to him, hold onto him and never let go. But I didn't want to risk him running away before I could explain, so instead, I remained shuddering on the floor.

"Yes, I've lied to you. I knew from the moment I met you that you were a demon. I was so thrilled to have finally found someone like me that I did the unthinkable. I never expected to fall in love with you, but once I had, I couldn't live without you. I love you so much and I'm so sorry for everything I've done, but Jeremy, please. You can't leave me."

"Watch me." He turned to go upstairs and my panic reached its peak.

"Please, Jeremy. You don't understand. You can't leave me... I'm pregnant." I knew it was a long shot he'd give a damn about a demon baby he didn't ask for, but it was my only shot at stopping him from racing upstairs and straight out of my life.

He stood in place with his back to me as I told him about the baby. And then, I told him a lie. "I'm pregnant, Jeremy, and once the baby was conceived, it started to draw on the life force of each of us. It's a blood bond they need to survive. If you leave and the baby doesn't have both his parents to draw from... it could die. Please, Jeremy. I know you'll never love me again, but please don't kill our baby by walking away from me now."

I knew he'd have no clue as to whether or not I was telling the truth, but I hoped the idea of hurting an innocent child would be enough to make him stay. He was such a wonderful man who would never hurt anyone, so I thought I had a good chance at making this work. But as he stood unmoving, still facing away from me, his next words brought that dream to a screeching halt.

"Meredith. You're a demon, a liar, and a murderer. You killed my wife and framed my daughter. How can you possibly think I would give a damn about you and that baby?"

Dammit! He was leaving me with no choice. As he started to turn around, I grabbed the pan from the kitchen counter. Scaling back my strength so I wouldn't kill him, I smacked Jeremy in the head, knocking him unconscious. I needed some time to think. I loved him with all my heart, and I wasn't ready to give up on my happily ever after just yet.

It didn't take me long to decide what to do. Honestly, it was the only thing I could do if I wanted to keep him here with me, and never have to worry about him leaving again.

I dragged him across the kitchen floor and leaned him against the wall, then grabbed a knife from the drawer and used it to nick my wrist. After lightly patting his cheeks, he started to move just enough to indicate he was coming to. That's when I placed my wrist to his mouth and smiled as he began to swallow my blood.

* * * * *

(Loraine)

I materialized into a room full of vampires with Rose crying in Christian's arms. I ran my hand down her back, trying to comfort her as I was filled with the knowledge of why she was in such pain. "There, there, baby girl. Everything will be alright."

"Are you sure? Is there any way you can go make sure Jeremy will be safe?" I knew Christian was speaking into my mind and was worried that Rose was right. Jeremy could be walking straight to his death. I nodded and in the next moment disappeared.

At first, I was excited because I thought I'd figured out how to go wherever I wanted, but instead, it turned out that Jeremy's anger and fear levels were what had called me to his side once more. When my body reformed, I was in Jeremy and Meredith's townhome.

He was peeking through the door that led from the kitchen into the garage. Suddenly, I had a mental picture of everything that was happening on the other side of the door. I'd never wanted anything more in my entire life than to be able to help my husband escape this evil woman.

I hovered over Jeremy as Meredith came bursting into the kitchen, and then in a flurry of blood and tears proceeded to tell Jeremy that she loved him, and that she couldn't lose him now because she was pregnant.

I wasn't sure if ghosts could pass out, but I must've disappeared when my anger took complete control of me. That was the only time my calming ability didn't work... when *I* was the one who needed it most.

When I finally rematerialized, I found Jeremy sitting on the edge of his bed with Meredith lying next to him. He was holding his cell phone in his hand, and I knew in that second, he was preparing to break the news to Rose.

Meredith had won.

CHAPTER THIRTY-FOUR

(Christian)

After Evie's announcement about love being the necessary ingredient to turn a dark-drifted vampire back to normal, everyone dispersed and went downstairs to feed. Evie still wouldn't risk us accidentally feeding on a demon, so we were stuck with bagged blood for the time being.

As the rest of the gang headed toward the stairs, Evie motioned for me to join her in her office instead. I took Rose's hand and let Evie lead the way.

"I think we're going to have to deliver the true death to Kennedy. With what we know now, if he hasn't drifted back already, I don't think he will."

I knew Evie wanted me to be the one to do it. Even though she still carried the poison of true death, this was her way of letting me take charge of the clan, even if it was just between us.

I didn't want to let her down. "Let's wait until the others are done feeding, then we'll go down while they open the club. Rose, you don't have to be there with us. You can wait in our room if you'd like, or stay up here with Dax and the others." I didn't want her bearing witness to any more death than she already had.

"Okay. I'll just stay up here with the others." She squeezed my hand and smiled at me with reassurance in her eyes. She knew I was nervous without me even needing to say so. *God, I love her.*

We sat in Evie's office and continued to talk about all the recent events while we waited for everyone to re-emerge from the pit: Terrance being in love and drifting back; Balam and the elders' assumption that creating a hybrid was the answer to our demon problem; Meredith's reasons for creating her army; and everything else in between.

Finally, we heard the stage lock into place, indicating everyone was once again upstairs. Rose stood up, kissed me, hugged me tight, then walked out of the office without saying another word. I think she was just as nervous about this as I was.

"Are you ready?" Evie asked.

"Yes." And I was. I'd finally started to trust and enjoy my new abilities. I knew without a doubt how to deliver the true death, even though I'd never done it before. I also knew we had no other choice. Kennedy wasn't going to drift back.

I walked to Evie's bookcase and pushed the button to open the secret door. We remained silent as she followed me down the stairs.

Once we reached the cell, we found Kennedy crouched on the floor finishing off the remainder of his blood bag. I didn't hesitate or try to make conversation. I just flew into the cell and grabbed the vampire by the throat and struck.

As I sank my fangs into Kennedy's neck, I released the poison of true death into his system, then pulled away as the poison began to spread through his veins. I backed out of the cell to stand next to Evie, watching the dark green poison creep across his skin, paralyzing him while turning his body to stone. Evie said nothing, but instead took my hand as we continued to stare at the green tendrils making their way to his heart.

Once the poison reached and solidified his heart, he simply turned to dust. The chains clattered to the ground and Kennedy was gone.

"He didn't suffer, Christian. Once the poison takes hold, it paralyzes them so they don't feel a thing." Evie was trying to pull me away from the cell, but I wasn't ready to go just yet.

"I know, Evie. Thank you. But can you please just give me a moment? I'll be up shortly."

She hugged me and left me alone. Or what I thought was alone.

"So, you're officially the new Sire now?" Terrance came sauntering down the hall from the direction of the supply room. I guess not everyone had finished feeding and returned to the club just yet. *Dammit.*

"I suppose the evidence speaks for itself." I pointed to the dust pile that used to be Kennedy. I hoped Evie was right about Terrance, and he no longer retained any connection to Meredith through their mind bond, or we'd be screwed. I really didn't want to have to kill him too.

"That's good. I'm glad. You'll make a great Sire, Christian."

His response caught me off-guard. I thought he'd be an asshole about it, but then I realized, this *new* Terrance must be coming from the calming effect Loraine had on him.

My God. That's it! That explains why he was able to fall in love with her despite Meredith's manipulations.

Loraine's ability allowed Terrance to retain that connection to his soul, and therefore fall in love with her. He must've always felt at peace when he was near her, which led to him develop feelings for her. In spite of everything, it was a blessing Loraine had been the one Terrance had targeted. If it'd been anyone else, we would have lost him for sure.

I smiled and thanked him for his kind remarks, and silently sent a thank you to Loraine as well.

"Evie wants to keep it under wraps though, so we can use it to our advantage against the demons. I need you to not say anything to the rest of the clan. Okay?"

"No problem, but if you want to use your command to guarantee it, I'm fine with that." Again, his response wasn't something I expected, but it seemed genuine. I decided not to use my Sire command to guarantee his silence. Besides, this could be the test that proved whether he was still under Meredith's influence or not.

As he followed me up into Evie's office, I began to wonder why Loraine wasn't here with Terrance now. She said she always appeared when someone was specifically thinking of her, so I figured that's why she'd been drawn to Terrance so much lately. He was probably *always* thinking about her.

As I shut the bookcase behind us, I got the overwhelming feeling something terrible had just happened. As we emerged from Evie's office, Rose was standing in the middle of the room while everyone else was busy doing their usual prep work.

She was speaking on her cell phone, and in the next moment Loraine appeared above her with a terrified look on her face. Rose threw her phone across the room and it smashed to pieces against the far wall. Then she let out a scream so loud, it had everyone frozen in shock.

I watched in horror as the love of my life started throwing chairs and upending tables in a fit of rage. "Rose, my God, what's wrong?"

When she spun in my direction, my heart dropped into my stomach. Her eyes were glowing a fiery red.

Time stood still as Loraine explained to me that yes, Rose and Jeremy were both demons, but that they'd only found out recently, and that's why Rose had been pulling away. She wanted to protect me and my clan by leaving. She continued to fill me in on why Rose's anger had finally been released; Jeremy was choosing to stay with Meredith because she was pregnant with his child. Their *pure demon* child.

The next bit of divine knowledge I received was from my own psychic abilities. I knew unequivocally that turning Rose was the only thing I could do. To save her, to save us, and to save her dad.

Without a moment's hesitation, I flew across the room and sunk my teeth into her neck.

Everything went hazy as I heard Evie scream in the background. "Christian, NO!!!"

CHAPTER THIRTY-FIVE

(Christian)

I always knew Rose would become my consort, but what I didn't know until the decision was made, was that by turning her... she would also become our hybrid.

As I drank from Rose, bringing her to the brink of death, all my thoughts were fuzzy from the effect her blood was already starting to have on me. But for Rose to become my consort, I'd need to perform the consort ceremony while delivering the sedative of eternal life. So, as I settled into my subconscious, I began to think of the words that would seal our consort bond, layering them with my Sire command.

"Your life to me, my life to you, through this bond our love is true. Whatever shall come, we share in whole. Life to death, eternity our goal."

I felt Rose's scanning ability snap into place as I fell to the ground with her in my arms.

* * * * *

(Rose)

After leaving Christian behind in Evie's office, I started to help set up the tables and chairs in the club. Suddenly, I felt my phone vibrating and looked down to see my dad's number.

The relief I felt was so overwhelming, I answered the call, buzzing with excitement. "Dad. You're alright?"

"Yes, Rose. I'm fine."

"Oh, thank God. I was so worried that crazy bitch would hurt you when you told her you were leaving. Are you on your way to The Rising Pit now?"

A knot in my stomach started to form when the line remained silent for just a little too long. "Rose, I need you to listen to me, baby. I know this will be hard to understand, but... I'm staying with Meredith. We're having a baby."

No words could flow past the anger now rising within me. I knew without a doubt Meredith had somehow tricked my dad into staying with her. *That bitch is going to pay.*

I didn't even bother hanging up the phone, but instead threw it across the room and watched it smash into tiny pieces.

I knew this was the end for me as I couldn't control my demon side any longer. I started seeing red as I threw chairs and smashed tables. I didn't care if everyone knew, because the second I left here, I'd be going to kill Meredith and would probably never return anyway.

Suddenly from behind me I heard Christian's voice. "Rose, my God, what's wrong?"

I spun around, trying to catch my breath and stared at him with my glowing red eyes. Even though I was angry, the sight of him had me wishing I had time to explain and apologize for everything. But I didn't.

Everyone was staring at me, but as I turned to run for the door, Christian flew at me with his vampire speed. The next thing I knew, his fangs pierced my neck as Evie screamed, "Christian, NO!!!"

My body went limp as the man I loved drank the life from me. Suddenly, I heard Christian's voice layering my mind. *"Your life to me, my life to you, through this bond our love is true. Whatever shall come, we share in whole. Life to death, eternity our goal."*

As I took my last breath, I felt a strange snap in my mind as we fell to the floor. The last thing I heard was Christian's voice inside my head.

"Rose, I forgive you."

Tish Thawer

"What do you do if
by being with the
love of your life, you
could throw them
into madness and
eternal darkness?
...this easily
five-of-five-star
[series] executed the
concept beautifully."

~ Ricochet Reviews

A black Rose dies...
Now it's time to run...
The one I love lost...
oh God, what have I done?

Death of a
Black Rose

Book Three of The Rose Trilogy

Death of a Black Rose

(Book Three of The Rose Trilogy)

***

Rose's eyes open and then she's gone.
My life will be over before too long.

CHAPTER ONE

(Christian)

The moment the sun set, I awoke—alone. Rose was nowhere in sight.

"Rose, are you here?"

When I received no response, I crawled out of bed and made my way into the bathroom. I looked from side to side, hoping to find some clue as to where she could be. The last thing I remembered was falling to the floor with her in my arms while our consort bond sealed her scanning ability into place. I felt the connection when it happened and sent my thoughts directly into her mind. I'd told her I forgave her, and I did. So, the question was... where was she now?

"She's gone, Christian."

I looked up into the mirror to see Loraine—Rose's mother—hovering behind me.

"I know. I can feel it. It's like our bond is being stretched." I sank down onto the bench where Rose always sat to do her makeup. I could still smell her scent in the air and my heart began to ache.

Loraine, who'd been killed by Meredith—the very demon that was currently bedding Rose's father—had recently started to appear in her ghostly form whenever she was needed or thought about. However, so far, I was the only one she could actually communicate with.

"Tell me what happened, Loraine."

"Well, after the two of you passed out upstairs, Evie had Dax and the others carry you both down to your room. They said it was too late to stop the process, and that Rose would have to feed from you to complete the transition once you woke. You both remained unconscious for the rest of the night and all day today, but hours before sunset... Rose started to stir."

My head snapped up. "That's impossible. If she was finishing her transition, she shouldn't have been able to wake until the sun went down. We should have woken at the same time."

"I know, Christian. I followed everyone down here last night and stayed with the two of you the whole time. Initially, I was shocked when I saw her start to wake, but what I came to understand is that her demon side allows her to rise before the sun sets. Demons aren't confined to the night like vampires, and therefore neither is Rose. Once she'd risen, it was like she knew exactly what to do to complete the process." Loraine shook her head, ever so slightly. "I watched as she drank from you."

My hand flew to my neck, and I could feel two small puncture wounds marring my skin. Apparently, Rose hadn't figured out how to use her sedative to heal me. That was something every Sire was supposed to teach their new sons or daughters, or in our case... wife. "She completed the process? She's a full vampire now?"

"I think so, but what I saw next scared me so much I must have disappeared. I only came back when I felt you thinking of Rose just now."

I jumped up from the bench, my fists clenching and unclenching as my panic rose. Glancing back at the mirror I caught sight of myself; my hair and eyes had drifted dark. "Tell me everything, Loraine. What did you see that scared you?"

Bright silver streaks flowed down Loraine's cheeks, and I realized she was crying. "She's bad, Christian. After she drank from you, I watched as my daughter's beautiful blonde hair turned dark as night, and her eyes became the deepest crimson I've ever seen. She's the hybrid now, and I'm scared for us all."

CHAPTER TWO

(Christian)

The decision to turn my girlfriend into a vampire was something I'd been planning to do for over a year. But what I hadn't planned on, was turning her the moment I found out she was a demon. Talk about a shock. It had been a huge surprise and yet another secret she'd kept from me. But in that moment, I didn't have time to be mad; the instant I'd seen Rose's eyes glow red, I'd been flooded with the information about her heritage and the unwavering knowledge that turning her into the hybrid was the right thing to do—the only thing I *could* do. But now, as I stood frozen in place, looking into the depths of my inky black eyes, I hoped I hadn't made a mistake.

"Loraine, what happened next?"

"She rushed around in a frenzy, throwing stuff into a bag, and then flew out of the club. I haven't felt a pull toward her since." Loraine sobbed, causing my heart to break even more.

I paced back into the bedroom, feeling completely lost—lost without Rose, lost in what I should do... just completely and utterly lost. Suddenly a knock on the door stopped my depressive spiral.

"Christian, may we come in?" Evie called.

I wasn't in the mood to face everyone right now, but knew I didn't have a choice. "Yes, come in."

The door slowly opened and Evie and Dax hesitantly stepped inside. I was relieved it was just the two of them. They eyed me cautiously as I sat down on the bed and buried my head in my hands.

"Are you alright?" Evie's voice was tentative.

She was probably scared I had permanently drifted dark and was in the throes of Rose's poisonous blood. "Don't worry, I'm fine." I tried to assure her.

"But your hair, your eyes..."

I flew from the bed, startling everyone, and started to pace again. "I've drifted dark because I'm upset! Rose is gone."

Evie's gasp signaled she hadn't registered the fact that we were alone in the room. Dax frowned and sank down onto the bed, claiming the spot I'd just vacated.

"What do you mean gone? What's happened? There's so much I don't understand."

I wasn't sure if I should tell them about Loraine, but in order for my explanation to make sense, I really didn't have a choice. "I know, Evie. There's a lot of information I have that you don't. Why don't we go upstairs to your office, and I'll explain?" I had to get out of this room. Staying in it without Rose here was triggering some dark emotions I couldn't face right now.

As we made our way out of my room and down the stark, white-tiled hall, I sent my thoughts to Loraine. *"I have to tell her everything. About Rose and Jeremy being demons, about you, about my decision to turn Rose into the hybrid... everything."*

"I know, Christian. I just hope they'll understand and not be scared into a reaction that would hurt Rose or Jeremy... or you." The look on her face was grim as she gently floated beside me.

Once we reached the private entrance that led into Evie's office, we all climbed the stairs, our silence filling the small space. As the bookcase closed behind us, Evie and Dax took a seat on the couch against the far wall, while I continued to pace. Loraine hovered by the door and nodded to me encouragingly. I wasn't sure where to start, so I tried to organize my thoughts into a timeline that would be easy to follow.

"As you're both aware, I developed extra *abilities* during my triggering which allow me to hear and know things that others don't. The latter actually floods my mind with information about situations with unwavering clarity and finality. This was how I knew what to do when Evie was knocked unconscious."

They both nodded but stayed quiet while I continued.

"Recently, my abilities, in combination with something else, have helped me to understand a lot about everything that's been happening."

Evie shifted in her seat as Dax put his arm around her shoulders. I was sure they knew what was coming next was going to be hard to swallow.

"For a few weeks now, Rose's mother, Loraine, has been able to visit and communicate with me from the other side."

Dax visibly sank further into the couch as he exhaled a shocked breath, and Evie's hair started to drift at a rapid pace. This was not going well.

"Don't panic. She's been a huge help. Please just listen and let me explain."

CHAPTER THREE

(Christian)

"When Loraine was alive, she possessed an ability that allowed her to calm people with her mere presence. It's because of this power I think she and I can connect. Basically, I'm able to see and hear her because we both share some sort of psychic ability.

"She explained that each time she materializes, her mind—much like mine, is flooded with information about current situations. It's like the gods give her a data dump every time she returns to this plane. This is how she found out that Rose and Jeremy are demons."

Evie and Dax visibly tensed up but thankfully remained silent and allowed me to continue without interruption.

"Rose had no idea about her heritage until the night she fought with Meredith. Ever since then, she's carried this secret and for the last few months, tried to distance herself from me in an effort to keep us all safe. It wasn't until Jeremy told her he was staying with Meredith because she's pregnant, that Rose lost control of her demon side. That's what you witnessed when she flew into her fit of rage.

"Now, I know you don't agree and have no way to understand my choice, but in that instant, I knew turning her and making her my consort was the only thing that would save us all. She's now the hybrid we need to defeat Meredith."

I took a deep breath and stared at Evie and Dax. My rapid revelations eased about a hundred pounds off my shoulders, but the unsure looks plastered on both their faces, combined with their increased drifting, left me unsure as to where things stood.

After a deep breath of her own, Evie spoke. "Christian, while I'm well aware of, and do understand your extra abilities, I'm sitting here looking at your dark hair and eyes and wondering exactly how turning Rose was the best thing for our clan? If her blood causes you to drift *permanently* dark, that means we will have lost our new Sire, and personally, I can't think of anything worse."

I knew she wasn't trying to reprimand me for my decision, but instead, simply sharing her concerns. And they were valid concerns, but again, the knowledge I possessed still led me to believe that turning Rose was the right thing to do.

"I can't explain how I know it, but I'm telling you, turning Rose will save our clan. Balam said we needed to create a hybrid to fight the demons, and then all of a sudden it turns out that the woman I love *is* a demon... Somehow, I don't think that's a coincidence. Call it cosmic intervention or fate, whatever, but I know I made the right choice."

Evie stood up and came to stand directly in front of me.

"Well, *fate* is a pretty big leap, and one that you've left us no choice but to take. But Christian, you're a vampire and the consort bond also means you can't be away from your chosen for very long. What happens if she doesn't come back? Do you realize you'll die because of your connection now?"

I turned away, catching a glimpse of Loraine before I answered Evie's question. Rose's mom looked as nervous as I felt.

"Yes, I'm very aware of our connection, and while it's being stretched, it's not severed, which means she's still alive. As long as I find her soon, we should both be just fine."

Evie looked at Dax and I watched him shake his head while she lifted an eyebrow. I knew they were scanning each other's thoughts and having a private conversation; probably about how they agreed I'd completely lost my mind.

"Look, I'm going to start my search for Rose immediately with Loraine's help, so if you can get Renard to cover my duties tonight, I'd appreciate it."

"Speaking of the clan, I think it's important you speak to them before you leave. Obviously, the cat's out of the bag that you're the new Sire, and they deserve an explanation," Evie stated.

"Yes, of course. You're right." As I turned and headed toward the door, I remembered something else I needed to share. "By the way, Terrance already knows I'm the new Sire. He was still in the pit when I delivered the true death to Kennedy."

Evie dropped her head, obviously frustrated I'd ruined our element of surprise.

"I'm sorry, Evie. I know this changes everything, but I promise it will all work out."

"I hope so, Christian. I truly hope so."

A knock on the door interrupted our conversation. "Come in," Evie called out.

Dominique entered the room with a worried look on her face. "Um... we've all fed from the blood bags downstairs and just wanted to check and make sure everything was alright since we didn't see any of you in the pit."

After a vampire named Kennedy bit a demon in the club last week, causing him to drift dark, Evie confined all of us to feeding from blood bags so as not to risk us biting an unknown demon by accident. She worried Meredith has started sending demons into the club to purposely pose as willing donors. But, unbeknownst to us at the time, the demon Kennedy had bitten was Rose—another tidbit of information I gleaned as our bond took hold.

Evie cast a quick look in my direction. "Yes, we're fine. Please let everyone know we'll be out in a few moments."

CHAPTER FOUR

(Christian)

I followed Evie and Dax out of the office and found myself under the scrutiny of the people I'd considered my family for centuries.

Bobby, my best friend, was sitting on the bottom step of the staircase that led to the second story of the club, while Renard and his wife, Loni, sat at one of the tables in the middle of the room. Dominique and her sister, Tori, were standing behind the bar as usual, and Terrance was leaning against the wall beside the entrance.

I walked across the room and up the steps toward the front door, putting myself slightly higher than the small crowd in an effort to make my first talk as Sire seem more official. As I moved close to Terrance, he kindly slapped me on the shoulder before I turned around to face everyone.

"Um... I guess you all realize I'm your new Sire." I cringed at their silent nods and *humphs* but continued. "Evie chose to perform the Passing of Powers ritual in an effort to prepare for our upcoming battle with the demons. We thought that having two Sires to fight against them instead of one was the best plan. I'm sorry we didn't tell you, but the idea was to keep it a secret so we'd gain the upper hand. Obviously, I kind of blew that."

Their blank stares had me swallowing hard against the lump in my throat.

"As you all witnessed, Rose is a demon, and while I'm sure you won't understand my reasoning, I know that by turning her into our hybrid and my consort, we will be able to defeat Meredith and her growing army."

Silence hung in the air until Dominique spoke up. "So even though you're showing signs of drifting dark, we're all just supposed to believe turning Rose will somehow save us?"

"I'm hoping you can trust me enough as your new Sire to do just that, yes. The abilities I've developed have given me clear insight into the fact that Rose will be our saving grace."

"Then where the fuck is she?" Bobby demanded. "Besides, like Dom said, you're standing there with dark hair and eyes. What's gonna stop you from foaming at the mouth now that Rose's demon blood is running through your veins?"

"I won't pretend I didn't start to feel the effects of her blood as I drank her to the brink of death. But the instant our connection snapped into place, everything changed. I knew I'd be able to survive this, and so will she."

It was then that Terrance spoke up. "Listen, if Rose's blood was truly affecting him like Meredith's did me, he wouldn't even be able to think or talk about her right now, so why don't you all cut him some fucking slack. He's our new Sire, and if he says things will be okay, then that should be good enough."

His statement caught everyone off guard. And while I was definitely grateful he'd come to my defense, it was still a pretty big shock. I wondered if the fact that Loraine was hovering near him was part of the reason he seemed so "pro-me."

After a few seconds of watching everyone contemplate his words, Dominique spoke up again. "I'm not trying to be a bitch here, but I have to ask, you said that you're *our* new Sire? I thought once a new Sire assumes power, they leave with their consort to start a clan of their own."

Thankfully, Evie responded to Dominique's statement. "Yes, Dom, that's usually the case, but since we are on the brink of something major that none of us understand, I thought it would be best if Christian and Rose remain with our clan until things have been resolved with the demons. Especially since Rose is now our best chance of winning against them."

"Fine. So back to Bobby's question. Where in the hell is she?" Dominique repeated.

The tension in the air was thick, and telling them Rose was now the hybrid had sucked. However, admitting I had no idea where she was, or what state of mind she was currently in, was going to be the hardest part of all.

"I'm not sure. Since Rose is able to rise before sunset, my guess is that she left to go check on her father."

The room erupted as everyone flew from their seats and started shouting.

"WHAT? That's suicide! She may be the hybrid now, but walking straight into Meredith's grasp has to be the dumbest idea ever," Bobby declared.

"What the fuck, Evie, how could you let this happen?" Tori demanded.

Renard and Loni were huddled together, probably plotting their exit strategy, while Dominique simply glared in my direction.

"STOP!" This was only the second time I'd used my Sire command, and while I definitely agreed with all of their concerns, I had to maintain a confident exterior. "All of your concerns are completely valid, which is why I'm going to have to cut this short. I'm headed straight there to make sure Rose doesn't run into Meredith right off the bat."

I didn't really know if this was where Rose had gone, but I sure as hell wasn't going to tell them that.

As I turned away, Terrance piped up and asked the one question I wanted to avoid at all costs. "Do you want me to go with you?"

Thankfully, once again, Evie came to my rescue. "Actually, I think it's going to be important Christian goes alone. For one, the less people for Meredith to take notice of, the better, but also because Rose and Christian haven't been able to come together as consorts yet. She left before he woke tonight."

Terrance nodded and luckily everyone else started to disperse to begin their nightly duties to open the club. Evie winked at me before engaging Dominique in a new conversation, providing me the time I needed to slip out the front door.

I didn't have to think about Loraine, because she was already hovering right beside me. *Do you really think Rose went straight to Jeremy's?* she asked.

I'm not sure, Loraine. But right now, it's the best idea I've got.

CHAPTER FIVE

(Rose)

Waking up next to Christian was nothing new. But waking up next to Christian with my teeth throbbing, and an uncontrollable urge to sink them into his neck, was definitely a shock.

I literally couldn't help myself as I bent his head to the side and sunk my newly developed fangs through the soft flesh of his throat. The sensation of his warm blood filling my mouth was absolute heaven. I could also feel our consort bond and instantly realized that was the reason I couldn't resist the temptation to drink. This was how all *newbies* completed their transition and drifted to their "normal" coloring.

I raised my head from the side of Christian's neck and knew something was wrong. Wrong, because I wasn't just a vampire... I was also a demon.

Flying from the bed, I looked into the mirror. My hair had drifted completely black and my eyes were a deep crimson. In the vampire world this meant I was bad. But thinking about Meredith, and the fact that she'd killed my mom and was now basically holding my dad prisoner—bad was feeling pretty damn good.

Racing around the room, I gathered some supplies and threw them into a bag. I looked over at Christian, surprised he was still comatose but then noticed the clock on the nightstand—it read 3:24 p.m., still hours before sunset. I assumed it was my demon side that allowed me to wake; the demon side that I'd hid from everyone until my father fell prey to that evil bitch. The moment he'd called and told me that he was staying with her because they were having a *baby*, I'd snapped.

With the memory now fueling my anger, I ran out of the club not caring if I was bad or not. I couldn't wait to get to my dad's and kill Meredith. And thanks to Christian, I was now the one person who could make it happen. I raced between the trees lining the freeway to Masen. The feeling of the wind blowing through my now black hair was so freeing I almost flew past my exit. I knew my dad lived off of 29th Street, thanks to Renard and Loni's recent reconnaissance.

I raced into the open space across from their brownstone, but realized it was early evening and both my dad and the bitch would most likely still be at work. As I contemplated my next move, the rumble in my stomach brought the fact that I was completely famished into sharp relief. The little blood I'd taken from Christian was just enough to complete my transition, but definitely not enough to appease my growing appetite.

After all those months of talking to Terrance, even though he'd been under Meredith's influence at the time, I did learn a lot about vampires. For one, they didn't feed from others of their kind, only humans, and only once per night. They programmed the sedative that flowed from their fangs to erase the person's mind and to heal their wounds. This made the experience something that was only a necessity for the vampires and never left the human hurt, or even aware it had happened at all. Too bad I'd run out before Christian had a chance to teach me how to do any of that. I figured it should be pretty easy, and since I didn't have a choice but to feed, now was as good a time as any to learn.

I looked around the park and saw a few people milling about. There was a young couple pushing a baby stroller on the far side of the small lake; an old woman sitting on the bench of the nearest shore, feeding the birds; but it was the jogger headed down the path that ran straight under the stone bridge that caught my eye. The bridge ran through a small grove of maple trees which shaded the entire length. It was perfect.

I made sure no one was looking my way, then raced to the other end of the tunnel and waited in the shadows under the bridge. As the man got closer, I could smell his cologne mixed with his sweat, but it was the sweet smell of his blood that had my fangs aching again.

As soon as he was within reach, I grabbed him and pushed him back against the curved stone wall. I moved so fast, he didn't have a chance to protest before my fangs were buried deep in his neck. I began to think of the thoughts to program my sedative, but instead got completely lost in the taste of his blood. I stifled his screams with my hand and continued to suck deep draws of blood down my throat. It felt as if his blood was a drug, one that I would never be able to break the habit of. It was more than a vampire necessity; it was like his blood was the life essence fueling my body and turning me into something that Meredith would fear. I loved it, and didn't stop drinking until the man fell to the ground.

CHAPTER SIX

(Meredith)

It had only been two days since I'd forged the mind bond with Jeremy by forcing him to drink my blood. He'd left me no choice when he prepared to walk out on me and our baby. Now, I only had to slip him a little of my blood every day to maintain control. And since before this little hiccup, we really were in love, it didn't take much to nudge him into feeling as if we were living out our happily ever after.

"Jeremy, darling. What time do you think you'll be home from work tonight?" I asked as I cleaned off the kitchen table.

"I'm not sure, honey. My boss said since I missed our last meeting in Seela, he wanted to make up for it today with a conference call." He shook his head, as if still trying to piece together the events of that day.

I still didn't know *exactly* how Jeremy had found out about our heritage or from whom, even though the answer seemed pretty obvious. All I knew for sure was that he'd cancelled his trip to Seela, came home early that day, and found me killing Damien in our garage. It had been the worst way possible to expose him to our demon side. But thankfully, that was all behind us now.

"Okay, well, just give me call when you're close to heading home so I'll know when to put dinner on."

"Don't you have one of your meetings tonight?" he asked.

I tensed up at the question, my eyes flaring red as I set the dishes in the sink. I hadn't talked to or seen any of the other demons who'd been coming to my meetings since after I'd received a call from Damien's cousin, Raúl. He told me Damien's body had been found down by the railroad tracks. I feigned surprise, of course, seeing as I was the one who dumped him there.

Damien had practically forced me to kill him when the power-hungry fool threatened to murder Jeremy. Plus, I refused to have a lieutenant who thought he could overpower me or uproot my plans. I told Raúl to let me know when the funeral was so I could come pay my respects, but my real reason for wanting to go was to get some time alone with him. I was hoping he'd agree to step into Damien's shoes as my second in command. I had to get back to building my army, because I knew Rose and her adopted vampire family would soon be closing in on me.

"No. This week's meeting has been postponed, so I'll be here waiting for you." I turned back to Jeremy and rubbed a hand over my belly.

With a loving smile, he laid his hand on top of mine and kissed my cheek. "Sounds great. I'll call you when my day is over."

Watching him head out the door with his coffee mug in hand, left me filled with satisfaction. He'd be sipping my blood all the way to work, and therefore, my mind bond would remain safely in place. The realization I would never lose the man I loved was almost as euphoric as when I'd drained the life from his wife.

Jeremy was the first demon outside of my family I'd ever run across. The moment we'd met, I knew I wanted him to be the father of my child. The idea of continuing my pure demon bloodline thrilled me, but the first step I'd had to take was to eliminate his wife. Her life essence had flowed into me and activated my ancient demon traits: faster speed, enhanced strength, and most importantly, my journey to becoming immortal. My grandmother's stories rang in my ears as I'd stood over Loraine's dead body; stories of our ancestors drinking human blood. It was in that instant I knew I'd found the key to becoming the most powerful demon in existence.

Now, if I could just go to this funeral and get Raúl to fall in line, I could start up the meetings again and continue to spike the punch with human blood. Most of the other demons didn't have a clue as to what they were drinking, but they had certainly enjoyed the "uplifting" effects it had on them. Raúl and a few other cousins had been in on the plan, and after demonstrating their slight increase in strength and speed, I knew dosing them in small amounts was the best way to build my unsuspecting army. However, before I could do anything else, I had to make the doctor's appointment that would confirm my pregnancy. I'd been so happy when my home test appeared positive, but with the distraction of killing Damien and having to establish my mind bond with Jeremy, the last couple of days had been a complete blur.

As I headed up the stairs to retrieve my cell phone, I realized even though Jeremy and I had just shared breakfast, I was still famished. The problem was... I wasn't hungry for food.

I was only drinking human blood as a way to maintain my demon traits, but right now I felt more like a vampire, like I was actually craving it. I entered our bedroom and picked up my cell off the nightstand, wondering if my appetite was something I should be worried about. It only took a moment for my uncertainty to grow, so instead of dialing the number for my doctor, I punched the numbers for my grandmother instead.

"Good morning, Grandma, it's Meredith. I was wondering if you'd be up for a visit today?"

"Of course, child. You know you're always welcome here. No need to call first."

The sound of my grandmother's voice was like a soothing balm to my soul. She was the one person in our family who had special gifts that were inherent to our demon race. But to me, her most special gift was how loved and comfortable she had always made me feel. I just hoped she'd remain as calm and comforting if I decided to tell her what was truly going on.

CHAPTER SEVEN

(Christian)

I continued to contemplate my little speech as I drove down the freeway in my '67 Comet Caliente. I had hoped it would ease the disappointment I knew my clan felt, but after scanning them as we spoke, the doubts and fears layering their thoughts were pretty overwhelming. In their eyes, not only was turning Rose a terrible idea, but the fact that I was the new Sire and they hadn't known about it was most likely going to cause a problem for quite some time.

In an effort to distance myself from these thoughts, I looked over at the passenger seat and saw Loraine staring out the windshield. It was so odd to look at someone and yet still be able to see right through them. The trees were flying by the window as ethereal wisps of her hair blew in a wind I wasn't even sure she could feel.

"Don't worry, Loraine. We'll find her."

She turned to face me and smiled a sad smile. *"I know, Christian. I'm just concerned about how she will be* when *we find her."*

I knew Loraine was talking about the fact Rose had drifted dark after completing her transition. Most people became light vampires, but there were instances where if the person carried sorrow and pain within them from their human lives, they would show signs of that by drifting darker initially. With everything Rose had been through over the last year—her mother's death, finding out about vampires, her attempted murder of Meredith, and the revelation that she and her dad were demons—um, yeah, I supposed I shouldn't be surprised she turned out darker than expected. Now it was just a matter of reaching her in time, before her emotions shut down, because at that point, she truly would be lost.

The horrible images playing in my head had me veering onto the shoulder. I couldn't imagine my sweet Rose as some dark, evil creature. The idea caused a serious knot in my stomach, because now, it was *my* responsibility to kill any vampire who drifted dark, even if it was the love of my life.

"Dammit," I cussed, banging my fist against the steering wheel. "Why couldn't I have been there to help her through her transition like every other Sire in history?"

Loraine's ghostly hand settled on top of my shoulder. *"Christian, I'm sorry. I didn't mean to upset you with my worries. And you already know the answer to that. Rose is special. She's now the hybrid and that means there's bound to be differences with her transition than any others before her."*

"Yes, but now, I'm just so scared that what seemed like the right thing to do at the time was possibly the worst decision I could've made."

Loraine's weak smile didn't offer much comfort, but apparently her calming ability still worked wonders, because as soon as the words left my mouth, the doubts about my decision eased, if only slightly.

Getting back on topic, I asked, "Have you felt any kind of pull toward Rose or Jeremy recently?"

"No. I haven't." She shook her head and dropped her hand back into her lap.

I wanted to reassure her everything would be okay, but I couldn't bring myself to lie to her. I honestly didn't know if we'd be able to find Rose or save Jeremy, but whatever our futures held, I had a feeling there was going to be a lot of heartache along the way.

* * * * *

(Rose)

After savoring the last drop of blood as it ran down my throat, I looked down at the man I'd just killed. I wasn't sure what to do or what I should be feeling. As a good vampire I should be mortified; as a bad vampire I should be reveling in the kill; and as a demon I should apparently feel the man's life force filling me with an immortal essence. But as the hybrid, I felt nothing. I wasn't remorseful, I wasn't sad, I wasn't happy, I wasn't... *anything.*

Black hair surrounded my face as I dipped my head and closed my eyes, trying to force myself back on task. I'd come here to end Meredith and save my dad, but I found myself no longer caring. I lifted my head and opened my eyes. Maybe I should destroy the bridge in an effort to conceal the dead man's body. Then again, why should I care if he was discovered or not? If anyone approached me for any reason, whether it was to ask the time or to accuse me of murder, I had nothing to fear. Nothing or no one could threaten me now.

Indifference layered my brain as I wiped my mouth, then rubbed away the traces of blood against my jeans. I walked out from underneath the bridge and everything looked different. It all seemed crisper and clearer... heightened somehow. I could hear squirrels scurrying throughout the trees, and the wheels of the stroller crunching over the rocks in its path. The old woman was still sitting in the same spot, feeding the birds, and even though I was at least one-hundred yards away, I could hear the low clucking noise she made under her breath as she scattered the seeds on the ground in front of her.

It was amazing. The sky was bluer than blue, and the trees swayed in time with music I was sure no one else could hear but me. For being dead, I suddenly felt so alive. I wanted to race around the park, up the trees, through the city, leap from building to building, crush cars with my bare hands, or maybe even stop a train. I laughed out loud at the thought, causing the police officer who'd rounded the corner to turn in my direction.

The low hiss that escaped my lips was a shock to both him and me. However, I was long gone before the cop had a chance to blink. I now watched from my perch in the top of the tallest tree as the idiot spun around, looking from side to side. It didn't take him long to find the dead man's body and within minutes the park was surrounded by flashing lights. Yellow tape went up and all the people I'd noticed before were being gathered and questioned. Each of them reported they hadn't seen anything or anyone unusual. A wicked smiled crept across my face at the idea any of them could have been my dinner, and yet none of them had even seen me.

I continued to watch as a crowd started to gather and the man's body was wheeled out on a gurney from underneath the bridge. It was in a black coroner's bag, just like you'd see on TV. I tried to muster some sort of emotion, but as I watched the corpse being loaded into the black van, I still felt nothing. It wasn't until I saw my dad's Lexus pull into his driveway across the street did I feel a twinge of anything at all. Unfortunately for him, the only thing I felt now was disgust.

I stared at the house as Meredith came out the front door and greeted my dad on the lawn with a hug and kiss. They stood there for a while, watching the scene in the park unfold. Finally, my dad walked across the street and asked a police officer exactly what had happened. The officer hesitated at first, but once Dad explained that they lived directly across the street, he started to share bits of information. After giving a serious nod to the cop, Dad walked back across the street and embraced Meredith once more.

Finally, a feeling sparked within me—one of rage. I had come here to kill Meredith and "save" my dad, but watching as the happy couple walked back into their perfect little home caused something inside me to snap. I could literally feel my emotions shutting down. As I watched them cross the threshold, I was suddenly over this entire scene—just like my dad had apparently gotten over me. As sad as that should make me, I couldn't bring myself to care anymore. I was a completely different person now, and it was obvious so was he.

I took one last look at my dad's house then disappeared into the night.

CHAPTER EIGHT

(Meredith)

Once I hung up with my grandmother, I showered and got dressed. I was still off from work due to the "illness" I'd faked a couple of days ago. I wanted to talk to her and make sure my baby was okay before I headed back to an office filled with nosy co-workers. Plus, I figured once I returned, announcing I was pregnant would make perfect sense as to why I had needed the time off.

On my way across town to Grandma's house, I tried to think of the best way to get the information I needed without openly admitting I was drinking human blood. As much as she knew about the ancient stories, I highly doubted learning her only granddaughter was openly practicing them would make for a very pleasant visit.

As I pulled my BMW into her driveway, I saw her peek out from the kitchen window and give a little wave. I walked straight in, knowing she'd have already unlocked the door for me.

"Hi, Grams," I called out.

"Hello, honey. Come on in. I'm making your favorite."

Grandma's back was to me as she continued to wash dishes in the sink. I could smell the herbs from the roasted chicken and stuffed green peppers drifting from the oven, but instead of my mouth watering as usual, my stomach rolled. *Dammit.*

It was becoming more and more obvious my decision to become immortal was starting to have negative effects, in addition to the positive ones. Yes, I may be strong, fast, and immune to harm, but apparently, I was also becoming something else in the process.

Not wanting to show my sudden concern, I took a seat at the kitchen table and said, "Smells good."

"I'm happy to see you, Meredith, it's been a while. How did you manage to make it over during the week?"

"Well, that's part of what I wanted to talk to you about. I haven't been feeling well, and I think it's because I may be pregnant."

Grandma gasped, and spun to face me. "What?"

I smiled and placed a hand upon my stomach. "Yep. I think I may be pregnant with Jeremy's child."

"Jeremy is the man you've told me about? The demon who doesn't know he's a demon."

"Yes." I giggled.

Grandma took the seat next to me and reached for my hands. I waited as she held them tight and closed her eyes. I knew she was trying to use her gifts to sense the baby, but I was a little nervous about exactly what she'd pick up.

After a few moments of strained silence, Grandma released me. "Well, you're right. You are pregnant." She sat back in her chair and smiled, but I could tell something was off when it didn't quite reach her eyes. "I'm not sure of the sex, and I can't quite get a good visual, but it's definitely a pure-blood demon. The question is... why do I also sense human blood in your system?"

Well, shit. So much for keeping my secret. I wanted to open up to her but was worried about her reaction to my news, so I decided to skew the truth just a bit. "Grams, please understand. I didn't mean for it to happen. Recently I was severely injured, but after remembering all the stories you told me about our ancestors, I drank human blood in a desperate attempt to save my own life. It worked. I healed almost immediately and gained major amounts of strength and speed." I waited to see what she'd say before I continued to dig this hole.

With a sadness layering her features, she sat there frowning like grandmas do. "Well, I can't say that I'm pleased, or that I have any idea what this will do to you or your baby. But I can tell that you are changing, and I'm afraid what you've started will not be good for our race." She pushed away from the table and returned to the sink. I felt like shit as she turned the oven off, obviously realizing I wouldn't be eating any of the food she'd cooked.

"I'm sorry." I didn't know what else to say, and I did feel bad for letting her down. But not only was stopping what I started out of the question, I literally didn't think that I could stop if I wanted to. Grandma was right, I had changed, and now there was no going back.

I tentatively approached my grandma as she methodically scrubbed the dishes in the sink, and gave her a small hug from behind. I wasn't sure if this would be the last time I'd see her or not, but I left the house without another word. I hoped she would be able to accept my decisions once I proved becoming immortal wasn't a bad thing, but a good one. Who knows, maybe she would start drinking human blood too, and then we could be together forever. The idea had merit, but I wasn't holding my breath.

I let the thought drop as I backed out of the driveway, switching my focus to happier things. It was only two in the afternoon, so I decided to head to the store to pick up what I'd need for dinner. I couldn't wait to welcome Jeremy home in the special way I'd done over the last few days: a glass of wine for him laced with my blood, candles, and sexy lingerie.

Our lives had become so much better since I'd started controlling him. I'd wiped his memory of me killing Damien and about us being demons. As far as he knew, we were just a happy couple in love who were getting ready to have a baby. I did, however, decide to leave the memories of when I'd comforted him after Loraine's death. That way, he'd truly feel the depth of our connection. But, the one thing I didn't hesitate on doing while creating our perfect world, was to erase all his memories of Rose. I couldn't risk any thoughts of her leaking through, especially if she was the one who'd told him about me and all that I'd done.

Shaking off the past, I finished my grocery shopping then headed straight home and began marinating the steaks when my cell phone rang.

"Hello."

"Hi, Meredith. It's Raúl. I was calling to let you know that Damien's service will be tomorrow afternoon at The Angelus Funeral Home on East 16th at four p.m."

"Okay, thank you, Raúl. I'll see you there." I hung up the phone, smiling. I was well aware that tomorrow would be hard for everyone in Damien's family, and therefore I'd have to be sure to put on an especially good act. My plan was to get through the service, then speak to Raúl alone. From the way he'd handled digesting the human blood at the meeting, I thought he'd make a good replacement for his dead cousin.

As I continued to contemplate my plan, I headed back to the kitchen to start the vegetables for dinner, but just as I sat the pan on the stove, I saw flashing lights outside the front window. I walked into the living room and saw the park across the street being surrounded by cops and other emergency vehicles. I stood watching as they taped off the area around the stone bridge, and then took a shocked breath when they wheeled out a dead body.

A few minutes later, Jeremy pulled into the driveway. I walked out the front door and greeted him with a hug and kiss. We stood there together, watching the police scurry around the scene. Finally, when a cop walked out toward his squad car, Jeremy crossed the street to speak with him. After a few minutes he walked back across the street, hugged me, then led me into the house.

"Apparently there was a man attacked under the bridge. The officer said his neck had been torn at and he died from major blood loss."

The instant I heard the words neck and blood, my eyes flared red. Thankfully, Jeremy was behind me as we walked back into the kitchen, and didn't notice.

I could only think of one thing that would tear out someone's neck and leave them to bleed to death. Well, besides myself—make that two things. I instantly worried this was a message from Christian's clan. I forced myself to remain calm and continued to prepare our dinner. I couldn't let Jeremy see I was actually on the verge of losing control.

"Did they say if there were any suspects?" I asked.

"No. The officer said no one in the park noticed anyone strange or heard anything. I guess we'll just have to watch the news and see if they found something to go on once they've completed the investigation."

"Well, I don't know about you, but the idea of people being killed in the park across the street from where we'll be raising our baby isn't the most comforting thing. Maybe we should think about moving."

Jeremy spun around, his eyes wide. "Really? You've lived here for so long. You'd really consider uprooting after just one crime in the park?"

"Well, yes! I may have lived here for a long time, but I've never been pregnant before, and certainly never had to worry about anyone else's safety but my own. But now... I can't imagine our child walking home from school and seeing something like this, or worse, being the victim."

Running was never really my style, but with the meetings on hold and the vampires obviously closing in, moving somewhere else might not be a bad idea right now. "What do you think? Maybe we could move into one of the high rises downtown that has around the clock security."

Jeremy walked over and pulled me into an embrace. "Honey, I'll move wherever you want as long as you feel safe. Plus, if we moved downtown, we'd both be closer to work, so it would offset the increased cost of housing if we didn't have to drive to work every day."

I was glad he was seeing things my way. "Thank you, sweetheart. I'll call the realtor tomorrow."

CHAPTER NINE

(Christian)

We arrived at the address Renard and Loni provided in their report, and I parked the car directly across the street from Jeremy and Meredith's brownstone. The block was quiet, except for a few cops milling around. They seemed to be gathering yellow tape from near the bridge. Police, crime tape... this was not looking good. I had a sinking feeling whatever happened, had something to do with Rose.

"Loraine, are you able to check to see if Jeremy and Meredith are in their home?"

"No, Christian. I'm sorry. I can only go where other people's thoughts pull me, and like I said, I haven't felt anything from Jeremy for a while."

"All right then, I'm going to wait until the police clear the vicinity, then go check out what's happening in the park. After that, we'll head over to the brownstone."

I figured I'd need to check out the park first, in case that's where Rose had confronted Meredith. But for now, I had no choice but to wait in the car. I thought about making small talk with Loraine but just didn't know what to say. I had so many questions about Rose and their family, but I didn't want to appear insensitive by making her talk about the loved ones she'd lost. So instead, I just sat there, watching the house for any signs of movement.

After a few minutes, Loraine spoke. "Christian. What do you think is happening to Rose? I mean, what's it like to change into a vampire and how do you think her being a demon has made things different?"

I wasn't sure how to answer, because honestly, I had no idea. So instead of speculating about Rose's experience, I stuck with what I *did* know.

Loraine's eyes remained glued to mine as I explained the process of vampire creation. I could see by the look on her face I hadn't really answered her question, so I added, "It doesn't hurt, Loraine."

A small smile crept across her sad face, telling me she wasn't convinced. I'm sure watching her daughter rise as a vampire and then drift dark wasn't an easy thing to process, but I didn't know what else to say to convince her everything would be all right. I thought about telling her the rest of the story, about how when a new Sire turns their first vampire that they were actually choosing their consort. But I didn't think the idea of Rose's and my life being connected to the point of dying if the other one does, was something Loraine needed to be reminded of right now. Besides, as I looked out the window into the park, I noticed all the people had finally left.

"I'm going to check out the park, I'll be right back. Do you want to go with me or stay here?" I asked.

"I'll stay here, I guess. But if you stop thinking about Rose or me, I'll most likely disappear. If that happens, just call me back when you need me again."

I was pretty sure this was Loraine's way of saying she needed some time alone. I figured the oblivion she faded away to would be a good break for her. As I made my way out of the car and into the park, I purposely guarded my thoughts. As I approached the bridge, I looked back and noticed she was gone. I hoped she found some peace, if only for a little while.

Regaining my focus, I continued to walk into the park. I could smell blood before I even reached the bridge, but it wasn't Rose's, though her scent was I the air. The blood, unfortunately, wasn't Meredith's either. I would have recognized the sharp tinge, since I'd gotten a good whiff when we'd left her bleeding on the floor all those months ago. No, this wasn't Meredith's blood, just some random human's which meant Rose had fed.

I was happy to know Rose was safe, but unfortunately I could also tell she wasn't anywhere in the vicinity. Our bond would have told me if she was, but instead, it still felt stretched, as if a great distance separated us. I took a deep breath, trying to hold it together. Even though Rose was long gone, I still needed to check to see if Meredith was alive or not. Maybe Rose had truly solved all of our problems within the first few hours of being the hybrid. One could only hope.

I left the dark tunnel under the bridge and flew across the street to hide in the bushes nearest Jeremy and Meredith's house. I listened for any movement or bits of conversation, but what I heard made absolutely no sense.

I picked up on the rustling of sheets, as if someone was climbing into bed, then Jeremy's voice rang out. "I'm so excited we're having a baby, Meredith. Becoming a dad is something I've always wanted."

What the hell? Um... Jeremy was a dad, and had been for twenty-one years. I continued to listen, trying to gain an inkling of understanding.

"I'm excited too, honey. I can't wait to be parents for the first time. I've always wanted a baby, and for it to be with you... my dreams really have come true."

I listened as they shared a quick kiss, then Jeremy continued. "I feel the same way. I just hope I'll know what I'm doing and will be a good dad."

Okay, this was fucked. I tried to think of why in the world Jeremy would be acting as if Rose never existed and was instantly hit with the truth. Rose had been right. Meredith had tricked Jeremy into staying with her. *Dammit!* This situation just went from bad to worse. Meredith had erased Rose from Jeremy's mind all together by feeding him her blood.

If Rose came here to confront Meredith and save her dad, only to realize her father had no clue who she was, I could only imagine the devastation she must have felt. If she was dark before, there was no telling what she'd be like now. The negative emotions caused by knowing your father—your *only* living family—had just been forced to forget who you were... *Oh man.* I was surprised Rose hadn't ripped off Meredith's head right then and there. Then again, what if Meredith wasn't here when Rose approached her dad? What if Jeremy turned her away, not knowing who she was? The picture I now imagined was one of Rose running off into the night, crying from a broken heart.

Dread settled in my chest as I flew from the bushes and back to the car. There was no reason for me to stay here any longer. I couldn't confront Meredith by myself, and I couldn't approach Jeremy either, because most likely, he wouldn't have any clue as to who I was either. I eased away from the curb, gunning it once I was around the block. I had to get back to The Rising Pit and tell Evie everything that happened.

On the way back to Seela, I tried to force my powers into revealing where Rose was, but it just wasn't working. Frustrated, I thought back through every conversation we'd shared, hoping to spark a clue as to where she could have gone. It would have been nice if I'd been able to read her thoughts before I changed her, or if Evie had been able to scan her at some point, but unfortunately that never happened either. I almost laughed out loud at our ignorance. Originally, I thought we couldn't scan Rose because she was purposely guarding her thoughts from us, but in reality, it was because she was a demon.

Demons, or zôts, were something none of us had ever encountered before. Until the situation with Terrance developed. Balam, Evie's Sire, had been helpful with his information, but this was also a first for the elders as well. Throughout the centuries it was thought that whenever a vampire drifted dark, it was a random event brought on by embracing their darkness that led to them reveling in the kill. Who knew the real reason was because they had accidentally fed from a demon? Our clan had experienced all this when Terrance was infected by Meredith. But luckily, he'd fallen in love with Loraine and became the only vampire in existence to come out of it alive. It had been Loraine's calming ability that allowed Terrance to retain a hint of lightness in his soul, and that was the *only* reason we ended up not having to kill him.

Now with Rose running around with a broken heart, I had no idea what we were supposed to do next. She was the only weapon that could destroy Meredith, and I had just lost her. *Can you say cluster-fuck?*

I could only imagine how dark I'd drifted with all these thoughts running through my head. So, when I pulled into the parking lot of The Rising Pit, I turned off the car, closed my eyes, and took a few deep breaths to calm myself. The news I had for Evie and the clan wasn't going to make them happy, and I didn't want to add to their stress by showing up looking even more out of control.

My meditative efforts were interrupted when Terrance knocked on the window of my car. I opened the door and stepped out, praying he didn't have more bad news.

"What's up?"

"I heard you pull up. So, what'd you find out?"

While I wasn't surprised by his question, I *was* confused as to why he'd left the club to ask me alone. I wondered what other factors had motivated this one-on-one meeting. I scanned Terrance's thoughts and found out exactly why he was here. He was trying to warn me.

Apparently as soon as I left, Evie and Dax discussed the situation with the rest of the clan. The outcome was that if I was unable to get Rose back safely, or if when I did bring her back, she was still dark and out of control, they were going to have to consider the possibility of putting an end to her, which would of course in turn, kill me as well.

I tried to show no reaction but fell back against the side of my car for support. I couldn't believe Evie would contemplate killing Rose and therefore me, or that she was second guessing my decisions. But, even worse, I was now considering getting in my car and leaving my family behind. That's what bothered me the most. I hated the idea of them being unprotected, but honestly, what did my presence do for them right now? Nothing. We would all remain sitting ducks until I got Rose back and we found out whether or not she was really meant to be our salvation. Continuing to search for Rose on my own was clearly the only choice.

"Terrance, please tell them I know what I'm doing, and I'll be back soon."

He nodded, and I could tell by the look in his eyes that he was well aware I'd scanned his thoughts. He clapped me on the back as I turned toward my car. "Just be careful, man. You're going to have to figure out a way to get some blood bags to keep with you, so you don't risk feeding off any demons Meredith has in the area."

"Thank you, and don't worry, I'll be fine."

The last thing I saw as I drove away from my home, and the family I'd spent over six hundred years with, was Terrance raising his hand in goodbye before he reentered the club.

CHAPTER TEN

(Rose)

I couldn't believe I'd ran so far from Masen already. Having the speed of a vampire and a demon truly made me the fastest thing alive. Looking around, I wasn't even sure where I was. I was standing in the center of a wheat field, lined on the far edge with tall oak and hickory trees. It was still night, but I could tell the sun would be rising in just a few hours. The idea I could sleep wherever, and whenever, I wanted, continuing on at my convenience, caused a smile to drift across my face. I would literally never have to worry about anything ever again.

I slowed my pace, enjoying the soft glow the yellow wheat gave off in the moonlight. My hand brushed the tops of the stalks as I walked toward the small forest. I could make out lights in the distance and figured it'd make as good a place as any to stop and feed. I didn't have any real direction I wanted to head, so the idea of starting my world-wide tour in the next town seemed like the most obvious thing to do. Who knew where it would lead me? Maybe I would stay for a few days and get to know the locals, or maybe I would book a flight and head overseas to check out London and Tuscany like I'd always dreamed of.

I came to the edge of town in a matter of seconds. I glanced at the highway sign and found I was in Mt. Vernon, a small town outside of Springfield, Missouri.

Okay, maybe I would just feed and catch a few hours of sleep and move onto somewhere else a little more exciting. From every history lesson I could remember, besides Missouri being the 24th state admitted to the Union, and the birthplace of Harry Truman, I didn't recall anything else about Missouri that would be considered *amazing*.

Oh wait! Yes, I did. Missouri was where Samuel Clemens, writing as Mark Twain, penned *The Adventures of Tom Sawyer* and its sequel, *Adventures of Huckleberry Finn*. Little did people know that the story was set around his real life in Hannibal, Missouri, including the caves where Indian, or *Injun Joe* had hid; they—and many other details from his books—were real and could be toured to this very day. Excited by my recollection, I was suddenly consumed by the idea of checking out and possibly hiding in these exact caves.

I stumbled at the thought... *Hide?* Why in the world would I need to hide? The emotions warring inside my mind were making me dizzy. Literally, I felt like I was weaving on my feet. I didn't think I needed to feed again, but one minute I was fine and fearless, and the next I felt paranoid and wracked with fear.

I made my way into town, using the shadows of the old buildings to conceal my movements. Mt. Vernon had a historical feel that seemed quaint and antiquated until you looked closer. In reality, it was just really old. No businesses were open, and no one was out walking to provide me with an easy meal, so I decided to find a place to sleep; I would just wait until the town woke and feed in the morning instead.

I raced through the dark streets, looking for the perfect place to spend the night. Finally, I saw a lumber mill at the end of the street. It looked promising and would provide plenty of places to hide. I leapt high into the rafters and curled up into a ball behind the large stores of wood, ready to welcome the oblivion of sleep. Too bad, all I got were nightmares instead.

Nightmares of stone and blood, demons and vampires, humans and death. I felt myself connecting to every aspect of these disturbing scenes as if I was the main character in each role: the human girl being sacrificed, the demon queen delivering the killing blow, the vampire princess drinking the blood. The images swirled and melded together, and then I was staring at a replica of myself flying up into the air. A scary-ass replica. I had dark hair and crimson eyes, much as I did now, but instead of my fangs being pointed and dainty, they were jagged razors, extending past my lower lips, but that wasn't the worst part. The thing that freaked me out the most were the black wings that had sprouted from my back.

Jolting upright, I quickly leapt into a defensive stance. I knew within seconds no one was actually attacking me, but as I settled back to sleep, I couldn't shake the feeling there was now something out there I might actually fear.

* * * * *

(Christian)

As I pulled onto the highway, I had no idea which way to go. Rose could have run north and already be in Canada, or maybe to the west and was hanging out in Arizona by now. But the one thing I did know was that Terrance was right; I needed to stock up on blood bags for my trip, and with the sun approaching in just a few hours, it was imperative I find somewhere safe to sleep. I didn't want to wake up in a morgue, which is what would happen if someone found me asleep during the day.

As I drove toward the nearest hospital, I thought about The Rising Pit and our lair deep beneath it. It had been the perfect cover for our family. We all worked in the club at night and retired to the pit below before morning. It was going to be weird not waking up in my own bed for the first time in years.

It only took a few minutes on the freeway before I came to the exit that would lead me to the hospital. Turning into the parking lot of St. Mary's Regional, I was suddenly hit with an idea. If Rose was really as bad as everyone thought, maybe I would just have to watch the news and look for an increased number of injuries or deaths to find out where she was. While I wanted to smile at the fact I now had a semi-decent plan, the idea of Rose killing and hurting people wiped the thought from my mind. How could I smile when the love of my life—the woman I'd longed to spend eternity with—was now lost to me and probably losing herself more and more with each passing minute?

I exited the car and walked toward the Emergency entrance. I hoped there weren't very many people in need of medical care this evening, because I really didn't want to have to waste time biting and using my sedative to erase my appearance here tonight from everyone's mind.

Luckily, the nurse behind the counter was preoccupied with the elderly man who seemed to be complaining of chest pains. I used the distraction to fly through the nearby door and search for the hospital's blood bank. It only took seconds before I found the refrigerated room. I quickly grabbed a large self-cooling container and filled it with bags; I didn't care what the blood type was. I felt bad about taking any of it, but I especially didn't want to take just one type, leaving them depleted for those in need of that particular kind.

I hadn't run into anyone, since to most, I was just a breeze of wind. But as I got back in my car, I wondered if there had been any cameras in the blood bank I should have taken out. Unfortunately, I didn't have time to worry about it. I figured if anyone tried to come after me, I would just have to risk biting them and erase the memory of why they were there.

I turned back onto the highway and tried to think of a safe place to sleep for the night, when suddenly my claircognizance flared to life. I instantly knew where I had to go... Jillian's.

Rose's best friend might have some ideas of where she would have fled to. Plus, somehow, I knew I'd be safe staying in her home for the night. I took the next exit and quickly found my way to Jillian's house. Her car was in the driveway and there was only one light on in the upstairs window. It was close to morning, so I wasn't sure if she had stayed up late, or if she was just an early riser. Either way, I knew this was exactly where I needed to be, but was still unsure why.

I parked across the street and quickly drained two blood bags before transferring the cooler to the trunk of my car. I wouldn't need any more blood until after I rose tomorrow night.

Walking across the street and up to Jillian's front door had me on edge. I wasn't sure exactly what to say, or if I would be forced to have some sort of confrontation with her parents, but luckily, when I knocked, Jillian opened it with a smile.

"Hi, Christian. I wondered how long it would take you to show up."

CHAPTER ELEVEN

(Meredith)

After hanging up with the realtor, I realized it was almost time for me to head to Damien's funeral. As anxious as I was to start the search for our new home, I simply couldn't miss the opportunity to talk to Raúl. If I got him to take over where Damien left off, we'd be back on track in creating my army within the week.

Jeremy had already left for work after a morning of utter bliss. We'd made love after waking, both excited about the new prospects for our future. It was a good day. I'd thought about introducing some human blood to Jeremy as well, to kick start his immortal genes, but I couldn't risk mixing it with mine in case it affected our mind bond in some unexpected way. So, for now, he'd just have to remain the clueless demon man I loved.

As I pulled out of the driveway, I took an extra moment to look back at my house. My happiness faded slightly at the thought of leaving my home permanently. Like Jeremy had pointed out, I had lived here for such a long time. But it wasn't the idea of moving somewhere else that was upsetting to me, but instead, the fact I was being forced to do so by a bunch of vampires who wanted me dead. To say it pissed me off was putting it mildly. I'd always thought of becoming immortal and creating my army as a defensive maneuver, but now, with the "message" they had left me in the park, maybe my efforts would need to become more offensive instead.

As I pulled into the funeral home's parking lot, I contemplated what a change of plans like that would mean. I'd always thought I'd just hole up and be prepared in case they came after me, but now... it looked like planning an attack may have to be my next move.

"Hello, Meredith. Thank you so much for coming." Thankfully Raúl was the first one to greet me as I walked through the white double doors. It wasn't that I felt uncomfortable being here, but just that I hadn't had much interaction with Damien's extended family besides seeing them at our meetings.

"Of course, Raúl. It's just so horrible what happened."

The slight tilt to his head made me nervous. Raúl and a few select others were very aware of what Damien and I had been doing, and suddenly I worried they might put two and two together and figured out it was me who'd killed their cousin.

"He'd be so pleased you came. I know he had developed some pretty strong feelings for you."

All I could do was nod my head and clasp his hand. I had no idea Damien had shared his feelings for me with anyone else. I wasn't comfortable with the idea of him talking about me to other people, which meant talking to Raúl later had yet another purpose. I needed to find out what Damien told them.

"Will there be a wake afterwards?"

"Yes, actually, it's in the same place where we held our meetings. My mother thought it was fitting, as he was truly responsible for bringing us all together. We'd all be pleased if you'd join us; we have a pretty big surprise to share with you."

Shit. I did not like surprises.

"Of course, I'll be there."

I sat through Damien's funeral, listening to sobs and prayers. So far, nothing was being said by the priest or family members that sounded like they knew who was to blame. Me! But who knew? Maybe they were holding back to keep up appearances for the non-demon attendees. I started getting nervous that once we arrived at the meeting site, they'd all end up turning on me. As anxiety filled my thoughts, I decided to find a human to drink from on the drive over to the wake. That way, if they did try anything, I'd be freshly juiced and unstoppable. None of them had been drinking blood as long as I had, and therefore, wouldn't even come close to my strength or speed. I hoped I didn't have to fight Damien's family, but if I was forced to... I would.

As the funeral came to an end, I made sure to catch Raúl before heading out to my car. "That was a beautiful service. Are you headed straight to the wake?"

"Yes, I have to help clear and transport all the flower arrangements first, but I'll be there soon."

I smiled and tried to gauge his reactions. "All right, is there anything I can do to help?"

"Yes, actually, we could use some cups."

"No problem, I'll stop and pick some up, then meet you there." This gave me the perfect excuse to delay my trip and feed.

As I left the local Wal-Mart, I saw a hitchhiker standing on the corner and picked him up. After a few blocks and a quick stop behind the nearest garbage dumpster, I'd quenched my thirst and was on my way again to the meeting facility. His blood was a boost to my system, and one that amped up my strength and eliminated my fears. I knew if anyone tried to hurt me, they would be in for a big surprise.

Once I arrived, I made my way inside and placed the cups on the empty table. I was used to being the leader of the meetings here, but today, until I could figure out exactly what was going on, I decided to lay low and took a seat in the far corner. I watched everyone mill around, exchanging hugs and stories about Damien, until finally Raúl and the last few members of his family came through the door.

After placing the flower arrangements and a few odds and ends around the room, Raúl's mother stepped to the front to gain everyone's attention. "*A-hem.* I'd like to thank you all for coming today. The service was beautiful and I appreciate all the kind words you had to say about my nephew. But now, I have some important words of my own to share. As most of you know, Damien's death was no accident."

Oh shit! I tensed up. If I was going to be hung out to dry, this was the moment.

"But his death did give our family an opportunity to learn things we didn't know, gain an understanding of our past, and provide a new course for our future."

What's with the damn riddles? I watched as Raúl and his cousins set the table with food platters and a large punch bowl, as I continued to listen.

"Damien was killed by vampires, and now we have a chance to learn from our ancestors and gain enough strength and power to exact our revenge."

My mouth almost hit the floor. I sat in stunned silence as I watched Raúl mix blood with the punch, just like I'd done the last time we were here. I stared as everyone grabbed one of the cups I'd brought and dip them into the blood-laced concoction. They all stood around shaking their heads and bobbing back and forth on their feet like they were a bunch of prize fighters preparing for their big bout.

Raúl caught my eye, and made his way over to me. "See, I told you you'd be surprised."

"Um... you could say that again. What's going on? Who told them about the vampires, and how did you convince them to start drinking blood?"

"I did. When the police found Damien's body, it was me and my mom who went to identify him. When I saw his neck had been bitten and shredded like that, I knew it was the vampires you told us about. I decided to tell my mom we'd been drinking blood in an effort to get stronger and become immortal like our ancestors. As she stood there looking at Damien and listening to the story, I saw something change inside her. Once we left, she said she was going to bring everyone on board so we could get revenge for Damien's death and help protect you in the process. She got the family together that same night and relayed everything I had told her and now... here we are. Everyone is ready to help you take on the vampires."

The amount of twisted joy I felt was unexplainable. I couldn't believe that by killing the one person who'd threatened me, I had just created a willing army in a matter of days. Everyone here was gaining strength in a controlled manner by ingesting blood in smaller amounts, which meant I wouldn't have to worry about being challenged again. This was perfect! The idea that Damien was killed by the vampires gave me a room full of demons with the motivation to do anything I asked, and I was so pleased I wouldn't have to hide or trick them into drinking the blood to do so. We could now openly plan our attack and discuss our experiences together.

Raúl was right, this was a big surprise... but one I didn't mind at all.

CHAPTER TWELVE

(Christian)

I wasn't sure what Jillian meant, or why it looked like she was expecting me, but I headed inside, hoping to find out why my psychic gift had led me to her doorstep.

"Thank you." I crossed the threshold tentatively. "You don't seem very surprised to see me after all this time, Jillian. Can I ask why that is?" I wasn't sure if confronting her right away was a good idea or not, but it was the path my mind was telling me to take, so I went with it.

She talked over her shoulder as we walked into the dark kitchen. "I'm not surprised to see you, Christian. I texted you to come over as soon as you could. Oh, and by the way, my parents are in Brazil on vacation to check out the place I'll *supposedly* be living in next year, so we have the house to ourselves."

I grabbed my phone and checked for the message I'd apparently missed. Yep, sure enough, there was her text. It struck me as odd that Jillian would be texting me at all, or why she seemed to understand we needed to be alone. I also didn't get what she meant by "...*supposedly* living in. next year." To say I was confused was a huge understatement.

"Have you heard from Rose recently?" I decided to not try and decipher her statements and got to the real reason I was here. I hoped Rose had once again reached out to her best friend, and that Jillian could therefore provide me a direction to head in my search. What I got instead was a complete shock.

"No, but William said Justin and I can help you look for her."

I spun around, knocking the bar stool over. Jillian was standing next to the refrigerator with a blood bag to her lips. "Want some?"

"Holy shit, Jillian! You're a vampire?"

"Took you long enough." She smiled and shrugged her shoulders. "After you and Rose disappeared all those months ago, Justin and I continued to see each other. It didn't take long before we really did fall in love. After I graduated college, he petitioned William to change me and then explained what was up. I, of course, jumped at the chance to be with him forever."

"How long? And do you know everything that's happened with Rose and our clan?" I assumed she did, since she was drinking from a bag.

"Yes and no. I've been a vampire for just a few weeks, but it was only earlier tonight that Evie contacted our Sire to explain about the demon situation. That's also when she told us about Rose, and how by becoming the hybrid, she was now our only hope in stopping them."

She took another sip from the bag, then hopped up onto the counter. "I can't say I wasn't ticked to find out that not only was my best friend a frickin' demon, but now some crazy ass cross-breed hybrid. But I was happy when William agreed to let us go with you, since after all, I *have* been her best friend for years. Evangeline told us you'd gone looking for her and agreed that maybe I could be of some help."

I couldn't process everything that had happened in such a short span of time. Jillian turned into a vampire, Rose missing, Evie contacting another clan to aid in our cause. It was so much to take in. But thinking about all Rose and I had been caught up in, it wasn't a surprise I'd missed so much of what had happened outside our own little world. I suppose it shouldn't be a shock Justin and Jillian had continued seeing each other, or that he'd petitioned to have her turned. But, I couldn't deny I felt a little pissed off that Evie had gone to their clan behind my back. *I* was the new Sire now, and that should have been something I decided to do, not her. Then again, after what I'd learned from Terrance, I supposed I should've expected it. If Evie felt they would eventually have to take a stand against Rose and me, she'd want to have backup lined up. *God, what a fucked up mess.*

"Well, I guess I should be grateful you and Justin will be joining me, but back to my original question... has Rose contacted you again? Do you know where we should be looking for her?"

"No. That's the part I have no clue about. I haven't heard from her since she threatened to kill me." Her fake giggle told me she, too, was upset about everything that had transpired.

I didn't know what she was talking about though, so I assumed it was just one more secret Rose had decided to keep from me. Shaking my head, I suddenly felt a tug in my chest as a tremor swept over my body. Our bond was wearing thinner and thinner by the hour, and right now I was starting to feel the effects. If Jillian could help in any way to find Rose sooner rather than later, I would be grateful for her assistance.

"You said that your parents are on vacation, and we have the house to ourselves?"

"Yes, I used my sedative to convince them I'd be living in Brazil to play for their country's volleyball team. They're ranked second in the world, you know."

"No, I didn't know that, but does that mean we can sleep here, uninterrupted for the day?"

"Yes. Exactly. Justin is gathering more blood bags for our trip, and will join us here tomorrow once the sun goes down. Now, let me show you to the guest room."

I followed Jillian down the hall to a nice room with simple furnishings. The blinds were already pulled, so I thanked her and fell straight into the comfortable bed. My head was spinning from everything I'd just learned, and the emotions it was causing within me had me drifting as I settled in. As much as I wanted to flesh out the next step of our plan, it was something I'd have to process tomorrow, because for the first time in centuries, I was actually tired.

CHAPTER THIRTEEN

(Evie)

After my meeting with William, the Sire of the closest clan, I rode back to
The Rising Pit in the passenger seat of Dax's SUV. I sat in silence because
I couldn't help feeling guilty. I knew it was Christian's place to reach out as
the new Sire, but with him in search of Rose, and the possibility of them
both turning dark in the process, I felt I'd been left with no choice. He
hadn't returned from his search, and honestly, I didn't have a clue if he
ever would. Therefore, as the clan's *original* Sire, their safety would always
be my responsibility and priority.

Dax didn't say a word as we pulled up to the club. Not wanting
oversensitive ears to hear my concerns, I remained in the car as I turned to
him. "I don't know what else to do, Dax. I'm not sure if I should call
Balam and tell him we had a hybrid, but lost her; or that we have a new
Sire in the clan but that he, too, is now drifted dark and gone; or if I
should just shut this place down and move everyone somewhere safer."

Dax took my hands in his and looked into my eyes. "Where would we
go, Evie? Where *is* somewhere safer? We now know demons litter the
world, so what makes you think we wouldn't run into another hive of them
where ever we ended up?"

I dropped my head into my hands, realizing he was right. There wasn't
anywhere we could go that demons wouldn't be a concern. It's just that
here, they were now a direct threat to our existence. Meredith was creating
an army to come after us, and if we didn't get Rose and Christian back
soon, I had no idea what we'd do. It was the reason I agreed to let Justin
and Jillian go with Christian to help look for her. I wasn't sure about it at
first, but when they'd explained Jillian had been Rose's best friend for
years, I thought maybe she could be of some assistance, so I gave them
Christian's cell number and hoped they would meet up soon.

"Let's go inside, honey. The sun's almost up and maybe by tomorrow
night Christian will have found her and all this will be behind us." Dax flew
from the truck and had my door open within seconds. "Besides, if we just

keep an eye on Meredith and her demon meetings, we should get the jump on anything she has planned."

He was right. I should send Renard and Loni back to keep tabs on her. It'd take a little time to set up, though, since I'd have to secure a place for them to sleep during the day without being interrupted. Hotels were fine once in a while, but after you stayed too long, people began to question a vampire's odd hours. No, I'd have to make sure they'd be safe, and then I'd send them on an extended stakeout until this mess was over.

"You're right. I guess that's all we can really do until Rose and Christian return."

We walked back into the club hand and hand. Dax had always been my rock. He was my consort and the man I would forever love. As we made our way down the spiral staircase into the pit, sealing the circular stage over our heads, I tried to imagine what Christian must be going through. To have woken up and instantly been forced to function without his consort; losing her before even having a single moment to bask in the joy of being together forever—I shook my head, a tear slide down my cheek as we entered our room.

"I don't think I can hurt him, Dax. If Christian truly turns dark because of all this, I don't think I can deliver the true death. He's been my son for hundreds of years and is the most kind hearted person I've ever known."

Dax embraced me as we lay down. "Have faith, Evie. Christian turned Rose feeling it was the right thing to do. We just have to trust him."

I let his words soak into my heart as I fell comatose for the day.

Just trust him.

* * * * *

(Rose)

I looked around the now illuminated lumber mill. Morning had come, but the nightmares I'd experienced left me feeling trapped and scared. I took a deep breath and eased out of my hiding place. No one was here, but I knew it wouldn't be long before the workers started to arrive to begin their day.

I figured feeding here would be a good idea, as long as there weren't too many people that showed up at once. Luckily, the supervisor was the first on site. I watched from my perch as he unlocked the gate and then the office doors. A few minutes later, he wandered out into the open space and I made my move.

Leaping down from the ceiling, I landed directly behind him and sunk my fangs into his neck. I tried to use my sedative again and program it so he wouldn't feel pain or remember anything. But just like before, the euphoria his blood sparked within me had my mind drifting, causing me to lose all focus until he was lying motionless on the sawdust covered ground.

As his blood pooled, mixing with the tiny wood flakes, I found the patterns it made amusing. I reached down to draw pictures in it, reminding me of the finger paintings I used to create in grade school. The consistency was the same, but before I could finish drawing my smiley face, I heard cars pulling up outside.

Bolting from the mill, I was gone in seconds and almost to the edge of town before I remembered I needed a map. I stopped at the gas station next to the freeway and casually walked in, paid for the small atlas with the change I had in my pockets, then paused under a nearby tree. Once I made sure I was headed in the right direction, I set off for the caves again. A smile crept across my face at the thought of the underground caverns. For reasons I didn't understand, I simply couldn't wait to get there.

CHAPTER FOURTEEN

(Meredith)

After Raúl's revelation, I mingled and talked to all of his family, especially his mother, Lupé. She was stern but had an excited edge to her, probably due to the effects of the human blood. She told me even though she was sad about losing Damien, she was happy to be out of the dark and felt this new way of life for her family was something the gods wanted to happen.

I wasn't sure about that, but it was certainly something that *I* wanted to happen. She suggested we move the meetings to her house, since it was further from the city and wouldn't draw attention. We'd be needing more blood, so being secluded while we continued to make our plans sounded like a great idea to me. I thanked her and announced that next week's meeting would be held at her house instead.

As I drove home, I couldn't help feeling giddy. When I'd left the wake, everyone had still been talking about how the blood had started to give them speed and strength. Some had even started demonstrating by lifting their relatives high into the air, while others just raced around the room, chasing one another in an endless game of tag. It was like watching children, and it brought joy to my heart. My race— demons thriving in the twenty-first century. Who could have guessed it? But as I pulled into my driveway, I thought about my grandmother's words, *"I can tell that you are changing, and I'm afraid that what you've started will not be good for our race."*

I could only hope she was wrong.

* * * * *

(Christian)

The last thing a vampire thought of before falling comatose was also the first thing they'd think of upon waking. I'd spent the last year making it a habit to think of Rose before I fell asleep. However, as I woke in Jillian's guest room, it wasn't the usual image of me embracing Rose that greeted me. Instead, it was one of me running after her.

I supposed it only made sense, since that's literally what I was doing—chasing after my consort in an effort to save her and myself. As much as I didn't want to admit it, I could feel I was losing her. Our bond was stretched so thin it was making me weak. I was pretty sure if she continued to drift dark, it would be as effective in killing me as if she'd actually died.

After straightening Jillian's guest room, I left the house and walked out to my car. I couldn't bear to think of anything happening to Rose without it sending me into a depressive spiral. I needed to get a hold of myself before Jillian and Justin saw I'd drifted dark again and reported it back to their Sire. I was sure if Evie found out I hadn't returned to my normal coloring yet, she'd assume the worst, and then not only would I be racing to find Rose, I'd be running for my life as well.

I grabbed a couple blood bags from the trunk and sat in my front seat, trying to gain some small measure of control. The blood helped, but as I imagined Rose out there feeding on her own, killing more innocent people, I knew I was far from okay. I had no idea what I was going to do once I found her, if she really *was* bad. I'd never heard of any Sire having to abandon their chosen consort in all of our vampire history, or if it was even possible.

No! Walking away was not an option; instead, if it came down to it, we'd both meet the true death… together.

I almost threw up at the thought.

I closed my eyes and tried to recall the last time Rose and I had been really happy together. I thought it was when she'd been hiding out with me after her attack on Meredith, but in hindsight I was wrong. She'd been struggling to keep her demon side a secret and had purposely pushed me away. I thought back to when she'd told me she knew I was a vampire and agreed to be my consort, but even then, it was after she'd lost her father thanks again to Meredith. I guess the last time we'd been truly happy was when I'd been in the dark about Rose knowing my secret. We'd dated like a normal couple and had genuinely fallen in love.

A sharp wrap on my window pulled me out of my reverie.

"Hey, come back inside so we can work out a plan, okay?" Justin's face was serious but didn't show signs of worry or fear, so I assumed my coloring had drifted back to normal.

I joined him and Jillian in the kitchen and sat quietly as they drank their evening meal.

"So, do you have any idea where Rose could be right now?" Jillian asked.

My first instinct was to get defensive, but I knew it wouldn't help. "No. I have no idea. She went to Masen, and I tracked her to her dad's house, but she was gone by the time I arrived. Do you have any thoughts?"

"Not really. I mean as kids we usually just hung around here or Masen, since both of our parents worked all the time. We didn't really ever take vacations and if we did, it was only to places like Disneyland or Six Flags. I can't really see her going there, though, 'cause she used to say, all that cheery, happy go lucky shit drove her crazy." Jillian laughed.

Well, great. The room fell silent as we all realized we didn't have a clue where to start. It was already looking like this was going to be a complete waste of time. Time I didn't have.

Jillian's voice interrupted my depressive thoughts. "Are you sure she left Masen? Maybe she was just feeding and hiding out until she could go back and finish off Meredith."

Her question made sense, but I also had to trust my instincts. "No. I can feel that she's gone. Our bond has grown really weak, as if it's being stretched by a large distance."

I hated admitting it, but what would be the point of keeping anything from them? Jillian was her friend and Justin had been the one to help her understand everything when Terrance had lied to her, so I knew they would help me if they could.

Just then, I got a lucky break. Loraine appeared above me, but for no more than six or seven seconds. In my mind, I heard, *"Caves, Christian. You have to start looking in caves."*

She was gone before I could ask any questions, and no matter how much I thought about her or Rose, she didn't reappear. I didn't understand where Loraine went when she disappeared from our world, but the fact I couldn't reach her now had me extremely concerned.

"What's wrong? You've started drifting again," Justin stated.

I didn't have time to explain about Loraine. "I have an idea of where we need to go. Where is the nearest set of caves to here?"

Jillian looked at me with a raised eyebrow, then headed straight to the computer in her father's study. After a quick internet search, we knew the three closest set of caves were in Virginia, Kentucky, and Missouri.

As worried as I was about Loraine, I knew it would do me no good to dwell on it. Plus, her clue about Rose was the first thing I had to go on, and I wasn't about to waste it. I wanted us to all break up and each take one location, but Justin suggested we remain together, in case one of them found her first. He thought I needed to be there, and I knew he was right. The certainty of knowing I would see Rose again made me happy, but the idea she could hurt her friends if I wasn't there to stop her, left me unsettled.

I forced myself to stop analyzing the situation and focused on our plan to get moving. I had to find Rose quickly, and we'd be a lot faster on foot. So, after packing our supplies, we all sprinted toward Virginia, hoping for a lucky break.

* * * * *

(Loraine)

Blood, wings, bats, caves, Rose—Blood, wings, bats, caves, Rose. It was the nightmare I'd been stuck in since I'd disappeared from Christian's car. I'd hoped for some relief from this god-awful situation when Christian left me sitting there alone. But instead of falling into oblivion like every other time I'd left the earthly plane, I'd been thrown straight into this reoccurring nightmare instead.

I could see tall stone temples and people in tribal clothing everywhere I looked. There were flashes of human sacrifices and a winged creature. I had no idea what I was seeing or when it was taking place, but the main focus I kept getting pulled back to, were the images being drawn on cave walls. So, when I'd felt myself being pulled back into my corporeal form, I knew that was the message I needed to deliver.

I found Christian in the kitchen of Rose's best friend, Jillian. As always, I immediately received the information I needed; Jillian was now a vampire and was here with her boyfriend, Justin, in an effort to help find Rose.

As soon as Christian spotted me, I'd already begun to fade and knew I better talk fast. *"Caves, Christian. You have to start looking in caves."*

I was gone a second later, once again pulled back and being forced to witness this gruesome scene. It had changed slightly, now focusing on the winged creature. The thing was obviously female and had long black hair and sharp jagged teeth. The fear radiating from the village it flew over was palpable. I could literally feel the terror of those poor people, and for the first time, I was happy I was already dead.

I was forced to watch as this beast annihilated an entire village, slaughtering men, women, and children. Their screams pierced my mind, and all I could do was cry. Village after village was decimated, and the monster grew more vile with each and every kill. It seemed as if the horror would never stop, then suddenly, it was over. For everyone. The next image I got was of an entire continent completely devastated. I knew what I'd just witnessed—an entire race being wiped from existence.

The scene started to clear, and I found myself finally fading into the oblivion I'd longed for. I tried to concentrate and piece together how any of this could be connected to Rose and Christian, but my mind was too fragile from all I'd seen. My body started to shake as I thought about that horrible creature hurting my baby. I couldn't understand why I'd been forced to see this, and could only hope it was leading me to some helpful information. I had to hold onto the hope that something good would come out of this, because if the death and destruction I saw here had anything to do with our future, I never wanted to return.

With an overwhelming sense of doom, I closed my eyes and let the darkness swallow me whole.

CHAPTER FIFTEEN

(Meredith)

Today was the day Jeremy and I were starting the search for our new home. Since everything was in order with Raúl and his family, I was excited to shift my focus to something else besides death and blood.

"Babe. You ready to go? The realtor will be here in just a few minutes," Jeremy called out.

"Yes, honey. I'm ready. You sound excited. Does she have some good prospects for us to look at today?"

"Actually, yes. I never thought house hunting would be something I'd enjoy after all these years, but I know a couple of the places have fantastic views, and I'm interested to see if she's managed to get everything on our wish list."

A fantastic new view was just what I needed, because every time I looked out the window of the living room or our upstairs bedroom, I looked straight into the park and was reminded of why we needed to move. It was imperative I get somewhere new and hide from Christian's vampire clan while my army continued to grow. We weren't ready to take them on just yet, but it wouldn't be too long before we were.

"Hey, Mer? Can you come here for a second?" Jeremy's voice had lost its cheerful tone, so I headed upstairs to see what he needed. As I rounded the corner of our bedroom, I found him standing next to his dresser, holding an old tattered wallet.

"I've been having trouble with this drawer and just figured out the reason why. This old thing was stuck behind it. Do you know who this girl is?"

He was staring at a picture of Rose. *Son of a bitch!* I'd forgotten all about this wallet. He had told me months ago that he'd lost it, so I'd simply bought him a new one and replaced all his cards and photos after erasing Rose from his mind.

"I'm not sure." I tried not to let my eyes flare or distress seep into my voice.

"Hmm. She looks familiar, but I can't quite place her," he continued.

I wanted to thank the gods when the doorbell rang.

"Well, time to go," he said. With a shake of his head, he tossed the wallet onto the top of the dresser and turned to grab his jacket from the end of the bed. "Ready?"

All I could do was nod. I followed him downstairs and grabbed our coffee mugs from the kitchen while he answered the door. Quickly using the small paring knife, I nicked my finger and added a few more drops of my blood to his coffee. Taking a deep breath, I grabbed my purse from the credenza and headed to meet him and our realtor, Cheryl, at the front door.

"Hi, Cheryl. Thank you again for driving us today. We're both very excited," I said.

"You're welcome, Meredith. But I think you're going to have a hard time choosing between the selections I've got lined up for you. So if you're both ready, let's get started. The first one I have to show you is a beautiful single-family home on the edge of downtown."

Jeremy locked the house as I headed to the car. I handed him his cup as he joined me, then climbed in the back seat of Cheryl's Mercedes. As I slid across the soft leather seats, I purposely let my skirt ride up and gave Jeremy a quick wink.

I regretted it immediately. He tripped on the curb and dropped his coffee. *Shit!* My little tease was supposed to put him at ease, not cause my problem to go from bad to worse. Now I could only hope my mind bond was strong enough to erase what had just happened in the house, but I wasn't entirely convinced it was.

As we rode to the first house, I made a plan to excuse myself to the restroom as soon as possible, so I could lace my cup instead, but as we pulled up to a stop light, Jeremy reached for my cup. "Do you mind? I'm parched, and it is your fault I dropped my coffee," he teased.

I sighed as I watched him drain the remnants of my cup. *So much for that idea.*

I couldn't feed him directly from the vein without causing a horrible mess and mass amounts of hysteria. So, after watching him discard the empty cup in the trash bag located on the floor of Cheryl's car, I simply hoped the house hunting would be enough of a distraction to keep his mind off of the picture of Rose.

"What do you think?" Cheryl swept her hand in the direction of the first house, and I wanted to kill her on the spot. It looked almost identical to Jeremy and Loraine's former home. The home they'd spent their entire marriage in, raising their daughter.

Jeremy stood silent and stared at the house for a few moments... a few *excruciating* moments. I was so worried the picture of Rose—and now the replica of their house—would sever our mind bond immediately, I really didn't consider killing Cheryl on the spot. But, if Jeremy was remembering anything, he didn't show any signs of it. I touched his shoulder and gently asked, "Should we go in?" His response made me the happiest woman alive.

"No, actually. This isn't at all what I'm looking for. I'm sorry, Cheryl, but can we just move on to the next choice?"

Cheryl nearly tripped over her high heels at Jeremy's request, but after regaining her composure, she simply said, "Of course," and motioned us back to her car.

He pulled me close once we were in the back seat again. I wasn't sure what thoughts were running through his head, but whatever the reason for him not wanting that house, put a smile on my face. Maybe I could trust him to want a future with me without controlling his mind after all. *Ha!* Who was I kidding? It really was laughable. Thinking back to the night Jeremy almost walked out of my life after catching me killing Damien in our garage, yeah... I knew I still had no choice but to manipulate him. If he were to remember everything I'd done, he'd leave me for sure.

We continued to ride in silence as Cheryl drove us to the next house on her list.

The building was one of the two new glass high-rises, smack dab in the middle of downtown Masen. The three-bedroom apartment was located on the twentieth floor and had amazing features. Granite counters, marble fireplaces, vaulted ceilings, and a master suite to die for. Jeremy walked through each room at least three times, then stood in the massive living room, taking it all in. I was staring out the wall of windows, overlooking what felt like the entire city, when he surprised me by asking, "Will this work for you?" I hadn't expected him to like it so much.

"My God, yes of course. It's beautiful."

Turning to Cheryl, he said, "We'll take it. How soon can we move in?"

"Jeremy, wait! We haven't even sold the house yet," I exclaimed. I wasn't sure what had gotten into him.

"We don't need to wait to sell your house, I still have the money from the sale of mine, so we can move in right away." He turned to Cheryl, pulling out his checkbook. "Which is something I hope we can do soon."

Cheryl handed him the keys, and pulled the paperwork out of her briefcase. "Of course. Just sign here and the place is yours." She winked, then whispered, "Just one of the benefits of prequalification."

Jeremy took the papers, signed them, then wrote out a check for the full asking price. "Thank you, Cheryl. Now... let's go celebrate. Lunch is on me."

I was about to ask why he was so gung-ho all of the sudden, but dropped it since moving this quickly only benefited me. We'd be out of the house and safe from the vampires tomorrow, and our new home was practically an impenetrable fortress. Plus, I'd get to start decorating our baby's nursery right away, where as in the old house, we would've had to redo an entire room by eliminating the study. Here, we had it all. It seemed now the only thing I had to worry about was getting some of my blood into his meal at lunch to keep this perfect charade going.

CHAPTER SIXTEEN

(Christian)

Before we left, I'd mapped out our search locations, starting with the closest and working to the furthest away. It only took about two hours for us to reach Virginia, and we were now standing outside Luray Caverns.

The caverns had closed hours ago, but thankfully, we didn't need lights or permission to get inside. After laying out a plan to explore the entire system and meet back in the specified location, we all broke off to our designated areas. I quickly moved into my section, already knowing we wouldn't find Rose. I didn't mention it because I didn't want to discourage Jillian or Justin, and I certainly didn't want to risk missing something by rushing or being overly confident in my gifts.

As I continued my search, I started thinking about Loraine's rushed message. I couldn't understand why we were even searching in caves to begin with. It's not like Rose needed to hide from anyone. If she was using her sedative when she fed, she could simply erase the experience from anyone she bit. But if not, and she was killing people instead, there'd be no reason to worry in that case either—dead people didn't talk. *Hmmm...* I thought of Loraine again. *Well...usually, dead people didn't.*

I tried to focus my thoughts on Loraine and pull her energy to me. I needed her to appear and hopefully provide a little more clarity, but unfortunately, I had no such luck. Instead, I just kept stalking through the underground cavern, looking for the woman I loved. I shook my head at the ridiculousness of it. What could a cave possibly have to do with Rose? I knew this was going to be a dead end, but I had to trust Loraine. Wherever she went, or whoever it was that gave her the divine messages, it was clear she had access to more information than me, even *with* my gifts.

I continued to contemplate the oddity of our situation as I walked deeper into the caves. Suddenly I found myself in a large open chamber. The ceiling was at least thirty feet high, and dome-shaped. As I moved into the area, I ran my hands along the walls while my eyes adjusted to the pitch dark. Continuing around the edge, I suddenly noticed the walls were smoother here, like they'd been worked by hand or worn over by years of water running over them. I didn't see any pools on the ground, and couldn't pick up any sounds of water, so I just kept moving along the wall. I wanted to circle the entire room to get an idea of the overall size, and to see if I could pinpoint a purpose to the space or any tunnels that branched off from it. As I reached the back portion, the surface under my hand changed slightly. It was still smooth, but I could sense something else. Squinting hard, I could make out ancient drawings that covered the cold stone wall.

The drawings depicted villages and fields of crops with people and animals scattered about. There were also moons and stars, and what I assumed were the tribesmen's interpretation of the constellations drawn onto the hard surface. I never expected to find petroglyphs in the caves of Virginia, which only heightened the joy this discovery brought me. I continued to look at the wide expanse of stone for a few more minutes before I heard Justin shouting my name. I called out and waited for him to find me.

"Whoa!" he exclaimed as he walked into the massive room. "Did you find anything in here?"

"Not really. Just some ancient drawings. How about you? Did you find anything?" I asked, even though I already knew the answer.

"No. I searched my area twice and there wasn't anything or anyone in the whole place."

Jillian walked into the cavern and added her report as well. "I didn't find anything either."

"Well, then let's not waste any more time. We have seven more sets of caves here in Virginia to check, so let's just go." I took one last look at the engravings, then followed the couple out of the cave.

Once we reached the surface, I took a deep breath and was overwhelmed with a sudden desire to call Evie. I wasn't sure why, but from the intensity of the feeling, I knew it was important to call. I pulled my cell from my pocket and dialed, hoping the necessary words would form when I needed them. Because right now, I didn't even know what I should say.

"Hello? Christian, is that you?" Evie sounded worried.

"Yes, Evie. It's me. I'm calling to let you know that Justin, Jillian, and I hooked up and are now looking for Rose together." As I listened to Evie exhale a sigh of relief, I felt bad for putting her through all of this. Even though it had been her decisions that led to leave, I supposed if I was in her position, I would probably be reacting the exact same way. If a new Sire and his hybrid consort both turn dark and then basically disappeared, the rest of my clan's safety would of course become my number one priority. Most of my anger faded away with that realization, but it still hurt she didn't trust my decisions and abilities as Sire. But then again, I was basically flying blind here, so how could I expect *her* to trust in me when *I* didn't even have a clue as to what I'd be led to do next?

Silence hung on the line as I searched for something to say; thankfully, in the next moment the words filled my mind and spilled from my lips. "Evie, I need you to contact Balam and ask him if he has ever seen any petroglyphs in the caves beneath Chichen Itza."

As the sentence left my mouth my head started to spin. I tried to piece things together; the carvings here in Virginia, Rose, Balam, Chichen Itza. I had no idea how any of it fit, but my gifts were guiding me in a way I'd never experienced. It was almost like I was being led by something other than my claircognizance. I suddenly wondered if Loraine had anything to do with the ideas now floating into my mind.

"All right, Christian. I'll call him as soon as we hang up. Do you want to tell me what this has to do with?"

"No, Evie. I'm sorry, but I can't tell you. I just need whatever information Balam has to share."

I wasn't trying to be an ass, but I simply couldn't discuss what I didn't understand. Maybe once I heard what Balam had to say it would all make sense, but until then, I didn't have a clue.

"I trust you, Christian. I want you to know that. I'll call as soon as I have something." Evie hung up first, because I was still too struck by her words to hang up the phone. *She trusts me?* That was good to hear. Now if I could just start to trust myself.

CHAPTER SEVENTEEN

(Meredith)

Today was moving day, and it was bittersweet. I hated being forced to leave my house, but I was happy to be moving forward with Jeremy and our baby. I only had a few more things to pack, and then Jeremy wanted to grab an early dinner while the movers finished the job. They would coordinate with the building's staff to get all of the big pieces into place, allowing me to spend the evening and the following few days unpacking and organizing at my own pace. I planned to return to work and announce my pregnancy and move by next week, but wanted to get the house set up first. The second I shared my plans with Jeremy, however, everything changed.

"No, I don't think so. I don't want you going back to work at all."

His statement shocked me. "What are you talking about? Why would I quit my job?"

"Because you're carrying our baby and you need as much rest as possible. I make plenty of money to take care of us, and once your house sells, our nest egg will be replenished. There's simply no reason for you to go back to work."

My first instinct was to feel softened by his concern, but as I looked at him and thought about his snap decisions as of late, I started wondering if there was something else going on besides him being an over-protective husband and father. The idea of not working definitely had merit. I could hole up here and not venture out into the world, except to further my cause with the demons. However, I felt the need to put up a little resistance, just to see if I could get any more information as to the true reason behind his feelings.

"But I love my job, you know that."

"Well, I love tequila, but I don't drink it, because it's not good for me. This is something I need you to do for me, Meredith. Just say you'll stay home and take care of our child."

Now I was getting worried. With his reaction to the first house on our search, and now with this over-the-top concern about the baby, I was starting to wonder if my blood was no longer doing its job. I decided to test my theory and used our mind bond to attempt to change his mind.

As he turned to grab the last box sitting on the kitchen counter, he hesitated slightly as I sent the thoughts into his mind, but then, after a slight shake of his head, he lifted the box and walked straight out to the car.

Son of a bitch!

I was on the verge of a serious panic attack. If Jeremy remembered Rose and the fact that I'd killed his wife and Damien... at worst, he'd kill me on the spot—or at least try to—and at best, the wonderful concern he was currently feeling would cease to exist as he ran out my door.

I wiped a single tear from my cheek as he returned from the garage. "Are you ready to go to dinner, honey?" he asked nonchalantly. "I thought we could head to The Melting Pot again."

Yuck. I was so sick of that place. I wasn't sure if it was the pregnancy, but if I had to dip one more thing into a bowl of melted cheese, I was going to puke. Why couldn't we just go to McCrady's? I was having enough trouble eating anything other than blood, but at least if we went there, I could get a good steak tartar.

"Never mind. How about we go to McCrady's instead?"

I spun around, squinting in confusion. If I was just able to change his mind about the restaurant, that meant the bond was still working. But if that was the case, then why didn't it work when it came to the baby? I tried something else completely random to test my theory.

"That sounds good, how about we take the bus instead of driving?"

"Sure, that sounds great. Let's take the bus."

What the hell is going on? I retracted my last thought from his mind and walked to the car instead. It looked like I was going to have to pay another visit to my grandmother and see if she had any idea as to what was happening. Because for the first time in a long time, I didn't have a fucking clue.

CHAPTER EIGHTEEN

(Evie)

Relief flooded me when I received Christian's call, but when he made his odd request, my nerves kicked back up again. As soon as we'd hung up, I dialed Balam as promised. I still wasn't sure if I should share *all* the details of our current situation, but as soon as he answered, I decided to stick only to the information Christian requested.

"Hola, Evie. How are you, my child?"

"I'm good, Sire, thank you for asking. I'm sorry to disturb you, but I'm calling with a special request."

With a light tone to his voice he asked, "And what might that be?"

"I need you to venture into the lower caves below the lair and see if there are any petroglyphs carved into the walls."

"My, my, that is a special and very *specific* request. Is there anything in particular I'm looking for?"

I knew this was his polite way of digging for more information, so I gave him what I could. "I'm not sure. In an effort to prepare our clan to stand against the demons, I've performed the Passing of Powers ritual with Christian. He is now our new Sire. I've asked he stay with us until the threat is eliminated, and following his psychic gifts, he's requested we check for carvings beneath Chichen Itza. That's really all I know."

After a slight pause, Balam replied. "All right. But the caves are extensive, and obviously since we can only look at night, it will take some time to cover them all. I'll gather a team and get started right away."

I was so pleased he didn't question me further. For one, I didn't have any more answers regarding Christian's request, and two, I didn't want to have to lie about Rose.

"Thank you so much, Balam. I'll be waiting for your call." I hung up before he had a chance to say goodbye.

I sat in my office, contemplating what it was that Christian could possibly expect Balam to find. It didn't take long before I was rubbing my temples, a massive headache starting to form. Pushing away from my desk, I walked out of my office and into the club. I spotted Dax and Terrance looking over the railing from the second floor and made my way through the crowd. I climbed the stairs and eased my way between my consort and his best friend.

My heart swelled as I looked at Terrance. We had almost lost him when Meredith had him under her control. It had been a blessing from the gods he'd fallen in love with Loraine, as it was *that* connection which had brought him back to us. I felt bad he would never get the chance to be with the woman he desired and who had ultimately saved his life, but I was so happy we had him back in our clan, I couldn't stop myself from shedding a tear.

"Evie? Are you alright?" Dax reached out and brushed the pad of his thumb over my cheek.

"Yes. I'm fine. Just a bit overwhelmed." I leaned into Dax's embrace, smiling at Terrance. "I'm so thankful you're back with us, Terrance. I'm sorry I haven't taken the time to say that."

"Thank you, Evie." He clapped Dax on the back. "I'm definitely happy to be able to hang out with this guy for a few more centuries."

Dax and Terrance had been best friends since the day we decided to turn him to save his life. When Terrance was infected and facing the potential of the true death, it had really hit Dax hard. This was just another reason I was grateful Terrance had pulled through. If he would've remained dark, I would have had no choice but to kill him, and I wasn't sure if Dax could continue to love me in the same way after that.

Dax must have been scanning my thoughts, because he whispered in my ear. "Nothing could ever change how much I love you."

The emotional rollercoaster I was currently experiencing must have gotten the better of me, because in the next second, I was overwhelmed with love and lust for Dax, crushing his mouth to mine as I pulled him into the nearest private room. Terrance laughed out loud and walked away.

After shutting the thick curtains behind us, I led Dax to the velvet couch. I'd always been so involved with being the Sire and making sure everyone else was taken care of, that at times, I forgot to take care of *us*. He always understood and knew it was just part of being the consort to a Sire, but at times like this, when I was emotionally drained, he was the only one who could fill me back up and restore balance to my life.

CHAPTER NINETEEN

(Rose)

After fleeing Mt. Vernon, it only took twenty minutes before I was standing at the entrance to the caves in Hannibal, Missouri. It was nine a.m. and the area was crawling with tourists. I was feeling possessive over the underground lair that awaited me and wanted everyone to leave so I could claim my new home.

Home. The word caused an odd reaction in my brain. First it became a question. Where was home? Then it became a slideshow of memories: a two-story house with a nicely manicured lawn, a night-club with a red sign flashing above its door, and finally an ancient cave where stone and fire surrounded me.

The images were knocked from my mind when someone accidentally bumped into me. A growl escaped me and the woman backed away with wide eyes. Trying hard to control my bursts of speed, I turned and ran toward the tree line that surrounded the area. I had to remain calm or else I'd end up ripping out the throats of everyone around me.

After I was out of range from prying eyes, I leapt into one of the massive oaks. I decided to get some rest while I waited for the daily tours to close. Leaning back against the rough bark, I balanced myself on the thickest branch. The awkward location didn't bother me in the slightest, and within minutes I was drifting to sleep.

A threatening roar ripped from my throat, and echoes of terror filtered to my ears as the villagers I now noticed screamed in reply.

I felt myself drifting above the scene. My fangs throbbed at the amount of blood that coated the ground and the strength that flowed through my body had me feeling like a god.

The scene remained the same until a large beast entered the other end of the village. I couldn't hear his words over the buzzing in my head, but I somehow knew he was talking to me. He had long jagged fangs, just like mine, and upon staring a little longer, I could make out large wings wrapped around his body.

As he moved forward, the tribesmen scattered in all directions like cockroaches scurrying away from the light. The massive winged beast stalked toward the center of town, heading straight in my direction.

"Ixtab!"

The roar in my head continued to increase as the creature got closer.

"Ixtab!"

I hovered above the beast and watched as he unfurled his wings. They were leathery—almost skeletal—and stretched at least six feet in each direction. He launched into the air, stretching his hands out to grab me.

I awoke screaming, finally free of the nightmare. Birds flew from the tree as the branch shook, setting loose its leaves as if to save them from my wrath. Breathing hard, I quickly scanned the area, making sure there wasn't an actual threat. After realizing I was safe, I leapt from my perch. My feet hit the ground, causing a slight tremor. I slowly walked out of the forest and approached the mouth of the cave. A tingling sensation radiated deep within my belly, spreading up and around to my back.

The temperature dropped as I walked further into the dark. My eyes adjusted instantly and a smile crept across my face. The stone walls were smooth yet jagged at the same time. The ground was compacted from years of tourist activity. There were lights and hand rails that ran throughout the trails, but as I walked deeper into the cave, I knew I'd find areas that were untouched by man. Those were the places calling to me.

When I reached what felt like the center of the tunnel system, I heard a trickle of water as I rounded the corner. After a few hundred feet, I came upon a room that had a small pond in its center. Looking to the sky I saw a waterfall that fell from an opening far above straight into the pond below. Besides the hole above, the room was a dead-end and therefore had only one main entrance, which meant it was easily defendable. I giggled and jumped into the air, grabbing the edge of the hole with my hands and lifted myself out of the opening to scan my surroundings. I found myself deep within the forest, surrounded by ferns and enough trees to blot out the sky. There weren't any trails as far as my eye could see, and the hole in the ground was the only additional entrance to the cave system I could find in the area.

I jumped back down and landed with ease. I knew this was going to be the perfect location for me to hide in. But the question of *why* kept drifting into my mind. I wasn't sure why I felt the need to hide and defend, but as long as this cave served my purpose, I'd remain here while I figured it out.

CHAPTER TWENTY

(Christian)

After I spoke with Evie and gave her my request, Justin, Jillian, and I took off like bullets from a gun. It took a bit longer to reach Kentucky, but we were now standing on the outskirts of Mammoth Cave National Park.

"Come on. Let's get inside and grab a map. We'll split up the sections like we did before," I suggested.

As we raced toward the visitor center, I tried to reach out to Loraine again. She had yet to reappear and my concern was growing. However, before I could sense anything, we were interrupted by a vehicle coming around the side of the nearest building. The headlights hit us before we had a chance to react.

"Hey, stop right there!" a voice rang out.

Jillian and Justin looked in my direction, and within a split second, my fangs were buried in the park ranger's neck. I didn't have time to deal with any shit that would slow our progress, but as I erased our presence from his mind, I scanned him to see if there was anything of interest I should know about within these caves. Surprisingly enough, there was. Apparently, just like the ones in Virginia, there were petroglyphs located in the depths of the caverns, far removed from the normal trails.

As we watched the ranger drive away, I told Jillian and Justin what I'd seen in his thoughts.

"I want to take that section so I can check out the drawings," I said as I pointed to the map. "Jillian, you take the section with the Frozen Niagara room, and Justin, you head to the Fat Man's Misery." They both nodded silently then kissed each other before breaking apart and heading to their designated areas.

My path led south. I followed curves and corners down and around the cold walls, all while hoping to glimpse something that spoke of Rose's presence. I'd gone about three miles in when I came around a sharp turn and caught myself on the edge of a massive hole. It was impressive and at first glance, could easily be compared to a bottomless pit. Suddenly, the images I glimpsed from the park ranger's mind dimmed in comparison to what I knew was hidden at the bottom of this abyss.

I jumped into the void without thinking twice. I fell for what seemed like twenty seconds with my eyes closed and my hair streaming straight above my head. Suddenly, my senses snapped into focus just before I splashed into a sink hole at the bottom of the pit. It was deep, but once I got my bearings, I was able to make my way to the water's edge and scrambled out onto what felt like a shell covered floor.

The loose shale that shifted under my feet had me wondering just how deep I was. It was clear water had constructed this entire wonder; the small river entering one side, spinning in the center, then disappearing back underground, was evidence enough. I was momentarily stunned as I thought about the water and stone, locked in a never-ending dance, resulting in this geological anomaly. I closed my eyes and let my senses expand. I listened to the constant ripple of the stream as it ran through the small pool, and after a few deep breaths, I felt a presence over my left shoulder. I turned back toward the pool to see Loraine hovering over the water, illuminating it and the space around us.

"Loraine. Thank the gods. I've been so worried."

I waited for a response but received none. Instead, Loraine's eyes were wide and her mouth open as if caught in a silent scream. The normal light that accompanied her ghostly form began to shine brighter and brighter, basking the entire area in a blinding silver glow.

"Loraine, what's happening? Please, are you alright?"

I shaded my eyes against her ethereal light as I tried to make sense of things. In the thick fog her spirit created, flickering images started to play out like scenes from an old-time movie. Images of blood and violence, rage and murder, complete decimation and utter chaos, all raining down upon hordes of screaming people.

The flashes were so distorted I couldn't piece any of them together, and I certainly didn't understand what they meant or how they related to me or Rose. Once I realized the flashes were all the same, repeating over and over, I decided to focus on Loraine instead of her confusing picture show.

"Loraine. Can you hear me?"

She said nothing.

"If you can't respond, at least give me a physical sign if you can hear my words."

A slight nod to her head was all I got in return. I supposed it should have eased my mind, but in reality, it just upset me even more. I didn't understand why we could no longer communicate. Before I had a chance to form another question, the pictures disappeared and Loraine herself started to flicker in and out. Within moments she was gone again.

"Dammit!"

I paced the cave and ran my fingers through my hair. I had no doubt I'd drifted dark again, and at this rate, I'd be surprised if I ever returned to my normal coloring. What was I supposed to do now? This turn of events left me frustrated and unfocused. I had to calm myself if I was to piece together any of the clues—if that's what they were—into information that could help me find Rose.

Sighing deeply, I forced my thoughts back to the reason I was in this hole in the first place... the petroglyphs. I walked around, my eyes slowly readjusting to the dark surroundings. The sink hole was in the middle of the round space, leaving the shale covered ground to circle the pool in a radius of about six feet. The walls surrounding the space were covered in strange vines which seem to burst through the hard surface on a life and death mission in search for the water below. I followed the curve of the room until I reached an area free of tangled roots. This particular expanse of stone was smooth except for the nicks and cracks, indicating the presence of the carvings I was looking for.

I squinted and ran my hands over the entire area. I could make out similar images to the ones in the cave in Virginia: tribesmen farming and herding animals, stars and comets filling their night skies, and adults caring for their children. But it was the warriors posed with spears pointing toward a winged creature that snagged my full attention.

The carvings were worn, but I could clearly see this beast was humanoid except for the massive wings protruding from its back. I followed the image to the right, trying to decipher the ancient story laid out before me. The warriors used spears and arrows to keep the beast at bay, but it wasn't until *another* winged being fought with it in the sky, that the creature actually left the village in peace.

CHAPTER TWENTY-ONE

(Meredith)

"Grandma, I'm sorry this upsets you, but I hoped you'd be able to help me understand what's really going on."

"I don't know what you want me to say, Meredith. I told you drinking human blood was going to affect you and the baby. I can only assume the connection you're describing is due to the link the baby has to its father. It's causing a bond between the two that is leaving Jeremy feeling very paternal and protective from the sounds of things. But as to exactly how it works... I have no idea."

Well, shit. While the information was vaguely what I needed, it wasn't exactly the greatest news. It seemed the initial lie I'd told Jeremy about the baby developing a bond to him was essentially coming true. The bond may not be required for its survival, like I'd falsely indicated, but it was certainly one that was making Daddy very "alpha-male."

"Thank you, Grandma. That's all I needed to know. I guess it makes sense the males of our race would develop a protective nature toward their children. Was Grandpa like that with Mom?"

"No, Meredith. My pregnancy was as normal as any other human's. That's what I'm trying to explain. You, my dear, are experiencing something completely unique, and whether that's good or bad, is something only time will tell."

The tone of her voice and the sadness layering her features portrayed just how disappointed in me she was. My heart began to break. But as she turned to walk away, the fissure stopped—my anger sealing it closed instead.

How dare she be mad at me! I was doing something no other demon had done in centuries. I was ushering our race back into a time of legends and gods. A time where demons didn't hide their existence, but lived openly, practicing the traditions that made us a race to be feared.

As my anger continued to grow, my fists clenched and I felt my eyes flaring red. I moved to confront my grandmother with these very thoughts when it hit me... *This is your grandmother.*

Now I was the one struck by fear. *What is happening to me?* How could I even imagine hurting the woman I'd loved my whole life? Not wanting to do that very thing, I raced from the house, tears filling my eyes. I knew this was the last time I'd be speaking to my grandmother... for her own sake.

People say when you're pregnant your hormones are out of control, but what scared me the most was, what if it wasn't my hormones at all? What if it was the fact I was becoming something I couldn't control myself?

CHAPTER TWENTY-TWO

(Rose)

It had now been three days since I'd settled into my new *home*. The cave served me well, as my meals—I mean the tourists— walked straight into my lap on a daily basis. I had stopped trying to use my sedative, as I simply couldn't get past the euphoric feeling caused by my kills. Instead, I enjoyed the feeling of the blood as it fueled me, boosting my immortal essence. I also started exploring the surrounding forest both day and night. The tall trees and fern-covered ground were filled with life and death, and I felt as if I fit right in. The only thing continuing to disrupt my existence were the reoccurring nightmares I had each time I slept, which lately had become more and more often.

It was as if I was being forced to watch a historical documentary of horrific proportions. One that left me feeling the need to search and destroy everything and everyone in my path. A strong desire to replicate the events I saw, had taken on a life of itself. Every time I woke from the terrible dreams, I found myself almost flying out of the hole in the cave, searching for the nearest *village* to exact my wrath upon. The feelings were so vivid, so tangible, it took hours after waking to shake them. And at times, my back even ached as if I had been the one flying the night sky, delivering death and destruction.

At the thought, I circled my shoulder blades in an effort to ease the tension building between them, then stretched my arms high into the air. I couldn't understand why I felt so sore and heavy.

Something skittering along the ground beside me. When I looked down to my left, I noticed something black, moving on the dirt floor. I jumped to the side in an effort to stomp on the creature, but was shocked when it moved in pace with me. I spun in a circle, trying to pinpoint its location.

It matched my movements, spinning and darting with every turn. I felt like I was moving in slow motion, like I was stuck in a dream where everything remained just out of reach. In an effort to protect my back from the curious critter, I moved to the closest wall. As I flattened myself to the stone surface, the realization of what was happening settled in.

Staring at the black *creature* now lying still upon the floor, I understood it wasn't a creature at all. It was me. The black shredded things pooled at my feet were actually dangling from the bottom of wings. My wings.

My scream filling the vast cavern was the last thing I heard before falling unconscious.

* * * * *

(Meredith)

After leaving my grandmother's and wallowing in the state of my situation for the next few hours, I'd received a call from Lupé verifying the plans for tonight's meeting at her house. The thought of getting together with the rest of the demons who supported my cause, brightened my mood considerably. Reaffirming what I was doing was for the good of us all, left me feeling rejuvenated. I had just enough time to return home, change my clothes, and to grab a bite to eat.

After passing security, I rode the elevator up to our apartment on the twentieth floor. Jeremy was going to be working late, which was customary whenever I had a meeting to attend. He always said, *"If you're not going to be there, what's the point of me being home alone?"* It melted my heart. But as I stepped through the door, I heard a rustling coming from the back of the apartment, instantly piquing my curiosity.

"Jeremy, is that you?" I regretted announcing my presence the moment I heard more vigorous shuffling and muffled voices. Quickly dropping my things on the living room floor, I crept down the hall toward my bedroom and suddenly found myself face to face with two vampires.

* * * * *

(Evie)

It was the night after I'd received Christian's call and his odd request. The club was open and the beat of the music was keeping time with my hammering headache. I sat at my desk, staring at the phone, wanting nothing more than to pick up the receiver and dial Christian's number. But, since I hadn't heard back from Balam, I truly didn't have anything to report; and if Christian had any good news for us, I'm sure he would have called by now. Forcing myself to move on with our daily tasks, I'd sent Dax to ask Renard and Loni to join me in my office.

Walking in hand-in-hand, they both took a seat on the couch and waited for me to begin.

"I've recently secured accommodations for you in Masen. We need the two of you to go back to where Meredith had her meeting and keep an eye on her. I want to know her every move and exactly how far she's gotten with her plans to feed her people human blood."

"No problem, Evie. We'll leave right away. Where exactly will we be staying?" Loni asked.

"It's a high-rise downtown, here's the address." I handed them a scrap of paper with the information on. "It's not a hotel, but since it's a new structure they have unoccupied apartments that are being rented out for long-term leases. I've secured one on the fifteenth floor for the next two months."

Renard's eyes went wide. "Two months? Bloody hell!"

I laughed out loud at his reaction. "I don't expect you to be gone that long, no. But it was the shortest lease I could get. Besides, once all this mess is over, I may just end up keeping it for getaways and to have a backup location in case we ever have to abandon The Rising Pit for any reason."

"Whew." Renard wiped his brow with the back of his hand. "You had me worried there for a moment."

After we settled the remaining details of their stakeout—including a two-week supply of blood bags—I watched as they drove away in Dax's blue SUV.

Returning to the club, Dax guided me through the crowd and back toward my office. "Don't worry, Evie, they'll be fine. And soon, we'll have the upper hand and know just what that bitch is up to."

"I hope so, my love. I hate feeling so useless, and waiting for Balam's response has left me on pins and needles for reasons I don't even understand."

"Well, it's only been one day since you asked him to look in the caves. You have to give him some time to complete the task, Evie. Worrying about something you can't control does no one any good." He placed a kiss on the top of my head. "Patience, my dear, patience."

Listening to Dax rationalize my frustration was rubbing me the wrong way. I knew he meant well, but hearing I just needed to sit and do nothing, wasn't helping my mood. So, in an effort to rid myself of my headache and my irritation, I left the club in Dax's capable hands and made my way downstairs. Perhaps a nice long bath would help to wash away my stress. Did I really think it would work? *No...* but it was worth a try.

* * * * *

(Loni)

The drive to Masen was quick, as rush hour ended hours ago. In just under two hours, we pulled into the underground parking lot of the new building downtown. It was an impressive high-rise, but to be honest, I was a little concerned. The whole thing seemed to be made of windows and while we didn't burn in the sun, I just wasn't use to being so exposed while I slept.

"Don't fret, love, we're on the fifteenth floor. Any bugger catching a peek up there would have to either be a window washer, or the Amazing Spiderman. Besides, that's what they make drapes for." Renard's flippant attitude reminded me of why I loved him so much. He always had a way of putting things into perspective for my overly stimulated brain.

"You're right, of course. Let's get settled in and then head over to Meredith's meeting facility. We still have a good eight hours before sunrise."

"Sounds perfect, pet."

We quickly made our way to the fifteenth floor and found our apartment at the end of the hall. The decor was nice, with replicas of fine art hanging on the walls and beautiful vases residing in lighted niches. The kitchen boasted granite counter tops and stainless-steel appliances, and the large jacuzzi tub in the master bath had me hoping our stakeout took all two months and then some. The place was gorgeous!

"Wow, swanky," Renard teased.

"It's nice, yeah?"

"Absolutely. But don't get any ideas, poppet, I don't want to be here any longer than necessary. The Rising Pit is our home, and I don't like being away from the family while all this stuff with Christian and Rose is playing out."

He was right, *again*. This wasn't a honeymoon, and it certainly wasn't a replacement home; it was just a means to an end, and that end was getting the low down on Meredith and her demons.

"Let's go," I said, feeling a renewed sense of determination.

Locking the front door and stuffing the key into his pocket, Renard grabbed my hand as we made our way back to the elevator. The doors opened and we stepped in, pushing the button for the ground floor. Unfortunately, the elevator was making its assent, so we'd have to wait for its skyward journey to end before we could be on our way downward. *We should have taken the stairs,* I thought to myself.

We stood in silence, bored as the people moved in and out of the box, entering and exiting onto their chosen levels. It wasn't until we reached the twentieth floor that something caught my attention.

CHAPTER TWENTY-THREE

(Christian)

I continued to study the petroglyphs in front of me, following the story they told over and over. It still left me no discernible information relating to Rose, though. However, I did feel trapped by the appearance of Loraine, as if leaving the only place I'd recently seen her would be a mistake.

"Justin, Jillian? Can you hear me?" I shouted.

It took a few minutes before I heard movements from above.

"Christian, where are you?" Justin asked, obviously confused.

"I'm down here. In the sink hole. I've found some more carvings, and think since it's getting close to sunrise, we should just stay here tonight."

"Do you want us to come down there with you? Is there a way out?" Jillian called.

"No. Just stay up there. We're far enough off the beaten trail no one will venture in here." My claircognizance was kicking in, and I knew we'd remain undiscovered while we slept.

"Okay. Sounds good. Neither of us found anything in our areas either, by the way," Justin added.

"I didn't expect you would." I tried not to sound disappointed. It wasn't their fault we were on a wild goose chase.

"Don't worry, Christian. We'll find her soon." Jillian's reassuring words helped a bit, but as I settled down onto the hard ground—the shards of shale poking into my sides—I concentrated on Rose, hoping something would spark. Unfortunately, the only sensation I got was that of our bond being stretched far beyond its limits. My body began to shake uncontrollably and it was in that moment, I wondered if I'd actually survive this situation after all.

* * * * *

(Evie)

After soaking my troubles away, I was headache free by the time Dax joined me once the club had closed. My evening was topped off by a much appreciated massage and the sensual attentions of my beloved mate before we fell comatose for the day.

The following evening, we woke and headed straight to the cooler. Everyone else had already fed and made their way upstairs, so it was just Dax and I in the storage room when my cell phone rang.

"Hello."

"Hola, Evangeline. I'm calling with news," stated Balam.

His serious tone put me on edge immediately.

"Just a moment, Balam. Let me get to my office so that I may take notes." I nodded at Dax and flew down the hall and up into my office in a matter of seconds, sealing the bookcase behind me.

"Apologies, Sire. Please continue."

"After searching the past two nights in the caves below, we did discover some ancient drawings in one of the oldest areas."

While I was excited to learn what they found, the hesitation I could sense in his voice had me worried that "excited" wouldn't be the appropriate word for what I was about to hear.

"Evie, I'm not sure if what we found will be of any help to you or your new Sire, but to say we have discovered some very important information about the demons, is putting it mildly."

The air rushed out of me and I began to drift as my Sire explained the extinction of an entire race.

* * * * *

(Loraine)

The terror was now something I couldn't escape. I was stuck in this hellish ether, forced to witness the end of a civilization over and over again. The images played continuously, until bits and pieces of information started to accompany them. Information I wish I could forget.

The story had been laid out before me; the demon princess Ixtab, the daughter of Yum Camil, was the Mayan Goddess of Death, Sacrifice, and Suicides. After reveling in her duties as the Death Goddess for centuries, she became bored and jealous of her brother, the bat-God Camazotz. She wanted to have wings and be able to fly like him. So, in an effort to do so, she performed dark magicks, offered many sacrifices, and finally—in a bizarre ritual—bit Camazotz, becoming the first ever hybrid—his vampire blood mixing with her own.

At first, nothing happened except her desire to drink human blood, but as she continued to perform her godly duties, killing more and more, she eventually developed wings and a thirst for nothing but blood and destruction. This was the hybrid's way of drifting dark.

After leveling villages and slaying her people, Ixtab left Xibalba and began her world-wide killing spree. Yum Camil sent his son, Camazotz, to stop her. He tracked her all over the world, engaging her in fight after fight as he tried to protect the innocent people of the human realm. Eventually, he successfully brought Ixtab back to Xibalba. When she realized she was trapped and could no longer leave their realm, she killed her brother and father in a fit of rage, effectively ending the Mayan race.

Trapped in Xibalba, truly alone and with her reign of terror complete—the Goddess of Suicide killed herself, leaving only the human descendants of Camazotz and Yum Camil to carry on in secret, hidden in the folds of time.

CHAPTER TWENTY-FOUR

(Rose)

I opened my eyes and felt death. The presence of it, the weight of it, the power of it. I couldn't believe how good it felt. I thought *the power of it* described it best. It felt like a surge within my soul... one that would only grow stronger.

Sitting up slowly, I took stock of my surroundings. I was still in the cave, laying on the cold ground. But spread out under me, cushioning me from the rough edges of the rock, were my wings.

I *hadn't* dreamt them. They were real.

Standing up, I looked over my shoulder, trying to get a better view. My wings were large, black, and fierce. They looked like dragon hide and had wisps that extended from the ends and edges, making what I was sure would be a frightening sight as I flew through the sky. A sight I had seen often as of late; a sight I had dreamt about for days.

Feeling the rush of anticipation, I extended my arms—not knowing how else to make them move. I laughed as my wings lifted, instantly catching the air currents surrounding me.

With one spin and a slight push off the ground, I was hovering in mid-air, as if flying was already second nature. *Wait... what if it was? What if the memories and feelings I've had lately were actually of me doing all those horribly beautiful things?*

Finally awake and aware of what I'd truly become, I shot out of the hole in the top of my cave and went searching for answers. Answers and blood.

* * * * *

(Evie)

"Christian, I need you to call me as soon as you get this message. It's URGENT!! I heard back from Balam, and we need to talk IMMEDIATELY!"

Dammit! I was so pissed right now. This was the fourth time I tried to reach Christian and was sent directly to his voicemail.

The idea of Rose drifting dark and turning into that... *thing*, was more than I could process. I needed to tell Christian what he was up against; tell him that his decision had been wrong; tell him that while being the hybrid *would* allow Rose to kill Meredith and her demons, but if we were too late, and she'd already transformed, she would most likely not stop there. She would turn on us all, wiping out vampires and demons alike. And worse, unlike Ixtab, Rose had run of the human realm; an entire world to terrorize.

I turned to Dax. "Do you think I should call William and see if he can reach Jillian or Justin?"

"Yes. That's a great idea. Maybe he'll know why Christian hasn't been answering."

I quickly dialed William's number, hoping he'd be able to set my mind at ease.

"William, it's Evangeline. I'm trying to reach Christian and have been unsuccessful. I was wondering if you've heard from Jillian or Justin lately?"

"No, Evie. I'm sorry, I haven't. The last time I spoke with them was right before they left. Justin had relayed they were taking off to explore some cave systems in the Midwest, but that was a couple of days ago, and I haven't had any reports since."

Caves? Perhaps Christian's gifts have already given him the knowledge of what's happening to Rose. The thought had me panicked and relieved at the same time.

"All right, thank you, William. I'll just keep trying him. Perhaps the caves are what's interfering with my calls. But please, if you hear anything, let me know."

"Of course, Evie. I'll try Justin again right now. Take care."

I hung up the phone and shook my head at Dax. Not that he hadn't heard the entire conversation, but because I just didn't have the words to express how devastated I was.

Rose was a descendant from the demon race, and now—since being turned by Christian, she was only the second hybrid to ever exist, linking her directly to Ixtab. If Rose was reveling in her kills, she would have already started to drift dark. If Christian didn't find her soon, we all might as well line up for the new Goddess of Death, Rose Reynolds.

* * * * *

(Christian)

I woke up in a panic. Most likely because the last thing I'd thought about was my imminent ruin before falling asleep. But I could feel it. I was running out of time.

I listened closely, waiting to see if Jillian and Justin had risen yet but was only met with silence. Using the natural nooks and crannies, I scaled the rock, hopping out the top in a matter of seconds.

I looked around and found Justin and Jillian huddled together, still asleep against the far wall of the small stone room.

I paced the tight area, annoyed I had no way of waking them faster. Frustrated, I slid down the opposite wall and closed my eyes. I figured I should put my time to good use, so after taking a couple deep breaths, I tried to connect with Loraine again.

Ten minutes of meditation, and I was no closer to receiving any answers. Thankfully, Jillian and Justin finally began to rise.

"Hey," Justin said upon seeing me.

I nodded my head in his direction as he stretched and stood.

"So, what did you find out from the drawings down there?" he asked.

I wasn't sure how to answer. Sure, I could describe the images to him, but what was the point? Besides the connection to the demented picture show my dead mother-in-law had shown me, what good had they served?

"Nothing really. Just drawings of the tribesmen's daily lives."

Justin tilted his head, and I wasn't sure if his hesitation meant he didn't believe me, or if he was waiting for me to continue. Unfortunately, I simply didn't have anything else to say. Instead, I removed three blood bags from my backpack and tossed two in his direction. "We need to feed and move onto our next stop... Missouri."

Jillian woke just as Justin and I began to drain his dinner.

"Morning!" she said with a smile.

She was apparently a "morning person." I probably would have been too, if I'd falling asleep with Rose in my arms. Sighing deeply, I shook my head. None of this was Jillian's fault, and I knew I had to stop feeling sorry for myself, but that would be a whole lot easier if my gifts had been more active lately. I wasn't used to being this disconnected. First with Loraine, and now feeling as if I was losing touch with all of my abilities. Who knew? Maybe I was.

"Any news?" Jillian asked.

"No. But I'm hopeful we'll find something at our next stop." I had to keep up appearances. If they knew how defeated I was feeling, they would report back to William, who would in turn tell Evie. Dealing with her reactions was the last thing I needed right now. I hung my head and took a couple deep breaths, but my anger at this entire situation must have caused me to drift again, because when I looked up at Jillian her eyes grew wide.

I frowned as they both stared at me with open uncertainty. I hope they knew no matter how depressed and upset I got, I wasn't that far gone. "What's wrong? Why are you both looking at me like that?" I asked.

Jillian spoke first after taking a few sips of blood. "Um... because you're glowing."

CHAPTER TWENTY-FIVE

(Loni)

The elevator door opened onto the twentieth floor, and my attention was transfixed on the blur that sped past. A blur that no one other than Renard and I would have been able to see.

We looked back and forth at one another as the crowd in front of us shuffled about. Whoever or whatever that was, would have been long gone by now, and since we needed to get to Meredith's meeting site, there was simply no time to investigate. But with a nod toward my husband, I verified I'd definitely wanted to check it out later.

We completed the torturously slow ride to the ground floor, then finally exited the elevator, then left the building. It was faster and way stealthier to run to our destination, so after a few short minutes on foot, we arrived at the building where we'd previously witnessed Meredith's meetings. Claiming our original stakeout spot, we peered through the window at the east side of the facility. The last time we'd been in this position, we'd watched as Meredith spiked the punch with human blood, but tonight, all we saw was a dark, empty room, devoid of any humans or demons.

"Well, shit," I said.

"Guess we should hang around to see if anyone shows up."

"Guess so," I replied.

After hours of waiting in the shadows, and no one making an appearance, Renard stood up and stretched his arms high above his head. "Looks like we'll have to come back tomorrow."

"Why? Let's just run over to her house and see if we can pick up her trail from there," I suggested.

"Evie made it clear we were to stay away from their home. Especially since Jeremy identified me the last time we were there. We can't risk either of them seeing us again, or we could blow this entire thing."

"Fine! So, what if she isn't here tomorrow either? Are we going to visit every night to make sure we don't miss her?"

"Yes. I suppose we will."

"Dammit!" I really didn't want to spend every waking minute sitting here in the dark, waiting for this bitch to show herself. Bouncing from foot to foot, I decided to run off my frustration by taking a quick lap around the building.

I was glad I did.

Smiling as I returned, I waved the piece of paper in my hand at Renard. It was the event schedule I'd grabbed from the glass case mounted next to the front door.

Taking the document from my hand, Renard quickly scanned the planned events for the next month.

"Meredith's name isn't on here anywhere. And even *if* she was using a fake name, all of these events are either wedding receptions or bar mitzvahs." After shredding the paper Renard shook his head. "It looks like she's moved her meetings, which means we're totally buggered."

Tonight had been nothing but a series of missed opportunities.

After racing back to our apartment, Renard called Evie and explained the brick wall we'd just hit. She wasn't happy, of course, but didn't want us to give up. We were to stay here, and for the next two weeks—which is how long our blood supply would last—go back to the meeting facility and talk to anyone we came across to see if we could piece together where Meredith was now. Evie refused to let us venture to their home, saying she wouldn't risk us being put on Meredith's radar any more than we had to be. Staking out the meeting facility was the safest bet.

It was three in the morning when Renard hung up the phone. I was frustrated and pretty wound up, so I contemplated how to fill the remainder of our night since sunrise was still a few hours away.

"Babe, do you want to go up to check out that blur we saw earlier? See if we can find out who or what's up there?"

"Not tonight, my sweet. I have other plans for us." He winked.

I settled into his arms and let him kiss away the disappointment I knew we were both feeling. We had two weeks to find Meredith, and during that time we'd also discover who was occupying the twentieth floor, so tonight... tonight was just about us.

* * * * *

(Meredith)

Staring into the eyes of two vampires in my own home sent me into a full-blown panic. But instead of launching an attack, my fight or flight response had me racing out of the apartment and back down the hallway. I assumed it was due to my *maternal state*. I flew past the elevator, heading immediately for the stairs. I was down twenty flights in a matter of seconds and ran directly to Lupé's house, collapsing at her front door.

"¡Dios mío! What is wrong, child?"

Lupé and her youngest daughter came running out of the house and quickly collected me in their arms, then helped me to the couch that sat at the end of the porch.

"Thank you." I hating showing any vulnerability in front of people who were supposed to be my lessers, but the surprise of what just happened overshadowed my need for pretenses. "The vampires found me."

Lupé gasped and her daughter, whose name I still couldn't remember, started crossing herself and praying under her breath.

"I'll call Raúl right away. We'll push up the meeting and dose everyone with a larger amount of blood, then we'll *all* escort you back to your apartment. We'll put an end to this tonight." She left my side and headed back inside where I could hear her dialing the phone.

I was so grateful for not only the physical support, but also for the feeling of being truly cared for. Though Jeremy treated me like a queen and always had loving things to say, in reality it was all a lie. But this— genuine concern from one of my own—it was real and made me feel good.

I smiled at the young girl and listened to her mother complete what I could only describe as a demon phone chain. Two initial calls went out, then, ten minutes later, people started arriving in droves. I watched in stunned silence as Lupé and her family quickly erected a large tent structure, filling it with tables and chairs in the front yard, while others carried in two humans who were obviously obtained to serve as our sacrifices tonight.

My strength returned and I licked my lips when I saw Juan, another of Damien's cousins, cut a man's throat, draining the life-giving fluid into the large pail placed at his feet. Sacrifices, blood, immortality... all present here in the woods with others of my kind; this was how our ancestors must have lived. The thought had me feeling extremely *primitive* and my craving for blood was quickly reaching an uncontrollable level. All I wanted to do was fly over to the dying man and latch my mouth over his open wound. But, if I wanted to keep the others drinking blood in only small doses, I knew I had to show restraint, however the stress of controlling myself had me shaking in my seat.

"Meredith, are you alright?" Lupé asked upon her return.

I met her gaze with my eyes glowing red. She simply nodded and walked straight over to the table, grabbed a cup, and dipped it into the vat of blood while shooing off everyone who began to question her as she made her way back to my side.

"I think you need this. Though I will have to answer questions from the others as to why they can't drink straight blood too."

After downing the savory contents of the cup, I smiled and said, "Thank you. I'll speak to them."

Lupé began to gather everyone under the large tent, and after Juan and Max, another cousin, disposed of the two bodies, I began my first speech as their true leader.

"Thank you all for coming on such short notice. I'm sure you have heard that the vampires found me, which is the reason for this rushed affair."

I placed a hand over my stomach in an effort to gain sympathy so that my next statement would be taken at face value.

"I asked Lupé to bring me a cup of blood directly from the pail in an effort to replenish and nourish my unborn child. The stress of running across town as we fled for our lives, took a toll on him that required a direct dose of blood to heal. Thankfully, the effects are fast acting, and the baby and I are now going to be just fine."

Sighs of relief and hushed prayers floated up from them, leaving me feeling hopeful.

"I want you all to make sure you have an extra cup of *punch* tonight, and then we'll head back into town to investigate together. I'm pretty sure the vampires would not have lingered, but you never know. The more of us there are, the better."

I suddenly stopped and thought about Jeremy. He wouldn't be home until later, seeing as he already arranged to work late because of my meeting, but what if he came home early and found his home infested with demons? No. I couldn't take that chance. I'd have to call and delay him even further.

"I have to make a phone call, so drink up, and then we can solidify our plans."

As the crowd began to gather around the punch bowls, I found a quiet spot in the back corner of her house to make my call. I took a few deep breaths in an effort to pull myself together before dialing.

"Hello, darling. How are things at work?"

"Hi, Mer. I'm fine, just busy. What's up?"

"Well, I was thinking, perhaps I should come meet you for a late rendezvous and we could take in the midnight showing of that new movie you wanted to see?" I tried to keep my voice even and upbeat.

"That sounds great, actually. I have a couple of new clients that just stopped by, and this will allow me plenty of time take them to dinner and give them my pitch."

Perfect. This also gave me plenty of time to investigate, destroy, and recuperate before I had to meet up with him.

"Where are you meeting your clients for dinner?"

"O'Connors, just down the street."

"Sounds great, darling. I'll meet you there at eleven."

I returned to the front yard and noticed everyone was clearly wired. The blood was doing its job. "Everyone gather around," I instructed from the top of the stairs. I paused as they moved closer to my makeshift podium. "I live on the twentieth floor of the new high-rise building downtown. I think it will be wisest for me to enter by myself, since the building has security. Then I'll make my way down to the entrance for deliveries and let you all in. We can take the freight elevator straight up to my floor without being seen. I'll go in first, followed by Raúl, Juan, and Max, then the rest of you follow, but remain in the front room unless I call for you."

Everyone nodded in agreement and seemed to be just fine with following my directions. This was exactly how it was supposed to work; the leader leads and the followers follow. Simple.

As fifteen or so demons loaded into the vehicles, I made sure I was in a car with Raúl, Juan, and Max. I needed to give a little more information to my main muscle.

"Okay, guys. Once we enter my apartment, you'll need to be ready. If the vampires are still there, they'll fight tooth and nail to defeat you, but our biggest advantage is that they won't bite us. They know doing so would give us the upper hand, as our demon blood would infect them."

They nodded their heads and bumped fists, as I continued. "However, we aren't restricted by their blood. We *can* bite them. So, if you get the chance to sink your teeth into one of them, do it. Draining them will be our best bet of survival, since it'll weaken them while fueling us."

The back seat was buzzing with excitement. The men were pumped and ready. Now I just hoped that my instructions were accurate. I'd never bitten a vampire before, but didn't think it would be any different than biting a human. Their blood should boost our speed and strength, while making them weaker in the process. It was clearly a win-win.

Once we entered the parking garage, claiming three spaces near the service elevators, I waved at the group of eager demons waiting in the cars as I strolled toward the front entrance. I was a nervous wreck as I walked into the lobby of my building but tried my hardest to appear calm and *normal.* I was worried my anxiety would spike, causing my eyes to flare for everyone to see, which I really needed to avoid. Normalcy was in high demand. I laughed out loud at the irony as I rode the service elevator down to greet my demon army.

CHAPTER TWENTY-SIX

(Rose)

Rain pelted my face as I flew through the air, but it did nothing to cool my rage. While I dipped and dove through the frigid spray, learning the nuances of my newly developed wings, my attention was suddenly drawn to the bodies scattered across the forest floor below. The overgrown ferns and mossy ground-cover hid them from plain sight, but the dried blood still clinging to their bodies drew me in immediately. There were at least twenty bodies strewn across the span of a couple of miles.

As I landed near a small group of them, I instantly knew I'd been the cause of their death. The jagged teeth marks left on their throats were a match for my now protruding fangs. Fangs that were longer and rougher than I remembered.

Shaking my head, I tried to recall inflicting this level of mayhem. A vampire only fed once a day, but apparently, I'd been killing at least six or more people at a time. Maybe that was why I was sleeping so much. I was ingesting too much blood. Even the thought of the word "blood" caused a smile to spread across my face and a tingling to race through my veins, but it also scared the shit out of me, and *that* pissed me off.

I should no longer fear anything, yet here I was, afraid of losing myself to whatever transformation had taken over my body and mind. I hadn't even been aware I'd been doing any of this; I needed to gain control, and fast. It wasn't that I minded the killing, as a matter of fact, I was enjoying it immensely, but what I did mind was not understanding or being able to control what was happening to me.

I flew back to my cave, descending through the hole and forced myself to think back to the last thing I remembered about my life before becoming the hybrid.

A man's face filled my mind's eye, a face I knew should be familiar but wasn't. I tried to muster a memory that would spark some emotion in regards to the image, but failed. I simply couldn't feel anything other than the pounding of blood in my head, drumming to an ancient tribal beat.

I laid down, closed my eyes, and let the darkness claim me once more.

* * * * *

(Christian)

Glowing?

"What are you talking about?" I asked.

"How else can I say it, Christian? You're fucking glowing!" Jillian replied.

I looked down at myself and found her statement to be true. My entire body was shining like a lighthouse beacon in the dark. The golden light was subtle at first, but then grew to an intensity that lit up the entire cavern.

"Holy shit!" Justin declared as he shielded his eyes.

I searched the space for Loraine, hoping she had something to do with this, but when pain started to wrack my body, I knew this couldn't be anything good. Whatever was happening to me had nothing to do with Loraine, but with Rose instead.

My gifts finally decided to kick in, and it became clear our consort bond was close to its breaking point. I was losing her. Our ethereal cord was ready to snap, and that meant I was going to die in this cave. Even worse, it meant Rose was on the verge of dying too.

I screamed.

"Christian, my God, what's wrong, what do we do?" Jillian yelled.

I had no answer for her as I fell to the ground. A painful pull within my chest had me wrapping my arms around my torso just before I passed out.

* * * * *

(Justin)

The second Christian fell unconscious his body stopped glowing. Jillian looked at me, obviously scared and clueless as to what we should do. I pulled out my cell phone to dial William for some advice, but quickly found I had no signal this deep within the caves.

"Let's get him back to the surface, so I can call William," I suggested.

Jillian shook her head and stared at me with wide eyes.

I picked up Christian and instructed her to clean up the blood bags and grab our backpack. We wove our way back out of the cave and reached the main opening within minutes. Thankfully, the park had closed over an hour ago, because the second we got service, all of our phones started blowing up.

Jillian and I quickly silenced ours, then I reached for Christian's, pushing the button to mute the incessant notifications. There were at least six messages for Jillian and I apiece, and over fifteen on Christian's phone. It was obvious whatever was happening was pretty serious.

I didn't want to be interrupted by another security guard, so I raced into the nearby woods and placed Christian against the base of a large tree. I immediately dialed William while Jillian paced, her hair and eyes drifting in rapid succession.

"William, it's Justin. What's going on?"

"Oh, thank God. Evie has some serious news she needs to relay to Christian, and she hasn't been able to get a hold of him. Are you still together?"

I looked at my unconscious friend and sighed. *This sucks.* "Yes, we are, but unfortunately Evie still isn't going to be able to talk to him."

"Why? What's happened?"

"We don't really know. After we woke this evening, he started… glowing, and then just passed out. He hasn't come to since."

The line was silent except for the sound of William's deep breaths. "Did you say he was glowing?"

"Yes, do you know what that means?"

"No, but it sounds like some next level shit is going on around here, and I don't want any part of it. I've never seen Evangeline this panicked before, and while I want to help her as much as possible, I refuse to put any of my family in danger. I think you and Jillian should come home."

Fuck! I didn't want to leave Christian, and I knew Jillian wouldn't want to stop looking for her best friend, but I had no idea how to convince William that everything would be okay, because honestly… I had no idea if it would be or not.

"William, Jillian and I are fine, and leaving Christian alone isn't going to sit well with Evie. With everything else going on, you don't want to start a feud between our clans."

"Christian has been a vampire for even longer than I have; he can take care of himself. Besides, Evie will understand my wanting to protect my clan, since that's exactly what she's doing too. No, you and Jillian will come home. Now!"

The last part of his statement was layered with his Sire command. Jillian dropped the backpack next to Christian's still form and within seconds our bodies were being pulled back to South Carolina of their own accord. I reached for her hand and watched the tears fall down her cheeks as we were forced to leave our friend alone in the woods.

CHAPTER TWENTY-SEVEN

(Meredith)

I knew my eyes were glowing red as we crept closer to the door of my apartment. I was so anxious about coming face to face with the vampires and the ensuing fight, that I could no longer stop my demon traits from presenting themselves. I didn't think the vampires would have stuck around, but if their intent was to end my life, then what better place to lie in wait than my own home? The question that nagged at me, however, was how in the hell had they found me so quickly after our move?

"Okay, this is it. Is everyone ready?"

My crew nodded their responses, and in the next second we all rushed through the front door, poised for battle. Immediately, the men followed me into the back rooms of the apartment, while the rest of my demon guard staked out the living room as planned. It didn't take long to realize we were alone.

"The place is clear," I called out, putting everyone's mind at ease. Lupé closed the front door, and we all gathered to discuss our next step. "Just look for anything out of the ordinary. A piece of paper or even a matchbook lying on the floor could be the clue we need in tracking them down," I ordered.

As everyone began to spread out, I returned to where I'd encountered the vamps in the first place. My bedroom was clean, and there was only the slightest hint of ransacking but nothing seemed to actually be missing. I was getting ready to look in the bathroom when my cell phone started to ring.

"Hello."

"Mer, it's me. I was just wanting to see if you were still planning to meet me at O'Connors? My meeting is done, so I thought I'd call and make sure you were on your way before I left."

I was happy to receive Jeremy's call and know that he was okay, and since this *mission* was obviously a bust, I had nothing to worry about here for the time being. But I was suddenly too exhausted to carry through with our plans for tonight.

"Actually, Jeremy, I'm feeling a bit tired and would prefer for you to just come home. I don't think I could sit through an entire movie at this point."

"All right, my dear. That sounds fine by me. I'll be home soon."

I hung up the phone and made my way back to the front room.

"Thank you all for accompanying me here to make sure I was safe. I'm so pleased by how well we came together as a unit to take on this situation. The time has come for us to become the hunters instead of the hunted, and when we do finally face the vampires, I know we'll succeed as long as we stick together."

Everyone smiled and clapped each other on the back.

"Let's plan to meet again at Lupé's next week. We'll discuss the next step in my plan, but for now, I'm going to call it a night. I will take extra security measures, so please don't worry about me."

Lupé stepped forward and gave me a hug. "Be safe and call us if you need anything at all."

"I will, thank you."

I watched as my small group of demons made their way back to the service elevator. I knew with Raúl as my second in command, and everyone on board with the way I was running things, we'd be able to take down the vampires when the time came. I was sure of it.

* * * * *

(Christian)

I opened my eyes and darkness surrounded me. I tried to use my psychic gifts to reach out for information, but couldn't. I knew I'd passed out and was now caught in some sort of in-between world. I wondered if this was what Evie had felt like when she'd fallen unconscious after linking to Terrance? I tried to calm myself and blank my mind, just as I'd suggested to her at the time. But unlike Evie's results, clearing my thoughts did nothing to release me from this nightmare. So, instead, I chose to fill my head with images of Rose.

I thought about the first time I'd seen her leaning out of that limousine, her long blonde hair blowing in the breeze; I pictured us sharing our first kiss in the back seat of my car and all the other times we made out during my breaks from work. I let my mind rifle through the next four months of what I thought was utter bliss when Rose had been in hiding with me at The Rising Pit; and finally, I landed on the image of me sinking my fangs into her neck as her eyes glowed red.

After everything we had been through, I was sure we were going to end up happy for all of eternity; vampires in love, living the dream. But instead, I was trapped in this unconscious hell, literally alone, feeling the cord of our bond preparing to snap, and my life about to end.

Just as I was about to take what I was sure to be my last breath, I started feeling a slight tug in my chest. The images started to flicker and suddenly a horrible beast replaced my beautiful Rose.

Its teeth were long and jagged and dripped with blood. It had hideous wings that sprang from its back and carried it up into the night sky as it screamed and screeched like a howling banshee. Its eyes were glowing red and its long black hair was stringy and flew in every direction. I instantly recognized it from the drawings I'd seen in the cave.

However, it suddenly became clear the beast I now saw in my mind *wasn't* a delusion or an image of an ancient demon from the past. No... it was the hybrid—it was *Rose.*

I screamed as the anguish of my decision washed over me in a tidal wave of despair. *How could I have been so wrong?* I cried out again as I opened my eyes and found the beast—my Rose—staring straight at me within this unconscious dreamscape.

She hovered in midair, piercing me with her ungodly gaze.

"Rose? Can you hear me?"

She tilted her head, like a dog does when spoken to.

"Rose. It's me, honey. It's Christian. Can you tell me where you are?"

The odd look on her face caused my heart to break and my despair to grow. She had no idea who I was. Maybe *that's* why our bond was breaking—*not* because she was dying, but because she was lost to me—lost to herself, and no longer the same person; no longer my beloved Rose.

I closed my eyes and let the tears come. I wondered if I would still die if our bond snapped even though she'd remain alive. Or would I simply continue to exist *without* my consort? She was the hybrid, and I was just the vampire who'd created her. I had no idea how our differences would affect our bond, but as I contemplated losing my true love forever, suddenly a golden light began to glow behind my eyelids. I opened my eyes, hopeful Rose was recognizing our connection, but what I saw next had me flying through the black space of this strange realm, screaming and crying and desperate to save my own life.

Rose had a hold of the end of our ethereal cord; our *actual* consort bond. It was a glowing thick rope that ran between me and her, anchoring into each of our chests right above our hearts... and she was preparing to rip it apart.

CHAPTER TWENTY-EIGHT

(Evie)

After receiving a call from William, I experienced a level of desperation I'd never known before. He explained Christian had passed out in the caves he, Jillian, and Justin were exploring in Kentucky. William told me he'd used his Sire command to order Jillian and Justin home, in fear of the unknown danger pursuing Rose would cause if they continued. I understood the desire to protect his vampire children, but the idea of my son being left alone in the woods, unconscious, had me wanting to sink my fangs into William's neck and let the poison of true death flow. I was much older than the young Sire and would prove the winner of any confrontation between us. Dax, of course, talked me out of any vengeance, and we were now racing to the spot we'd been told Christian would be.

After three hours of shadow hopping, we found Christian still unconscious at the base of a tree outside of the Mammoth caves just as William had indicated.

"Do you think we should try to scan him?" Dax asked.

"Honestly... I have no idea. I can't deny I'm nervous to use my scanning ability after what happened to me with Terrance. And with Rose being a demon turned hybrid... truth be told, I'm a little scared to try."

"I don't blame you, sweetheart. Let's just get him home so we can keep him safe and watch over him until, whatever this is, passes. I won't risk you being hurt."

With that settled, Dax gently lifted Christian into his arms, while I gathered the backpack that was lying at his feet. It would be slow going as we headed back to The Rising Pit, but at least I knew everyone in my clan was safe for the moment.

* * * * *
(Loni)

Tonight, we took our time as we made our way back over to the meeting facility. There was a wedding reception taking place and after questioning a few of the guests, we quickly deduced no one present had any connection to the demons we were looking for.

"This is bullshit. I don't care what Evie says, we just need to run over to their house and see what the hell's going on," I snapped.

"As much as I hate disobeying Evie, she didn't use her Sire command to truly keep us at bay, so I think you're right. Because this," he pointed toward the building, "is a complete waste of time."

I was glad my husband saw things my way, but after sprinting across town to Meredith and Jeremy's brownstone, I was now in an even worse mood than before. There was a "For Sale" sign in the front yard and the place was completely empty.

"I don't fucking believe this!" I shouted. Screw being quiet; there was no danger here, since no one was around. "This is ridiculous. First Jeremy moves from Seela, and we almost lose him. Then, Meredith moves her meetings and we're left scrambling. And NOW, we try to track them down at their actual home, and it's a fucking ghost town. What the hell are we supposed to do?" I blew out a frustrated breath and plopped down on a grassy knoll in the park.

"First things first, Loni. Let's return to the apartment. I'll call Evie again and let her know what we found out. She'll be upset we went against her wishes, but once she realizes the importance of what we found, she shouldn't be too hard on us."

After wallowing in my pity party for a few more seconds, I jumped up and walked hand in hand with my husband through the streets of Masen. Renard phoned Evie once we returned to our temporary home, and just as expected, she was upset, but understood. We were all frustrated by Meredith's disappearing act, but Evie told us to stay put until she had time to do a little more digging on her end.

"So, babe, do you want to go see a movie or something? Or we could check out the twentieth floor like I wanted," I asked.

"I know you want to see what was up there, but it's not like we've been threatened since being here, and honestly, I'm just not up for any more drama tonight. Can we just go see a movie and enjoy ourselves until Evie has some news for us?"

The moment he pulled me close and placed a kiss on my lips, I forgot all about the blur we'd seen on our first night. "You got it sugar, that sounds great."

I changed out of my *secret mission* clothes, sliding into my skinny jeans, converse sneaker wedges, and a black tank-top that was a little dressier than my previous attire. There was no need to rush at this point, it was barely after eight, and we'd already eaten from the blood bags before we'd left the apartment initially. So, with no more pressing business, we headed out to enjoy the rest of our evening, hand in hand.

CHAPTER TWENTY-NINE

(Meredith)

After spending the day rearranging furniture and finally unpacking the last few boxes from our move, I'd showered and was ready to spend the evening with my wonderful fiancé. I had already slipped Jeremy some of my blood in his morning coffee as usual, so I hoped I could make plans for tonight without any hindrance from our mind bond going *wonky* again.

"Darling, what would you say if we headed out for a drink and the movie we missed last night?"

"Sounds perfect. Let me just grab my jacket."

Good. I already knew a glass or two of sparkling cider wasn't going to quench my thirst, so I'd just have to excuse myself during the movie to "use the restroom" and find myself someone to drink from who would.

As we locked up our apartment and walked toward the elevator, Jeremy's cell phone started to buzz. After a quick look at the text, he nodded his head and smiled.

"What's that about, dear?"

"The clients I met last night liked my proposal and want to expand the campaign a bit. They asked if I could meet them at O'Connors again to get the rest of their ideas before they leave town tomorrow morning. Do you mind if I take care of a little business tonight before our movie?"

"Not at all."

I loved seeing my future husband be so successful in his work, but it was the fact that this gave me the perfect opportunity to excuse myself from their meeting and find someone to drain that had me agreeing to the interruption of our date night without hesitation.

I couldn't deny my thirst was becoming a problem. One that had me on edge. I kept thinking back to my grandmother's words, *"...I can tell that you are changing, and I'm afraid that what you've started will not be good for our race."* I didn't see how becoming an immortal could be a bad thing, but the closer I got to immortality, the more out of control I felt.

I continued to contemplate the best way to maintain the course I'd set for myself and my race, without losing myself in the process. But every time I started to think about cutting back on the blood I was consuming, the physical reaction I experienced was a big indicator it simply wasn't an option.

After parking the car, Jeremy and I walked down the street and around the corner to the restaurant. The warm breeze blowing the scents of the city in my direction had me craving the taste of blood even more. While we waited in the lobby of O'Connors, I scanned the crowd to see whose neck I would be feeding from tonight. The hostess might have moved to the top of my list if she hadn't rushed Jeremy and me to a table almost immediately.

"Would you like to order a drink while we wait?" Jeremy asked as he pulled out my chair.

"Actually, if you could order me a glass of sparkling cider and have it placed at the bar, I would appreciate it. I'm going to excuse myself to the restroom and allow you to conduct your meeting in peace." I leaned down and kissed his cheek. "Just come find me when you're done."

The quick wink he gave me and the sensuous smile that layered his handsome features had me excited for the rest of our evening.

I made my way to the restroom, slipped on my gloves, and claimed the largest stall at the end of the row. I hid inside with the door unlocked, anxiously awaiting my next meal. Luckily, it didn't take long until a middle-aged woman strolled into my grasp. I snapped her neck before she even realized I was there. The taste of her blood was so appealing, I knew I'd never be able to go back to not drinking straight from the vein. *God, I sound like a fucking vampire.*

After I swallowed the last drop, I laid her body on the tiled floor of the restroom, taking a moment to smear some of her blood on the toilet. I hoped it simply looked like she'd fallen and broke her neck.

I removed my gloves and placed them in my purse. Then, making certain I was alone, I washed my hands and exited the restroom. It had only taken two minutes to drain my victim, and as I took a seat at the bar, my glass of cider was placed in front of me. I took a sip and closed my eyes as the smooth flavor blended with the blood still coating my throat. I'd never done drugs as a kid, but I was pretty sure this was what being *high* felt like.

I continued to sip my drink while glancing at the menu the bartender slid in my direction. An amused giggle boiled to the surface, which I quickly coughed away. I found the idea of eating solid food hilarious at this point, but my humor faded when I thought about how difficult this was going to become. How would I explain to my fiancé I no longer wanted to eat? I supposed I could always order a plate and fake my way through a meal like a toddler trying to push his peas around the dish. But sooner or later, Jeremy was going to notice.

Relishing the last drop of my blood-tinged cider, I set the empty glass back onto the bar. I glanced at my watch then turned to look over my shoulder toward Jeremy's table. My smile fell and my eyes flared red when I focused on his clients. They were the same two vampires who had invaded our apartment.

* * * * *

(Rose)

"Rose? Can you hear me?"

A strange voice pierced the dark. I turned in its direction and tilted my head. There was a figure in the distance.

"Rose. It's me, honey. It's Christian. Can you tell me where you are?"

I frowned as I tried to place this person; place his voice. I knew he should be familiar to me, but I couldn't find the connection. He started crying and a flicker inside my chest flared. I looked down and saw a strange golden cord attached to my heart. It spanned the distance between us, connecting me to this man... this *stranger*.

My anger boiled to the surface. I had no control over what was happening to me, and it now looked like someone else was trying to control me as well. *No!* I reached down and grasped the glowing rope and pulled. The man flew through the air screaming, but then fell to the ground the instant the cord snapped in two.

CHAPTER THIRTY

(Loraine)

I materialized on a strange realm. A realm I didn't recognize. But it only took seconds to understand my purpose here.

Christian was lying on the ground and Rose was hovering in midair, opposite him. My beautiful daughter was now a frightening beast and her hands were still wrapped around her end of their ethereal cord. I looked down and saw their bond snapped in two, lying at my feet. I quickly picked up both ends and felt the surge of energy flow through me. Christian floated into the air, dangling from his end, while Rose was held in place by hers.

I wouldn't let go, and if this was the end for me, I was okay with that. I closed my eyes and held on tight. I was now the astral bridge between my daughter and her consort. Christian may be the one person who could save my daughter, but it was clear I had to save their bond in order for him to even have a chance.

We hovered in this empty space, frozen in stasis, until a jostling on Christian's end grabbed my attention. I opened my eyes and could thankfully now see past this dreamscape as if I was looking through a cloud. I watched as Evie showered Christian with concern and care, while Dax lifted him into his arms. As they began to walk away, I felt a pull as if we were all being forced to float along behind them. I glanced in Rose's direction and noticed the movement had caused her to stir as well.

* * * * *

(Rose)

I was locked into a paralyzed state the moment the white woman held the glowing cord in her hands. The energy linking me to that man surged from him, through her, and straight into me. An odd sensation flowed from the woman; a strange connection that washed over me; a connection penetrating deeper into my being with every passing second. I couldn't understand it, and that made me want to rip these people to shreds.

I was stuck on this astral plane but could also feel the connection to my true body. I realized I was flying through space; flying somewhere this woman was leading me. I assumed this was how I'd flown and killed those people without realizing it before; my mind was stuck in this dream-state while my physical body was fully functioning in the real world.

With my mind a flurry of dazed confusion, I shook my head and confirmed once we got to wherever I was being forced to go—and my mind and body were joined again—I was going to destroy everyone in my path. The images of death and destruction I'd dreamt about were now the same picture I was planning to paint.

* * * * *

(Evie)

I continued to cry as Dax placed Christian on his bed. He hadn't woken once during our journey home, and I was at a complete loss as to what we should do next. I debated calling Balam again, but thought it highly unlikely he'd have any advice regarding our current situation. When he'd explained the story of Ixtab to me, his final words had been, *"Good luck, my child. I fear you are facing a very difficult time."* What a fucking understatement.

Dax wrapped his arms around me and asked, "What should we do, Evie? I feel so useless. Are you sure you don't want me to try to scan his thoughts? Even if I'm knocked unconscious, you can always link to me and guide me back the same way I did for you."

I spun around in his arms and looked up at him through my tear-filled eyes. "No, Dax. I won't risk it. We have no idea what's causing Christian's condition, so that solution may not even work. No. We just have to wait until he comes out of it on his own."

I turned back to Christian and simply stared at my first vampire son, hoping for nothing less than a miracle. We stood over him for what seemed like only minutes when a scream pierced the air. In reality, an hour had passed while we stood vigilant, and it was now just past three a.m. as Dax and I raced from Christian's room and flew up the stair into the club. Luckily it was Monday and The Rising Pit was closed, so there were no patrons to slow us down.

"What's happened?" I demanded.

"There's something scary as all shit out there. It's got big wings and is hovering in mid-air, just out in front of the club," Tori replied.

I walked to the entrance, already dreading what I was about to see, and peered out the small round window in the front door. The image that greeted me had me sinking to the floor and shaking my head in denial.

Dax flew to my side and threw the lock. "My god, Evie, what is it?"

"I know what's happening to Christian. He's dying, and we are *all* next."

CHAPTER THIRTY-ONE

(Meredith)

Staring down the vampires in the middle of a restaurant was the worst-case scenario. Especially since this time, my fight or flight response was definitely leaning toward the *fight* side of things. I was ready to tear this place apart to get those assholes away from Jeremy. Luckily, they saw me before he did and immediately brought their meeting to an end. One shook Jeremy's hand, while the other gave him a pat on the back, then shot me a smug smile. *Oh, these guys are going to pay!*

As I watched them slink out the exit, I realized I didn't recognize either of them as being part of Evie's clan, which meant someone else was onto me. *Shit!*

I thought of chasing after them and getting some answers, but as I watched Jeremy stroll through the crowd to reach me, I knew this fight would have to wait. I wouldn't risk destroying the life I was building by jumping the gun with one rash move. I truly loved this man and would live and die for him, therefore I had to plan my attack with the utmost care. But now, having been located again, I knew I couldn't avoid it any longer. I'd have to call Raúl and boost him and the rest of the army's intake of blood. I needed them stronger and faster, and I needed it now.

"Meredith, are you alright?" Jeremy's question snapped me out of my internal strategizing.

"Yes, I'm fine. How did your meeting go?" It was imperative to get all the information I could on these two vampires, and then... let the hunt begin.

* * * * *

(Christian)

The surprise I felt when I came to left me shocked and confused. I was still stuck in whatever unconscious state I'd encountered Rose in, but was now being held in place as Loraine hovered between the two of us, holding our broken ethereal cord in each of her hands.

Rose was hovering in midair on the opposite end of the glowing rope. Realizing there was no escape from the strange embrace we were all locked in, I took this time to really look at her; to try to find some semblance of the woman I loved hiding beneath this beast. Her hair was dark as coal and she had long, jagged fangs. Her wings were large and rough, with what looked like a stringy gray and black film dangling from the ends. She looked gaunt and bone thin, like she was wasting away, or possibly becoming something more animal than human.

I jerked my head away and closed my eyes at the thought, letting the wave of despair wash over me. I'd been completely wrong. I never should have changed her. So much for trusting my gifts. *What a joke.*

My eyes jerked open with a surge to my chest. Loraine tightly held our severed cord while staring directly at me. Suddenly, it was as if I could see through her eyes, and what I saw brought sweet relief to my previous hopelessness.

Dax and Evie were carrying me through the woods, and thanks to my claircognizance, I instantly knew we were headed home. I immediately regretted mocking my gifts as I looked across the misty space and watched as Rose closed her eyes and floated along with us.

It was in that instant I knew we still had a chance to survive. All of us. I sank into my meditative state and threw my energy and thoughts directly through the cord at Loraine.

"*Loraine. Can you hear me?*"

"*Yes! Oh, thank goodness, Christian. Are you alright?*"

"*I am now. Everything is going to be fine. But I do need your help.*"

"*Of course. I'll do anything. Just tell me what you need.*"

"*All right. I need you to open yourself up to me. Try to see my energy as it flows from me, through you, and into Rose. Can you do that?*"

"*Yes. I think so. When I grabbed the broken rope between the two of you, a surge of energy shot through me and has continued to flow at a steady pace ever since.*"

"*Good. That's exactly what we need. I'm going to try to fuse my thoughts to the energy that is flowing between us, and hopefully this will allow me to reach Rose's mind.*"

"*Okay, Christian. I'm ready.*"

Loraine closed her eyes and took a deep breath. Her ghostly form glowed a little brighter, and I knew this was going to work.

I centered myself and brought the image of when I held Rose in my arms as I changed her to the forefront of my mind. I layered it with the words of the consort ceremony and in a surge of energy, cast my thoughts outward, through Loraine, and directly into Rose's heart.

CHAPTER THIRTY-TWO

(Meredith)

As the lights dimmed in the theatre, the idea of actually sitting through a movie right now struck me as utterly ridiculous. I was contemplating using my mind bond to force Jeremy to scrub the rest of our evening and call his "clients" back to meet him again. Unfortunately, I knew nothing like that would work. I was sure Jeremy would have a message saying they decided to go with another firm for their marketing when he returned to work on Monday. Now that they'd located me, they wouldn't need to keep up their fake roles any longer.

"I'm excited to see this movie, sweetheart. Thanks for waiting for me at the restaurant," Jeremy said.

"It's no problem, darling. I'm happy your new clients love the plan you've put together for them. Where are they from, anyway?"

"They said they were leaving in the morning to head back home, but they never actually mentioned where *home* was."

Dammit. I needed information, but they'd been careful to not give Jeremy any that I could use. As much as I wanted to buck and rage at that fact, there was no point in worrying about it now. So instead of contemplating about the looming fight, I decided to curl up next to Jeremy and enjoy our time together. Because tomorrow, I'd be immersed in blood and battle plans.

* * * * *

(Loni)

Renard and I arrived at the theatre, grabbed some candy, and claimed our seats in the highest row possible.

"When was the last time we actually went to see a film?" Renard asked.

"I don't know, which means it's been *too* long." I leaned in and kissed him long and slow. I loved making out at the movies. It brought back memories of when we'd first met at Grauman's Chinese Theatre almost eighty-six years ago.

Breaking our kiss, Renard laughed. "You don't want to miss the beginning, do you? It's starting."

After placing one last peck on his lips, I turned my attention to the screen and spent the next two hours completely engrossed.

The movie was better than I expected and had even brought an unexpected tear to my eye a couple of times.

"Are you ready to head back to the apartment, or would you like to take another stroll through town before morning?" Renard asked as we made our way to the exit.

I was just about to voice my answer when I stopped dead in my tracks.

I found myself staring directly at Meredith and Jeremy. They were in the crowd just ahead of us, making their way to the side door that led directly to the parking lot.

Holy shit!!

"Renard, look. That's Meredith and Jeremy. They're right there in front of us!"

"Calm down, Loni. Don't give us away. Let's tail them. Then we'll finally have some positive news to report to Evie."

We hung back and melded into the shadows of the dark theatre. With each step the couple took toward the exit, we mirrored them from our veiled position. It didn't take long until we all emerged from the building, at which time we raced around the corner, ensconcing ourselves in the dark alley next to the parking lot.

"Do you still have them?" I asked.

"Don't fret, love. You know I'm good at my job." Renard winked. "We won't lose them."

Jeremy and Meredith walked down the street hand in hand, until they rounded the corner and came to the parking garage of a tall office building. The deep expanse of shadows the garage provided allowed us to get even closer. We continued to watch as the couple entered their car and pulled out of the structure and onto the street.

We tailed them for a few blocks and were stunned when we all arrived back at *our* apartment building.

"What the fuck? How is this even possible?" I asked Renard.

"Guess we know who the blur on the twentieth floor was now, don't we?"

I squinted my eyes and scrunched my nose at him. I'd *told* him we should have checked that out before. I couldn't believe the demon bitch we'd been looking for this whole time was literally living right above us. I was in shock. We hung back until the elevator closed, then watched as the numbers ascended, finally confirming our assumption when they halted at 20th floor.

We immediately raced up the stairs and practically flew into our apartment. Renard had his cell phone out before I'd even shut the door.

"Evie. We have news. Wait... what? Now?"

I didn't like the panic in Renard's voice.

"All right. We'll be right there."

"Why didn't you tell her about Meredith? What's going on?" I asked.

"We have to leave... NOW!"

CHAPTER THIRTY-THREE

(Meredith)

After returning to the apartment, I was resolved to the fact that my attack on the vampires needed to happen sooner rather than later. I refused to continue being stalked, which was exactly how I felt, now that *another* set of vampires had found me.

It was time to take our stand.

I used my mind bond to send Jeremy straight to bed, then made my way to Lupé's with multiple donors in tow.

"Meredith, you need to control yourself. There are too many dead bodies piling up," she declared.

I looked across the lawn and saw my entire demon army drinking human blood straight from the source; I could only smile at my guaranteed victory. "I'm sorry you disagree with my methods, Lupé, but you are the one who suggested we bring everyone in to help get revenge for Damien's death, and now that I want to actually attack the vampires responsible, you're getting cold feet?"

I didn't wait for her response before placing my mouth back over the open wound of the woman currently dangling from my grasp.

"You have become lost in the blood, child. You are not thinking clearly. You can't just go to The Rising Pit and declare war. You have no idea what will happen if you do."

"That's where you're wrong. I know exactly what will happen. We'll engage them in a fight and once they ingest our blood, we'll be able to forge a mind bond with them. I'll then force their Sire to eliminate her entire clan. Piece of cake."

"Piece of cake? Meredith, you know that won't work. They won't bite any of you. They are *very* aware of the poison our blood holds for them. No." She shook her head. "This plan is bound to fail, and I won't be a part of it."

I was sick to death of having to explain myself. I let my eyes flare and dropped the now dead woman onto the ground. Taking a step toward

Lupé, I made sure to keep my voice low and stern when I gave her my response.

"Who said anything about them needing to bite us?"

* * * * *

(Rose)

I could feel my physical body had come to a stop. I was hovering in midair in both the real world and this dream-like state.

I watched as the man sat on the ground, crossed his legs, and closed his eyes, while the white woman remained immobile between the two of us. She, too, had closed her eyes and was now emitting a glowing light.

Uninterested in what either of them were doing, I closed my eyes as well. However, the moment I did, I was hit with a massive surge of energy.

I shuddered as if I'd been struck by a physical blow, but once I recovered, images started to invade my mind, accompanied by words that caused my heart to race.

My thoughts grew calm as I heard his voice inside my head. *"Your life to me, my life to you, through this bond our love is true. Whatever shall come, we share in whole. Life to death, eternity our goal."*

My -body shook again. The phrase repeating as images spun inside my head. Moments of me—the me I used to be—and this man locked in a passionate embrace; the two of us kissing, naked in bed; myself working at a club, the club I now recognized as The Rising Pit. All these memories threatened to overwhelm me if not for the mantra repeating in my head.

"Your life to me, my life to you, through this bond our love is true. Whatever shall come, we share in whole. Life to death, eternity our goal."

Finally recognizing the man, I called out, "Christian!" Staring at me from across this open expanse was Christian; my lover, my Sire, my *life*. He had turned me into the hybrid in hopes of stopping Meredith, the demon controlling my dad. Everything rushed back to me in a split second. More and more energy surged between the two of us as the cord that held our bond in place started glowing ever brighter. Pulsing, bright golden strips of light, raced from him to me.

The white woman's form grew brighter and brighter, blazing like the midday sun. As a massive burst radiated from her, she fell to the ground, our cord fused together once more.

Christian ran to the woman. "Loraine!" he cried out.

Loraine? Oh, my god... it was my mother!

"MOM!!!" I screamed raced forward.

* * * * *

(Christian)

The moment Loraine opened herself up to my energy, I knew I'd be able to save Rose. I felt our connection strengthen with each passing moment.

I sent random images of us together, along with the words from our consort ceremony on a repeating cycle into her mind. Images and words I hoped would bring her back to me.

Once I felt my energy fuse with hers, I opened my eyes. I wanted to cry at the scene before me. Bright golden streams of light were shooting down our ethereal cord, brightening Loraine as they passed through her on their journey toward Rose. *My Rose.*

She was currently looking right at me through silvery-blue eyes. Her hair was starting to lighten but quickly drifted past her usual blonde, settling instead on pure white. Her wings, too, were transforming, losing their hideousness and changing into something daintier and more angelic, though they remained black as night.

She was a sight to behold.

I shielded my eyes as the light Loraine was emitting reached its pinnacle, bursting from her and knocking her to the ground as our ethereal cord fused back together.

I raced to her side as Rose cried out, "MOM!!"

CHAPTER THIRTY-FOUR

(Rose)

Everything happened so fast. Memories of my life flooded my mind, and now I was staring at the ghostly form of my dead mother, lying on the ground before me.

"Christian, how is she here? What's happening?"

Christian reached up and smoothed my hair with his hand. The emotion in his eyes had me melting at his touch, but both of our focus was brought back to my mother as he began to explain.

"Rose, I think your mother just saved us. She was the conduit that kept our bond whole until I had a chance to bring you back."

I looked at my mom and was flooded with such gratitude, but also a horrible sadness. I wanted to scoop her into my arms, but knew I couldn't. My hands would mist right through her.

"Is she really gone this time?" I asked.

"Yes, Rose. I think she is."

* * * * *

(Christian)

I held Rose in my arms on the astral plane as she mourned her mother's death for a second time. When Loraine's body finally shimmered and dissolved into the ether like a million tiny fireflies, I worried that Rose wouldn't be able to handle the overwhelming grief of such a tragic event. But as I held her tight, and thought about the transformation she'd just gone through, I knew the love we felt for one another was strong enough to weather anything.

"Rose. I think when you're ready, if we just concentrate on our conscious selves, we should be able to break free from this place and awake back in our actual bodies."

"Okay, Christian. I think I'm ready," she replied.

We both stood and held hands, closed our eyes, and allowed our thoughts to meld. I tried scanning her, and for the first time ever, I could actually read her thoughts. I could see her physical form hovering just outside The Rising Pit.

My eyes flew open, and I found myself lying on my bed. I raced from my room and up the stairs and straight out to my beautiful wife who was waiting for me outside, transformed.

The moment I stepped in her direction, her eyes too snapped open and she slowly drifted to the ground. Evie and the rest of the clan gathered behind me. Apparently, they too had witnessed Rose's transformation from inside the club.

"Christian? Are you alright?" Evie asked in a low whisper.

"I'm fine. We're *both* fine." I nodded at Rose.

A smile crept across her face and within seconds she was nestled in my arms again. I hugged her fiercely, taking care not to crush her soft black wings.

"Christian. I love you so much!"

"I love you too, Rose. I'm so sorry about your mother. I wish there had been time for you to actually speak with her."

She didn't say another word but simply buried her head in my chest and let her soft tears continue to fall.

* * * * *

(Meredith)

The moment I grabbed Max and forced my bleeding arm into his mouth, everyone started screaming at me.

"Shut up! You will *not* question me! I am your leader, and I know what I'm doing will work."

I threw Max to the ground and tested the mind bond I'd just forged with him by instructing him to pick up the knife that rested on the decrepit picnic table nearby.

I was thrilled when he did exactly what I wanted.

A hush came over the crowd and everyone stared at me with a mix of fear and respect. I knew this was the demon equivalent of being a vampire's Sire. Once my demons ingested *my* blood, they'd do exactly as I commanded. The similarities between our races where shockingly obvious the closer I looked.

"I know you won't agree, but by Max making this sacrifice, we will be able to defeat the vampires in one swift move. All we need to do is get his blood into their Sire, and I'll be able to control them all."

The shocked expressions and wide-eyed stares I received in return pissed me off. How dare they not fall in line with my plans? What about this didn't they understand? The loss of one would guarantee our victory. *What the fuck is their problem?*

"Meredith. Max isn't just a soldier in your army, he's my nephew and a part of this family. How can you even consider doing this?" Lupé questioned.

"Just like this."

I sent the command for Max to cut his own throat and rushed to his side to place a collection bucket beneath him as he fell to the ground.

Silence hung in the air for two heartbeats, then screams turned into howls, and in the next second I was being rushed by the entire crowd.

CHAPTER THIRTY-FIVE

(Christian)

Once everyone recovered from the shock of the scene in front of them, we all made our way back into the club.

"So, you're saying that Rose is cured from the hybrid's version of drifting dark?" Dominique's question was layered with skepticism.

"Yes, Dom. That's what I'm saying. The spark of love I was able to ignite within Rose is what brought her back to us. Just like what happened to Terrance because of Loraine."

Rose remained quiet as everyone stared at her. I hated she was so uncomfortable, but with everything that had transpired, her altered appearance was a lot to take in. She was beautiful, yet fierce, and the lust I felt for her in this moment was beyond compare. I could no longer sit here and answer questions from the clan, I had to be with my consort... to be with *my wife,* before one more second passed.

"I'm sorry, but if you'll all excuse us, we'd like to be alone. Rose needs some time to adjust and process everything that's happened as well."

Rose must have been thinking the same thing because she smiled and reached for my hand, allowing me to lead her to the spiral staircase under the stage that descended into the pit.

"Thank you." Her voice was tentative.

"You're welcome." I squeezed her hand and hoped the look on my face portrayed the immeasurable amount of love I felt for her.

Once we reached our room, I only turned on the light in the corner. The moons and stars still hanging from the ceiling started to sparkle and shine. "Is this going to be okay?"

I wasn't sure if it was too fresh a reminder of her mother, or if it would act as a comforting gesture like I hoped.

She didn't answer, but instead guided me to our bed and pulled me down beside her. We laid in silence and watched the crystals twinkle and spin. Minutes passed before she spoke.

"Christian, I did some really bad things while we were apart."

"It's okay, Rose. I forgive you. I forgive you for everything. For keeping secrets, for lying to me, for leaving me the moment you awoke as a vampire. I *completely* forgive you. While your mother was here, she was able to fill me in on everything. I know you were only trying to protect me."

I felt her release a breath and prayed my words brought her some measure of comfort. I hated the idea she felt guilty for her actions.

I was just about to express my own apology for not being there for her, when suddenly, she crushed her lips to mine.

* * * * *

(Rose)

I wound my hands through Christian's hair as I climbed on top of him. The feel of his strong arms around me as his hands explored my curves had me writhing against him. We kissed and fondled each other with an intensity that rivaled the great love stories throughout history, and while I knew the timing was probably wrong, I simply couldn't wait.

Lifting his shirt above his head, I took a moment to revel in the sight of his chiseled chest. His thick muscles and smooth skin created the perfect canvas for my mouth. Christian's breath grew heavy as I licked and nipped my way across his pecs.

In a rush of speed, Christian ripped my blouse open, taking care to not snag my wings. His tongue went straight to work. With my legs wrapped around him and his mouth at my breast, I closed my eyes and let myself fall into his expert hands.

We made love with a passion that transcended time as our minds and hearts truly connected. Our consort bond flared to life and set the room alight. Maybe we glowed because I was the hybrid. But to be honest, I liked to think it was because our love burned hotter than anything either of us had ever encountered before.

* * * * *

(Meredith)

It took some doing, but I'd finally fought off most of the idiot demons who decided to challenge me. My numbers had dwindled because of this little hiccup, but I still had plenty of demons who were now truly scared of me and wouldn't think of going against me again. With that settled, we'd be able to move forward with my plans to attack the vampires tonight.

"We simply need to fill these syringes with Max's blood and whoever gets close enough to Evangeline just has to inject her. Once that's done, I'll be able to use my mind bond to control her since the blood is so fresh."

They all nodded their heads. After filling twenty shots, we all loaded into Raúl's SUV and took off for Seela. I was so pumped to put an end to these pests tonight, I didn't even bother washing off the blood that saturated my clothes and skin.

We exited the freeway a couple of miles before the turnoff to the club, using the back roads to get close, then ditched the SUV.

"It's imperative they don't hear or see us until I give the signal to attack," I explained.

My demons once again nodded their understanding.

We quickly made our way through the forest to the club. I watched from the shadows as two vampires exited a blue SUV and made their way toward the front door. The same SUV I'd seen outside my old house just last week.

I burst from the bushes and flew to within inches of the couple. They spun around and assumed a fighting stance, then called to their Sire—exactly as I wanted them to do. Their eyes grew wide as my army joined me in the parking lot of The Rising Pit.

In seconds, Evangeline and the rest of her clan emerged from the club and faced off with us.

"How dare you come here!" Evangeline bellowed.

I laughed at her stupidity. "Did you think I wouldn't come for you after you tracked me down and threatened my life with Jeremy?"

"We didn't threaten anything. You are the one who started this war when you infected Terrance and killed Rose's mother."

"Speaking of Rose... where is my precious, soon-to-be step-demon?"

A vicious roar pierced the air, causing my entire army to cover their ears. I looked up to a see a winged creature with sharp fangs hovering directly above us. A few of my demons started to make a run for it and the rest of us watched as it snatched them up and ripped them limb from limb in one swift move. There was no escaping whatever this was...

"Oh my god... *Jeremy?*"

CHAPTER THIRTY-SIX

(William)

I waited inside the apartment I'd secured on the eighteenth floor for my vampire strike team to return with the prize I'd sent them to claim. They walked through the door with Jeremy in tow just after three a.m. All I had to do now was change him into a hybrid, just as Christian had done to Rose, then I too would be able to protect my clan in this upcoming battle against Meredith and her demons.

I'd been so grateful when Evangeline had informed me of the situation and explained her plans for securing a place in Masen to gather intel from. It was then, I decided, to do exactly same thing, only for a different reason. I'd sent Bryce and Nicholas with a picture of Jeremy, one I'd gathered from Jillian's scrapbook of her times spent with Rose and her family.

I'd been thrilled to receive the report they'd actually run across him on their second night as they rode the elevator to the apartment. I'd instructed them to make contact while I handled the situation with Justin and Jillian's return. But instead of Jeremy walking into their initial trap, it had been Meredith who'd found them in her apartment instead. After that mishap, they made the wise decision to only encounter Jeremy at his work, so as to avoid another confrontation with the demon bitch herself.

Finally, tonight, they had tracked the two back to their apartment and after watching Meredith slink away, they had been able to get to him without any interference. He was now standing in my room with wide eyes, a gagged mouth, and his hands tied behind his back. I hated securing him like this, but since we couldn't bite him and use our sedative to keep him calm, we were left with no other choice.

"Jeremy. Please don't be afraid. We're not going to hurt you. We're only here to help reunite you with your daughter, and in the process, save our family."

I nodded to Bryce to remove the gag.

Jeremy stood calmly as he looked between us. "What the fuck are you talking about? I don't have a daughter yet. My fiancé is only a few weeks pregnant."

I immediately realized trying to explain our situation wasn't going to help. I only hoped that during his transition process, his memories would fully return. So, without delay, I launched myself at him and buried my fangs into his neck. The sedative of eternal life flowed into his veins as his body went slack in my arms. As soon as he took his last breath, I placed him on the couch and entered the bedroom we had prepared.

I immediately lay down on the operating table and let Nicholas hook up the transfusion equipment. From Evangeline's explanation, I knew Jeremy's demon blood would cause me to drift dark. Therefore, my plan was to remove it from my system as fast as I could by performing a quick blood wash. Hopefully it would work, and I could avoid losing myself, ultimately end up facing the true death at her hands.

Just before my mind started to blur, I instructed the boys, "If this doesn't work, take Jeremy to The Rising Pit and tell Evangeline everything. Let her know where I am and that I accept what she has to do." Their clipped nods indicated they understood.

I closed my eyes and tried to blank out my thoughts while the medical equipment did its job. I didn't want any undue stress to impede the process, because the faster we knew if this was going to work, the faster we could move forward with helping Jeremy adjust to his new life as our hybrid.

I felt groggy... hazy, but tried to remain still as the second round of machines kicked in. I could feel the blood moving in and out of my veins in a rhythmic push and pull. Suddenly, I was lulled to sleep like a baby listening to a lullaby.

Upon waking, the first thing I thought of was how Evangeline was going to be upset by my decision. I hoped I could make her understand she wasn't the only Sire who had a clan to protect. I looked around and found Bryce and Nicolas staring at me from the other side of the room. I assumed the fact that I remembered their names and what we were doing here was a good indication that the process had worked.

Bryce walked over and flipped off the equipment's switch as Nicholas asked, "How are you feeling?"

I sat up to gain my bearings. "I feel great actually. How long have I been out?"

"You dozed off briefly and drifted dark and back again a few times throughout the process, but overall, it's only been about an hour."

"Wow. That's great. That gives us plenty of time to get to The Rising Pit. I need to speak with Evangeline right away. Let's get Jeremy loaded into the truck and out of here while he completes his transition. I don't want him waking up in a building full of people, or with his demon fiancé directly overhead and hell-bent on finding him."

All three of us rushed around in a frenzy, packing up the medical equipment and wiping the place clean. Unlike Evangeline, I didn't plan to keep this apartment for further use. We loaded the truck, securing Jeremy in the back seat, and headed directly to the club.

* * * * *

(Jeremy)

After returning home from the movie, I was ready to join my beautiful fiancé in bed when suddenly I was overwhelmed with exhaustion. The minute my head hit the pillow I was out like a light. Which was now one of the many reasons I was completely confused by my current predicament.

I was bound and gagged and standing in a different apartment with Bryce and Nicholas, my new clients, looking at another man I had not yet met. He was speaking to me about my daughter and how I could "save his family." *Good lord, I must be dreaming.*

Bryce removed the gag from my mouth, and I told them I didn't have a daughter. They all looked at me with a sense of confusion.

Suddenly, the strange man launched himself across the room and bit the side of my neck. I didn't even have a chance to move before he was on me. I felt the warm trickle of some sort of serum filter into my veins. It immediately caused me to relax and forget any thoughts of fighting back. My mind became a haze of images as I felt myself bleed out.

I assumed I'd wake up back in my bed with Meredith tucked by my side, but what I found when my eyes opened was a man shoving his arm into my mouth as the vehicle I was in jostled down the highway. I had no control over what I was doing and no idea where I was, but as the warm liquid flowed down my throat and the salty taste of his blood hit my tongue everything snapped into place.

I wasn't dreaming. William was my Sire, and I was now a vampire. *No... that's not right.* A hybrid. I was a demon and so was my daughter, Rose. My wife, Loraine, had been human and we'd been perfectly happy until *Meredith* ruined all our lives.

I raised my head from William's arm and screamed into the air. I could see everything clearly now, as if my transformation wiped out all the lies that previously layered my brain. I remembered the conversation with my daughter in which she explained everything to me. Meredith had killed the love of my life, then later set up Rose, causing her to go on the run. We were all demons and Meredith had obviously succeeded in controlling me, just like she planned.

Another howl burst from my mouth as a darkness settled within my chest. I would hunt and kill this woman, this *bitch*, who ruined my entire life. A demon whose blood I could currently smell riding the air currents around me.

I snapped my head up and took in my surroundings. I was in an SUV that sat parked on the edge of The Rising Pit's parking lot. It only took a moment for me to pinpoint Meredith. She was standing in front of the club, surrounded by vampires and demons.

With an animalistic roar, I burst through the roof of the truck and found that not only had the transformation changed my thoughts, it had changed my body as well. I had massive white wings that carried me into the air and sharp fangs that came to smooth points just below my lips.

I hovered over the scene for a split second before the demons started to run. I knew they were part of Meredith's army just from the smell they all carried. I swooped down and ripped the first two apart before landing only yards away from the woman who'd destroyed my life.

CHAPTER THIRTY-SEVEN

(Christian)

I glanced at the clock to see if Rose and I had enough time to make love again before the sun rose. It was only 5:30 a.m. and the sun wouldn't be lighting the sky for another two hours. *Yes!*

I stared at Rose's naked body as she returned from the bathroom. Her wings shifted softly as she walked, and her pure white hair held a silver shimmer that reminded me of Loraine. She was so beautiful, I knew I'd never be happier than I was in this moment.

"I love you, Rose, and I'm going to tell you every single day."

"Wow. Every day for forever? That's a lot!" She giggled, as her eyes brightened.

Talk about a new twist in our drifting. It now seemed that whenever our emotions flared, we both took on the golden hue from our consort bond. I was wondering what the others would think about it when a massive roar sounded above us.

Rose's head snapped up as she sniffed the air, looking very much like the hybrid she was. "Demons!" she exclaimed. Her wings flared and eyes went wide, and in the next second we both flew into our clothes and raced out of the room.

As we stepped through the front door, we were met with a raging battle.

My clan was standing near the front of the club, watching as a winged creature dove through the crowd, ripping multiple demons to shreds. Meredith was in the middle of the chaos, struggling to hide behind anyone close enough to offer her the slightest bit of protection. It didn't take long before the ground was littered with bodies, and she was the only demon left standing. We all watched as she made her plea.

"Please, Jeremy. Don't kill me. Remember, I'm going to have your baby."

Holy shit! This was Rose's father. I stood in shocked silence and wondered how Jeremy had become a hybrid. I was about to pose the question when I looked at Rose and knew it didn't matter.

She was smiling from ear to ear with tears in her eyes.

* * * * *
(Rose)

Seeing my dad as a good hybrid, like me, made my chest burst with pride. I'd missed him so much, and after almost walking away and losing myself, and him, to this disgusting woman in front of me, I could hardly contain myself.

"Dad!"

I ran to meet him in the open space between my clan and the carnage before us.

"Oh, Rose. Are you okay?"

I buried my head in his chest and felt myself grow a little warmer as tears of joy filled my eyes. "Yes. I'm fine, *now*."

I hugged him tightly before pulling back to get a good look at him. "How are you? And how in the world did you become a hybrid?"

Before he answered, he flew to Meredith, who'd taken a few steps toward the surrounding forest, and lifted her into the air by the throat. I laughed out loud as she dangled from his grip like a wet noodle. She kicked and yelled, but Dad silenced her with a quick shake as he bared his fangs and growled in her face.

Turning his attention back to me, he called out, "William! Could you come out here please. It looks like you have some explaining to do."

We all watched as William and two of his vampires climbed out of the truck that was parked at the lot's farthest edge. A truck with a huge hole in its roof.

"William, will you be so kind as to explain to everyone how we arrived *here*?" Dad asked as he motioned to himself with his free hand.

William proceeded to explain that after Evie told him about the demons and what her plan was, he'd decided to follow in her footsteps, using Jeremy to protect his own clan. He'd specifically paid special attention to how she worried that Christian had turned dark due to Rose's blood and formulated a way to avoid that part of the process. By performing a blood transfusion and immediately cleaning the demon blood from his system, there would be no contaminates to cause him or Jeremy to drift dark once he awoke and fed from him. His plan had worked perfectly, but it was when Jeremy's anger and emotions flared over the realization of all Meredith had done, that his wings literally sprouted forth the moment he burst through the roof of their truck.

"Wow." I didn't know what else to say. Christian and Evie had made their way forward to join me during William's rapid explanation. As Christian placed his hand around my waist, I felt him nudge my mind with a question; one I repeated to Dad immediately.

"So, what are we going to do with her?" I pointed to Meredith, who was still dangling like a rag doll in my father's grip.

"I'll leave that up to you, Rose. She killed your mother and has been after you and your clan for months. Not to mention tricking and controlling me. It's your choice," Dad replied.

Everyone stared at me while I contemplated my decision. A day ago, I would have ripped out her throat and drawn pictures in her blood and not even blinked, but now... I wasn't sure how I felt or what the right thing to do was. But, before I could truly process my feelings, something strange started to happen.

Meredith started convulsing, causing my dad to lose his grip. She hit the ground hard, but instead of fleeing, she remained coiled in on herself as her entire body twisted and popped. The sounds of her bones snapping and cracking, accompanied by her horrible screams, filled the air as blood started pouring out of her mouth, nose, and ears.

Everyone took a step back in an effort to distance themselves from the gruesome scene. The startled expressions around our group confirmed no one had any idea what the hell was going on.

I quickly put my scanning ability to use to see if I could understand what was causing such a horrible reaction. Christian, Evie, and Dax must have been doing the same thing, because as I looked up, we all shared a sense of shocked understanding.

"What's happening, Rose?" Dad asked.

"It's the baby. Your transformation into the hybrid has affected him through your bond. He's changing and it's caused Meredith's body to reject him and the blood she's ingested. I'm sorry, Dad, but neither of them are going to make it."

A stoic expression settled on my father's face, mimicking the feelings of the entire clan. I was about to say something like, *"Maybe it's for the best,"* when suddenly, I caught a whiff of more demons. I snapped my head toward the forest and watched as two elderly women emerged from its edge.

With their hands raised, one announced, "We come in peace."

As they approached the macabre scene, horror showed in both of their eyes. They stood over Meredith, crying as they watched her contorted form struggle for its last breath.

"I'm Meredith's grandmother, and this is Lupé, an elder and demon in Meredith's *army*." Tears slid down her cheeks as she gazed at her now dead granddaughter. "Lupé came to me tonight and explained Meredith's plans." She shook her head. "I tried to warn her drinking human blood would be the downfall of our race, but I had no idea it would end like this. Her greed for power and immortality caused her to experience a severe case of bloodlust, one she could no longer control."

The older woman wiped her face and reached for Lupé's hand before continuing.

"Drinking blood is something demons are no longer meant to do... that is your lot in life, not ours. Meredith chose not to heed my warnings and paid the ultimate price, but it's our hope that with this *ending* we can start anew. Lupé and I will *never* allow our kind to drink again and will share what's happened here with the elders of our race. We have no quarrel with you or those like you. Will you accept our offer of peace and agree to a truce between us?"

Evie started to walk toward the women but paused when she reached Christian's side. Placing her hand on his back, she smiled and gave him an encouraging nod.

Christian walked toward the women and extended his hand. "We accept."

And just like that, the threat which had plagued my family for the last year had come to an end. Christian hugged me, then released me into my dad's embrace. The rest of the clan, including William and his vampires, starting piling the body parts on top of Meredith's remains as the demon elders simply walked away. We all stood back when Terrance flicked his lighter and tossed it onto them. It was fitting, after everything Meredith had put him through, too.

We all watched as the flames licked the sky.

I knew there were other demons out there, but with the ability my father and I possessed to *literally* sniff them out, none of them could threaten us ever again, even if they did choose to break the truce. I looked at Christian and gave him a slight smile, as our battle came to a fiery end. My entire family was finally safe, and while our wings limited my father and me to only coming out at night—just like true vampires—we were free to live our lives together and without fear, and *that* fact alone made everything right as rain.

The End

Author's Note

As I stare at the words, *"The End,"* I feel a hint of sadness but also one of renewed wonder at the thought of my next adventure. While it's hard to say goodbye to Rose and Christian, I feel they will always be a part of me in whatever story I'm trying to write. I will carry with me the strength these characters have in whatever else I do, for they are such an inspiration to me. The devotion they have for one another is so subtle throughout the series, sometimes you forget they are basically newlyweds. Instead, they seem like that old married couple who has been through so much together, they could complete each other's sentences, or come to an understanding with just a simple look. That is Christian and Rose; truly, madly, deeply in love with one another, and I with them.

Goodbye my friends. <3

For more Rose Trilogy **Bonus Content** visit:
http://www.tishthawer.com/rose-trilogy-bonus-content.html

(Enter the password: "Christian" to gain access.)

About the Author

#1 Bestseller in Historical Fiction
Top 100 Bestselling in Paid Kindle Store
Best Cover Award Winner
Readers' Choice Award Winner
Best Sci-fi Fantasy Novel Winner (x2)

Author Tish Thawer writes paranormal romances for all ages. From her first paranormal cartoon, Isis, to the Twilight phenomenon, myth, magic, and superpowers have always held a special place in her heart. Best known for her Witches of BlackBrook series, Tish's detailed world-building and magic-laced stories have been compared to Nora Roberts, Sam Cheever, and Charlaine Harris. Tish's books have been featured in British Glamour and Elle Magazines. Tish has worked as a computer consultant, photographer, and graphic designer, and has bylines as a columnist for Gliterary Girl media, RT Magazine, and Literary Lunes Magazine. She currently resides in Missouri with her husband and three wonderful children, and operates Amber Leaf Designs, an online custom swag retail store.

You can find out more about Tish and all her titles by visiting: www.tishthawer.com

Also by Tish Thawer

The Witches of BlackBrook

The Witches of BlackBrook - Book 1
The Daughters of Maine - Book 2
The Sisters of Salem – Book 3
Lost in Time – (A Legends of Havenwood Falls novella,
and a Witches of BlackBrook side-story)

The Women of Purgatory

Raven's Breath - Book 1
Dark Abigail - Book 2
Holli's Hellfire – Book 3
The Women of Purgatory: The Complete Series bundle

The TS901 Chronicles

TS901:Anomaly – Book 1
TS901:Dominion – Book 2
TS901:Evolution – Book 3

Havenwood Falls Shared World

Lost in Time – (A Legends of Havenwood Falls novella,
and a Witches of BlackBrook side-story)
Sun & Moon Academy – Book 1: Fall Semester (A HWF Anthology)
Sun & Moon Academy – Book 2: Spring Semester (A HWF Anthology)

The Ovialell Series

Aradia Awakens - Book 1
Dark Seeds - Novella (Book 1.5)
Prophecy's Child - Companion
The Rise of Rae - Companion
Shay and the Box of Nye - Companion
Behind the Veil - Omnibus

Stand-Alones
Guiding Gaia
Handler
Dance With Me
Magical Journal & Planner
Elf in a Cell

<u>Anthologies</u>
The Monster Ball: Year 3
Fairy Tale Confessions
Losing It: A Collection of V-Cards
Christmas Lites II

CPSIA information can be obtained
at www.ICGtesting.com
Printed in the USA
LVHW092004301121
704872LV00012B/207/J

9 781087 916668